HOLLOW SACRIFICES

THE ORDER OF THE HAWK TRILOGY
BOOK 2

C.L. SHARP

Cover Illustration and Design by Moonchildreams

Interior Chapter Art by It's Just Peachy Pages

Editing by Haleigh St. Paul at Grim Girl Edits

ISBN: 979-8-9922229-3-7

AUTHOR'S NOTE

Greetings Reader!

Thank you for your interest in Hollow Sacrifices! This trilogy takes place in an urban setting and addresses many modern issues throughout each book. I believe in the importance of providing a warning in case any of the below topics can be triggering to you, the reader.

Content Warnings:

- Explicit language
- Descriptive sex scenes
- Violence
- Death of loved ones in a tragic situation
- Brief mention of infertility
- Brief mention of rape resulting in pregnancy
- Characters that deal with Anxiety and PTSD
- Discussion revolving around suicide and depression

Safeguarding your mental health is extremely important, so please continue at your discretion. I hope you enjoy Talliana's story!

Wishing you a good read,
C.L. Sharp

To the ones who have ever felt broken.

And to those tired of pretending not to be. Let those cracks shine.
They're fucking beautiful.

Katarina Lehmann, one of our youngest Healers at the age of eight, has started showing an affinity for water. She cannot control it as well as the other Water Elementals her age, but there is no doubt of her ability.

We, the elders of the German community, have decided to keep a close watch on young Katarina. Never before have we seen a Hawk manifest more than one ability. If the Great Hawk has seen fit to bless her with two abilities, then we will ensure the gift is not squandered.

- Journal of Friedrich Meyer

CHAPTER 1

TALLIANA

July

GRIEF IS LIKE THE tide. It ebbs and it flows. It can be a gentle caress over your feet, or it can be a raging beast that pulls you into the ocean to drown you. Only the moon can control the tide.

But I am not the moon.

I am the ice that cuts and the frigid water that burns. I can't control the tide, but I sure as hell can create a barrier around all the things I can't afford to feel. But today, maintaining that barrier is almost impossible.

I've been sitting here for a while, watching the sun rise and the dragonflies skip along the water. It's a peaceful morning. The only sounds are the birds chirping, the lake lapping at the small bank, and the breeze rustling through the willow trees. But in my head? I hear the sounds of swords clanging, guns firing, people screaming in pain, and the whisper of his words, "I'll never leave you." Words uttered only moments before he did just that.

Closing my eyes, I try to will it all away. But the noise inside my head doesn't budge. It's been two years, and I had hoped by now that it all would have faded, even slightly, but it hasn't. The March on Massachusetts is a day that will forever live in my mind and play out as vividly as if it were happening again right in front of me.

"The moments that shape who we are will never fade. But their sting does lessen once you allow yourself to heal," Coventina says in response to my thoughts.

Sitting up, I turn toward where she is lounging about a foot away. Her iridescent scales shimmer in the sunlight and her pale green hair flows around her, making her look as beautiful as ever, but her gaze is a mix of sorrow and annoyance.

"I can't afford to heal. You know that," I argue. This is something we occasionally fight over. She thinks I should take the time to heal, but I don't want to. I simply don't want to get better, because I need the anger to fuel the darkness, and I need the darkness to end this war. If I did heal, and the anger and overwhelming need for vengeance did fade, I might not be powerful enough to make it through to the end. I need just enough to get me to the moment of ensuring my people's peace, then I will find peace of my own.

The dragon doesn't respond, just puts her head back down in a resting position. Not in a sign of defeat—far from it. She is choosing not to argue today on the anniversary of Trey's death and our bond.

I turn away from her toward the gravestone I've been resting against. The granite slab looks as polished as it did the day it was placed. Between Mrs. Waterstone and myself, we keep it in perfect condition. My finger traces the letters etched into the stone, and his name blurs as I allow myself to shed a few tears for the time that was taken from us.

My mouth opens without my permission, and I talk to him, like I have done hundreds of times. "Hey there, handsome. It's been two years, and I still miss you so much. Everyone told me it would get easier with time, but it hasn't. I've only grown more determined to get through the day without my barrier falling to pieces," I admit. "Oh, Marcus and Aurora's youngest, Aisling, got her ability last week. She's a Dream-walker, too. The poor girl looked terrified when I saw her a couple of days ago." Laughing lightly, I rest my hand right over his name, *Treyton Waterstone*, as if it is a way to touch him. "She's in for a long road, but she's strong. I have no doubt she'll be great at it. I'm happy for her, but it was a struggle not to think about our plans—our hope that one of our kids would have inherited that ability, too."

A weight settles on my chest, thinking about it again. So, in an effort to distract myself, I turn my focus to the wild red poppies that sprouted around Treyton's grave only a week after his burial. Impossible—it should have been impossible for those to grow that quickly and between the willow tree's roots and rock-filled dirt no less, but the magic in this forest must have recognized Trey's sacrifice and honored him with the beautiful, bright flowers.

I continue to talk to him for a while, telling him about Greer's and my last mission, things happening around the community, and anything else that pops into my head until I run out of updates to give him. "I love you always and forever, Trey. Have a good rest, and I'll visit again soon." I kiss my hand and place it back on the gravestone in farewell.

Brushing myself off as I get to my feet, I turn around to find Draven and Greer behind me. I jump back in alarm, almost falling backward over the gravestone.

Shadow dragons can hide themselves and their bonded Hawk in shadow and appear out of nowhere. Almost two years of these shenanigans, and they still manage to surprise me.

"I hate when you two do that!" I scold.

Greer and Draven both laugh heartily at me.

I swear, Draven's laughter is the strangest sound I have ever heard. It's filled with the joy of a little boy, but it's coming from an intensely deep voice. His charcoal-colored scales shimmer as much as Coventina's do as his body shakes. That is pretty much the only similarity between the two siblings, though. Where her scales are rounded, his are pointed. While she has smaller wings and a tail shaped like a mermaid's, his wings are large and imposing and his tail is in the shape of an arrow. They both have two horns on the tops of their heads and smaller ones that continue down their necks, but hers are rounded whereas his are pointed. Coventina's demeanor is often stoic and serious, and Draven is energetic and light-humored. They are as different as Greer and I, so it's fitting.

According to Coventina, she is the older sibling by a couple hundred years. Draven is only one hundred years old, making him essentially a preteen in dragon years. I have asked about their parents before, but Coventina won't tell me about it or give me many details. She did tell me once, after a year of pestering, that there are not many dragons left in the world, just two dozen or so, and most don't leave their homes. She also confirmed what we all suspected, that she and Draven are the only bonded dragons in the world and will likely be the last.

"Don't you two have something better to do than scare me every chance you get?" I ask incredulously.

"Actually, we flew to the city and back to bring you these." Greer searches around in her bag attached to Draven's saddle and pulls out a white paper bag.

"Donuts?! You shouldn't have!" I exclaim. These donuts are my absolute favorite. I never get them since we don't have a donut shop, and the packaged donuts from our community grocery store are a pathetic substitute.

Greer jumps off Draven, landing on her feet, and hands me the bag. I snatch it, pull out a cream-filled, and sink my teeth in. My mood lightens considerably as my mouth is filled with the sweet vanilla taste. I may have changed a lot in the last two years, but my love for confectionery treats has remained.

I don't have to ask Greer why they did this for me because I already know, and she knows that I know. It's a true testament to how our relationship has been lately. I've done everything I can to pull away from everyone these last two years, not uttering a word to anyone about the darkness or what I let it do for our people. But Greer sees it. How could she not, when she watches me use it on so many of our missions? She tried talking to me about it for a while, but eventually stopped asking after each question only made me pull further away from her.

Once my donut is wholly devoured, I pull another out and toss it at Coventina. She catches it easily with her massive mouth. She generally has a strict diet of fish, but she never says no to a donut. I toss one at Draven, too, and hand Greer one. There are two left, which I will save for later.

"What are your plans for the rest of the day?" Greer asks between bites.

"I don't know yet. Maybe go for a swim." I smile at Coventina.

"Of course. Can't keep you two out of the water in the summer." She rolls her eyes.

"Well, what are your plans for today? Going to go scare a helpless old lady in the community next?"

"We already met our daily quota for that with you," she quips. I give her a bland expression. Greer always had sarcasm and the occasional joke before, but Draven has brought so much youth and fun into her life that she has loosened up a lot. Even if her scary factor has doubled.

A week after accepting Draven's bond, Greer developed his ability to shadow-wield, a rare Air Elemental ability. For her foresight ability, she can actually see real images now depicting a person's future emotions instead of just sensing them. Her eyesight has also been enhanced so much that she can see almost as well as Draven. I guess that helps when you are traveling within shadows.

"I think we'll rest for a bit, though. Maybe check on Ash," Greer answers, taking Draven's saddle off and throwing it over her shoulder. He shakes like a dog dispelling water and walks toward his cave, which is about a half-mile hike away.

Ash has taken to the two dragons well and loves them almost as much as we do. He often goes on flights with Greer and always brings them treats like they are spoiled pets. For the first year after our bond, he unearthed every single text we have on dragons and has shared a ton of information he has found on them with us, since the dragons aren't exactly forthcoming in their personal details or history. Ash is also the one who designed our saddles and had them made for us, and they have proven to be invaluable. We are more than capable of riding the dragons without them, but they have two seats with straps to buckle us in and extra hooks to carry bags if ever necessary.

Greer starts to walk away back down to the house, when I call out to her, "Thanks for the donuts!"

She holds a hand up over her head in a *"Don't worry about it"* kind of gesture and keeps walking. I turn to Coventina. *"Ready?"*

"Always."

7

I pull off my t-shirt and shorts, revealing the bathing suit underneath, then throw off my sandals and run toward the lake. Coventina is already in, diving under the water. Without hesitation, I wade in and jump right at the edge of the natural bank. We swim in the lake so often that I no longer notice the cold water. It's actually refreshing today now that the sun has fully risen, and the air has turned from warm to hot.

I hold my breath and sink in a few feet, then stretch out my hand and catch Coventina's leg as she zooms past me. She slows down just enough so I can pull myself onto her back and wrap my arms around her neck. Once I have a good grip, she flies through the water at an incredible speed. After half a minute passes, she surfaces the water, allowing me to breathe.

"*Do you want a bubble today?*" she asks me, twisting her head back to look at me.

"*Yes, please,*" I respond through my mind. She blows a bubble toward me like she has done a hundred times, and it forms around my head, allowing me to breathe underwater.

She dives again, and we do laps around the lake without surfacing. I watch the different fish that swim past us, all trying to avoid the large predator. Coventina often flies to other lakes and bodies of water for meals, using this one for the occasional snack. She does this so that no lake completely runs out of fish, although Dad ensures someone is always stocking the lake just in case.

After a few laps, I practice trying to move around her back, to her legs, then to her tail without falling off as she moves through the water. These maneuvers are likely pointless, but it's a great workout. Once I'm completely exhausted and constantly losing my grip, Coventina takes me back to the surface and drops me off at the bank of sand. I pull myself out of the water and wrap up in the towel I grabbed this morning on the way over here. I collect my clothes and, with one last look towards Trey's gravestone, head back to the house for a shower.

CHAPTER 2

TALLIANA

"YOU LOOK BEAUTIFUL, TALLI," Mom says with a sigh. She's standing behind me at her vanity, smoothing one last piece of hair into place on my head.

"This is too much," I mumble, voicing my real thoughts. The dress, the hair, the make-up, this whole event...it's just too much. My body is draped in a light-blue silk dress that is made to look like water moving around my skin. My auburn hair is swept to one side and pinned, so that my mostly exposed back is on full display. The moonstone necklace Trey gave me is still around my neck, a permanent fixture I refuse to take off.

"It does feel that way," she agrees. "But the community wants to celebrate, and we can't deny them that."

"They want to celebrate one of our most horrific attacks in recent history," I argue as I struggle to slide the strappy heels onto my feet.

"They want to celebrate the second chance they were given and who gave it to them."

"I don't want to be celebrated."

"I know, but it will be over quickly. Just smile through the speeches, mingle with some people for an hour or two, and you can go. Greer, too, for that matter. This day may be mostly about what you did, but it's also to celebrate how you've both kept the community safe in the years since. You both are a blessing from the Great Hawk to our people; let them pay you the love and respect they believe they should."

I nod, knowing that any further argument is pointless. Now that Mom has finally finished fussing over my appearance, I leave the bathroom as she calls Greer in next. She is glowering in the hallway, black shadows hanging around her like a fog. She has to dress up like a doll, too. A fact that does make tonight slightly more bearable. For me, at least.

"Have fun," I tell her as I head down the stairs. She grumbles in response and loudly shuts the door behind her.

Dad and Ash are waiting in the living room, fully dressed in suits. "You look stunning, honey," Dad says when he sees me.

"Radiant," Ash agrees.

I offer them both a smile, but I know it doesn't quite reach my eyes. Ash notices and pulls me into a hug. He whispers in my ear, "You say the word and I can be violently ill and in need of healing."

Pulling away, I laugh and genuinely smile at him. His hair had been getting longer and curlier lately, but much to Greer's dismay, he had it trimmed earlier today, making him look a bit older. His black rimmed glasses, the same ones he has had since high school, are low on his nose, so I push them back into place before standing at his side and resting my head on his shoulder.

"You have a very important job tonight, Ash," Dad states.

I lift my head and look at him, and Ash does the same, suddenly very tense. "I...no one told me about a job...I'm not prepared. What is it?" Ash struggles to ask.

Dad grins at him, humor dancing in his eyes. "You have to escort both of our ladies of honor tonight, since Talli declined her own escort."

I scowl, but Ash relaxes and laughs it off. "I hope you don't mind me saying, but I don't blame her, considering who was chosen for the job initially."

"The guy was an asshole who talked down to Ash as if being a human is a flaw. He represents the worst of our people, and I wouldn't tolerate it," I defend myself.

"If I had known he was like that, I wouldn't have chosen him. But a simple 'no thank you' would have sufficed. Pinning him to the wall by his clothes with ice daggers was a tad extreme," Dad scolds. His tone suggests seriousness, but his expression betrays him. He looks like he is fighting back a laugh.

"Pinning his skin to the wall would have been a tad extreme. What I did was kind, considering what I wanted to do."

It doesn't take long for Greer and Mom to come down the stairs, and we head to the Range where the evening's festivities are set to take place. Greer huffs the entire walk, adjusting her black dress, which was created to look like shadows, every few minutes. The leather bodice hugs her well, while the skirt is full of tulle and flows around her like a ball gown. Her raven black hair is pulled up into a bun, probably to show off the charcoal gray dragon scales she has on the back of her neck, the mark she received when she bonded with Draven. I have a similar one, but with blue-green scales just above my hip instead.

Ash keeps stealing glances at her, his hand on the small of her back, trying so hard to be a proper escort to her. I'm sure he will commit the vision of her to memory, knowing he might never see her dressed up like this again. I keep looking at her because the expression of disdain and discomfort on her face is making me feel less alone in this whole thing.

"*Complain all you want, but Draven and I are the real show ponies,*" Coventina growls into my mind. She's perched on my shoulder in her lizard form and will likely stay that way for a while until Dad calls for her and Draven to shift. He had to promise some excellent meat in exchange for their attendance tonight.

"*Show ponies? Where did you learn that term from?*" I ask.

"*That's what the feline called us earlier.*" She means Melisandre, Dad's bonded panther. She is only a few steps ahead of us, walking at Dad's side.

"*Well, she's not wrong. I guess we are all going to be uncomfortable tonight.*"

"*If someone even dares to try to touch me, they will lose their hand,*" she warns.

"*I'm of the same mind,*" I agree.

We arrive at the large clearing where our community usually practices all manner of combat training, including archery, knife throwing, shooting, and more. Although tonight, it's almost unrecognizable. String lights surround the area, giving it a soft glow against the dark night. There are rows of tables filled with food and refreshments and a large stage at the edge of one side for Dad and the other elders to give their speeches. It's not common for all of our people to gather at one time like this, but I have little doubt that most are here. Even young mothers, with their babies snuggled up tight to their chest, and children running around hyped up on sugar, awake far past their bedtimes.

Greer, Ash, and I stay together as we work our way through the crowd. Even with Greer getting attention herself, they truly are my anchors through every "thank you," "may the Great Hawk bless you," "you saved my family that day," "you saved me that day," "you and your dragon are the miracle we have been waiting for," "have you met my grandson," and so on and so forth. Not only am I forced to mingle with the residents of this community, but I am also forced to mingle with elders from many other communities who came for the event.

Once I am beyond the point of being overwhelmed, I tell Greer and Ash that I need a moment, and I slip away before they can follow. I need complete solitude to collect myself and ensure my barrier is still firmly in place. Winding my way through the hordes of people, I finally reach the end of the Range and walk a minute down one of the paths leading up to it. Once most of the noise has faded, I find a solid tree, lean against it, and sigh in relief.

I have just enough time to get a handle on myself again before I hear footsteps coming my way. I brace for the worst case, but it's Seth who comes barreling down the path toward me. The German shepherd's tongue is dangling out of the side of his mouth, bouncing with his pace, and I swear he gives me a real smile as he reaches me.

"Oh, Seth. You are a sight for sore eyes," I exclaim as I wrap my arms around his furry head. Planting a firm kiss on his snout, I straighten to see Mr. Simon at the end of the path, smiling at me warmly. "I didn't think you were going to make it," I call to him.

"I found an earlier flight. I didn't want to miss all the fuss," Mr. Simon replies, walking the rest of the way to me and his bonded creature.

I wrap my arms around his middle, hugging him tightly. Mr. Simon has been away for two months, visiting some European communities with his fiancé, Trisha Garner, the head Healer for the New Hampshire community. I've missed him dearly; the whole community has. Not only has training with just Greer felt wrong without him barking out orders and drills at us, but I've missed his comforting presence during mission debriefs as well. I love my dad, but if I could call anyone my second father, it would be Mr. Simon. I used to consider him like an uncle, but our relationship has grown so much in the past years as I've worked to become a weapon for the Order.

"Alright. Let's get you back before you make this old man cry."

Pulling away, I grin up at him. Even in heels, he still towers over me. The bottom of his neatly trimmed beard doesn't even brush the top of my head. "Two months out of the states doing nothing but focusing on your pre-marital bliss, and you're going soft on me," I tease.

He laughs and tells me about his trip as we head back to the Range.

Just as Dad ends his well-crafted speech about what happened at the March on Massachusetts—how Coventina and I heroically flew into the air and I wielded water for the first time, using the rain to heal all our people, and how they captured and chased out the remaining living Brethren—he gives me a nod and Coventina jumps from my shoulders and shifts into her dragon form, eliciting a loud gasp from those standing near us in the middle of the crowd. One man shifts too closely to her side, and her head whips around, growling at him. His hands immediately go up in surrender, and he backs away from her. Everyone does.

"Then my fellow Hawks, another dragon showed up and found my other daughter, Greer of the Meyer bloodline, worthy of his bond," Dad goes on.

Draven shifts next, a couple of yards away from us, causing more gasps and a few shrieks. He responds by smiling, showing off his rows of sharp teeth.

"The dragons have found us worthy again of their aid, and together, we will see an end to this war, and our children will finally be able to sleep in peace."

The crowd erupts into cheers and screams of excitement.

What a show Dad put on. What a fucking ridiculous show. The war ending is something to be excited over, but none of the people know what it might take to end it. They don't understand the cost of life. They don't understand what Greer and I do on our missions...

"Your Dad is inspiring. The truest leader among our people," a male voice says from beside me. I turn, finding Reef standing next to me. His light-brown hair is down for once, straight as straight hair can get, brushing past his shoulders and almost completely hiding his bonded otter, Odel, who is wrapped around his neck like a scarf. His hair is usually in a bun, I assume for Odel's sake, showing off the sharp edges of his jaw. He looks over to me and winks, before refocusing on the stage where Dad is exiting, and the celebration starts to resume around us.

"Well, he sure can get a crowd going," I mutter.

Reef fully turns to me then, his silver eyes sparkling as he looks down at my dress. "Has anyone told you how enchanting you look tonight?"

"Here we go." I cross my arms and roll my eyes.

"You look enchanting, princess."

"Does that line work on all the girls?"

"Girls, yes. Women like you," he shrugs, "sometimes."

Reef is a Water Elemental who transferred here last year from the California community to study under Dad and Mr. Waterstone. He's the ambitious sort, a little younger than me, but he is kind and appears to genuinely want to help our people. But it didn't take him long to admit that he was interested in me, and that immediately puts a person on my "avoid at all costs" list, because those who are interested in me either want me for my bloodline or my bonded.

Narrowing my eyes at him, I ask, "Is there something I can help you with, Reef?"

"Hearing your angelic voice saying my name is help enough. Have a good night, princess."

I pull a little bit of moisture off of Coventina's scales and hurl it at the back of his head. He catches the water easily with his ability and holds up his pointer finger, willing the water to spiral around it as he walks away.

Mom walks up to me from that direction and says casually, "Reef looks nice all dressed up."

"I hadn't noticed." I really hadn't. All I saw was his hair, and all I thought was how weird it looked down. I start walking back toward the house, ready to crawl into bed, even though the celebration will most likely last most of the night.

I'm not surprised when Mom walks with me, if only to continue our conversation a bit longer. "I wish you'd give him a chance."

"Yeah, well, I wish Trey was still alive, but we all can't get what we want." I don't think as the words fly out of my mouth, but I should have, because Mom stops dead in her tracks, causing me to stop and look back at her. Her expression is terrifying, and I know she is hiding the worst of it to avoid causing too much of a scene.

She glides up to me as her cornflower-blue eyes pin me to the spot, somehow still appearing graceful in her outrage, and tries to look calm as she says in a clipped tone, "Today is a very emotional day for all of us, but that is no excuse for your behavior. You can grieve for as long as you need to, but this isn't grief. This isn't the daughter I raised." Mom walks away toward Dad, who gives us a questioning look.

I feel my face burn with embarrassment. I hadn't meant to take out my frustration on Mom; I know she is doing what she believes will make me feel better. That is her exact ability after all, and I don't deny that it is likely right, but I need her to understand that I don't need to feel better right now. I need to fight.

I climb onto Coventina's back, failing at my first attempt in my silk dress. I pull myself up with both arms instead and sit with my legs to one side since I can't spread them enough to straddle her.

"*Please fly carefully,*" I beg her. She doesn't reply, but lets out a loud huff, warning people to back off, then she takes off. My body is thrown sideways, and I'm forced to wrap my arms around her body in order not to fall off. As soon as we level out in the star-covered sky, I push myself back up and grab ahold of one of her small horns at the base of her neck.

"*Any requests?*" she asks.

"*I don't care. Just fly for a while,*" I reply.

She keeps the flying smooth and slow so I don't lose my balance again. I breathe in deeply, enjoying the crisp evening air. It's a bit chilly up here, but I don't mind the cold. Taking the rare, people-free opportunity, I try to think through all my disagreements with Mom lately. She was never this pushy before, but I don't think she has ever been this worried before, either. She has every right to be, but I need her to stop pressuring me into a relationship.

They started showing up a month after I woke up. Any eligible bachelor who was within twenty years of my age. They each came with resumes and ploys to try to make me fall in love with them. Frankly, I could look like a troll, and I have no doubt that they would all still have come, because I am just a trophy to these men. Marrying the woman with the dragon bond would be a hell of a thing. Obtaining me means obtaining the most powerful Hawk in the world as their wife. Mom and Dad initially fought them off, but now they have switched to hand-selecting them. Only letting the "best" resumes through. It's ridiculous, really, for them to think I would consider any real relationship. Too much is at stake. I don't need a partner, I need a distraction who doesn't know me and who doesn't want to know me.

Last year at the beginning of the school, my second year in college, I opened myself up to some advances from human men. I had four one-night stands until it started to circulate that I was an easy target. The whole debacle resulted in a small memory tampering of the men I had been with and the men who caught on to the rumor. Now, regardless of good or bad intentions, I turn down anyone who approaches me. It's better this way. Despite what Mom's ability is telling her.

Black shadows appear next to us, and Greer is there on Draven's back, Ash right behind her. Unlike me, she is able to straddle Draven's back in her flowy dress.

"Thought we would find you up here," she shouts.

"Do you want to talk about it?" Ash asks, also shouting into the wind.

"I snapped at Mom. It was wrong and I wanted to get out of there," I explain.

"I'm sure all our parents will be busy tonight with the celebration. Let's go back to the house, build a pillow fort in the living room, and watch a movie," Ash suggests.

Greer looks back at him. "Last I checked, we weren't twelve any-more."

Ash shrugs. "Last I checked, I'm tired of being an adult. I miss twelve-year-old us, the three of us, with little worries and no secrets."

I know he didn't mean it, but that latter part stings. I am the one keeping secrets from both of them, and they know it. But isolating myself is the only way to keep everyone safe.

"Okay, as long as we can become adult us again when we get into bed tonight," Greer replies.

It's too dark to tell, but I have no doubt Ash's cheeks are turning pink. "I can agree to those terms," he answers sheepishly.

"Well, the shy looks you both will be giving each other will defi-nitely make me feel like we are twelve again," I quip.

Deep laughter fills my head, and I know it's Draven laughing at my bad joke. It forces me to crack a grin. Then Greer. Then Ash. Soon, we are all laughing, and the tension I've been feeling all night loosens just enough.

CHAPTER 3

TALLIANA

"GET UP!" COVENTINA SHOUTS into my mind, jarring me out of sleep. I sit straight up in bed and immediately start yanking off my pajamas and slipping into my leathers. Greer is doing the same, and I know she got the same alert from Draven.

"What is it?" I ask frantically.

"The New Hampshire community. The alarms were tripped," Greer answers.

Shit.

At least they're the closest community to us so we can get to them quickly. Greer and I run out the back door to the shed where we keep the saddles. We fasten them onto the dragons, jump on their backs, and are in the air heading toward the fire in a matter of seconds.

I feel a faint buzz in my head for a second before it clears, and I know our communication path is open. Greer and I found out shortly after her bonding with Draven that our dragons can open a sort of channel in all our minds, so when going on missions, we can all communicate with one another. I can hear and talk to Greer and Draven just like I do to Coventina. It's incredibly convenient, but it's something else that makes us a novelty.

Ash went nuts over the information, but came up empty in his attempt to find anything on it in his books, and the only explanation Coventina provided was, "Dragon magic is superior and doesn't follow the same rules."

"*We'll be there in ten,*" Greer says through the channel.

A year ago, the Order began installing alarms in our neighboring communities. When triggered on the perimeter of the fence, these alarms would send out an alert to all resident phones, making everyone's escape to safety much faster. It also sent the alert to Greer's and my phones so that we can show up to help. However, only a few months later, the Brethren started disabling phone towers before an attack to prevent the alerts from going through. The Hansens, who are responsible for creating the system, changed course, and with the help of Ash, the alarms now trigger a high-pitched frequency that most bonded creatures can pick up from long distances.

Our losses from direct attacks at night have almost disappeared for the communities close to us with the new system up and running. Only four communities so far. Our community tested it first, and we've been able to get it into New Hampshire, Connecticut, and Vermont. New York and Maine are in the process of installation. It will likely be installed at a few more communities, but distance will have to be considered. Sure, dragons fly fast, and we can get to the surrounding states within a few minutes, but if we go much farther, we will end up being too late. Already, we don't always make it in time before the fire starts. But even if we make it after the attack is handled by the local emergency officers, my water-healing ability is unmatched by any elixir. Best case, we get there just to turn around and go back to bed. Worst case, we fight the Brethren.

Following the March on Massachusetts, attacks have become significantly more frequent. Fortunately, they are not so frequent that Greer and I never get sleep. Not-so-fortunately, that may change once the alarm system is in more states.

The smell of smoke reaches my nose, forcing me to regain my focus. They've managed to set a fire.

"Talli, I'll cover with shadows and take out the threats. You take care of the fire," Greer directs me in my mind.

"Roger."

I lift my hands to the sky and pull out the moisture in the atmosphere, shaping it into raindrops. Coventina circles the area where the fire is, staying above the shadows and out of sight. My hands are still suspended above my head, commanding the water in the sky. I throw my hands down, and the newly formed rain falls, covering the earth below us. It puts out the fire in seconds, but I keep sending water down for a full two minutes in case there are any flames I can't see from here.

As soon as the shadows clear, we descend and land in the middle of a street next to Draven. I dismount to find everything orderly. Greer is talking to one of the community elders, Walter Channing, and three guards are lining up Brethren to take to the community prison for questioning and memory-wiping. The Brethren prisoners are white as a sheet, staring at the dragons in front of them. All the communities keep our dragons as a close secret, but it is always reassuring to see the disbelief on prisoners' faces that tells me they clearly had no idea they existed.

Luckily, only one house caught on fire, and it appears to be only slightly singed on the bottom floor, while the rest of the house looks intact. Emergency officers are now inspecting it for damage. On the other side of the street is a group of people dressed in nightclothes and looking shaken. I scan for injuries on them and don't find any from here.

"Talli, over here!" Greer calls for me, and I jog over to her. When I reach her and Elder Channing, she tells me, "There are five injured with bad burns. They are in house number 7854, the blue house a couple down on the right."

"On it."

Quickly locating the house, I get ushered in before I can even knock. I'm directed to the kitchen in the middle of the home and find the injured sitting around the large walnut dining room table. Someone is bent over one of them, trying to rub something on a burn spot. Trisha Garner. This must be her house.

"Ms. Trisha, let me help," I say, announcing myself to her. She whips her head up, causing a few strands of pale blonde hair to come loose from her hair clip. Her face lights up with a smile as soon as she sees me.

"Well, if it isn't the local superhero!" She steps back from her patient, giving me space.

I ask someone to get me a bucket of water, and within a minute, I have one in front of me. I get to work right away, willing the water into small spheres that I place onto the burns of the first injured person in front of me. The water washes away the damaged skin cells and causes new ones to generate at an accelerated rate, leaving no scar or mark behind.

Once all five are healed, I breathe deeply to calm my rapid heartbeat and take the offered water bottle in Trisha's hand. After I've drunk half the bottle, she nods her head to the back door, indicating that I follow her, and I do. I've known Trisha for a long time. A friend of Mom's and Mr. Simon's fiancée, she is the kind of woman who always has a fresh plate of cookies ready to give to anyone who walks through her door, and there are often people visiting her home.

"Sorry I missed out on the celebration a few days ago. Spending hours on an airplane is rough on this old body. Simon said both you girls looked beautiful," she says as she takes a seat at her patio table. I always thought she looked amazing for her being in her late sixties, but under the moonlight, she looks delicate and small.

I don't sit, because as much as I care for Ms. Trisha, I don't want to stay long. Not only because it's the middle of the night, but because every time I'm in battle mode, the darkness is not far from the surface. I feel it now rolling around and clenching onto my muscles, ready to spring into action. "I understand."

Her green eyes study me for a moment, so similar to the way Mom's do when she thinks something is wrong. "Talliana, those burns weren't bad. You could have let us handle it," she says softly.

"Two of the people would have been left with scars. Why not save them that pain?"

"I know they appreciate that, but you put too much on your shoulders. You *and* Greer. Your mother has confided in me what your father has you two do when everyone looks the other way."

"He asks us to save lives by killing those most willing and capable of mass slaughter. The Order has done that before."

"Before, when there were no other options. We have options now," she argues.

"Memory-wiping doesn't always take away someone's wickedness. Some people are just evil, and their soldiers will always find a way to bring them back. They must be permanently taken out." This is an argument I have had in my own mind a hundred times, trying to reason to myself why I follow my orders to kill men and why I let the darkness within me walk free. But I have seen it happen. We attempted to erase the memory of one of the lieutenants, and they reappeared in uniform a month later, as if nothing had happened.

"And that is somehow solely your and Greer's responsibility?"

For the second time this week, I snap. "I will do anything to end this war. Even covering myself in blood. No one else will die because I wasn't strong enough to do what it takes."

Turning on my heel, I leave the house and return to Coventina. I pass by twenty different families that make a point to thank me and look at me like I am some literal superhero walking through their streets, just as Ms. Trisha called me. My skin itches with discomfort. I don't deserve this kind of awe. I'm not a superhero. I'm a soldier following orders. If they really knew what I was...if anyone knew...

"All good?" Greer asks as I approach her.

"There will be no scars left behind tonight."

"Good. Let's go home."

I nod my agreement and decide not to think about my conversation with Ms. Trisha anymore.

CHAPTER 4

CASPIAN

"It's time. Is everything taken care of?"

"Yes, sir. I have an apartment, a part-time job, and I'm enrolled in most of her classes," I respond, standing at attention in front of my father's desk. His large frame fills up his seat, and his stern, calculated expression sucks all the air out of the room.

"Good." He nods and adds, "I expect a monthly report. Remember, we have worked hard to keep your identity hidden for years, so any communication with me must be secured through text unless I initiate the contact."

"Yes, sir. Of course."

"Good luck, son. It would be a disappointment to have to go through all this trouble again if you get yourself killed, so don't." His tone is almost bored, despite it being the nicest thing he has ever said to me. I can count on one hand how many times he has called me son.

"I won't fail."

"Well, that would certainly be a first." My fingers twitch in an urge to clench into a fist, but I don't let any other sign that the comment affected me show.

KNOCK. KNOCK.

"Come in," my father calls out, hands laced in front of him on the desk. A sergeant walks in, his maroon uniform looking wrinkled and damp, like he was thrown into a pool a few hours ago and didn't bother to change. I step automatically to the side to give him more space.

"General Campbell, the attack on the New Hampshire community was a failure, sir. We injured five, but no confirmed deaths," the newcomer reports.

My father's dark-green eyes flare with anger at the news, and he guesses, "The mysterious rain again?"

"Yes, sir. The sky was completely clear, but shadows moved in from nowhere, and it started raining."

"Caspian, you're dismissed." My father waves a dismissive hand at me, and I turn to exit the room, shutting the door behind me.

Whatever this defense mechanism is, we need to figure out how to dismantle it soon. The first time we saw it was during the failed Cleansing of Massachusetts two years ago. We didn't see it again until about eight months ago, and even though it isn't consistent about when it comes after the fire starts or if it comes at all, it manages to take out the fire in a matter of seconds once it does. Very few attacks in the northeast have been successful lately because of it. It's just one more reason why my mission is so important.

I have been training and preparing for this for three years. Make her fall in love with me, earn her trust, and she will tell me everything. I'll use that knowledge to win the war. It seems simple enough, but after watching this woman for a while, I know there is absolutely nothing simple about Talliana Hoffman.

She is the most beautiful woman I have ever seen, but she is ruthless. She and her sister, Greer, are responsible for over a dozen assassinations of our top men. The Order is not known for resorting to murder, but it seems that whenever it is deemed necessary, these two are sent to take care of it. My father doubled his personal guard because of them.

After the Cleansing of Massachusetts, I narrowed down my list to six different girls as my target for this mission. Any daughter of an elder in any of their communities would do, but when we discovered the identity of the notorious assassin taking down all our people a few months ago, my father set his sights on her as my target. He believes that she must know more than any of the other girls we've considered, given her role as assassin and the fact that she's the daughter of a Massachusetts community elder. However, she might prove impossible to crack. Well, impossible for any man *other than me*.

A cocky grin spreads across my face as I nod to the soldiers that I pass on my way out of our command center building. Outside the door, I find my Jeep, which is packed up and ready for the long drive to Massachusetts.

When I was sixteen, I started earning soldier wages like all the men here, and I saved every penny for two years to purchase the only love of my life: my Jeep. I climb into the leather seat and turn on the engine. I don't suppress the joy I feel at hearing it roar to life. I made sure she was fully tuned up and polished for this mission. She needs to be in perfect shape for this, just like I need to be.

I won't pretend that this will be easy, but if this is the challenge my father wants me to overcome in order to gain his approval and secure my spot as his lieutenant general, then I will do it. Failure is not an option. It is either succeed or die trying. Granted, dying by Talliana's hand might be one of the most beautiful ways to go.

When I saw her last, I was at her college getting registered for classes. She looked at me once from across the room, and I felt like she saw right through me and into my soul. She didn't hold the gaze for long, but if I'm not mistaken, I saw a blush on her cheeks as she turned away. Talliana might be a killer, but she is a woman susceptible to my charms, just like the rest.

And she will be in pieces by the time I am done with her.

Ever since I was a child, my emotions have always led to catastrophe. Others told my mother that I was an ill-mannered child who should be punished for my behavior. She agreed with them and did all that she could to control me, but it turns out I can't be controlled.

- Journal of Katarina Lehmann

CHAPTER 5

TALLIANA

August

I RECEIVED A TEXT from Dad thirty minutes ago with a message I always dread getting: "Mission. My office. 30."

That's his only warning before he sends Greer and me out on a mission. It's an order to drop everything and run to his office for the details. Sometimes, we get a couple of days before we have to leave, but most of the time, it's a that-night situation. Summer classes just ended, and I barely have had a chance to breathe. I was hoping to enjoy this small week break before fall classes start, but there goes that plan.

I get to Dad's office door and see Greer already standing outside of it, her hands clasped behind her back in a good-soldier-ready-for-orders position. Our eyes meet for a minute, and I tune into her. She lowers her shield enough to give me the impression that this will be a rough one.

I nod and move next to her to mirror her stance, waiting for the other meeting Dad is in to finish. We only wait a minute before the door opens, and Mr. Waterstone walks out. He stops before us, giving us a reassuring smile, then offers, "Good luck, girls."

The Waterstones are doing okay, it seems. But since Asher moved in with his actual parents after graduation, right before Trey died, it's like they lost two sons at once, so I don't see either of them very much anymore. Granted, I started avoiding most people in our community after everything that happened.

Once he turns the corner around the hall, Greer and I shuffle into Dad's office, taking immediate note of Chief Lu and Mei-Lien. Looking at the two of them sitting next to one another, it's like seeing a mirror image. I used to think that Mei-Lien didn't look much like her mother, but since she cut off the streaks of color she always had at the end of her hair, she looks just like her. Same black cropped hair, same stern expression, and same rigid shoulders.

They are sitting at Dad's conference table, which has a few maps spread across it. The monitor above the table, mounted on the wall, has pictures of several men whom I don't recognize.

"Come take a seat," Dad directs us. Greer and I both sit, taking seats opposite the two Lu women. It's only now that I notice Reef is also here, darkening a corner of the room. Dad stands from his own seat and examines the monitor for a moment, pulling my focus away from the quiet observer.

Greer breaks the silence by saying, "Please tell me we are finally getting Mackay."

Dad smiles. "We found an opening."

The name causes me to jolt in my seat. Robert Mackay.

I have listened to Greer rage over him for the last couple of months. A colonel for the Brethren who is responsible for all the attacks in the southeast of the country. She has said that he is horrible and particularly adept at finding creative new ways to eliminate us, but I feel entirely out of the loop on this one because she never explained in detail exactly how.

Everyone in this room is heavily involved in military affairs, whereas I'm busy focusing on my studies to become a doctor, specifically a pediatrician. A pointless endeavor probably, but one that keeps me distracted and my family less worried about me. I only get brought in when a target needs to be taken out. Sometimes, I wonder if I should try to be more involved, but I do prefer it this way. No need to know very human details about a monster. It's easier.

Dad must see the look on my face and says, "Mackay is the colonel who oversees the southeast. He is by far the worst colonel we have seen in a while. He's the man..." Dad swallows before continuing, "He's Penn's real father."

My eyes widen. Uncle Cyrus's adopted son's birth mom was a teenager when she was brutally raped by someone during an attack. I always figured it was a random soldier, not an officer. She decided, after everything, to put the baby up for adoption within the communities, and Uncle Cyrus and Aunt Janet didn't hesitate to take him after trying to have kids of their own.

"Penn's birth mother is not the only one he has done this to. Most of the women have been killed afterward, but she is one of the very few survivors who managed to get away." Dad clears his throat. "I don't feel inclined to go into further details of how bad this man is, but I'm sure if you girls wish it, Mei-Lien can fill you in later. She will be joining you on this mission."

Again, I feel stunned. I look over at Greer, and the only indication of surprise is a slight lift to her thin black eyebrows.

Dad goes on, "Mei-Lien has been tracking his movements for three months, and she cracked his pattern of attacks. Mackay moves around every few days to different spots, and we know his next target will be Florida."

I can see on his face that this is personal for Dad, as it is personal for Greer and me. Dad is from the Florida community. He grew up there until he came here to Massachusetts after high school. It's also where Uncle Cyrus, Aunt Janet, and Penn live. Our family is at risk.

"Cyrus is there waiting for you three to relay the full plan. He understands the purpose of the mission and each of your roles. He and a small team he is putting together are the only ones that do."

I speak up then, too curious to wait. "May I ask what Mei-Lien's role is? Does she know what Greer and I will be doing?"

Dad's amber eyes meet mine, and his severe look is disapproving, but he does answer. "From what we can tell, Mackay is one of the closest field colonels to General Campbell. We believe his knowledge to be invaluable. There will be a small window, but Mei-Lien's role is to compel as much information out of him as possible before you two take him out. And yes, Mei-Lien knows exactly what you girls do for the Order," he pauses, and his face softens. "The sacrifice you both make."

I almost snort, but I control the urge. Sacrifice is a strange word to use. Satisfaction feels more accurate for me, but I don't voice that thought aloud. Instead, I ask, "How does she plan to travel with us? Last I checked, Onyx doesn't have wings." Onyx is Mei-Lien's bonded black cat. Aside from the dragons, he is one of the stronger bonded creatures in our community when it comes to boosting Mei-Lien's abilities. Small in size, but mighty in power.

Greer chimes in then and says, "Draven and I can take her. He's used to the extra weight and will manage it fine." Greer takes Ash for flights often, and Draven is definitely the bigger of the two dragons.

"Thank you, Greer. That's helpful," Dad replies, then pins me with a glare.

Warning received.

Mei-Lien gives Greer a nod, which she returns. I narrow my eyes at the exchange. Greer has mentioned finding some common ground with Mei-Lien since they both work as police officers for the community. But it almost seems friendly between them.

"*Jealousy doesn't suit you,*" Coventina mocks.

"*And why would I be jealous?*"

"*Mei-Lien will never replace who you are for Greer. Even if they spend a lot of time together.*"

"*They spend a lot of time together? How much time?*"

Yep. That is definitely the sound of jealousy rolling through my mind.

"*They are partners now.*"

Immediately, I turn my head to Greer, and I stare at her in surprise. She didn't tell me that. She only told me that she was getting used to having Mei-Lien around, and that they were civil. Greer must feel my eyes because she turns to look at me. I shift my surprised expression to one of anger. The darkness stirs inside of me, answering my call. Her brows furrow, then raise as Draven likely tells her that Coventina shared her secret. I watch her groan and drop her face in her hands.

"Greer? Is there something wrong?" We both turn our attention back to Dad.

Greer straightens. "Nothing, sir. I think it's just the start of a migraine."

"Well, I'm sure Talli can fix that for you after we are done here."
Dad swings his gaze to me.

"Of course," I reply, making my tone neutral. As Dad turns back
around, I meet Greer's eyes and promise her hell after we leave this
meeting.

Dad wraps up, and we are dismissed to pack and leave by eight
o'clock tonight. Greer stops to talk to Mei-Lien on the way out to
confirm the plan of when and where to meet us. I stand to the side and
pretend not to overhear the brief conversation by flipping through my
phone.

"Something bothering you, princess?"

I growl in response to Reef's question.

"Alright. Alright," he holds up his hands in defeat. "Good luck on
your mission."

"I won't need it," I reply to his back as he walks away.

Greer and I walk out of the building. She was already here when we
got the text, so she jumps into our car—really Mom's old one that they
gifted us to share—to ride the short distance home. She shuts her door
and immediately explains, "Look, it just happened a couple of weeks
ago, and I was going to tell you as soon as I had a chance."

"It's fine. You don't have to answer to me. If you want to work
alongside the bitch that made our life a nightmare growing up, that's
your prerogative." I don't look at her and focus on driving instead,
pretending it takes more than half a brain cell to get us home.

Her sigh is audible. "Talli, she's different now. She's grown up. We
all have. She has been a great partner so far, and her abilities make her
invaluable to the community."

"I'm sure," I answer dryly.

"We have worked through all our issues, and you should use this
mission as an opportunity to do that, too. Give her a chance."

I glance at her but decide to wait to say something until we pull into our driveway two minutes later. Placing my hands in my lap after turning off the car, I look at her fully. "All of your issues? Including what she did at prom? Did she ever tell you why she did it?"

My mind flicks back to that night when Mei-Lien forcibly kissed Ash in front of Greer to compel his lost memories back. At the time, I decided that Mei-Lien's confession to me was not a secret I should share, but maybe now I should.

Greer looks at me skeptically. "She didn't explain the full extent, no. But I have my suspicions. Why? What do you know?"

Drastic times call for drastic measures.

"She did it for you. She had feelings for you, Greer. She practically told me herself after Ash ran off to find you."

I wait for the shock to cross Greer's face, but it doesn't come.

"Nice of you to keep that from me for all this time. That is what I suspected, though." The snark is apparent in her tone.

"It wasn't my secret to tell. She hadn't even come out yet." Mei-Lien came out a few months after the March. She started dating a girl from our class shortly after, and I believe they are still together. From what I've heard, though, it wasn't without difficulty. Belonging to a people who believe in maintaining strong bloodlines through matching with other strong Hawks and having kids...her identity wasn't well received by some people. Greer occasionally has the same issue, dating Ash, but people don't have the courage to cross Greer or me. Ash also does more for this community than most of the actual Hawks that live here, so that also deters them, thankfully.

Greer nods her head at my reason. She could respect my choice on that.

"Plus," I add, "I was a little pissed off that you never told me about yours and Ash's first kiss."

"Okay, let's not drag up all our dirty laundry today. Otherwise I really will have a migraine. This mission is a serious one. Mackay is the biggest target we have ever had. We need to keep focused."

This conversation isn't even scratching the surface of our dirty laundry, as Greer put it. The reality is, her not telling me right away about Mei-Lien doesn't even surprise me. Our conversations with each other have grown shorter while our secrets have grown bigger these last two years. We don't share everything like we used to, and it's entirely my fault. Greer was one of the first people I shut out, and it's fractured our relationship.

"I agree. I'll play nice."

"Besides, you should be thrilled to know that you could take Mei-Lien down in a matter of seconds if you felt so inclined. She is no longer superior to you in hand-to-hand."

That does make me feel better. I mean, I figured as much, but I've trained solely with Greer and Mr. Simon since my destiny was revealed, so I wasn't positive. A pleased smile crosses my lips. "Alright, let's get this asshole."

It is a perfect night for a flight. The midnight-blue sky is clear, and the stars are on full display. I feel as though I could touch them, if I could only reach far enough. But they are out of my reach, like everything else I truly desire. I decide instead to ignore them and focus on the rising warmth in the air.

The Florida community is right outside the Everglades, so close that the man-eating...everything surrounds the whole back side of the community, much like our community backs up to the forest. Luckily, that means few Brethren are actually stupid enough to attack from that side. But apparently, we aren't smart enough to find a better place to discreetly land.

Ten minutes into the walk toward the community entrance, and I've nearly stepped on three snakes, all of which Mei-Lien has pointed out to be poisonous or deadly in some way. Despite my confidence that my ability could heal whatever happened, I still don't feel like experiencing what it would be like to be attacked by one of these things. How do people live like this, with the constant fear of stepping on a slithering nope-rope? I feel so grateful to live in Massachusetts, where the snake population is much, much smaller. Not counting Midori, Chief Lu's bonded, of course.

I move to take another step forward and see a black one dart out from that spot. Stumbling back and nearly falling on my ass, I let out a shriek.

"So much for being discreet in our visit," Greer mutters.

I glare at her and shake off the feeling of my soul leaving my body.

"*You do know that snakes are distant relatives of mine. If you harm one, I might be inclined to defend it,*" Coventina threatens lightly.

"*What about defending me? You're my bonded!*"

"*Hmm...blood or bond...I might have to think that one over.*"

The thought crosses my mind to swat her off my shoulder, where she is presently perched in her lizard form.

"*I will drench you in swamp water.*"

I look to my right, where a swampy pond currently is, and decide to keep any other ideas of upsetting the snarky dragon out of my mind.

Uncle Cyrus met us where we landed, bearing a string of fish and a whole dead chicken for Coventina and Draven. He's been making happy chatter since, cheerfully carrying Mei-Lien's over-packed bag for her while she carries Onyx around her neck. The pair look a bit worse for wear. Between never flying on the back of a dragon before and the flight being a couple of hours long, I don't blame them for being in rough shape. I do, however, feel slightly satisfied with their discomfort. Is that childish of me? Yes, yes it is. Do I care? Eh, not really.

Uncle Cyrus falls into step beside me, holding up his giant flashlight to help me avoid more close calls. "How are you doing, kid, really? Your Dad tells me plenty, but he doesn't let you visit enough." His tone is light despite the serious question. He looks even older than he did the last time I saw him two years ago at graduation. His beard has grown long, nearly brushing his stomach, and the creases around his face have deepened.

"I'm okay. Busy. Between college and all the missions we go on, free time isn't really an option," I reply.

His bonded great blue heron, Bluebell, is perched on his head, bobbing as he walks. It's a weird sight to see, but I've known Bluebell my whole life and this is a typical spot for her, just like my shoulder is for Coventina. I peek down at her to check her mood, and I'm rewarded with a long tongue fluttering out at me.

Still feeling snarky. Got it.

"Heck of a way to spend all your time. Aaron doesn't let you have any fun? How about any time for someone special in your life?" His eyebrows lift in a playful suggestion.

What is it with everyone and their need for me to have a man in my life? A relationship does not solve all the world's problems, and it certainly will not solve mine.

"I don't have time for either."

"Eh, you'd make time if you found someone special enough. I'm sure they are waiting for you just around the corner. It's healthy to have someone to talk to and share your burdens with."

Around the corner? More like behind me, in my past and long gone, I think despairingly. "I have Greer. We are in this together," I answer instead, though that really isn't the full truth.

"Of course. You two share the burden of your unique duties to the Order, but that's not quite what I mean."

"I know what you mean. You may be right, and there may be someone out there for me, but they'll have to wait a bit. I'm not ready for them yet."

If ever at all.

"No one is ever truly ready when they meet their person. The key is to welcome them into your life anyway." He playfully winks at me.

I look at my uncle and scrutinize his posture. Then I decide to ask, "Did Dad put you up to this?"

His laughter causes the sounds of the surrounding wildlife to quiet for a moment before they resume their nightly performances. "He may have mentioned all your mom's failed attempts at matchmaking. I was voting for the Henry kid from Texas. He seemed nice. But no, he didn't put me up to this. I'm just trying to give some good old-fashioned uncle advice, since I can see clear as day you're struggling. I know you're growing up, but I barely recognize you. We used to joke that your mom slept with the wrong twin because you were always so bright and painfully cheery, like me. Not dull and serious like your dad. Sorry to break it to you, kid, but you're getting dull."

"Okay, first, gross. Second, I'm not dull. I'm busy. Third, gross. Fourth, Henry had enough personality for two people and was insufferable to be around. I'm insulted that you thought he would have been a good fit." Henry is one of the ones I wish I could forget. He was shorter than me, loud, thought everything he said was funny, and all around not well-mannered.

Uncle Cyrus laughs even harder at my apparent disgust, his head bobbing, making Bluebell bob around even more. "Fair enough."

The large trees start to thin out, and we come to an actual path leading us to the community's front gates. As we walk up, one of the smaller gates on the side blocking the sidewalk swings open, allowing us entry. An empty golf cart is parked on the curb. Uncle Cyrus places Mei-Lien's bag on the rear-facing back seat and beckons us all to get in. He comments, "They are all the rage in Florida."

As we drive past all the brightly colored houses in the community, we notice all the golf carts parked in front, just like he said. They didn't have these the last time I visited four years ago.

The ride to my uncle's house takes only a few minutes. It's late, and the three of us with our respective bonded creatures all settle in without hesitation. Greer and I are in one guest room and Mei-Lien is in the other. Tomorrow should be a relatively easy day; we will walk through the plan, then up before the attack happens after midnight, and into the early hours of the next morning.

"You doing alright down there?" Greer calls from the top of the bunk bed we are on—a bunk bed we have shared many times in our lives.

"Yeah, I'm alright," I reply.

"Liar."

"Nosy."

"At least I'm not a busybody like the rest of the family," she counters with humor.

Greer overheard the conversation with Uncle Cyrus, then.

I sigh loudly. "Yeah, you're not a busybody, and I'll always be immensely grateful for it. I just don't understand why everyone else has to be. Or, at the very least, why are they only meddlesome regarding me? Why are you exempt?" I ask the boards of wood above me.

"Probably because I have Ash. They aren't worried about me becoming an old, lonely crone. Unless I mess things up with Ash, then I'm more apt to become exactly that."

I get out of bed and poke my head over the top bunk railing to look at her.

"Don't look at me like that. It was an innocent comment meant to make you feel better. Don't read into it." She glares at me. I see right through it, though, and I keep looking at her. I don't know why I keep pushing her. I normally don't, but I guess maybe I'm finally tired of not talking to her after the Mei-Lien thing.

I know I have effectively unsettled her when she dramatically drops her head into her pillow and says, "You're a busybody just like the rest."

I shrug. "Guess it's in my blood. New ability unlocked, busybody." I pump my fist like a cheesy video game character.

She laughs and admits, "Things really are okay. I think we are just coming out of the honeymoon phase of our relationship. Our conversations are getting more serious about the future, and we don't agree on much. He wants to get married and think about kids, but I'm not there yet. I'm not sure I'll ever be there. He wants them, Talli. I can't move forward with him if I'm not positive I can give them to him."

"I don't think he expects you to walk down the aisle next week and pop out babies within a year," I try to reassure her.

"Yes, I know that."

"Has he said that not having kids is a deal breaker?" I ask.

"No..."

"Then how do you know?"

The guilt sliding off of her is palpable. It tickles my skin and causes me to shiver. Realization hits me. "You sensed his emotions while you had this conversation, didn't you?"

She sinks her face into her pillow.

"More than once?"

Her face sinks in a little more.

"And he found out, I take it?"

She nods, then lifts her head and looks at me with red cheeks. "We were arguing, and I mistakenly used something he felt against him. Now, he hasn't talked to me since the morning after the celebration."

I had vaguely wondered why Ash hadn't been around, but I was barely home myself, finishing summer semester classes. Greer was acting relatively normal, too, but she can shield her face as well as she can her mind. I should have seen through it. A better sister would have.

"Why didn't you tell me sooner?"

"I was embarrassed," she admits, and throws her face back into the pillow.

"Yeah, I would be, too. You broke his trust." Me, the pot calling the kettle black. I tried sensing Trey's emotions a hundred times once we got him back, but I was never particularly successful at it.

"Not helping," she groans into the pillow.

"I'm sure he just needs some time. I'm assuming you have apologized?"

"A thousand times."

"And promised you would never do it again?"

She groans again. Clearly, she still needs to complete step two.

"Greer..."

"I can't promise that, and breaking a promise is worse than the invasion of privacy."

45

"Hmm...is it? I'd argue that you should never do either in a relationship."

"Coming from the woman allergic to anything past a one-night stand."

"Well, excuse me for trying to lend my ear to what has you upset." I climb back into my bunk and under the covers. Her head appears upside down, and I have to work to not laugh at how silly she looks.

"I'm sorry. Please come back and make me feel better." Her plea sounds pathetic, and I know she did it on purpose.

"I'm comfy now, so you have to stay like that if you want to talk."

"Deal. Now tell me what to do to make him talk to me."

It doesn't take me but a moment to come up with a solid plan for her to win back my best friend. "As soon as we get home, wait until it's dark, throw some rocks at his window, and then play a sappy song on your phone. Also, hold the phone up like an old boom box when he looks out the window. That should do the trick."

I touch my head, ensuring I didn't grow another one, as the look she is giving me suggests I have. I further explain, "It's silly and romantic, and an old movie reference. All the things that make you incredibly uncomfortable. It shows that you're willing to go the distance for him."

She thinks on that for a minute, then replies, "I can do silly and romantic. Should I scale the wall next and climb into his window?"

Her excitement at the prospect is alarming.

"Uh...maybe ask his permission first?" I suggest.

She nods, and her head disappears.

Another thought occurs to me, and I hope I don't regret opening up this can of worms. "And Greer?"

Her head pops back into view.

"I really, really don't want to know what bedtime looks like for you two, but maybe spend the next few times not letting him do all the work."

The look of murder that crosses her face tells me my guess is correct.

"Are you suggesting what I think you're suggesting?" Her eyes narrow on me.

"I'm suggesting Ash likes to please, and you like to let him."

Her face turns into a grimace, and she promptly agrees, "Good point." Then she thinks for a moment, and she flashes me a coy smile. "Got any suggestions for me?"

"Goodnight, Greer." I turn onto my side, facing the wall, and pull the blanket up to my ears, which are likely turning pink.

"Goodnight, Talli. Sweet dreams." Her tone is wicked with delight, and on that note, I clamp my eyelids shut and try not to think about how long it has been since I have had sex.

Too fucking long, in case the world was wondering.

"*I wasn't*," Coventina quips.

CHAPTER 6

TALLIANA

WE WAKE IN THE morning to a giant pile of French toast and bacon that Aunt Janet made for us. Once my stomach is full and my mind is capable of focusing, we spend the morning reviewing the plan. As much as I dislike the overabundance of snakes here, I always enjoy visiting. We are still on duty, but it's a nice break from being at home.

After lunch, we get Coventina into Uncle Cyrus's pool for a swim. It's like a bathtub for her, with no room to move around, but she's enjoying the cool water. I can tell because her mood is always considerably lighter when in the water. I am lounging next to her on a float, soaking in the sun that will probably leave me red as a lobster, with a raspberry lemonade in one hand and a book in the other. I wish it were a more interesting read, but it's called *Salem: What We Did Wrong*. I found it this morning in Uncle Cyrus's Hawk collection, hoping it might offer me some insight. Ash and I have torn through the entire

Massachusetts collection looking for answers in the past to help our future. Will we find the answers in a book? Probably not. But anything to try to spark an idea. Mei-Lien is on the deck in a similar state as I am, just on a lounge chair instead, Onyx curled up between her legs. Greer is...well, I actually don't know where Greer is.

"She is currently being mauled by the sticky, tiny human," Coventina helpfully chimes in.

Penn must have gotten home then. According to Aunt Janet, his terrible twos haven't passed yet, and the boy is four. He can be a sweet little boy at times, like this morning when he brought me flowers before leaving with Aunt Janet to go to daycare for a little while. Granted, they were pulled from his mother's garden, but the gesture almost left me in tears. Then he ran at Greer full speed, screaming at the top of his lungs, and jumped at her like a proper wrestling partner. Apparently, they are back at it.

I have approximately two more minutes of peace before I hear a shriek, and I see Penn throwing off his shirt and shorts and running straight for the pool in his underwear. Before I can react, he surfaces, hanging onto Coventina's leg, and she lifts him out of the water. He giggles and climbs up her leg and onto her back.

Aunt Janet runs out the back door and puts a hand on her chest in relief when she sees her son safely perched on the back of a dragon. Not a sentiment most parents would share, I'm sure.

"Oh, thank God," she breathes out. She allows herself a moment of relief, then places her hands on her hips and turns on her scolding mother mode. "Penn Oliver Hoffman, you know you aren't allowed to run into the pool without me or your father in there to watch after you."

Penn looks guilty but not even a little remorseful as he replies, "Sorry, Mama, but Talli and Covey are in the water. I knew they'd catch me."

The kid makes a point. I was totally unprepared to catch him, but it seems Coventina was. The scolding is wholly forgotten in the next moment, though, as Penn is trying to ride the dragon underneath him like she is a pony. Coventina starts making small waves in the water, moving up and down like a horse on a carousel. This is undoubtedly a sight to behold.

It's good to know that Coventina is good with kids. Not that it matters. I don't plan on having any, not anymore. Grief pangs in my chest at the thought.

I look over my shoulder and see Greer sitting on the edge of the pool now. Her hair is pulled out of her tight bun in random places. I silently hand her my book and drink. She tosses the former to a chair in a water-free zone, then finishes off the latter in a big swallow. I jump off my floating donut tube and start splashing Penn with little water squirts that I am creating with my ability. He flinches and giggles as they hit him from different directions. Next, I create various shapes and animals from the water, seeing if he can guess them.

"Dinosaur! Fox! Birdy!" His little voice squeaks as he guesses.

Before I know it, I've drawn in a crowd. Everyone is now sitting around the screened-in porch, trying to guess. I haven't laughed this hard in a long while. It feels good.

After dinner, I catch Mei-Lien looking at some photos Uncle Cyrus has on the walls and mantle in front of her. I stand beside her and notice she is looking at a picture of Dad, Uncle Cyrus, and my late Aunt Delilah.

"That's my Aunt Delilah. She passed away when Dad was a teenager."

"I know," Mei-Lien replies.

She notices my stare, clears her throat, and says, "Elder Aaron...I mean, your dad told me about her. When I struggled with my ability, he told me stories about what she went through when she was learning. It helped me not to feel so alone."

That made sense. Aunt Delilah had a compulsion ability like Mei-Lien. The ability is not a common one, but highly sought after once it does manifest in someone. Communities often argue over who needs it more. It's not so bad anymore, with the memory elixir easily accessible, but the demand is still present since they can force Brethren to talk or hide their memories, like Mei-Lien will do on this mission.

"I'm glad his stories were able to help you. Usually, they bore Greer and me to death." It's an attempt at humor.

See? I can try to get along with her.

A small smile touches Mei-Lien's lips. It quickly turns down, though, and she asks, "How did she die? He never told me that part."

"It was during an attack on the community. She tried compelling one of the Brethren, but another one came up behind her and threw a burning piece of wood at her. She burned to death." The thought makes me queasy, even though it is not an uncommon way for our people to go.

"I'm so sorry." Mei-Lien looks at me then, and I feel it. Her sorrow for a woman she didn't even know but feels connected to.

I shrug despite my surprise at her feelings. "She was my aunt, and I'm sad over her death, but it was before I was born, so I never knew her. She's just another tragic death on the long list of them."

Mei-Lien nods, then swallows hard. "Talli, I...I am sorry for everything. I was a bully in high school, and you didn't deserve my ridicule. Especially in the last year. You were going through a lot, and I made it worse."

I meet her brown eyes, then take a deep breath. "I forgive you." As the words leave my mouth, I realize they are true. I do forgive her for what she did. A part of me will always be a little hesitant toward her, and I'll never want to be her friend because of it, but I am willing to let go of my anger over it.

She nods again, and once it becomes uncomfortably awkward, she blurts out, "You were the first person I told."

Surprised by her words, I reply, "I don't remember you telling me anything." She is talking about at prom when she insinuated having feelings for Greer, but she never actually said anything.

"Well, not in so many words, no. But it was one of the scariest moments of my life because I knew you would put it together, who I am. I kept waiting for you to tell someone, but you kept my secret, even from Greer."

I turn fully to her. "You are Mei-Lien. You've always been Mei-Lien. That discovery didn't change who you were in my eyes. I still hated you just the same, but I understood you a bit better." I grin at her, and she matches it. Then I continue, "Trey did overhear, but neither of us spoke about it to anyone else because it wasn't our secret to share. I did give myself grief for not guessing beforehand, though. The rainbow hair should have been a dead giveaway."

She absently touches her now short black hair and admits, "I think I miss it."

"Then fix it the minute we get home."

Her smile is warm, but before she can turn and leave, I ask, "Can you do me a favor, though?"

"If I can, I will."

"Leave the past where it is. None of us are the same people we were in high school, and we will never be again. I also...I can't afford to think about it much. Who I was before."

Her face reflects her understanding. Very few of us are the same after the March on Massachusetts happened, and I have no doubt that she is one of the few who know the entire truth about what I'm meant to do.

Mei-Lien gives me a weak smile devoid of all its previous warmth, and she walks away. A small part of me wants to feel bad for ruining a decent moment between the two of us, but the broken-hearted ice bitch that makes up the rest of me doesn't care. The *darkness* that's attached to her doesn't care. War is war. There is very little time for apologies or decent moments.

I turn my focus back to the picture in front of me. Aunt Delilah is between her two younger brothers, an arm wrapped around each one. Uncle Cyrus is making a silly face, and Dad is grinning from ear to ear. The twins had to be fourteen years old, by my guess, making her sixteen. Aunt Delilah is smiling, but something is off about it, as if it's forced into a smile from a grimace.

"I can hear the wheels of your mind turning. What's up, kid?" Uncle Cyrus comes up behind me, peering over my shoulder at the picture. "Ah. Do you want to know the irony of the three of us? I was the outcast, and Aaron and Delilah were more like the family's twins. They both got your grandpa's Intelligence classification, while I got your grandma's Elemental one. They rarely left each other's side, always whispering secrets and keeping me out of the loop. It wasn't until later that I realized I was grateful for it."

"Why were you grateful?" I ask.

He picks up the picture and studies it, then answers, "They were constantly testing their abilities, seeing how far they could push themselves. I caught them one day trying to find new ways to manipulate folks in the community. I tried telling our ma and pa, but their concern disappeared overnight as if I had never told them. I stopped trying after that and kept my distance. Shortly after, we had that attack that killed your aunt, and Aaron moved away the moment he graduated from high school."

He hands the picture back to me, and I see now what's wrong with Aunt Delilah. It's not her smile at all; it's her eyes, which look almost black. My heart hammers in my chest.

"What is it?" Uncle Cyrus asks, picking up on my reaction.

"What color were Aunt Delilah's eyes?"

"Amber, like your dad's and mine."

I hand the picture back to him. "What color do you see in this picture?"

"Amber. I'm not sure I am following, kid."

I take the picture back, and they are, in fact, amber now. The darkness inside me stirs and stretches, as if it had just woken up from a good nap.

I can't breathe.

"Talli?" Uncle Cyrus asks, his salt-and-pepper brows pulled together.

I put the picture down and force a reassuring smile. "I'm fine."

Leaving the room as fast as my feet will take me without running, I go outside and gulp in the humid air, trying to slow my heartbeat. I hear the slight patter of Coventina's little lizard feet as she stands beside me.

"*Aunt Delilah was like me, wasn't she?*"

"*It would appear so.*"

Aunt Delilah had the darkness inside of her, too.

CHAPTER 7

TALLIANA

GREER, MEI-LIEN, AND I fly to the cabin where we suspect Mackay to be located. The Brethren love their isolated cabins in the woods to set up a temporary base. They have them scattered all over the country. I know, because I have personally attacked a few of them.

We land in a clearing three-quarters of a mile away as midnight strikes, and we are greeted by Uncle Cyrus and two other men. I met one of them, Sam, earlier today while we were getting ready for the mission. He's a Strategist with a red fox bonded. His hair is the same shade as the fox's, but it's not natural. Apparently, he had dyed it to match. The freckles and pointed face *are* natural, though, as he made sure to tell me. Right when I felt unsure if I should laugh or not, Uncle Cyrus came up from behind us and exploded into laughter. He's always had a weird sense of humor.

The other man on this mission...I try to hide the catch in my breath as my gaze meets a familiar pair of green eyes. Then I see the black curls on his head and know it's Waylen.

I busy myself, unstrapping my bow and quiver of arrows from Coventina's saddle and ensuring all my knives are in place. Coventina and Draven take off and start circling the area with their glamour on.

"Mackay is here. We have a confirmed sighting. Everyone understands their roles and the plan?" Uncle Cyrus asks. All his usual light humor is nowhere to be found. He never actually goes on missions anymore, hasn't since they adopted Penn, but he told us that he wanted to be here when Greer and I make history by taking General Campbell's right-hand man down. Though I suspect that the real reason is to ensure this monster, Penn's birth father, is put in the ground for what he has done to so many women.

Everyone echoes an affirmative, and we all quietly walk into position around the cabin, circling it. I have to suppress my groan when Waylen follows me, claiming the title of my watch partner. We don't say anything as we take up our spots, sitting beside each other, shoulder-to-shoulder but facing opposite directions so no one can sneak up behind us.

The plan is to surround the cabin, waiting for most of the Brethren to leave for the attack on the community, then move in on Mackay while he doesn't have as many men around to protect him.

"Long time no see, Red," Waylen whispers as he leans back a little. I shiver at the feeling of his breath on my ear.

"Waylen. Still causing trouble every chance you get?" I ask.

"I wouldn't be here if the elders didn't trust me explicitly. You could say I've grown up since you last saw me." His southern twang is light, but there.

Waylen, admittedly, was my first crush, and I've known him since I was little. We used to visit every year around Christmas, and he was my playmate. He had a way of talking me into mischief and getting us both in trouble. The extreme opposite of Treyton in many ways. He was also my first kiss. An awkward kiss at the age of fourteen, but my first nonetheless.

When I don't respond and just nod, he adds, "You've grown up a lot too these last four years. It seems we are both badass adults now."

I grin at him. I can't help it. He has always had a way with words. I briefly wonder if he's gotten better at kissing since he was fourteen.

Dangerous. Such a dangerous thought. I shove it out of my mind before it has a chance to steal my focus.

"Anyone foolish enough to claim you yet?" I ask innocently.

"Nah. I had a girl for a while—two years—but she kept rushing me toward the chapel, and I was not ready for that yet. I'm still young, ya know? Anyway, she found someone who was and married him within a year. Crazy. I don't know how people do that, but people get married and have kids like the world is ending around here."

I understand that. It is common in all the communities, and it's the exact thing my parents are suggesting I do. Truthfully, though, it is more Mom than Dad. He seems to be just trying to manage the situation, rather than push me toward it.

"I'm sorry to hear that."

"I heard what happened to your man a while back. I'm sorry, Red. I bet he was something if he had you."

"He was. He was exceptional." That is all I can manage to say, still keeping my voice at a whisper level.

"A group of us jumped in a van and headed north as soon as we heard about the planned attack. We knew we would be too late by the time we got there, but I guess we felt we needed to go anyway. You were out cold still when I tried to see you," he admits.

"No one told me you visited. I'm sorry. If I had known, I might have planned a trip down at some point." I'm not sure that's true, but maybe I would have.

"It's okay. You've been busy being important, riding your dragon, and saving the day and everything," he teases.

"You've been keeping tabs on me?" I tease back.

"Hard not to when all old Cyrus can seem to talk about is his two nieces that kick ass every day while we train."

I smile. Of course Uncle Cyrus would be bragging about us to anyone within earshot.

Waylen and I continue in companionable conversation, catching up in soft whispers while we wait for something to happen. One hour passes. Then two. Four hours pass without movement or attacks on the community. Uncle Cyrus calls it, and we all head back to his house to rest.

Mei-Lien is frustrated, swearing it would have been tonight, but clearly, they postponed their usual rotation of attacks. We knew it was a possibility, but all our nerves are shot after waiting all night in the bushes for nothing to happen.

The following night, we resume our positions around the cabin, with Waylen, yet again, following me. It's comfortable now, though, and our friendship and light teasing are coming back naturally again. At about two in the morning, a group of Brethren leaves the cabin.

Finally.

"*All clear*," Draven says into my mind once they're gone.

I nod at Waylen, and he reaches in front of himself where he is sitting, placing his hands flat against the sandy dirt. His eyes close. One heartbeat. Six heartbeats. Fifteen heartbeats.

"There are four inside the cabin, and I don't sense anyone else," Waylen whispers. Waylen is an Earth Elemental. One of the many tricks to his ability is that he can use the ground to sense where things or people are. He did this as a kid, always cheating at hide-and-seek because he could tell where I was.

I relay the information to Greer, as Waylen relays it to Uncle Cyrus through the communication device he has attached to his ear. Slowly, we tighten our circle. We all have our weapons ready as we close in on the cabin that houses our target.

Just as we are about to reach the door, it swings open, light pouring out into the dark. Mackay steps out with his hands raised.

"Ah, Hawks, nice of you all to finally join me," he greets with a smile, his voice as slimy as the rest of his appearance. He has slicked-back hair and a mustache that has iconic bad guy written all over it. Three guns appear beside him in the doorway, all aimed toward us. I look over at Waylen and see a red dot on the back of his head.

Snipers.

It's a trap. And we walked right into it.

"*Greer, there are snipers!*" I scream at her through our mental link. She looks over at me, and shadows start to grow at her feet.

"Don't do that," Mackay tsks, then continues, "If anyone moves a muscle or does something funny, my men in the trees will shoot you all dead without hesitation."

Greer's shadows retract back into nothing at her feet. Mackay looks us all over, then settles his eyes on me, my bow with an arrow still pulled back and ready to fly in my hands. I get his meaning and slowly, reluctantly, lower my bow. Greer's sword lowers to her side, and Mei-Lien, Uncle Cyrus, Waylen, and Sam lower their own weapons. All at once, we drop them.

"*What's the plan?*" Coventina asks.

"Stay close, you two, but don't do anything until we say. We don't want to risk anyone getting shot in the head," Greer answers.

"I can cover the area in shadow so they can't see," Draven offers.

"It won't be fast enough," Greer replies.

Think Talli, think!

We all wait in tense silence, and then Mackay says, "I am so thrilled to meet the famed assassins of the Order." He looks at Greer, then at me. "I admire your work, but unfortunately, I need it to end. Having all my coworkers killed off is bad for business."

They know who we are.

Did they already know? Or did he guess right this minute? He had to have known already. Our faces are compromised. Shit. I glance back at Greer, and I know she is thinking the same thing, her face showing a hint of panic.

The darkness reacts to my own panic, thickening and preparing for a fight. My fingertips tingle with raw power.

"What do you want? Clearly it's something, since you haven't killed us yet," I sneer. My tone drips with annoyance. The façade I usually put on when face-to-face with the Brethren. I want them to think I only view them as bugs under my shoe. Bugs I am prepared to squash.

"Information, of course, little witch. I need to know how to destroy your people."

The three guns behind him are now attached to three men walking toward us, zip ties at the ready.

"You won't get anything out of us," Mei-Lien responds.

"Draven, we need a distraction," Greer says.

Waylen is the first to get his hands zip-tied. The Brethren come behind me next, and...Draven's roar is like a thunderclap. Everyone looks up, aside from the six of us who know better.

"What the hell was that?" Mackay asks.

Draven roars again, and Waylen stomps his foot down, causing the ground to shake so violently that everyone topples to the ground.

BANG.

Waylen, the only one still standing, falls. My ability tells me he was shot in the shoulder. He's still alive, but I have to get to him soon.

I grab an arrow I dropped earlier and drive it through the man's leg, the one about to tie my hands. Then, I grab his gun from his holster and fire.

BANG.

The man racing toward Greer drops. She is deep in concentration, trying to wrangle the snipers out of the trees with her shadows. If the sounds of distant screams are any indication, she is managing well.

Taking note of the situation, Uncle Cyrus jumps in front of Greer and creates a glittering shield around her.

BANG.

Sam goes down. Shot in the abdomen. I race toward him, but see Mei-Lien running toward Mackay with her knife. The third man intercepts Mei-Lien, and she fights him hand-to-hand.

I make a quick decision between running after Mackay and helping Sam. I race to Sam and pull out the canteen of water strapped to my side, immediately getting to work healing his gunshot wound. Waylen is next. He has time. I can feel it.

The ground shakes, but I ignore it.

"*We have Mackay blocked,*" Coventina says.

BANG.

I look over and see that Mei-Lien managed to get hold of the third Brethren's arm and compelled him to shoot himself in the foot.

The last bit of Sam's skin seals shut, and I hand him the gun I have. I run toward Waylen. Looking up, I see Greer and Uncle Cyrus fighting four new Brethren surrounding them.

What the hell? I look around and see ten more men running from the trees.

Shit.

Grabbing a gun that's discarded on the ground, I reach Waylen in the next second and hand him the gun. I heal him while he opens fire on anyone coming upon us.

"*We need some dragon help over here!*" I scream.

"*Coming!*" Coventina answers. A moment later, she lands next to me. I finish healing Waylen as she starts shooting water balls at incoming Brethren.

Every time I look, more are coming. We need to get out of here, but not before I take Mackay out, information or not.

"*Where's Mackay?*"

"*Northwest. Draven's guarding him.*" Coventina responds.

I get to my feet and head in that direction, but I spot the charcoal-colored dragon by Greer's side, fighting off incoming Brethren. I keep running but ask, "*Draven, where is Mackay?*"

"*Mei-Lien was doing her compelling thing on him and told me to help everyone else,*" he answers.

Oh no.

Greer takes down the man she is fighting and runs in my direction. We both have the same thought. Mei-Lien can't defend herself while trying to concentrate on compelling information out of someone.

Greer and I slow to a stop at a small clearing in the moss-covered trees, seeing the situation in front of us. Mei-Lien is on her knees, hands bound in front of her, with two guns pointed at her head. Using the humidity in the air, I form an ice dagger in my hand.

"Move, and she dies. Drop your weapons," Mackay calls out.

Greer and I both drop our weapons. The sound of running comes from our right, and two more Brethren emerge from the forest, guns in hand.

"*Get everyone to safety,*" I order the dragons.

"*Already doing so,*" Coventina replies.

A gun is pressed to the back of my head. I don't have to look to know Greer has one against hers, too. I desperately try to think of a way out that doesn't involve any of us getting shot, but I can only think of one, and there is no time to find another option.

I will not let any of us fall today.

"*Talli, what are you planning?*" Greer asks.

"*When everyone drops, grab Mei-Lien and run. I'll be right behind you.*"

"Now..." Mackay starts talking, but I tune him out. Looking inside of myself, I call on the darkness.

Time to come out and play.

It's always a gamble to call on it. Sometimes it listens to my will and allows me to use its power with control. Other times, it shoves me into the back seat and does what it wants.

I anxiously await its decision as it rolls and tumbles through me, coating everything aside from my heart, which somehow still has a dim light shining around it after these two long years. The darkness's power surges through my veins, but I don't feel its nails clamp down onto my muscles, rendering me helpless to its whim. It's letting me have control.

Thank you.

I've never tested this skill before, but it will work—the darkness will ensure it. I feel a buzzing in the back of my head and a tingling in my fingers. It's in agreement. This is the only way.

"*Talli, wha*—" Greer starts, but I shut down my mental connection to everyone and stretch out my fingers as wide as my joints will allow.

Inhale. Exhale. Inhale. Exhale. On the third inhale, I lock onto the targets and pull hard with my closing fists, using every drop of dark-coated magic inside me.

Water shoots out of Mackay and the other three guards' pores. I release my pull, and the water drops to the ground with the four empty bodies.

"What the hell did you just do?" I hear Greer scream out loud. She doesn't wait for an answer but runs to Mei-Lien.

Good, because I can't answer anyway. I'm too weak.

Mei-Lien is shaking on the ground, going into shock. I watch as Greer navigates around the deformed bodies and grabs Mei-Lien with her shadows. With a last look at me attempting to move my feet, Greer runs with her deeper into the forest.

The darkness recedes its power, and I stumble and fall, hitting the ground hard. I'm so tired. My eyelids waver, wanting to close.

"*Get up!*" Coventina yells. I push myself to my hands and knees. An arm wraps around my waist, and before I can weakly thrash, I hear, "I got you, Red."

Waylen.

I could sob from relief. He picks me up and swings me over his shoulder. Then he starts running with me bouncing against his rigid back. I slide in and out of consciousness until we stop, and I open my eyes to see Coventina. Waylen is putting me in her saddle.

My face gently rests against her soft hair. I have no energy to hold myself up. I feel Greer climb in behind me and buckle us both in. I smile at Waylen, who is still standing right there, panting from exertion.

"You always find me, don't you?" I ask him sweetly, then everything goes dark.

CHAPTER 8

TALLIANA

My eyes open, and I wince from the splitting migraine I feel pounding through my head.

Where am I?

Oh, that's right. I see I am in the guest bedroom at Uncle Cyrus's house. I lost consciousness. I sit up, one hand on my head, and look down to see Coventina in her lizard form curled up on my stomach.

"*You need more sleep.*"

"*How long have I been out?*"

"*Eighteen hours.*"

"*I'm fine then.*"

"*You need at least another twenty-four. You almost completely drained yourself. Again.*" Her tone is pure annoyance. After the March on Massachusetts, she wanted me to promise her I would never push myself that far again. I didn't promise because I knew better.

"I'm much stronger than before, so I'm fine. I just need a hot shower, and I'll be right as rain."

Coventina jumps off my lap and onto the bed as I swing my legs to the side of it. The door opens, and Greer comes in.

"Snitch," I say out loud to Coventina so Greer can hear it, too.

"You are not leaving that bed until you explain what you did out there," Greer tells me firmly, arms crossed over her chest—the usual Greer is pissed stance.

I sigh loudly. "I want a shower."

"After." She turns on the bedside lamp, and I see Draven perched on her shoulder. I guess this is going to be a family conversation, then.

My initial reaction is to brush her off, avoid the topic, push her further away, but it's been nice starting to talk again. So reluctantly, I explain, "I learned how to do it while we were in China. Mrs. Chan told me how, before we left. I've never practiced or done it before, but it was there just in case."

A couple of months after we bonded with Coventina and Draven, Chief Lu came clean about one of the China communities' best-kept secrets: they had a Water Healer. A woman over a hundred years old, but alive and willing to teach me what she knows. Water Healers were supposed to be extinct, but apparently, China had been hiding what they thought was the last one, until I came along.

We spent three months there, and then Dad sent us to Russia for Greer to learn under the fiercest Shadow-wielders known to us. Greer lasted about two weeks in the cold before we jumped onto our dragons in the middle of the night and went home when no one was looking. Ash found some texts on shadow-wielding for her to learn from, instead, since no one else in the United States has the ability.

"So, you...just..." she starts.

"I pulled all the water out of their body," I confirm.

"Why didn't you tell me you could do that?"

"I never intended to use it. I never wanted to use it. When I knew Mei-Lien was going to die, and us potentially with her, my intuition kicked in, and I knew it was the only way."

"Your intuition? Do you think I still don't know what you mean when you use that word?"

I avert my gaze.

"You scared me," she admits quietly, and I look at her again. "I've never seen you use your power like that. I've seen that *thing* in your eyes before. I've seen you lose yourself to *it*, but this time? I felt the same thrum of your magic when *it* amplifies you, but I didn't see *it*."

"That's because it was my choice this time. When you see it, it means I no longer have free will, it's in complete control of everything. But times like today...it lets me use it."

"What you did...is that something you could do without help?" Greer asks carefully.

"I think so, but not more than one person at a time."

She nods and looks down at her feet. Before I can change the subject, she says, "I get it, Talli. Why you wouldn't want people to know. While you were resting, the four of us agreed to never speak about what really happened. As far as anyone else knows, you used water daggers to kill those men."

What she isn't saying is that if anyone found out I could kill someone in an instant like that—let alone a few someones simultaneously—I could be locked up for having that kind of power. That, coupled with everything else I can do, is beyond anyone else we know of in history.

"Four? What do you mean four?" I ask.

"Waylen and Uncle Cyrus. Waylen saw what happened, and Uncle Cyrus...well, he demanded to know." I groan and fall back into bed, but she continues, "I almost asked Mei-Lien to tamper with both of their memories, but Uncle Cyrus was the first to swear us all to secrecy and promise to not even tell Dad. And Waylen...I'll leave that up to you, but Uncle Cyrus vouched for him, and he has been nothing but worried about you since we got back."

"I trust your judgment, Greer. I trust it more than mine. What happened here? Was there an attack?" I ask, referencing the Florida community.

"No, it was just a trap for us. Mackay hid all his men in the trees where they couldn't be seen or easily sensed. Speaking of that son of a bitch, Mei-Lien got some information out of him before his backup arrived. So the mission was successful for the most part," Greer explains.

"Good. I guess we can go home then?"

"We will head out tomorrow night. Dad approved the extra day when I told him I needed it. He didn't need to know that you were in rough shape."

"Yeah, probably not. If a few water daggers drained my magic, he would know something's up."

I notice some bruising around her chin, and before she can protest, I pull the water out of the cup on my nightstand and press it to the bruise with my ability. I do it five more times when I sense more on her. Only bruises, though, so that's good.

"Thanks," she says, rubbing her chin.

I nod, and she goes to the door. She stops and turns back to look at me before opening it. "You would tell me if you needed help? Or at least let me know if I needed to be past simply worrying?"

"Of course," I answer as I bury the guilt inside of me. The fact is, I am not alright, I do need help, and she should be past just worrying, but I'm dealing with it. Greer may be a Shadow-wielder, but she is the picture of control. It's that control of her emotions and abilities that keeps the darkness away from her. Me, on the other hand? I have little to no control. The darkness is my bedmate, and it keeps me cold every second of every day. But I've come to prefer the cold.

She gives me one last assessing look and leaves the room. A minute after her, I head straight out and go to the bathroom to take a shower. Afterward, my body feels significantly better. Of all the things my bond has gotten me, self-healing with water has been the best, without a doubt.

"*Aside from my friendship, of course,*" Coventina quips as I wrap myself up in my towel.

"*Of course. I love having you in my head,*" I reply sarcastically, but I do actually mean it, and she knows it.

"*The crush is in your room. He almost squashed me when he sat on the bed.*"

I blush at the name she gave him. "*Thanks for the warning.*"

I should be concerned that Waylen is waiting for me, but to my own surprise, I'm not. I leave the bathroom and head into Greer's and my shared room. Sure enough, he is lounging on my bottom bunk. The towel is still wrapped around me, and I shut the door. Long gone is the innocent, shy girl I used to be.

"Oh, sorry, Red. I knew you were in the shower, but I didn't...I thought you'd have clothes. I..." Waylen stammers as he suddenly gets out of my bed and goes to the door. I've known him my entire life, and he has never struggled with his words before.

"Waylen, it's fine. What's up?" I cut him off.

He turns back to look at me, and his eyes darken in the good way as he lets himself take in my towel-wrapped body. He clears his throat and catches my eyes before saying, "I came to say thank you. You saved my life and Sam's. All our lives, really. Seeing you in action, well, it was pretty amazing."

I tuck a piece of damp hair behind my ear. Flattery and gratitude have always made me a bit uncomfortable. "Thank you for coming to my rescue, too. I would have been a sitting duck if you hadn't come along."

"It was nothing. But really, Greer wouldn't have left you. She saw me coming for you, and that's why she left."

He takes a step toward me.

"It was something. Why didn't you go with Covey to safety?" I ask.

"I think she tried to get me, but I'm not sure since she was glamoured, as you call it." I forgot he isn't bonded, so he wouldn't have been able to see the dragons like the rest of us could while they were glamoured. Luckily, his ability still allowed him to sense where they were through the ground. He continues, "Instead, I checked for your shape and found you, but you were surrounded. I decided to go try to help you. Though, you didn't need my help, did you?" He laughs a little under his breath.

Two more steps.

"It was very gallant of you to come running to save me, even if I didn't need it," I tell him softly.

He nods. "I'm not sure how often you two do this kind of thing. I will take a guess that it's often enough." Another step. "But I'm sure it takes a toll. If you need to blow off any steam before you leave," he says, right in front of me now, his chest brushing up against the hand holding up my towel, "my house is just down the street. Number 3584. I'm the only one living there, so come by anytime."

He reaches his hand out to push the hair sticking to my shoulder back, gently touching my bare skin in the process. It warms in response to his familiar touch, and the rest of my body aches to feel that warmth all over.

"Waylen, you deserve better than someone just wanting to use you. Because believe me, I'm not what you want. I'm not what anyone really wants," I explain.

"Nah. I don't believe that. I think you tell yourself that to justify keeping your heart guarded. I get it, though. I've done the same since my girl left me." He brushes his hand down the length of my arm, and then continues, "I won't pressure you, but you will not hurt me if you decide to come. Maybe I want to use you as much as you want to use me. We'll call it a friends with benefits type of situation. No expectations."

Now that...that I can do. Before I can say anything, he turns around and heads back to the door to leave. His hand is on the handle as I say, "Wait. There's one thing I need to know."

His eyebrow lifts, and I ask, "You know what I did to those men. You saw it, and you're not afraid of me?"

He gives me a smile, one I know well, the one he always gives me when he knows I'm on the hook for any scheme he comes up with. "I've always been afraid of you, Red. But it's because you are a weakness for me—something that clouds the tiny bit of good judgment I actually have. But I could never be afraid of you because your abilities are powerful or because you do what you have to. It only makes me admire you more." He leaves without further explanation, and I'm left feeling puzzled and very aroused.

Once I'm sure Greer is asleep, I creep out of bed, getting my first shoe on. "Give Waylen my regards," Greer says into the dark room.

Damn it. I put on my second shoe a bit louder than the first. There is no point in denying it or being quiet at this point.

"I'll be back before dawn."

"I'm not judging," she replies innocently.

"You are always judging."

She snorts and doesn't say more. I roll my eyes at her dark form and head out.

As I walk to Waylen's house, the night air is warm and sticky. Part of me knows this is a bad idea, but the part I'm choosing to listen to is bouncing at the thrill of what is about to happen. It's been a while for me, and before Treyton, Waylen was the one I always dreamed of. Curiosity might be the death of me, but I'm desperate to know.

I knock at number 3584, a house that looks the same as all the others, but this one is a simple cream color. A moment passes, and then the door opens. Waylen is in loose black sleep pants, hanging low on his waist, and no shirt. I stifle a groan as I look at what's on display. He has always been thin and lean, and not much has changed...aside from the six-pack, the well-defined arms, and the fact that his boyish good looks are now pure manly sexiness. His grin makes me want to melt on the spot, but instead, I walk inside and let him close the door behind me.

"I have to come clean before we do anything," he states, and I turn around to face him.

"Oh yeah?" I ask, caught off guard.

"Since we shared that first kiss, I've always wondered if you still tasted like strawberry ice cream."

I laugh. That was not at all what I was expecting. "Waylen, I tasted like ice cream because I had some that day, remember?"

His smile widens. "I theorize you still taste like ice cream any-way." His slight southern accent comes out on *theorize*.

"Care to test it out?" I tease.

The ground underneath my feet rumbles a little, and I grin. He swaggers up to me, using his ability to make it seem like each step is making the ground shake, and his mouth crashes into mine. I let him slide his tongue into my mouth and taste me. He does a thorough job, his hands grasping my waist as he does so. Then he pulls back, licking his lips, and says, "Mmm...strawberry ice cream. Your mouth is even a bit chilled."

I smack his chest, and he pulls me back up against him and kisses me again. He has vastly improved his kissing since we were fourteen. Granted, I would be worried if he hadn't.

I feel my self-control slipping, and even though I've known where this was going to go since he asked, I'm still worried about breaking my one rule. So I pull away and ask, "What about the connection?"

"We are adults. Doing it once will not hurt us if we don't let it."

That's all I need. I put my mouth back onto his, letting go completely. He pulls away again and breathlessly asks, "Tell me what you want, Red."

I'm taken by surprise by the question. I have never been asked that before.

"I want to be touched," I answer, thinking about his warm hands. It's vague, but understanding coats his face, and he picks me up, an arm under my legs and one behind my back. I laugh, and he captures the sound with his mouth. He walks us through his house, up the stairs, and to his bed without ever opening his eyes.

I feel his comforter underneath me, and he does exactly what I ask. He touches me. His touch is so familiar and comfortable that it does something to me. It breaks down some of the walls that are built up inside of me, and I am reminded of who I am.

I am Talliana Hoffman: a daughter, a sister, a friend, a Healer, and so much more.

Release finds us both as we are gasping for air, and together, we collapse. A few minutes pass, and I can't help but ruin the happy, sex-dazed mood by asking, "What did you mean earlier?"

"Which part?"

"When you said I am your weakness." I prop my head up on my arm to look at him.

He sighs. "There isn't anything I wouldn't do for you, Red."

What? No. No. He said...

"I know what I said about no attachments, and I meant it, but you had to have known I've loved you, I think, our entire lives."

I reel back, not prepared for that confession. I don't know what to say. I enjoyed myself—a lot. And what passed between us felt different, unlike all the other guys I hooked up with for the sake of it. But love? It doesn't feel the same way it did with Treyton.

"Don't fret. I don't want anything more than this. Like I said before, I'm not interested in starting a life with anyone at the moment. Especially after fighting for my life the other night. Maybe if this all ends one day, I will, but not sooner."

I get it. That's how I have been feeling, but maybe...maybe that's the wrong way to look at it. We need people to help us through the hard stuff, like what Uncle Cyrus said when I got here.

"Can I tell you a secret?" I ask, coming to a decision.

"Of course," he replies a bit eagerly, sitting up.

I sit up to face him, pushing back my realization that I'm still naked. "No one knows outside of a select few, but I'm supposed to end this war one day." His eyes widen, and I press on. "When Covey bonded with me, she told me that together, she and I would end it."

He takes a moment to think about that. "What about Greer? Is she included in this, too?" That is an astute question.

"Not that the dragons have shared, no. We just have a vague vision from her late father telling her she is meant to help me. But since I've learned about Covey's prophecy, I've kept far away from anything resembling a real relationship. I've been terrified of losing someone else. But everyone around me keeps putting on the pressure to find someone, and I don't know what to do anymore," I confess to him.

He places his hand on my cheek and says, "Talli, all you can do is what feels right. It's your life and your destiny. No one can make you do anything either way."

He's right. His words are so simple, but they are exactly what I need to hear right now.

"Thank you, Waylen. I've missed your friendship." I lean in and kiss him again. Not one full of lust, but one full of friendship and gratitude. I pull back and then flash him a cheeky grin. "Just so you know, I had the biggest crush on you when we were kids."

He grins right back at me. "I know. You were never very good at your shields growing up."

I feign offense, then laugh. I know it's true. I wore everything on my face. Still do, half of the time. I worked very hard for a long time to keep strong shields, but I gave up after I lost Trey. I no longer saw much of a point to it. I don't care what people think of me.

Getting up, I get dressed. Waylen sits on his bed, watching me, and I let him.

"Thank you for tonight. I'll try to visit again soon."

"I'll hold you to that," he says with a smile.

I turn to walk out, but he stops me, like I stopped him earlier. "Oh, and Red? Once you know how to end this war, give me a call. I want to be there to help you take them down."

I turn and meet his beautiful green eyes. He is earnest, and my heart swells with respect. Nodding, I walk out the door feeling different. Once on the sidewalk, halfway back to Uncle Cyrus's, my breath catches as I feel something in my chest.

It's the connection to Waylen snapping into place.

I slowly look inside of myself, and instead of trying to ignore the attachment to my most vital organ, I look toward it. The other is still there—the ghost of a rope frayed and unraveled next to that tiny thread that now belongs to Waylen.

A tear falls. Then another. As much as the weight of that thread attached to my heart next to *his* threatens to shatter me, it is a reminder that my heart still works.

Even if it's broken.

CHAPTER 9

TALLIANA

DESPERATELY, I RUSH INTO my bedroom and shut the door behind me. Aside from those first few tears after I left Waylen's house, I've been holding in the emotions starting to overwhelm me until we could get back home to Massachusetts. Greer went straight to Ash to serenade him outside his window when we landed, as she should have, and I'm so grateful for it. I need to be alone while I deal with...myself.

I feel like a cauldron about to boil over. My ice barrier is no longer holding back everything I have been trying not to feel for the last two years. Looking around frantically, I try to decide what to do, when I catch sight of my reflection and stop. I stand in front of my floor-length mirror which I once cherished and used every day. Now, I don't think I've genuinely used it in years except as a clothes rack, that is.

I don't know what possesses me, but I pull each article of clothing down one by one. My favorite green sweater, a purple blouse, my navy hoodie, and a top that always made me feel like a mermaid each time I wore it. Piece by piece, I feel like a brick made of ice is being torn down from the wall I have built around myself.

The reality is that since Trey died, I haven't cared what I looked like, not like I used to. Clothing, makeup, jewelry—everything that felt like my external identity, my armor for everyday life—it all felt trivial and unimportant. It was a part of me that I let myself lose along with Trey.

With the mirror bare in front of me, my entire appearance on display, I don't recognize the person I see. She has dull hair, a tired face, and a body of lean muscle with no soft edges. Her stance is alert and battle-ready, her eyes full of something, a darkness swirling there. She has felt loss and heartbreak. She has seen evil and killed people. Her only focus is her end goal, not caring about anything along the way. She...I cup a hand over my mouth, holding back a sob.

She is me.

All her...all my beauty is gone. I close my eyes and feel a tear run past my hand, still closed over my mouth. I've killed so many without thought or remorse. I literally sucked water out of people's bodies and left them as half-empty sacks of skin. Something I told myself I wouldn't do, a line I never wanted to cross. I kill with the intent to make it quick and painless, but that was anything but painless. I can't even blame the darkness for forcing me to use my ability that way. No, it was my choice. I did that.

I fall to my knees in front of this ultimate truth-telling device. Something that has never deceived me or filled me with pretty words or fake compliments. I hug myself, hunch over on my knees, and take a sledgehammer to the barrier I've put up around my true self—the wall I've helped the darkness build after I lost Trey. Each sob that racks my body is another strike to that wall. Each tear is a new stream of water that flows out of the cracks I'm creating.

I take every blow and don't stop until the wall is rubble at my feet. My body is flooded with every emotion, feeling, and thought I've locked away over the past few years. Looking around at the mess inside myself, I turn back to where my fortress once stood and see a girl curled up into a ball on the floor, crying. She's so young and full of life, yet so sad.

"*You found her. The sad one,*" I hear Coventina say.

"*What happened to her?*" I ask, but I already know.

"*Her head needed her to move on and continue living, but her heart wasn't ready. So, she was locked up in a cage made of ice and darkness and never allowed out. But you did it. You rescued her. You freed yourself. Now, let yourself heal.*"

I open my eyes to see that girl in the mirror in the same position. My sad, dark-blue eyes turn hard as I stare myself down—stare the darkness down.

I will not lock myself away again, and I will not hide who I really am. I will allow myself to heal, feel, and love. I will end this war, but I will allow myself to live again until I do. Simply existing until then is no longer enough.

I stand, a different sense of purpose straightening my back. One that is full of hope. One that includes my happiness. One that sees me through this darkness boiling inside of me, and to the light that is fighting for space.

Waylen helped me remember who I was inside, but it took my strength to set her free. Now, I need to figure out how to tame the darkness so it doesn't consume me again.

I have no doubt it's easier said than done, but I'm ready. I'm ready to stop shutting everyone out. I'm ready to be open to feeling love and everything messy that comes with it.

I'm ready to live again.

"*Took you long enough,*" Coventina mutters.

The next day, Greer and I walk together to Dad's office for our mission report. Her steps are unmistakably lighter this morning, and they feel contagious.

"So...did you sleep well last night?" I pry.

"Yes, I slept well. Thank you."

"Did Ash sleep well, too?"

She looks at me and grins fiendishly. "Yes, I would say he slept very well."

I return her grin. "I am so happy for you both."

"Me too. I meant to ask you yesterday, but there wasn't much time. How did your little meetup with Waylen go?" Her tone is teasing but genuine.

"Oh. Well, it was good, but it's clear that we're just friends. I needed something to remind me of who I am, though, and surprisingly, Waylen was the answer to that."

"That's good to hear. Being the positive one around here is exhausting. So good to have you back!" She puts her arm around me and pulls me to her side as we laugh together the rest of the way to the community building.

Once in Dad's office, the usual crowd fills the room: all three elders, Mei-Lien, Mr. Simon, and Reef. Everyone's bonded is here, too, aside from Coventina and Draven. They needed some rest after the long flight last night.

Greer gives the full report of what happened, minus the truth of how I killed those men. Mr. Simon summarizes the report provided by Uncle Cyrus earlier over the phone. Then Mei-Lien presents the little information she gained from Mackay before he got the upper hand, which includes where General Campbell usually operates from. The prison in Colorado. The same one where Treyton and the Hansens were held. It was something we already suspected, but now we have confirmation.

"Well done, the three of you. The mission did not go as planned, but you kept each other and the team safe while still managing to get some information. I am very proud of each one of you." Everyone looks pleased, but Dad turns his attention toward me and asks, "Talli, I have to ask, though: those water daggers you used to kill those men, how did you know they would be fast enough? There were guns at your heads."

I look to Greer, but I know she can't be the one to answer this for me. I straighten my back and explain, "Greer was being modest in her report, giving me all the credit for saving Mei-Lien. She used her shadows to knock the guns out of the men's hands behind us, which distracted the men who were holding Mei-Lien long enough for me to get them with my water daggers. Then I turned around and killed the men behind us with them, as well."

"I'm sorry, I didn't think the detail was necessary when Talli is the one who truly took them out," Greer explains to cover her ass for not including that fake detail initially. I feel her suppress the urge to glare at me.

Dad nods, accepting the explanation, then replies, "Well, good teamwork. I want you two to lay low until we know for sure if your identities have been compromised."

"Yes, sir," we say in unison.

"Go rest and enjoy your day."

Once we are all dismissed, I let out a breath of relief, and Greer seems to do the same. When we get outside, she goes her own way to meet Ash at the library while I head back to the house.

I hear my name being called, so I turn to see Mr. Simon trying to catch up to me. "Talli, may I walk with you? I have some questions about your report."

My body tenses. Of course Mr. Simon caught our lies. He can detect even the smallest ones underneath an extremely well-built shield with his ability. He didn't rat us out, though, so I nod and allow him to fall into step beside me. Seth finds a place between us, and I scratch his head, causing his tongue to tumble out of his mouth. The gesture makes me grin.

"Care to tell me why you and Greer lied about how you killed those men?" Mr. Simon accuses, getting right to the point. This man will never change. Being a former investigation officer for the U.S. Army, there is no beating around the bush for him.

"Not really."

He pins me with a parental look, so I respond, "It was collectively decided that it was best to keep what happened within the team."

"So, Cyrus knows the truth and is also lying?"

"Yes," I confirm.

"And I suppose he was the one who decided it was best not to be honest?"

I huff. "Don't say it like that. Greer and I agreed once I woke up. We likely would have made the same decision regardless."

"Once you woke up? What did you do to knock yourself out like that?" He stops me then and turns to me. "Talli, it's me. I know you've been pushing everyone away over the last two years, and I don't blame you. Really, I get it. But I'm worried about your safety. You know that I won't share what happened with anyone."

"You're not going to let this go." Not a question. I know he won't.

"The alternative is that I call Cyrus."

I groan and look around to make sure no one is close to where we are on the street. Suddenly, I regret this whole not-shutting-people-out thing. "I..." I clear my throat. "When Greer and I were visiting the China community, the Water Healer I studied under told me about a way I could use my ability. I swore never to use it, but the only other choice was to let one of us die, and I couldn't let that happen."

Mr. Simon studies me closely. "Go on."

"I pulled all the water out of their body to kill them," I blurt out in a rush.

His studying gaze turns into a wide-eyed stare of horror.

"That's why I didn't want to tell you or anyone else. What I did was horrific. It also makes it clear that I can kill anyone I have my sights on without touching them. In a matter of seconds," I tack on.

Mr. Simon scrubs his face with his hand, then looks at me seriously. "This is the first time you have used this ability?"

I nod.

"I assume you know that light would not allow you to do something like that. Only darkness can wield magic with that much destruction," he warns.

"The light would allow me to, I feel confident of that. But it's not strong enough to do it to the extreme that I did...to as many people as I did..." It's only a theory, but I'm pretty certain of it.

"How long?"

I know what he is asking. How long have I let the darkness run rampant inside of me.

"Three years. I started feeling it after Trey was taken. The March on Massachusetts was the first time I let it take over," I answer honestly.

"Talli. I can't express to you how dangerous using it can be. You could lose all control one day if you let it continue."

"I know. I have...But! After this whole *situation*, I've decided to start working on controlling it. The fact is, I need it to end this war. It's the only way to do it. I just haven't figured out how yet. In the meantime, I will do whatever the elders ask of me and keep my head down. I am already considered a valuable object to so many because of Coventina, but if this or my *other* ability got out, they would either put me in prison or create a breeding program just for me."

"Your father wouldn't let that happen," Mr. Simon argues.

"No, I don't think he would, either, but he already uses Greer and me as assassins for the Order. Who's to say what he might do, or have me do, if he learned about this? He has sent me to the labs three times this summer to be evaluated by the Hansens for the *other* one. I know it's just a matter of time before they figure out a way to use it. I mean, I want to do whatever it takes to end the war, but I...I have a bad feeling about it. So I can't risk this."

"I don't like admitting it, but I agree."

I swallow hard. I knew he would, but hearing him say it out loud makes my stomach churn. I am powerful, more powerful than any other, and using darkness to fuel that power to a level never seen before while living among people who believe in control and limitations, who abhor the darkness—our original sworn enemy—is dangerous. If the Order found out what I was and the extent of magic I wield, prison or a breeding program would be the kindest outcomes I could ask for.

It is more likely that I would be cut down without much hesitation. Greer would likely be next, simply for being associated with me.

"*Draven and I would tear the flesh off the bones of anyone who dared to try,*" Coventina comments inside my mind.

"I know your schedule will be busy with classes starting again next week, but will you make time for an extra training session with me? An hour every week," he clarifies.

"I don't think—" I start, but he cuts me off. "I want to help you learn to control it."

"How?"

"I know of a book. I suspect it will give us some answers."

I stare at him. Ash has pulled many books over the last two years, looking for anything that references darkness for me, but he hasn't found anything that hasn't just made me ask more questions.

"What book?" I ask, finally.

"It's actually a journal—the personal journal of Katarina Lehmann."

Katarina Lehmann was the first Water Healer in our history. That's intriguing, and I'd be very curious to read what it says, but how could her journal help me?

"Okay. I'll look over my schedule and let you know."

Mr. Simon gives me a small smile. "You are not alone, Talli. I have your back always. You only have to ask." He turns and walks back down the sidewalk with Seth by his side.

For the first time in two years, I really don't feel alone.

Chapter 10

CASPIAN

I throw the last box toward the door of my small apartment, feeling immense relief to be done. Eying the gray couch next to me skeptically, I turn and allow myself to fall back onto it, bracing my body for the chance that it will fall apart the moment my weight hits it. To my surprise, it doesn't, and I exhale in relief. Relaxing into the cheap cloth fabric, I try yet again to keep my thoughts from running away with me.

The couch was delivered two hours ago in another box that needed unpacking. The fucking thing even had to be put together. A couch! Apparently, furniture bought online has to be assembled, as I've learned the hard way today. I put together a bed frame, a dresser, a nightstand, a coffee table, and a couch in the last twenty-four hours. Tomorrow, I'm sure I'll add a dining room table and chairs to the list once they get delivered. I grumble at the mere idea of reading another set of instructions with no words and bad images that don't even make sense.

I swivel my body to change into a lying position on the couch, my head up against the armrest and my legs, from the knees down, dangling over the edge of the other armrest. Furniture bought online is also much smaller than it appears in the pictures.

Reaching for the back of the couch, I idly search for a blanket to ball up and use as a pillow for my head, only to remember I haven't bought any yet. Or pillows for that matter. My day is not over, it seems. A trip to the store is still in order to pick up blankets, towels, and a few things for the kitchen.

Juliet, our housekeeper, made me a list of things I'll need. I'm grateful for it, otherwise I would spend a week running to the store over and over again to get things I am missing. I will miss her company, the only mother figure I had growing up, but I will not miss having my every move watched and reported back to my father. Granted, I have no doubt I still have spies on me even now.

I sit up, determined to get the shopping trip over with as quickly as possible so I can end my day. Standing, I go to the kitchen counter to grab my keys when my phone rings. I pull it out of my pocket and see the call is from Matthew—the closest thing I've got to a friend back in Colorado.

"Hey man. What's going on?" I answer.

"You're not going to like this," he replies.

I tense, unsure I can handle any more stress today, but I don't have much of a choice, so I ask, "What is it?"

"Mackay made an attempt at your girl."

Ice floods my veins. No. He isn't that stupid. My father's leash on him is loose compared to most, but surely he knows better than to interfere with his plans.

"He's dead, by the way. Word is, his soldiers found his body and four others in a pretty gruesome state," Matthew explains.

I feel air filling up my lungs again at the knowledge that he wasn't successful, so I take a deep breath. "How?"

"Like dehydrated mummies. They are still trying to figure out exactly what happened. But one of his men confessed to Mackay's plan, and they confirmed a sighting of her."

New trick, Talliana? What can't you do?

"She got away, I take it?"

"Oh yeah. Without a doubt." Matthew hesitates, then adds, "Are you sure you don't need any backup? I can enroll in the school too, pretend to be a friend of yours."

"No." The word comes out too rushed, so I try to recover by saying, "I appreciate the offer, Matthew. But she would read you from a mile away. I can't risk you blowing my cover."

"Yeah, you're right. She can probably smell fear, and I'm fucking terrified of her. If she actually did *that* to Mackay somehow...I have always envied how much attention you get from women, but I don't envy you this time."

I snort. "Be sure to remember my sacrifice when we win this war because of it, and keep me updated if you hear anything else pertaining to my target."

"Sure thing, Caspian."

"Thanks." I hang up the phone and scrub my face with my hand.

Your girl, he had called her. She is undoubtedly not *my* anything, aside from being my target. I can't help but feel impressed, though. She took down Mackay. That did everyone a favor, ridding the world of that sick bastard. There are a lot of bad men that work for the Brethren, but he...he was on his own level of evil. He crossed lines that no one else dared. Even my father propagates the belief that having sex with a witch is condemning yourself to the worst kind of fate—a fate he is allowing me to condemn myself to. But this mission is important, and I have to do everything in my power to succeed.

My dick hardens in response to my line of thinking, the traitor.

Shopping. I need to go to the store.

My thoughts now set back on task, I leave my apartment to pick out some blankets and towels I think a murderous witch would like to wrap herself in.

I DIDN'T MEAN TO, BUT IT JUST HAPPENED. OTIS GOT HURT, CUT HIS LEG DURING HIS SWORD PRACTICE. I WAS WORRIED HE'D GET AN INFECTION, SO I USED MY WATER ABILITY TO CLEAN HIS WOUND, BUT THEN HIS LEG STARTED TO GLOW. HIS SKIN STITCHED ITSELF BACK TOGETHER, AND NEITHER OF US COULD BELIEVE OUR EYES. I HEALED HIM! NO ELIXIR OR SALVE NEEDED. THE OTHERS SAW THIS, TOO, AND IMMEDIATELY RAN TO THE ELDERS. I'M AFRAID MY WORRY OVER MY FRIEND'S HEALTH HAS LED TO MY WHOLE LIFE CHANGING.

- JOURNAL OF KATARINA LEHMANN

CHAPTER 11

TALLIANA

September

WALKING TOWARD THE DAY'S first class, I do my best to focus on my newly found optimism. I have goals and plans. I am going to get a handle on the darkness inside of me, and with that control, maybe I will finally find the solution to ending this war.

I briefly met with Mr. Simon last night, and he showed me the journal. It turns out Ms. Trisha is one of Katarina's descendants, and her journal has been kept in the family for generations. She never read or did anything with it until she heard I was also a Water Healer. At that point, she became interested in what it might say. It turned out to be about her struggle with the darkness, and Ms. Trisha disregarded it as nothing more than the ramblings of an abused woman. But she did mention it to Mr. Simon a while back, and now that he has learned the whole truth about me, he has decided that we should study it for helpful information. Skimming it last night, it did feel like Ms. Trisha described, but Mr. Simon has hope. So I am choosing to have hope, too. One thing is clear, though: Katarina Lehmann was dark like me.

Are all Water Healers susceptible to the darkness? I never saw it in Mrs. Chan, but I wouldn't be surprised if she, the only other Water Healer alive, was. She never explained whether using water healing—an ability that should solely be about restoring—as a weapon was something passed down from generations or something she had discovered herself. Either way, I have little doubt that she recognized the darkness inside of me. Why else would she teach me to use my ability in a way that is only powerful once backed up by the darkness?

What if instead of being susceptible to the darkness, it's more of a precursor to becoming a Water Healer? Like the darkness doesn't just fuel the ability, it's a requirement for it. That thought makes my stomach churn. If I had to choose between my water healing and being free of the darkness, I would choose water healing without hesitation. Again and again. There is a small comfort, as messed up as it is, that Water Healers aren't the only ones who can be targeted by the darkness, if Aunt Delilah is any proof of that.

How many others in our history have struggled with this?

Mr. Simon told me he would hold onto the journal for now to see what he could decipher first, since I'm busy with school. I am grateful for the offer, nervous yet hopeful to see what he will find. Although the idea of being in the possession of another person's journal, a person like me, makes me itch with the urge to want to read it myself. I have a million questions about how she dealt with the darkness, but I have to resign myself to trusting Mr. Simon to tell me what I need to know.

I want to tell Ash about it. I know he would be anxious to study it, too, but I don't want Greer catching wind of this through him just yet. She will want to be involved, and I'm not entirely ready for that.

"Iris?" A voice comes from behind me, one that sends a warm shiver down my spine.

I stop and turn toward it. "Excuse me?"

The man I'm now faced with is familiar, but I can't quite place him in my memory. He's tall, well over six feet. His golden-blond hair is a wavy masterpiece on his head, like the fresh-out-of-the-shower shaggy look is precisely what he is going for. His hazel eyes are a swirl of greens and browns with a softness in them that I can feel deep inside me. Most men's gazes feel like a violation, trying to take each piece of clothing off me with their eyes. But his? His gaze is a warm caress that causes my body to automatically inch closer to him in response.

"The song you were humming. 'Iris' by the Goo Goo Dolls, right?" He gives me a gentle smile, and my stomach dips. I didn't realize I was even humming.

Snapping out of the trance he put me under, I reply, "Oh! That's embarrassing. Was I humming loudly?"

"No, I just happened to catch it on the wind. It's a favorite of mine."

Wow. He is refreshingly respectful and has good taste in music.

"It's a favorite of mine, too." My tone borders on shy, and I want to smack myself for the ridiculousness of it.

People are clearly peeved at us for blocking the middle of the hallway, but they are quiet about it as they move around us like water moving around two rocks. Finding his eyes again, he catches me there, locking me in a gaze I can't pull away from—not an awkward one per se, but a charged one. I am about to break it, but he beats me to it.

"Caspian." He holds out a hand between us.

I take it and smile as I reply, "Talliana. Do we have a class together? Because you look familiar." I gently and somewhat reluctantly take my hand back from his.

"Yes, several, actually. I'm the big guy in the back who always looks confused." He softly laughs at his own admitted struggle.

That's right! I do know him. It's only the second week of the fall semester, but I have seen him. I also believe that the first time I saw him was in the Registrar's Office; I briefly admired how attractive he was in my head, then quickly got distracted by everything else.

I give a little laugh in politeness before replying, "I do remember you. It sounds like you already know I'm the obnoxious teacher's pet in the front."

"I doubt there are many in our program who don't know who you are. There are few women, and you're the only redhead." His smile widens as he finishes, "Also, I find that you know everything to be amazing, not obnoxious." His tone feels genuine but teasing.

"Well, you would be the first. Speaking of class, though, we should probably get to it," I say, pointing behind me in the direction of the classroom.

"Yes, good idea."

He takes up space beside me, and I try not to focus on the heat radiating from his arms resting at his side, so close to mine. We quietly walk the short distance together. I set my bag and books down at my usual front-row desk while he walks past me to take a spot in the back.

Once I settle into my desk, I can't help but look behind me. My eyes meet Caspian's, and he smiles at me. I spin back around as I feel my cheeks start to burn. Thankfully, the class begins, and I try to focus on intestinal pathologies, but those eyes. Colors that remind me of the trees in the forest behind the house. I feel like they are resting on the back of my head, but I'm probably being silly. The urge to drop my pen and take a peek rises, but I push it down. That would be an obvious move.

Focus. Focus. Focus.

This class is going to take forever.

It does, in fact, take forever for the professor to dismiss us.

It is so out of character for me, but for once, I don't think I heard much of the lecture. I pack up my book and notebook in my bag. As I stand up, swinging my backpack over my shoulder, it collides with something.

Horror. Absolute horror renders me frozen in place as I realize I hit the beautiful, large blond on the shoulder as he was walking past me.

"Oh my God, did I just hit you?"

He laughs it off, then replies, "Bad timing. Don't worry about it." His eyes meet mine as he rubs his shoulder with one of his hands and adds, "I'll see you around, Talliana."

I open my mouth to respond, but he is already walking out of the classroom door. What is wrong with me? Like seriously, what has gotten into me?

"Everything okay, Talli?" Tucker asks, coming up to me. His white cane bumps the back of my leg, and I'm careful when I turn around to face him.

Tucker is a Hawk from the Massachusetts community, a class ahead of mine. Many people from our community go to this small college. It's the closest to the community, and with several of us studying various things here, it allows us to watch out for one another. Well, in Tucker's case, he keeps his senses open.

There are three of us enrolled in undergraduate programs that will lead to medical school one day, but I see Tucker the most. He is a kind

Healer with light-brown hair and an excellent bedside manner. The community will be lucky to have him at the medical center once he finishes school.

"Yes, I'm fine. Tucker, do you know Caspian or anything about him?"

He leans back on a desk behind him and answers, "Not much. He just started here this year. Transferred from another school, as far as I know. I don't usually hear him chatting much with others, but with the type of guys that go here, I don't blame him."

Tucker, as well as I, know the type of guys that go here. Rich daddy's boys make up most of the medical programs. Tucker is the one who overheard the rumor about me being an easy target last year. He came to me about it and helped me solve the problem by calling on his cousin, who has a compulsion ability, to come help from the Michigan community. I told him that I owed him for saving me the embarrassment of having to ask Mei-Lien for help, but he refused to accept any favor.

"Thank you for the information and for checking on me," I tell him sincerely and touch his arm gently with my hand.

Tucker once confided in me that since he is blind, people often avoid physical contact so that they don't startle him. But he actually prefers physical contact because it helps him create a better visual of that person in his mind. His healing ability is not too different from what mine was before my bond to Coventina. Whereas I could sense where someone's pain is in their body, he can sense internal and external temperature just using his hands. It's really fascinating to watch him pinpoint problems because someone's temperature feels off.

He smiles brightly at me. "Glad to help."

Greer's open palm collides roughly with my shoulder, and I'm thrown onto my back on the mat.

"What is up with you today?" Greer asks, extending a hand to help me up.

I shake the daydream of sun-kissed skin and a warm smile out of my vision and see Greer glowering at me. She has had me on the mat at least a dozen times now, and we've barely started.

I idly rub my shoulder and answer, "I'm distracted. Sorry."

"That's obvious, but what's distracting you?"

I smile wide. "Hazel eyes, golden-blond hair, and a smile that could warm up the Arctic."

Greer narrows her eyes at me. "You're pulling my leg."

"I am not! He's real, and I met him yesterday. I can't quite get him out of my mind, either. It's stupid, really."

Greer's face lights up. "What community is he from? Did Mom finally get it right this time?"

"No, I met him at school. He's in some of my classes." I tell her about everything that happened, even though what did happen was minimal.

"You know, Dad and Mom will have a heart attack if you marry a human and mess up the bloodline."

"Yeah, yeah." I bat my hand in her direction in a dismissive gesture. "I'm not thinking about marriage or a relationship. I literally only know his name and that he has good taste in music."

"And that he's going to be a doctor," Greer points out.

"And that. But my point is, he hasn't even asked me out. He likely never will, either. He is just something to admire. From afar."

"Uh huh. Let me know how that works out for you."

I bristle and place my hands on my hips. "What are you trying to say?"

"All I'm saying is that if you want something, you don't quit until you have your way, which is not a bad thing. I just know that if you want him, you'll find a way to get him."

"Wow. Alright. I guess you have a point there. But! I don't think there is anything wrong with working for what you want in life. Especially when so much of my life is already forfeited." I cross my arms over my chest.

Greer sighs. "I agree. If you want to mess around with a hot blonde, you should do it. Just don't get too wrapped up over a human you won't be able to keep. You don't need another broken heart."

She's right. The last thing I need is to wound my already fragile heart. I am going to get control of my darkness, and with that, I hope a solution to the war will present itself. It would be idiotic to do anything to jeopardize the focus I am trying to obtain right now. My temporary happiness is not worth the risk.

Deflated, I return to the mat and wait for Greer to join me.

"Talli, I didn't mean..." she starts.

"It's fine. You're right. I can't risk my heart again."

"Talli..."

"No, Greer. How would it be fair to anyone for me to even think about getting tangled up with someone right now, human or Hawk? Despite what Mom and Dad believe. It's not just a broken heart I'd be risking. It's this entire war. It's our people's lives. I don't have the luxury of being selfish anymore." Before she can argue further, I pull the water from an open cooler perched on one of the benches. I form it around my fists and ready myself. "I'm done talking about this, and I'm done having you go easy on me. I don't need coddling."

Greer also moves into position and forms shadows around her fists, mimicking me. She sighs again, and I lunge for her with my water, decidedly done with being distracted and ready to take out my frustration instead.

CHAPTER 12

TALLIANA

"DID YOU FIND SOMETHING?" I ask as a way of greeting Mr. Simon. We decided to meet at the Range behind the community building, because at this time of night, nobody will be around to overhear us.

Mr. Simon straightens, seeing Coventina walking into the field with me. She elegantly strides to a spot a few feet from where Seth is lounging and lies down in the grass. Her iridescent scales look dull under the pale-yellow light from the lanterns we have set up all around the area. Seth lifts his head to look at her. Coventina gives him a glare, and then he promptly puts his head back down, nose pointed away from her.

I shake my head at them both and look back at Mr. Simon. He pulls the journal out from a pocket inside his jacket and opens it, searching for a specific page.

"Yes, I found quite a bit, and I have mapped out some steps that I believe you should take," he answers.

"Okay. Tell me what to do."

"Breathe."

Breathe? Seriously? "I already do that."

"I mean that breathing exercises seem to be the first step in control. When you feel like you are losing it and your emotions start getting away from you, stop and breathe. In through your nose and out through your mouth. It turns off your sympathetic nervous system, that fight-or-flight instinct," he explains.

"Okay, that makes sense. But I actually do breathe when I feel overwhelmed or out of control. Thinking back, it's probably the one thing that has kept me in control in the past."

"Good. Then you've already got a head start, but you should practice it more. It needs to be a muscle memory to start deep-breathing the second you feel the darkness stir within you. I want you to be at a point where you don't even have to think about it. You just do it," he advises.

"Yes, sir. I can do that. Stop and breathe. Easy enough. What's next?" I ask, anxious to keep moving.

He closes the journal and responds, "That's it for this week. Once you have breathing under your belt, we will move on."

"I don't have time for this. I need to learn control now. At least tell me what step two is." My annoyance rises, and I feel the darkness stir inside, delighting in my negative emotion.

Mr. Simon gives me a pointed look, and I start breathing. When I finish, I say, "See? I'm already a natural."

"Talli, I know we are doing this training unofficially, but I am still your trainer, and I need you to trust me. When you started learning how to fight a few years ago, did I throw you right to the wolves to learn? No. You strength-trained with Greer first. Breathing is your strength training."

"Technically, it was Greer who made me do that first," I point out.

"Yes, and who did she learn it from?"

I groan. "Fine. Point taken."

"Breathe, and I'll see you as soon as you have that mastered." Seth gets up and follows Mr. Simon out of sight down the path.

"*Want me to drench him next time?*" Coventina asks.

I look at her and answer, "*No, he is my superior officer, and I should listen to his guidance. You'll also risk getting the journal wet.*"

We both laugh, as we head back toward the lake, taking the opposite path that Mr. Simon took.

"*What do you think about all this? Learning control?*" I ask her. She has been quiet on the subject, not adding her usual commentary when I think about it.

"*Seeking control is very wise. Accepting help is even wiser.*"

I narrow my gaze at her. "*Why must you be cryptic at the worst of times? You're full of opinions when I don't want them.*"

"*It's just one of my many winning personality traits.*"

I snort.

She huffs back and says, "*If I gave you all the answers, then you wouldn't feel very deserving of the credit once this is over.*"

"*I couldn't care less about the credit or the fame.*"

"*Yes, because you would much rather live a simple life with a simple male, making as many sticky little spawns as possible.*"

I burst into laughter. "*I saw you with Penn. Don't deny that you would love it if I had sticky little spawns.*"

"*You mistake tolerance for love.*"

"*Whatever you say.*"

"Is this seat taken?" I look up from my reading and see Caspian hovering with a food tray, that warm smile on his face again. Does the man have any other facial expressions? Why do I feel desperate to find out?

I've been trying to avoid him this week, but like magnets, we keep running into each other. His arm will brush up against mine when we pass in the crowded hallway, our eyes will lock when I reach behind my seat to get something out of my backpack, and my stomach dips whenever he is close.

"Uh, no," I reply hesitantly. I place my bookmark in the book I'm cradling in my lap and close it, setting it back in my bag. I realize now that I was so engrossed in my book—one I actually wanted to read this time—that I hadn't touched my food. With that thought, I pop a french fry in my mouth. Yep, it's cold, but I keep eating it anyway.

"I hope I didn't interrupt your reading." He runs his hand through his hair and takes a bite of the spaghetti on his tray.

He likes pasta, noted.

"You didn't. Well you did, but my food is getting cold, so I need to start eating anyway." I take a bite of my chicken sandwich, and it's cold too. Damn it.

After a minute of heated silence, he asks, "So, what else do you like besides music and knowing everything?"

"You're going to make a great doctor with that bedside manner," I quip. He makes a laughing noise in his throat since he has food in his mouth. I decide to answer, "Reading, as you can tell, swimming, running, and movies. How about you?"

"Me? Well, aside from music, I like soccer and hockey. I also enjoy movies and can be a tiny bit of a geek when it comes to sci-fi," he answers, holding his thumb and pointer finger close to emphasize 'tiny'.

"Hmm...so you're a man who appreciates all the arts. Sounds like a fictional character from a book. Too perfect to be real." His eyes light up, and he curves his lips into a smirk.

Oh God. I just called him perfect. I quickly backpedal. "Not that I'm saying you're not real or anything, but I feel like every guy I've met is either hardcore into sports or gaming and movies."

I can't tell if that helped or made things worse. My cheeks feel warm, and I can see him contemplate how he wants to respond to my admission. He tilts his head and replies, "Maybe you've been meeting the wrong kind of *men*."

The smirk is still on his face, and I feel like crawling under a rock.

"So, do you play soccer and hockey with teams or for fun?" A valid question and a decent change of direction, I think.

"I played soccer in high school on a team, but hockey has always just been a fun sport for me. I mean, what's not to love about ramming other people into a wall to chase after a little puck?"

"That's true." I laugh, but my brain pictures him skating as fast as lightning, taking out other guys left and right while looking perfect. I swallow hard, pushing that image away for another day, and ask, "Did you see the Bruins pre-season game last night? I really thought they were going to crush the Penguins, but they totally lost focus in that last period."

He blows out a breath and gives me an admiring look, sitting back in his seat. "A girl who is smart and watches sports. Sounds like a fictional character to me," he teases.

"Maybe you've been meeting the wrong kind of *women*," I echo his earlier statement.

He laughs, dimples appearing in his cheeks. "I think I have been until now."

He says it so casually, so openly, that I feel like I have to blink to make sure I am not just imagining him here. "I have plenty of flaws too, believe me," I blurt out as if it's a defense mechanism against attractive men.

"You can tell me, but I'm not sure I'll believe you."

I open my mouth, then close it. What am I doing? Why am I telling him my flaws? He is flirting with me, and I'm about to give him my list of why he shouldn't. When I definitely want him to be.

I decide to start with the first, most human thing I can think of. "Well...I can be a bit stubborn at times." He gives me a disapproving look, so I add, "And! I am awful at accepting help from others. Like, tragically determined to do everything myself."

"Being stubborn is not a flaw. It just means you know what you want. As far as not accepting help," he shrugs, "well, you don't want to be a burden on people. I'd argue that's more admirable than allowing everyone to do everything for you."

I don't think I've ever felt more seen in my life. My skin flushes. I do know what I want, but I can't have it. I push my hands into my lap, trying to maintain some level of control over my body's reaction to this man's words. I clear my throat and ask, "Since you are such an expert, pray tell, what are your flaws?"

"Hmm. I think that's third-date territory."

Laughter bursts out from me. He is either cocky or trying to be funny. The grin on his face could be taken either way, and I'm not sure which one I would prefer.

"Well, I didn't come over here just to make you laugh. That was a great added bonus, though. I actually wanted to see if you would be interested in these." He pulls two tickets from his back pocket and holds them up for me. Before I have to ask what they are, he explains, "I work at the Sneezing Panda downtown, and we host a lot of bands. Tonight, we have a local indie band playing that I think you would enjoy. Anyway, I have some tickets I can hand out, and I thought you might like them. If you're not busy."

My first instinct is to accept. Checking out a band at a club with a high chance of seeing more of Caspian is extremely tempting. I never do fun things like that. But everything Greer and I discussed last week is still ringing in my ears. I need to tread carefully.

Caspian sees me hesitate and adds, "I'll be working tonight, so the tickets are for you, and if you want to bring a friend. There's no pressure if you want to take the tickets and decide not to come."

Tonight is movie night with Greer and Ash, but maybe I can convince them to do something different. "Do you have three tickets?"

He reaches for his pocket again, producing a third one with a smile, then hands all three to me. "Band starts at eight o'clock. Maybe I'll see you there." With that, he grabs his tray and strides off.

I watch him walk away, admiring every inch. He wears those jeans so well. I think over our conversation while I pick at what's left of my food.

Third date territory. I scoff. The desire to read into this man's every word is overwhelming, but I have to tamp down the urge.

CHAPTER 13

TALLIANA

"You're putting a lot of thought into an outfit for a 'friends night out.'" Greer is sitting at her desk, watching me get ready.

Greer and Ash actually seem excited about the change of plans for tonight. The three of us never go out anymore and have fun, so I marketed the idea as a chance to spend time together outside the community.

"We never do this, and I want to look nice," I shoot back at her while I try on another outfit. The pile on my bed has grown to an outrageous height, indicating that I desperately need to clean out my closet. I haven't really done any shopping since high school, so everything feels dated and a bit too girly. Not at all how I want to look.

"So, it has nothing to do with the fact that Caspian will be there tonight?"

I had to tell her how I got the tickets. She laughed when I told her, but she okayed it the minute Ash said he wanted to go. Out of the three of us, he leaves the community the least. Whenever he does, it is to other communities for his work, and he only goes with Greer and Draven.

Last year, Ash got a job in the Research and Development division of our community for defensive technology. He travels to other communities to investigate problems they may be experiencing and to conduct research on topics relevant to a particular project. He also takes online classes in Information Technology, with the thought that "it couldn't hurt," as he puts it.

"I just want to get my poor best friend out of the community for some fun since you keep him hidden away from the world."

"I do it to protect him. Especially if our identities are compromised now," she argues.

This quiets me. I understand. Ash could be in danger because of us. Anyone Greer and I choose to be with could be in danger.

"Talli, I'm sorry about our last conversation about Caspian. I never meant to make you feel bad. If you really like this guy..."

"He's a friend, Greer. Let's leave it at that."

Who am I kidding? I don't dream about my friends' eyes, their smiles, or what their muscles might look like under their shirt.

"Uh huh." Greer sees right through me.

I am looking myself over in the mirror, trying to decide if this outfit will make the cut, when there is a knock on the door. I call out, "Decent!" and Ash walks in.

He looks at me and then at Greer. "What number are we on?"

"Twelve," Greer responds with a snort.

Ash lets out a slow whistle, and his eyes crinkle behind his glasses. "I am dying to meet this guy if she is this worked up over her outfit."

"I hate you both." I shoot daggers at them with my eyes.

"Talli, put that red top on from outfit three with the black jeans from outfit seven. Then, put on your black heels. Put your hair in a high ponytail, and he will not be able to resist how badass and sinful you look," Greer lists out casually with a devilish glint in her eye.

Ash and I look at her, awestruck. Never has she shown an interest in clothes before, and yet she just whipped up the perfect combination without a sweat.

"What? I am the one with a clear head here, and I know your clothes as well as you do." She stands from her seat and grabs Ash's hand, leading him out the door as she throws over her shoulder, "We'll meet you downstairs in five minutes!"

As they leave, Ash asks, "Why don't you ever look sinful for me?"

Greer's cackle echoes through the hall, bringing a smile to my face. I guess things really are settling back into normal for them.

I quickly get dressed and do my hair exactly as Greer ordered, surprised at how perfect the effect is. My hair is much longer now than it used to be. Even in the high pony, the ends still brush my back. It appears I haven't taken much time to shop or get a haircut.

I sigh at myself in the mirror. *Friend.* Caspian has to be my friend because he can't be anything else.

CHAPTER 14

CASPIAN

"Hey, Caspian, did you see the girl who walked in a few minutes ago? She's causing quite a commotion," Gabriel says, bringing me a tray of clean glasses to stack at the bar.

Gabriel is always bringing news of hot girls who come in. I wonder if he thinks that if I go after them, it will save him the embarrassment of being turned down when he tries. I always seem mildly interested to keep up the appearance of a young single man, but I always tell him I pass.

"Oh?" I reply, not moving my eyes from my task.

"Yeah, a hot redhead. This one might even be up to your high standards."

"Yeah?"

Redhead. I whip my head up to look at him. "Wait. Did you say redhead?"

She's here.

"Ah. That's your type! I always wondered why you pass up on everyone else." Gabriel looks satisfied.

Gabriel isn't a bad-looking guy, with shiny brown hair and a decent build, but he lacks confidence and the ability to talk to women. He holds himself all wrong and acts like a boy, even though we are the same age. Since I started here last month, I keep telling myself I will teach him one day how to attract a woman the right way, but in truth, I have never made time for it and probably never will.

I have prey that I need to catch.

"Gabriel, I invited a redhead tonight. Where did you last see her?"

"Over by stage right. Some guy was trying to talk to her but failing spectacularly." His expression is smug, and he is undoubtedly pleased to see other guys fail like him.

"Take over for me? I'll be back in a minute," I say, already throwing the towel that was over my shoulder down.

"Take all the time you need."

The club isn't big, but the bar is tucked in the back corner, and you can't see the entrance or the right side of the stage very well when there is a crowd. I should have stationed myself better.

Walking toward stage right, I stop dead in my tracks when I catch sight of that thick red hair. There she is.

I. Am. Fucked.

There has never been a doubt in my mind that she is a beautiful woman—one I am very attracted to—but God, after talking to her earlier, hearing her laugh, and now this...She has a pull that makes me believe sirens must be real, and she was born from one.

Her red shirt, if you can even call that a shirt, hugs every perfect curve and shows a lot of her bare back. I see why she has caused a commotion. Her breasts aren't any more exposed than most women who walk through here, but the way they are displayed gives a perfect preview of what's underneath while still leaving enough to the imagination. And those black pants. They look more like liquid than fabric. I have spent time admiring her ass plenty over the last few weeks, but now the urge to grip it is overwhelming. I want to touch every inch of her.

Get it under control, Cas. You need this to go a certain way. She likes nice guys, respectful guys, sweet guys. You have a mission, a goal. Don't let her bewitch you.

I take a breath and continue walking toward her.

Toward my death sentence.

CHAPTER 15

TALLIANA

"I THINK GREER'S OUTFIT choice worked too well," Ash comments with a hint of humor.

It's true. I haven't been left alone since we walked into the Sneezing Panda. I never really doubted how I looked, but I could never doubt it now. Still, I feel self-conscious. Maybe I should have gone for a softer look.

"I'm a bucket list item for these guys. They see the red hair like a beacon and lose all their senses for a night. It's not even that red," I argue. Yes, I am considered a redhead, but my hair is auburn. I straddle the line between redhead and brunette, if you want to be technical.

"It is with that shirt."

Ash is not helping. At all. I straighten my top for the tenth time since we got in here and try not to look obvious as I search for Caspian. Still no sign of him.

"He's probably working. Relax," Greer whispers and places her hand on my arm.

"As I have said, I am here to have fun with you two. It would just be easier if I didn't have to fend off every idiot in this place."

"I can take off my jacket and help draw some attention away from you," she offers, starting to pull it off. Underneath, she is wearing a loose black V-neck T-shirt—nothing as overtly alluring as me, but I have no doubt she would draw some attention, too, if Ash wasn't so close to her.

Ash pulls the sleeves back up her arms and zips her jacket to her neck, wrapping an arm around her possessively. She laughs and turns to run her fingers through his curly brown hair, pulling him into a long kiss.

I turn away and mutter, "Gross," which makes them kiss more.

Oh no. Here comes another one. This one is tall and thin, easily resembling a twig, but determination pours out of him, and...yep, that's lust.

"Hi there. I couldn't help but notice you look like a third wheel in need of a fourth." He gestures to Greer and Ash behind me.

"Oh, that's okay. I'm very comfortable being a third wheel. I've had lots of practice," I reply, praying to the Great Hawk that he gets the hint faster than everyone else.

Of course, he doesn't.

"Are you sure? I'm good company. We could have a great time tonight." He winks at me and takes a step closer.

A throat clears, causing me to jump. It almost sounds like a growl full of predatory warning. Caspian emerges from the crowd and comes to my side. "Excuse me, miss, is this man bothering you? I'd be happy to toss him out." He looks at the guy in front of me with a serious expression while maintaining a relaxed posture.

"Aren't you the guy working behind the bar?" The guy's tone is dripping with annoyance.

"Yes, and this is my guest for the night. If you continue to harass her, I'll make sure you never pick up women from this club again."

The guy turns quickly and walks off without another word.

My blood boils. Did he just show up like a fucking knight in shining armor? How dare he!

As soon as Caspian turns to me, about to say something undoubtedly heroic, I cut him off sharply. "I am not a damsel in distress in need of your rescue. I was handling him just fine."

His smile turns into a confused expression, and his comfortable stance slumps slightly like his ego is deflating.

Good.

"I'm sorry. You never took me as someone who needed rescuing, but I've seen that guy in here a lot harassing women. He doesn't let up without a fight. I thought I would save you some time." His eyes are earnest.

Okay, maybe I'm being harsh, but I need to set a boundary now. "I can take care of myself," I reply a bit more softly.

"I promise I'll never save you from another asshole again." He places his hand over his heart, then his face turns thoughtful, and he adds, "Except for Jeffrey Hamilton. He is always bugging you and asking to get punched with the way he treats everyone." Jeffrey has bugged me since day one of college, and my refusal only makes him more persistent.

I laugh, my mood lightening, and I cave. "Alright, Jeffrey is the exception. You can rescue me from him any day."

"Consider it done."

Our eyes meet, and he catches me in another moment. We quietly look at each other, the air around us feeling charged with electricity.

My skin tingles, and it feels the same way it does when the darkness boosts my magic. I'm not sure how much time passes when Greer moves to stand beside me, squeezing my arm, with an awkward smile plastered to her face.

"Hi. I'm Greer, Talliana's sister, and this," Greer yanks Ash from behind me and continues, "is Asher."

Caspian pulls his gaze from mine and turns to her, smiling. He casually shakes her hand, then Ash's. "Nice to meet you, Greer and Asher. I'm Caspian."

"You can call me Ash. I'm Greer's boyfriend and Talli's BFF," Ash explains to him, matching Greer's awkward smile. Since when has he ever used the term 'BFF'? I narrow my eyes at them both. What is wrong with them?

Caspian smiles broadly at him and turns to me. "Talli, eh?"

I nod, trying my hardest not to hide my face in my hands at the awkwardness that is my two companions.

"You can call me Cas then."

"Wow! Seems everyone has a nickname. Well, except for me," Greer responds, and my eyes widen. Ash even looks at her at that. I need to find a hole and promptly bury myself in it.

"*I'll start digging*," Coventina chimes in.

"Yes, it seems so," Cas replies with warmth. "Well, I have to get back to work, but please find some seats. The band will be starting soon. Can I send any drinks over?"

"Just three Pepsis would be great," I answer.

Greer is turning twenty-one in a couple of weeks, but Ash and I are still underage. I don't think that would stop Cas from sending over alcoholic drinks if we wanted them, but Hawks avoid alcohol to keep our senses sharp anyway.

"You got it." Caspian turns entirely to me and leans in a few inches. "I hope you don't mind me saying, but you look gorgeous tonight." And with that, he hurries off. My blush must be obvious because Greer and Ash are wearing shit-eating grins when I turn to them.

"What?" I demand, exasperated.

In unison, they exclaim, "Nothing!" and start walking towards some seats.

The club has comfortable booths along the walls, all semicircles facing the stage up front, then some small tables and seats scattered around toward the back behind a dance floor. The style in the club is not what I would have expected based on the name Sneezing Panda. The upholstery for the booths and the seats are made of bamboo-green velvet, and the wood that makes up the tables and bar is heavy and dark. Aside from those elements, nothing else uniquely matches the name. No cuddly black and white bears anywhere. I'm seriously disappointed.

Greer and Ash find an empty booth, the last one, and we slide in with Ash in the middle. That is deliberate on Greer's part, I can tell.

"Greer, what was with the weird? I have never seen you act so awkwardly," I ask, staring her down.

"Nothing! I like him, that's all."

She's lying. I look to Ash, the weak link. He looks between me and her a couple of times, and finally gives up. Keeping his voice low, he says, "She had a vision."

My eyes widen. She saw something about Cas. "What did you see?!" My heart rate picks up, and my leg bounces under the table.

"I am not telling you," she replies, and I know it's because of the stupid foresight rules. She can't tell someone about their future unless she wants to risk completely messing it up. "I just think *that* one," she says, pointing her eyes toward where Cas is at the bar working and helping customers, "is special."

My heart threatens to leap out of my chest. "I...I..." I stutter, unsure how to process this bit of news. This is a serious turn of events.

"Talli, I am telling you that you should give him a chance," Greer tells me softly.

I flick my eyes back to him. All the muscles in his arms bulge slightly as he shakes a cocktail shaker, his plain white t-shirt—the apparent uniform for the club—looking perfect on him. I bite my lip, and, not moving my eyes away from him, I ask Greer, "What about 'don't get too wrapped up on a human'?"

"I take it all back," she answers.

Her words ring in my ears, my head, and my chest. What is happening right now? Am I actually considering this? Could I actually allow myself...God, I am ready to be happy. I don't know how or why, but maybe I shouldn't question it. Maybe I should let myself have this one thing.

"Are you *sure*?"

Ash answers this time. "Hey, one step at a time. Get to know him, and if it's right, we'll figure it out, because the three of us are in this together. But you deserve to be happy, Talli."

A lump forms in the back of my throat, and the water in my eyes threatens to spill over, but instead of letting the tears fall, I grab Ash's hand from under the table and give it a squeeze.

There will be no figuring it out together, though, because it can't go past short-term—a fling. No one should be allowed to fall in love with someone who doesn't have a real future. And I certainly don't. We are benched right now anyway for missions, so what harm could a small fling do? As long as love never enters the equation.

Our drinks arrive along with some mozzarella sticks we didn't order, but when I try to ask Caspian about them, he winks at me and goes back to work.

"Do you suppose this is something he just does? Gives a woman tickets to come see a band, free mozzarella sticks, forces them to watch him work all night, then he'll invite me back to his place after his shift," I ponder out loud as my eyes track him like a predator studying its prey. He seems to do a bit of everything around here. One minute, he is behind the bar helping with drinks; the next, he is delivering food, settling unhappy customers, and helping the band during a song break.

Ash chokes on his soda, and Greer laughs. "If it is, I'd say it's working."

Straightening my back, I force my gaze away from him and toward the table instead. Then, feeling a sudden urge of spite, I say, "He's going to have to work much harder than that."

The band has been on for a little while now, and they are what you would expect as a young band performing in a small club, playing a mix of their own titles and covers of popular ones. Caspian was right, though, and I really do enjoy them. When a popular, upbeat song comes on, I suggest, "Let's all dance."

Greer groans. "No."

"Please."

Ash starts scooting out of the booth, pushing her out in the process, until she is standing with her arms aggressively crossed over her chest. I grab her arm and Ash's hand and pull them into the fray. As the music plays, I let my body move in time to it, relishing in how free I feel. For once in my life, I don't want to hide. I want to be seen in this moment. Because right now, I am not who I have been; right now, I am who I want to be. Just a normal woman letting loose and having fun dancing at a club.

The night moves in a blur as I dance with Greer and Ash. Ash figured out, rather clumsily, how to spin both of us into his arms at the same time, and my stomach aches from laughing so much. Finally, we decide to head back to the booth and take a break when the lead singer of the band announces they have a special request and...no, it can't be.

They start playing "Iris."

I turn around to see if I can find Caspian, but my breath hitches when I find him right behind me, watching me intently. "Why?" I ask, not sure what else to say.

"I owe you an apology for earlier," he answers softly.

"You already apologized."

"I knew I could do better. Care to dance?" He stretches out a hand to me. Looking around, many couples are starting to dance in a slow sway, including Greer and Ash, who look more content than I have ever seen them. I turn back to the prospect in front of me. There is no pressure in his look, only hope.

"Yes, I would like that." Taking my hand in his, he pulls me close and rests his other hand on my bare back. I flush, very aware of how perfect every callous on his hand feels, but when my eyes find his, I am lost. I let him pull me around the floor, following his every step and sway.

With only the need for more—more of him—driving my actions, I pull my hand out of his and wrap my arms around his neck. He takes a step closer to me, and our bodies are now completely flush. My senses become overwhelmed with the scent of oak and sunshine, and I want to wrap myself in it. How a man can smell both woodsy and like summer, I don't know, but it's intoxicating.

As the song plays, every word feels as though it is somehow meant just for us. I don't know this man, not really, but every instinct is pulling me to him. I am broken, but I want him to know who I am. All of me. Someday.

My mind physically recoils at the idea and the impossibility of it, but there is something else inside that yearns for it, for him knowing exactly who I am. Or rather, *what* I am. I know I should be afraid of that, afraid of whatever this is that's happening, but all I feel is wonder.

Who is this man?

The song comes to a close, and everyone claps at the band's performance, but I don't loosen my grip around his neck or move away.

"I'm glad you came tonight." His silky-smooth voice rolls over me like warm water.

"Me too."

"The band is done for the night, but they play every other Friday. Let me know if you ever want to come again. I can get tickets for you and your friends anytime." His grip loosens from around my back, and the spot where his hands were is suddenly cold. I follow suit and let go as well, allowing some space between us.

"Thank you," I reply.

"Well, I'll see you around, Talli."

That's it? No, 'what are you doing tomorrow?' Just let me melt into your hands and leave me hanging? "Okay," I answer instead of voicing my thoughts. He gives me one last warm smile and heads back to work.

Greer touches my arm. "Time to go?" Her voice is soft, picking up on what just happened.

I nod, suddenly feeling very tired. I turn to head back to the booth, but Ash is already waiting with our bags and jackets in his arms. He hands each of us our stuff. With one last glance at Caspian collecting empty plates and drinks, I leave, not quite sure how to feel anymore.

CHAPTER 16

CASPIAN

IT'S AN EFFORT TO make myself put one foot in front of the other, when I know each step is taking me farther away from her. There were so many things I could have done in the moment we just shared, things that could have sped up this entire relationship, and my body was screaming at me to consider the most reckless options, but I couldn't risk it. Not when my common sense felt like it was floating away from me.

My hands still tingle at the feel of her soft, ivory skin. The chill of it was such a startling contrast to my natural warmth. I can even still smell her somehow, the scent of rain-kissed leaves overwhelming my senses. It was impossible to work while she was dancing with her friends. Every time I caught the color red in the corner of my eye, I had to stop and look. Her movements were so fluid and free, it was hard to look away once I started.

I shake my head and start collecting dirty dishes from empty tables. I'm being ridiculous, and I need to focus. Everything is going according to plan, even with that slip-up earlier.

I honestly thought I had her type pegged—the hero types—but I missed the mark. No, she doesn't want to be rescued. Why would she when her teeth are sharp enough to take down anyone who gets in her way? *Huh*. She's different than what I expected. Granted, most Hawks are. As a child, my father always painted them as ugly, hateful monsters, so that's what I've grown up believing. But I'm finding out that description doesn't quite match.

How is it that the same woman who was in my arms, staring up into my eyes only moments ago, is also responsible for murdering dozens of my men? For leaving Mackay, a man feared almost as much as my father, as a dehydrated mummy, as Matthew so eloquently put it? This has to be a trick or enchantment that forces me to ignore the worst parts of her.

A pat on my back jars me from my thoughts, and I almost swing around and put the idiot on the ground, but clench my fists instead in an effort to control myself.

Gabriel's grin is all I see as he comes from around me. "Dude! You had her wrapped around your finger. Why didn't you go in for the kill?"

The word "kill" makes me suddenly uncomfortable, though I know what he means. "I have a plan with that one." I focus back on the task of picking up, but like a little fly, Gabriel follows me with a look of awe on his face.

"Oh, master, teach me your ways." He pretends to bow to me, and if I were in any other mood, I would have laughed at his hopelessness, but I'm still tense from the feel of Talliana pressed up against me.

Reminding myself not to be an asshole by telling him to fuck off, I stop what I am doing instead, and give him a serious expression.

"Some girls, you can say a few pretty things and hope they spread their legs for you. A woman like *her* is like a game of chess. If you really want them, sometimes you must sacrifice a few pawns," I explain.

He looks confused and then grins, nodding like he understands, which I have no doubt he doesn't. He leaves me then, back to work and back to my calculating. The words I just said feel almost strange. When I started this mission, they would have completely lined up with how I view all this, a chess game to get her to share all her secrets with me. That is how my father always explained war to me. But now, the description of what just passed between us feels sour on my tongue. This doesn't feel like a chess game.

Not anymore.

My mother told me today that I'm to be betrothed as soon as someone's blood is deemed a worthy match to my own. I don't understand why she is allowing this. Surely, she understands I am too young? I am not ready to become a stranger's property. She told me that the elders wish to see if they can duplicate my ability, but why can't they wait? Why don't i have a say in my own life?

I told her that if i were to be anyone's property, i wish to be Otis's, but she dismissed me. She always dismisses me. Everyone dismisses me. But not Otis. I know he is my true love, and he will fight for me like he always has.

- Journal of Katarina Lehmann

CHAPTER 17

TALLIANA

October

"I SWEAR THE BREATHING has been officially mastered," I say to Mr. Simon when I see him.

He laughs. "Don't worry, I have something different for you today."

Bending down, I give Seth his greeting scratches and then face Mr. Simon, ready for step two in control. "Lay it on me."

"Focus on someone you love."

"You're kidding."

"Talli, before you can control the darkness and learn how to use it, you have to learn control over your explosive emotions. Allowing yourself to feel extremely angry or afraid is what feeds the darkness," he explains.

"So, in other words, I need to stop laying out an all-you-can-eat buffet for it."

"Right. If you can control how much food you put out for it, that leads to controlling how much power it gives you. Eventually, you should be able to metaphorically take the food away to stop it if it gets too out of control."

"Okay, I can get behind food analogies."

"Good. So, in step one, you breathe through the emotions to get enough oxygen to your brain to think. Then, take that moment of clarity to focus on someone you love, or even someone who makes you feel good emotions—ones of light."

I close my eyes and do what he asks. *Someone who makes me feel good emotions.* I can't stop my mind from immediately conjuring Caspian. I lose myself in all the feelings that flood my body. Happiness, excitement, and a need to touch him, even though he isn't mine to touch.

"I think that is plenty of focus." Mr. Simon breaks my concentration, and my eyes fly back open. Placing the back of my hand on my cheeks, I realize they are heated. "Sorry."

"Don't be sorry. If there is someone on your mind who makes you smile like that, then that's a good thing." Mr. Simon's grin could almost be considered cheeky. Almost.

"It really is nothing. At least right now, it's nothing," I say quickly.

"Hmm. Well, that's all I have for you right now."

I grumble under my breath but nod nonetheless.

When Coventina and I reach the lake, the urge to jump in takes over my sense of reason. The water looks so beautiful, with the full moon reflecting off its surface. I can feel my water ability tingling at my fingertips, begging me to use it. I strip off my jacket and pants, revealing my bathing suit underneath, bolt for the water, and dive in.

Coventina is behind me, scooping me onto her back and throwing me straight up to break the water's surface. I throw my hands down, creating a water vortex that catches me. I will it to hold me in place for a moment before having it propel me over the water's surface. I move my hands straight out from my sides, then up, allowing it to suck me back under the water. I look around and grab Coventina's leg as she zooms past me.

I swim and play under the moonlight with my magic until I feel like a walking prune. Swimming toward the shore, I see someone crouching at Trey's gravestone. I pull myself out of the water, and Orsen Waterstone stands up and turns around to see me.

"Talliana, I am sorry if I disturbed your fun." He gives me a soft smile, and I reach for my clothes.

"Not at all. We were done, actually," I reply, matching his smile and pulling on my clothes. They immediately cling to the wet bathing suit.

"It's hard to stay away from the water during the full moon, isn't it? It's the one night most Elementals struggle to sleep. Our magic feels too strong to ignore," he comments.

"Yes, very much so. It's like an energy underneath your skin that feels so different from healing."

Coventina exits the water behind me, and she comes to stand next to me. Mr. Waterstone bows his head to Coventina, and she returns the gesture—a sign of respect between the two. I notice Lemon, Orsen's bonded retriever, sitting a few feet away. Her golden fur looks as soft as always, even in the moonlight.

He pulls some of the water from the lake behind me, creating a spinning sphere in between his hands. "We Elementals are partial to our own element, but water is truly the most beautiful and powerful. I can't begin to imagine how it must feel to heal with it. It must be extraordinary."

"It is," I agree skeptically. Mr. Waterstone has never been a man who has made me feel uncertain, but I am unsure where this conversation is going.

"You are truly blessed by the Great Hawk, and this community is blessed to have you." He meets my eyes and drops the water to the ground. "I know you feel his loss strongly, like Angeline and I do, but it's okay to want happiness for yourself again. I see so much of your father in you, his stubborn determination to solve the world's problems alone. Angeline and I were talking about it last week, and we want to make sure you know that the community supports you. You saved so many lives that day. Don't let the one you didn't save hold you back from your destiny."

My chest grows heavy from his words. I don't know what to say. Coventina brushes up against my shoulder, supporting me from one side.

"Thank you, Mr. Waterstone," I choke out. "That means a lot to me."

He nods and smiles at me. I return it, and then Coventina and I walk back to the house together.

First, Uncle Cyrus, Greer, Mr. Simon, Ash, and now Mr. Waterstone? It's like everyone woke up one day and decided it's time to check on me. Granted, I have spent the last two years like a ghost, avoiding everyone and everything, especially my true self. But now that I'm trying to get back to myself, to gain real control over this darkness and live as much as possible before I end this war, it's like now people can actually see me again.

"I'm just a walking advertisement for my feelings now, aren't I?" I ask Coventina.

"Your people love you and are worried about you. You're their savior."

"We're their savior, and that was only one battle, not the war."

"It will come. Be patient."

I huff, and she huffs back.

It's not that I'm ready to forfeit what might be necessary to end all this, but I wish I knew how much time I have left.

CHAPTER 18

CASPIAN

SHE'S RIGHT WHERE I knew she would be. Mondays, Wednesdays, and Fridays are for running laps around the college track outside, and today is Wednesday.

It's been almost two weeks since she came to the club, and I can tell by the way she keeps stealing glances at me that she has been waiting for me to do something. I don't think patience is a quality of hers, but I'll give her credit for the restraint she has shown so far.

Well, today is her lucky day. She gets to watch me run.

It's early October, and even though there is a slight chill in the breeze, it's still warm enough outside to build up a good sweat. It's also warm enough for Talliana to wear running shorts and a loose tank top over her sports bra.

God, she is stunning. The warm sun bounces off her hair, highlighting all those red strands I want to run my fingers through.

Talliana's eyes meet mine, and that's my cue. Sticking my headphones in my ears without turning on any music, I start running around the loop when she is on the other side of it. For the first lap, I keep myself exactly on the other side of the track from her. Then, once I start the second lap, I increase my speed. By the time I'm halfway into the third lap, I am coming up behind her. When I'm even with her, she looks over at me, and I wink, slowly moving ahead of her.

To my absolute delight, she increases her speed, too, trying to outrun me. I let her get a little ahead of me, then pick it up another notch. I flash her a grin when I get beside her again, daring her to challenge me.

She nods, knowing precisely what I am thinking, and then I push myself to my full speed as we enter the next lap. She stays at my heels the entire way around, then shoots off like a lightning bolt at the last few yards, beating me without question.

Talliana throws up her arms in celebration as she slows down and starts laughing. I find myself laughing with her as I pass the finish line myself. She drops to the grassy center of the track, her chest moving dramatically up and down as she takes deep breaths. I do the same, pulling my headphones out and trying to slow down my rapid heartbeat.

"So, what did I win?" she asks, sitting up.

"I didn't realize we were competing for a prize." My tone is light and full of humor. I still can't wipe the dumb grin off my face.

"I don't compete unless there is a prize." She looks at me, and I can't help but want to read into the potential double meaning. Is she insinuating that I am a prize?

I'm all too aware of the lack of coverage my running shorts afford me. I sit up in a weak attempt to hide how turned on I am right now and match her gaze. "What do you think a running contest win is worth?"

Her feline grin stretches, and feigning thinking about it, she answers, "Definitely something full of calories. I need to counteract all the work I just did."

Who is this woman?

"You want me to take you to dinner?"

"No, I want you to buy me dessert," she replies, jumping to her feet.

I chuckle. "I can do that. Meet me in front of the Sneezing Panda at nine o'clock tonight, and I'll get you the best dessert you've ever had."

"I'm holding you to that." She jogs off, leaving me still sitting in the grass.

Disbelief hits. She just distracted me and then talked me into a date without me fully realizing it. I came here to play her, and she completely played me. *Oh no, Talliana Hoffman, you don't get me that easily.*

I get up and start heading to my car, a plan forming in my mind, when I almost bump right into someone.

"It's Caspian, right?" the man in front of me asks.

I assess him—light-brown hair, medium build, non-existent threat level. However, his white cane could do some serious damage if he were fast enough. I have noticed him talking to Talliana on occasion, though that's not unusual. Most of the other guys in the classes we share have a habit of trying to talk to her.

"Sorry, man. I didn't mean to almost run right into you. But yes, that's right. I'm Caspian. You are?"

"Tucker." He offers a hand, and I take it with a firm grip. I force myself not to squeeze.

"What can I do for you, Tucker?" I ask casually.

"I am a friend of Talliana's. I..." he hesitates, clearly unsure of how to word whatever it is that he wants to say, but eventually continues, "she has been through a lot and is currently going through a lot. If you are looking for an easy target, I'm asking you nicely to move along."

Easy target. I know Talliana is no easy target.

It's evident that Tucker has no practice at doing something like this. His stance and demeanor tell me that he is uncomfortable. And he isn't a random classmate, he's a Hawk. I can respect what he is trying to do. He isn't interested in her for himself, he's trying to watch her back.

"It's not like that. I really do like her, and I'm only interested in pursuing a real relationship with her if she is interested in the same thing. I promise I don't have any intentions of hurting her."

His head nods slowly. "Okay. You seem like a genuine guy, so let me warn you: she will hurt you in the end. If you *are* looking for something real, a good woman to settle down with one day, you will want to keep looking."

Annoyance prickles at the back of my neck. My first instinct is to view him as an obstacle and physically remove him from my path. But if he is a friend of Talliana's, then I need to act like a man who is truly after her heart.

"Look, I appreciate the warning, I do. But Talliana and I are both adults—adults who have only chatted a couple of times so far and who are going to make our own choices. You have her back, and you're a good man for it, but let's not get ahead of ourselves planning the wedding before the first date."

Tucker examines me for a moment. It's something I can feel rather than see since his eyes are unmoving behind his dark sunglasses. He's trying to read my emotions, no doubt. I keep myself calm and try not to tense up at the intrusion he is likely trying to commit inside my mind. Finally, he nods and walks around me without another word. I can't tell if I passed whatever test he was putting me through or if he determined I wasn't worth the fight. Either way, I have a date I need to prepare for and a woman I need to woo.

Time to call in that favor I set up last week.

At nine o'clock, Talliana shows up as promised, wearing dark-wash jeans and an oversized sweatshirt that says "I'd rather be reading" on it. Not club attire and nothing like what she wore the first time she was here, but I still have the same overwhelming urge to touch her.

I give her a lazy grin instead. "I'm hurt." She looks confused, so I add, "You'd rather be reading than getting dessert with me."

Her smile is sheepish as she explains, "Last time I was here, I got too much attention. I thought tonight I would avoid that as much as possible. Save you from being tempted to rescue me again."

"I hate to be the bearer of bad news, but a sweatshirt is not enough to save you from being the center of attention in any room." Her freckle-dusted cheeks turn a little pink, and I have to force my face steady so my smile doesn't grow too wide—creepy-level wide—at the reaction. "Don't worry, though, you don't even have to set foot in the main part of the club. Follow me." I gesture down the alley that leads to the kitchen in the back of the building.

She hesitates a moment, but I meet her eyes and say, "Trust me."

"One would usually be advised not to trust a man when he wants to lead you down a dark alley at night. But no one's given me that advice, so I guess I will," she jokes and follows me.

I lead her to the kitchen door and knock. Gus, the club's chef, greets us in his long black apron covered in flour and I'm not sure what else, and lets us inside. The smile he gives me, then Talliana, is wide, so I usher her to the other side of the kitchen before he has a chance to say anything.

I offer her a seat at the small table I had placed here earlier for just this reason. Going to the fridge, I grab out two slices of cheesecake and place them on the table to unwrap them and add some whipped cream.

"Maybe that one *is* worth the effort," Gus whispers as he walks past me and back to the sizzling pot on the stove. When I asked him to make the cheesecake last week and pop it in the freezer so that I could impress a woman, he'd laughed at me, then said that if I needed anything more than my looks to impress her, she wasn't worth the effort. Apparently, he'd changed his mind.

When I started at the club, Gabriel informed me that Gus had an appreciation for blonds. I thought he was joking until Gus made that comment and started eyeing me like he was undressing me in his mind. Nonetheless, I offered him all my tips from bartending for the next week, and he promptly agreed to help. I can already tell this will be tips well spent.

I walk the cheesecake back to the small table and watch in satisfaction as Talliana takes a bite and her whole face lights up. She savors it, then promptly takes another bite before admitting, "This is amazing. Best cheesecake I've ever had."

"I'm glad you like it. Gus calls it his Cinnamon Roll Cheesecake."

She nods enthusiastically and asks, "Do you treat all your friends to cheesecake like this?"

"No, you're the first person I've taken back here."

After a moment of quiet while we both eat our dessert, she asks me to tell her more about myself. I give her the basic rundown, keeping to the truth as best as I can. Like how I'm from Colorado, my father was a mostly absent one, my mother died when I was little, and I have no siblings. In return, she answers all my questions about her family, which I already know, but it's not hard to pretend to be interested in hearing her explain it to me.

We get lost in conversation until finally, a couple of hours later, I walk her back to her car. On the way there, she asks, "What do you do in your free time besides school and work?"

"I don't quite have enough time to play sports, or rather, I haven't figured out how to have the time yet. So I mostly go to the gym and pick up overtime at work when I'm bored."

"Oh, you're one of those," she chuckles.

"One of what?" I ask, genuinely confused.

"Gym guys. You probably spend way too much time looking at yourself in the mirror while lifting an obscene amount of weight."

I laugh. "I do lift weights, along with doing other things at the gym, but I wouldn't consider myself one of those gym guys who obsess over it. You're one to judge, though. You seem very organized with your running schedule."

Talliana gives me a knowing look, and I realize I just gave myself away. I knew she had a running schedule and joined her today on purpose. Bracing myself to be called out, she surprises me by saying, "I do more than run. I also go to the gym to work out. And before you ask, yes, more than just cardio. I mostly enjoy sparring with Greer."

My eyes brighten at her admission. Looks like she just accidentally gave herself away, too. "Sparring? Like Karate or Krav Maga?" I ask innocently.

She backpedals. "More like basic self-defense. It's a scary world out there. Lots of men who want to take you down dark alleyways at night."

I laugh, genuinely laugh, at her comeback. How can someone so evil be so funny?

I can't resist the urge when I offer, "If you ever want to learn a little more than the basics, I'd be happy to show you some moves sometime."

"You know how to fight?"

Oh, you have no idea, Talliana.

"My father hired someone to make sure I could always deal with a bully." I fake my nonchalance.

"Okay. That might be fun." Her cheeks redden, a much brighter color this time, and she closes her eyes as if she immediately regrets her words.

We reach her car, but she doesn't go for the door handle right away.

"Really? That easy to convince?"

She leans back against her car, putting herself in a tantalizing position. "Call me curious."

"Okay, Curious. My gym has a private space I can reserve for us. When do you want your lesson?" My body moves on its own, taking a full step closer to her. She tracks the movement carefully, and if my eyes aren't playing tricks on me, I see her back arch slightly. She wants me to touch her. But I need her to yearn for me, just a bit longer. So I shove my hands in my front pockets to keep myself in check.

"Sunday morning?" she suggests.

"Eight-thirty?"

"Sounds great."

I pull my phone out and offer it to her, clearly suggesting she put her number in it.

"You can't just tell me the name of the gym?"

"What if you forget after I tell you?" I tease her.

"I don't forget things." She meets my eyes in challenge. I accept, and we watch each other for what feels like an eternity. It's really only a moment though, until she takes my phone from my hand and does what I ask.

I grin when I realize she put her contact name as "Teacher's Pet." I immediately type out a message with the gym information in it, sign it as "Big Guy in the Back" and hit send.

She checks her phone and giggles. Such a perfect, innocent sound. Then she opens her car door and tells me, "See you in class tomorrow."

"Yes, see you there." I watch as she drives away.

Perfect. Innocent.

No. Those delicate hands have been used to murder so many of my people, and I can't lose sight of that. Even when her attention fills me with a strange feeling, one I like.

I do have to wonder if being an assassin is her choice. Granted, anyone can say no. And if she is being used because she is powerful, then she, more than anyone, should be able to say no. But it might not be that simple. I understand what it's like to want to say no but not be able to.

I am surprised, though, by how playful and eager she is, considering how dismissive she has been with other men's advances. I thought this would be much harder, but I could almost sit back and let her take the reins.

Almost.

I still need to play a specific role, one that is quickly evolving. I planned to come into this as the non-pushy, sweet, caring guy, but I'm finding she wants someone who speaks their mind, happily engages in playful banter and teasing, and admires all of her, mind and body. She needs someone to see and know her for who she is, not just what she is.

Oh, Hawks. Don't you know that you can't leave a weapon like that uncared for?

I will make sure to be all she needs, and she'll come to rely on me until she cannot possibly imagine letting me go.

CHAPTER 19

TALLIANA

"GET UP! IT'S CONNECTICUT!"

I groan and stretch, hoping I imagined the wake-up call from Coventina.

"Talli, get your ass out of bed," Greer snarls at me.

Shit. Guess not.

I force myself to throw off the covers and get ready. I am lacing up my last boot when I hear, "Maybe if you weren't out so late, you would be more prepared." Greer stands over me, arms crossed, waiting for me to finish.

"Started your period today, huh?" I retort and hope it really is my imagination this time when I hear her growl at me.

Connecticut is the last community I want to visit right now. We refer to it as the frat boy community for a reason. It's made up mostly of men in their twenties and thirties, and it is not a female-friendly environment. Only men are in charge, and they all act like it's a boys-only club. The women are more like accessories and a maid service to them. Our community has stepped in several times, with the assistance of Florida, to help women who want a new placement.

Greer and I respond to the fire in our usual shadows-then-rain fashion, but when I land with Coventina, Greer is immediately at my side. "Something feels wrong. These men we caught are feeling way too smug about it."

Alarm shoots through me. The Brethren feeling smug is never a good sign.

I walk past her and up to the man with the straightest back in the line-up. He is bound and gagged, and Greer is right there to hold him steady. I place both my hands on the sides of his face, press my fingers into his temples, and pry into his memories using my inner eye.

It only takes me a second to find his last memory before the attack. I rifle through a few others to ensure I have everything, then pull myself out of his mind. I look right at Greer. *"It's a trap. They're trying to draw out the new security system, as in us, to figure out what it is and stop it."*

"They probably have cameras somewhere," Greer guesses.

"I see eight flying machines in the sky," Draven's deep voice cuts into my thoughts.

"Drones," Greer and I think in unison. Greer climbs into Draven's saddle, and they are instantly gone to take them out.

"This is a trap," I tell one of the community's elders, and they immediately order some men to start searching the area for more Brethren. Hopefully, they or Greer will find the source of the drones and eliminate that camera footage. We do not need the Brethren finding out about the dragons.

"*Glamour up, Covey.*" Without a word, she does what I ask and puts on her glamour. Only Hawks with bonded creatures can see her now, meaning she is invisible to the cameras.

"Neat trick."

I turn around to find Zander, the most pompous ass I've ever had the pleasure of meeting. His shiny, ginger hair is in perfect arrangement, and his over-the-top clothes are pressed in crisp lines, even at three in the morning. He is the youngest community elder in our history and only three years older than I am.

"Which one? The one where we saved your asses? Or the one where I made you disappear from my life?"

His laugh is like nails on a chalkboard, and as if it were a strange bird call, his bonded pheasant lands on his shoulder, lifting its head in a snobbish gesture.

"The offer of marriage still stands, by the way." I roll my eyes. "But no, I was talking about your deduction of what the Brethren were up to."

"It was a hunch," I reply coolly.

"Why did you have to touch him then?"

"A Healer trick that is above your pay grade." The lie rolls right off my tongue.

"Ah, but nothing is above my pay grade. Maybe you should do that little trick on me, so I can see it for myself."

Disgust hits me in a wave, and I wrinkle my nose in a sneer. "I wouldn't enter your mind even if there was a knife to my throat."

His anger at my words is evident in his dull eyes, but his words stay calm as he says, "You know, before I gave you my proposal—the second time—I had you watched for a little while." Now it's my turn to be angry, but he continues, "I couldn't help but notice your tendency toward human men. You really should be with someone at your own speed. Imagine how powerful our offspring would be."

Okay, now I'm repulsed. The darkness stirs inside, but I breathe before it can latch onto me. *In and out. In and out.* Then I picture Greer and Ash...and Caspian. The darkness settles again.

Good. This is good.

Deciding to change tactics, I coo, "So, you think you would be at my speed? That you could pleasure me with your little wind magic?"

Zander takes a step closer, and his bonded flies away, almost hitting me in the head on the way. "You would be amazed at what I can do with my little wind magic. I know all the right places to blow." His tone goes low, and he blows wind that lightly whips around my neck, tossing the loose strands of my hair back.

In a flash, I press an ice dagger to his neck, then plaster on my most innocent smile and say in a suggestive tone, "You know, I recently started seeing a human man. He's tall, blond, very muscular, and really knows how to treat a lady. One of my first impressions of him was that he reminded me of a Greek sun god. Fucking gorgeous." I take a few steps back, and Zander's smile drops into a frown. I continue, "But you, Zander? My first impression of you was that you reminded me of an undercooked noodle."

Coventina lightly blasts him with water. He falls to the ground and is only sent back seven or so feet from me. She could do a lot worse than that. Draven lands behind me, and Greer climbs off, coming to stand next to me. I realize now the men who were watching the prisoners are in fits of laughter at their fallen elder, not even trying to hold back.

Greer watches Zander try to get his feet under him so he can stand. Surprisingly, I see a shadow fly from her feet toward him and create a line in front of his legs. He is seething when he catches sight of us, but when he goes to stomp in our direction, the line of shadow trips him, and he goes down hard on his face.

"What was that for?" I ask her.

She shrugs. "I've just always wanted to do that to someone."

I laugh. "Cameras taken care of?"

"Yeah, a few grand worth of technology down the drain. I stole the computer, though, to see if we could get anything off of it."

"Good. Let's go home."

On that note, we fly away before Zander can figure out how to use his feet again.

"*He saw me use my memory-seeing, but I don't think he figured out what I was doing,*" I tell Greer down our mental connection.

"*Should we turn around and make sure?*" she asks.

"*No. Even if he did figure out what I am, no one would believe him.*"

"*I have to disagree, considering the impossibility that your existence already is.*"

"*You mean the impossibility that Draven and I exist,*" Coventina grumbles.

"*Don't worry, we haven't forgotten. You both are big, bad, scary dragons. Our lives would be worthless without you,*" I reply sarcastically through the channel.

Draven laughs, and Coventina responds, "*Your sarcasm is not amusing.*"

"*I find it amusing,*" Draven says, still laughing.

When Draven finally calms down, Greer brings the conversation back on topic. "*Dad won't be thrilled.*"

"*What's new?*"

Unfortunately, about a year or so ago during an intimate moment with one of my classmates that I later regretted, I touched his face and found myself in one of his memories. It was of a sweet-faced blond girl who looked at him like he was the reason for the Earth's rotation. The shock of what happened and what I saw sent me running out of his dorm room. He was the last human I had sex with. It turns out that accidentally seeing someone's memories of an ex-girlfriend is a real turnoff, even for a one-night stand.

Coventina being the cryptic pain in my ass that she is, had simply said, *"Finally,"* when it happened and went on complaining about how long it took me to access my third classification. Two classifications is unheard of, and they only happen in the rare case of a Water Healer. But three classifications? It should be impossible. Not only that, but I also gained an Intelligence ability that is extinct among the Order.

Only a handful of people had the ability during the seventeenth century, but we have no idea who they were because their identities were kept a secret. No one knows for sure why the ability disappeared, but the history books suggest that the Great Hawk took it away, deciding it was too powerful and didn't have enough limitations to keep it in check. With all the secrecy surrounding the abilities of Memory-seers, only myths and guesses remain for us to figure out what I can do with it. Something tells me I'm barely scratching the surface of the ability's power.

Only the elders of our community, Mom, Greer, Ash, the Hansens, and Mr. Simon know about it. It was decided that if it got out that the ability resurfaced, everyone would either be fighting to use me for their own desires, or I'd be *evaluated* for being too powerful. I'm not sure which would be a worse fate. If the memory-seeing and what I can do with my water ability got out, then, I really would be locked up or killed by my own people.

CHAPTER 20

TALLIANA

WALKING UP TO THE gym's front desk, I look at the thin brunette sitting at the computer behind the counter. "Excuse me, I'm looking for Caspian Stewart. He has a training room reserved."

She looks up, and her drawn-on eyebrows pinch together. She chews her gum for way too long before she answers in a tone that suggests she has a nasal infection, "Go straight back, up the stairs, and into the third room on the right."

"Thank you," I reply and walk around the counter. Before I get too far, I tune into her and feel the burn of jealousy. I tune back out and follow her directions, hoping she didn't lead me astray out of spite.

Why do I have a feeling that Caspian is the type of man who often leaves a trail of jealous women wherever he goes? Well, he is gorgeous, well-mannered, has a voice that women dream about, and that ass...*Focus Talli*.

To my relief, she didn't lead me astray. I peek my head in the doorway to see Caspian stretching with his back toward me, and speaking of that ass...

I lean against the doorframe and shamelessly watch him as he moves. His sleeveless navy-blue shirt is just loose enough around the arms so I can see the muscles in his shoulders flex as he stretches his arms and back. He reaches his hands high and then moves them down to his ankles, his body following until his head is down between his legs and facing me.

His eyes crinkle, spotting me, and he slowly moves back to a standing position. He turns to me and asks, "Enjoying the show?"

"Taking notes."

"I didn't realize the lesson had begun."

I push off the doorframe and go to the corner to drop off my bag. I turn back to him and say, "Something you should know about me is that I am always learning."

Caspian smirks, and I remove my athletic jacket, revealing my favorite sparring outfit. It's aqua blue, and the sports bra and tight leggings hug my body perfectly.

He gets his water bottle and sips at it, trying not to be obvious as he watches me braid my hair to the side. We meet in the middle of the mat and he explains, "First, I'd like to go through some basic moves to see where you are." I nod, and he continues, "I'm going to grab you, and I want you to try to get out of my hold." I nod again.

Don't react. Don't throw him across the room. You are a human—an ordinary human woman with average human woman skills.

Choosing the most basic route, he grabs my wrist. I twist my hand from a palm-down position to palm-up, pushing hard against his wrists, and pulling my hand free.

"Good."

"That's self-defense most toddlers can perform out of instinct," I retort.

He smirks. "Okay. Let's kick it up a couple of notches."

He wraps an arm around my chest, pulling my back up against him and pinning my arms to my sides. There are a few ways to get out of this one. I choose the simplest.

Throwing my right elbow back, I jab him hard in the stomach and then twist in his arms, pushing hard against his chest. He loses his grip on me, allowing me to spring free.

We do several more moves, and even though I restrain myself during each one, I haven't let him get the best of me yet. I know at some point, I will have to let him win, but I am having a hard time controlling myself. This is simply too much fun. Although, if I keep beating him, he might stop trying to teach me, and that's the last thing I want right now.

I have never been one to view sparring as something that could turn me on; it's always been the exact opposite. But practicing self-defense with Caspian, having him...touch me...Our bodies are growing steadily more familiar, and we are starting to anticipate each other's moves. It feels like we are back on the dance floor, swaying to our favorite song. But this time, no curious eyes are watching us. It's just him and me.

The heat inside the room is climbing rapidly, so we both take a quick water break. Setting my bottle down, I lift my eyes to see Caspian stalking toward me. His eyes are narrowed, and his shoulders are hunched. This catches me off guard, so much so that I let him back me up against the wall. He grabs my wrists with alarming speed and pins them above my head.

Oh fuck.

I can get out of this easily, of course, but my body screams at me to do no such thing. My chest moves up and down from my accelerated heart rate, causing my breasts to press into his chest. It takes every bit of self-control I possess not to outwardly groan at the sensation.

What would he do if I did?

"Out of moves?" he asks. A sensual smile lights up his face, a stark contrast to his darkening eyes.

The challenge is clear, and I take the bait.

I give a little push with my wrists, pretending to test out his grip. Then I strike out with a knee-to-the-groin move, only to be blocked by his leg. He uses that same leg to push mine out, and he copies the movement with the other one, wedging both his legs between mine.

My whole body flushes with heat, and desire builds up between my legs. I'm *really* turned on now.

His face moves a fraction closer as he whispers, "You can do better than that."

My mind wants to take the bait again, show this cocky ass exactly who he is dealing with, but my body remains unmoving. Maybe if I stay still long enough, he'll move even closer to me. Or better yet, he'll remove one of his hands from my wrists and use it to trace the curves of my body instead.

"Is this too much for you?" The question could be taken as being considerate. It's almost as if that's how he meant it, but his husky tone makes it sound like a taunt. I try to bring my dirty mind back to the challenge and contemplate my next move when we hear the door open. Caspian lets go and takes a step back, turning to see the front desk clerk looking alarmed.

"Elaine, sorry. I was teaching my friend self-defense, and I lost track of time." He effortlessly delivers the explanation with his usual warm smile.

"Oh, it's okay, Cas. The next group can wait a couple extra minutes while you and your friend...pack up." All alarm has gone out of her expression. She could be thinking any number of things about what was happening in this room, but there are two cameras in here, so I have no doubt she won't hesitate to look at the footage when we leave. If only to watch Caspian...*Cas* and imagine herself in my place.

She walks out the door, and I move to collect my stuff. "Thanks for the lesson. I think you had me stumped there at the end." A lie, but it's best he doesn't know how easily I could have put him on the ground.

"It was fun. You are a lot more skilled than most. I'm sorry if I came on a bit...aggressive toward the end." His smile is not the least bit apologetic.

"No need to apologize. I enjoyed it." I immediately wince, regretting my word choice.

"Oh, so you like it rough?"

My cheeks burn. "That's not what I said. I enjoyed the challenge is what I meant."

To my relief, he doesn't push further, just asks, "You're very competitive, aren't you?"

"What gave it away?"

He laughs at my immediate admission. Honestly, I don't even know why I'm being so competitive. There is just something about him that draws that side out of me.

We leave the room and apologize to the group that is impatiently waiting for us. We are five minutes late, which is apparently the equivalent to the end of the world to these people.

"I like your tattoo by the way," he says on the way down the stairs.

I look at him, confused, because I don't have a tattoo. "My what?"

He points to my side. *Oh.* Coventina's bonding mark. I have a habit of forgetting it's there. "Oh yeah, thanks. I got it a while ago."

Once we get outside, he smiles and asks, "Do you want to grab some brunch with me?"

I check my phone and see three missed messages: one from Dad and two from Mom. I groan, regretting the decision I have to make.

"I wish I could, but I have a bunch of messages from my parents. I take it that I am needed at home. Raincheck?"

"Of course. Family is important. I'll see you tomorrow at school."

I match his smile and give him a little wave, watching as he walks away.

Ugh. This better be important.

I check Dad's message first.

Dad: *Hey, we need you home. We have guests coming.*

I check Mom's next.

Mom: *Don't hate me. I invited some friends from the Vermont community over for the day, and they are bringing their very attractive son. I promise this one is so much better than the others.*

Mom: *Please come home and put on something nice.*

I should have just pretended like my phone died and gone out with Cas. He is much better company than any guy Mom could invite over. I head back to my ride, walking toward the heavily-forested park that's behind the gym.

I wonder if Cas has driven off yet. Maybe I can catch up to him.

"Contemplating running from your problems?" Coventina asks as I come upon her lounging in the shade of the trees with her glamour up, since it's broad daylight.

"Can you blame me?"

"No, but maybe it's time to tell them you are with this human."

I strap my bag to the saddle and climb on her back. She takes off, and we head home.

"I'm not really with him, though. We're only hanging out. He hasn't made a move suggesting he wants to be anything official yet."

"*Human nonsense. Your body wants to have his babies, and his body suggests that he wants to give you babies. There shouldn't be anything more complicated to it than that.*"

I laugh, though the image of making babies with that man, well I'm going to just stop there.

"*Is that how dragons date? You tell each other you want to have babies, and you just...erm...do it?*"

"*No. We aren't like humans who can mate with anyone. We bond to one another, which keeps us tethered for our entire lifespan. I have never desired to tether myself to another and never will.*"

"*Maybe you haven't met the right dragon yet?*"

"*Low on my priority list.*"

Yes, I understand that perfectly. It really isn't important when saving our people and ending this war is the priority right now. Why doesn't anyone else understand that? But thoughts of Cas and having his body crowd around mine, pinning me against the wall, breathing in my air...I don't allow myself to feel helpless or vulnerable anymore, but with Caspian? He is the one man who makes me want to be vulnerable and let him take over the precious control I hold onto so tightly.

"*My question remains.*"

"*I don't know how they will respond if I tell them I am considering dating a human. It's best to wait until I'm actually dating him. Better to ask forgiveness than permission and all that.*"

She chuffs at me, indicating she disagrees, but she doesn't say another word about it.

I clean myself up and put on a decent outfit. Looking in the mirror, I spread out the skirt of my simple green dress with my hands.

This is dumb.

"I think it's time you tell them you're seeing Caspian," Greer comments, echoing Coventina's suggestion from earlier.

I turn to her. She is sitting on the edge of her bed with Ash sitting on the floor under her with another book I borrowed from Uncle Cyrus in hand. Greer's legs are laying over Ash's shoulders, her arms are crossed and resting on his head, and her own head is resting on her arms. It almost looks like she is sitting on his shoulders, but the bed is bearing her weight. These two are always cuddling or touching each other in the weirdest of ways. They are both looking at me from where I am standing at my mirror, but Greer's brow is arched, waiting for me to say something.

"What are you two doing today while I'm entertaining a suitor?" I ask in a posh tone, ignoring her comment.

Greer snorts, but Ash drops the book and laughs. He asks, "You're enjoying those historical romance novels I got you?"

"Yes, I love reading about all the grand balls, the line of suitors, and how the main characters always have a way of wrapping them all around their pretty fingers. They handle it all much better than I do."

"Ironically, they also always have their eyes set on someone they believe they can't have," Ash points out. My humor dissipates.

Greer adds, "*Believe* being the key word here."

"Maybe if someone would tell me why they *believe* he is someone I can *fully* have, then we can save ourselves all this drama," I retort. I told Greer after the first night at the club that I intend for Cas to be nothing more than a fling, which she promptly disagreed with because her vision suggested otherwise.

Greer buries her nose into Ash's hair and seals her lips.

157

"Great. Now, if you both excuse me, I have someone I need to scare off. Enjoy your lazy Sunday afternoon," I say to them both, but only Ash smiles reassuringly.

As I enter the kitchen, I see Mom finishing up icing a cake. Seriously? A cake?

"So, tell me about today's victim." I lean on the kitchen island, watching as she works her magic.

Mom's look is anything but amused as she answers, "I really think you will like this one, Talliana. Can you please try?"

I roll my eyes. "Yes, ma'am."

Right on queue, I hear Dad's voice outside, and the door opens. He must have escorted them to the house himself. Of course.

Mom gives me a pointed look, and I straighten my posture. I feel exactly like the young girls in the book I am reading.

"Hello, Red."

I spin around to find Waylen standing in the doorway. Surprise floods my veins. I can't believe she is trying to set me up with Waylen now. Still, I can't help the smile that spreads across my face when I see him again.

"Mom didn't tell me it was you who was coming. I completely forgot your parents moved to Vermont."

"Oh, and here I thought that pretty dress was meant for me."

His green eyes crinkle, and I know he is teasing—our last conversation replaying in my mind. Something tells me he was dragged into this just like I was.

"I told you you would like this one," Mom says openly, making Waylen grin wider. Then she leaves us to meet his parents in the living room.

Waylen approaches me, stopping a step away from me. "Did you tell her about everything that happened on your last visit?"

"Oh my God, no. She has no idea. She knew that you were on the mission team, but that's it. Why are you here?"

"My parents dragged me along. I thought it was just for a friendly visit until Mama made me put on this ridiculous suit this morning. I promise I have no intentions of asking for your hand today," he explains.

I take in his appearance and said suit, and it does look silly on him. Waylen has never been the kind of guy who wears suits. He looks much better in black sleep pants. My cheeks blush a little at the thought, and I reply, "Good, because I have no intention of saying yes."

Waylen grins at me, and I realize how easy life would be with him. He could be a best-friend kind of love. He would stand by me and support me; he would do anything I ever asked and more. Our sex life wouldn't even be bad, either. We have plenty of chemistry, but thinking about that night with him compared to what I felt this morning pressed against Cas, there is no comparison.

"You are always thinking in that mind of yours," he says with adoration in his tone. Suddenly, I realize this is all a bit too close for me. He seems to sense the same and takes a step away. I open my mouth to suggest that I show him around when Mom calls from the living room, "Talliana, Waylen, come here and sit with us for a bit."

"Want to have some fun?" he asks.

"What do you have in mind?"

He grabs my hand, interlocking our fingers. "Follow my lead."

"Just like the good ol' days then," I respond with a smile.

Waylen and I certainly do have fun. Both of our mothers are giddy with happiness seeing our hands clasped and how close we sit next to each other on the couch. It's funny how Mom and Dad hated how much time I spent with him when I was little. Now, they expect me to tie my life to his.

Waylen first endures a list of questions from my parents, and then I endure some from his. It would have been painfully awkward if I were sitting beside anyone else, but Waylen takes everything in stride. Greer and Ash come down and join us all for an early dinner and dessert. When Mom's cake becomes the center of attention among the parents, the four of us go to the backyard to hang out. Ash has never met Waylen before, but takes to him easily. I think Waylen has that effect on people.

When the time comes for him to leave, my chest feels lighter, and my cheeks hurt from all the laughter. I see him to the front porch while our parents say goodbye at the car. He turns to me, snaking his arms around my waist. Not pulling me completely to him, but close enough.

"Ready for the grand finale?"

"If you kiss me right now in front of our parents, my mom will be looking at wedding dresses by tonight, I swear."

"Cheek?"

"Yes." I smile at him. He leans in and gives me a soft kiss on my cheek. We separate, and I watch him get into the car with his parents. I wave while Mom and Dad climb up the stairs to me.

"I never thought I would see the day that that boy would become a contributing Order member," Dad comments.

I roll my eyes, and Mom smacks his chest. We walk into the house, and she responds, "I think Waylen has turned out to be a wonderful young man. Too bad Talli doesn't know what's good for her."

I whirl on her. "What?"

"I'm not blind," Mom replies.

"And Melisandre isn't deaf," Dad adds.

Mom puts her hands on her hips, "Maybe if you two stopped playing games, you'd see something could grow there."

I groan. Stupid eavesdropping cat. Turning to Dad, I decide enough is enough and ask, "Weren't you the one who helped bring arranged marriages to an end within the Order? What happened to the man who believed in choice?"

"Do you see me drawing up marriage contracts? No. We are giving you a choice, Talliana. These men started showing up for you the minute word got out about what happened during the March. Your Mom and I are just trying to control who comes knocking."

"We want you to be happy," Mom says, tone low.

"Why do I need a man in my life to be happy?"

"Because that is what will make you feel better, I promise you," Mom answers.

"Your ability can be wrong every once in a while."

"Talliana. I am your mother. I don't need my ability to see that you have been a ghost of your former self since losing Trey."

My eyes sting. That's how they see me then—someone who is broken and needs repairing. I'm a savior to some and a lonely, broken girl to others around here.

"What about you, Dad? Do you think a distraction is the best thing for me right now?"

He meets my venomous glare and answers evenly, "A distraction? No. Someone who might give you a reason to fight harder? Yes."

Mom swings her gaze to him, mouth partially open. I mimic her shock.

"*I think he needs a reminder of how sharp my teeth are,*" Coventina snarls.

I cross my arms over my chest. "Fine. You both want me to have someone so bad? Then I have someone. You can stop worrying about me now."

"What does that mean?" Mom asks.

"Hey Mom, can..." Greer comes down the stairs, stops when she sees us, then turns back around. "Never mind!" she throws over her shoulder and hustles back up the stairs.

"It means I am hanging out with someone right now, and I am going to see where it goes."

"Who?" Mom asks.

"I met him at school," I answer quietly.

"A human? So you haven't started a new study group like Greer alluded to," Dad guesses.

"Yes, Dad. He is a human, a very nice one that I really like. He is in my program and studying to be a doctor like me."

"Do you think that's wise? Talli, I'm not sure you understand this, but you can have your pick of any single man in the Order. Why are you entertaining the idea of a human? How do you think that relationship will work long-term? You can't lie to him forever." Dad's voice is calm but agitated.

"You're the ones telling me to find someone, so I have. You can't be upset if I am doing as I'm told."

Mom's face softens. "What is it about him that you like?"

"Caspian is interested in me and sees me as just a woman he likes. At least, I think he does. Every other man in the Order is interested in me as a prize. I'm the woman with the bonded dragon and rare ability to them. I'm not Talliana, and I never will be. Waylen is the only exception to that rule, and we have already established ourselves as friends and nothing more. With Caspian, I don't know how long-term will work. I try not to put too much thought into long-term plans anymore. I'm just trying to focus on getting through each day and solving the impossible riddle of how to end this war."

"How do you think adding a human boyfriend is going to help? At least if you matched up with a Hawk, you could have someone to confide in and talk to," Dad argues.

"That's the whole point. I don't want someone to talk to about it. I have Greer and plenty of others. I want someone who I have no choice but to be my real self with, someone who allows me to be who I was before Trey died."

"And you want to be with someone you can't form a heart connection with?" Mom guesses, her tone full of solemn understanding.

"Yes. That helps, too. But, speaking frankly with you both, I am not asking permission. I am an adult who has more than earned the right to choose what I do with my free time."

I stare them both down, waiting for the next argument. Moments pass before Dad exhales and responds, "Fine. But the next date you two go on, he'll pick you up here. I want to meet him and vet him first."

"As long as you promise not to just scare him off for the sake of it." I don't think much could scare Cas, but I feel it necessary to add that anyway.

"I promise."

I look at Mom, but she doesn't say a word. So I huff, say goodnight to them both, and march myself upstairs.

I never knew such cruelty existed until Klaus became my husband. Our marriage vows had barely been exchanged before he forced himself upon me. I cried for hours in the bath afterward, then scrubbed myself until my skin was red and tender. Is this what marriage is supposed to be like? My mother says it is, but something inside tells me she is wrong.

Marriage with Otis would have never been like this. I don't understand why he left. Why he didn't fight for me like he promised. His note said he had to leave because he couldn't bear to watch me be wed to another, but i don't believe him.

- Journal of Katarina Lehmann

CHAPTER 21

TALLIANA

CLIMBING THE STEEP PATH up to the Range, I try to settle my mind before meeting with Mr. Simon. I need him to see that I can do this and that I'm ready for the third step. If I handled Zander this week without cutting his tongue out, then it's safe to say I am ready.

Step three is going to be harder, I have no doubt, but so far it has been smooth sailing. It helps that Greer and I haven't had any scheduled missions, only a few middle-of-the-night emergencies. Laying low has been a nice break, but it's also been leaving me anxious, like all the progress we have been making is stalled.

I reach the clearing and find Mr. Simon flipping through the journal. Coventina leaps from my shoulder, shifting into her dragon form to take up her usual spot a few feet away from Seth.

"Good evening, Talli," Mr. Simon greets.

"Good evening," I reply.

"How're the first two steps coming? Ready for number three?"

"Great. Amazing really. I am definitely ready for step three."

He sets the journal down on the table behind me and stands straight. "This is going to be trickier. You need to visualize yourself putting the darkness into a box."

"A box?"

"A box," he confirms. My face scrunches, and he continues, "Close your eyes and, using your inner eye, look inside yourself and find the darkness."

That I can do. I've done it hundreds of times. Closing my eyes, I look inward, searching for the darkness. When I find it, it looks like a sleeping beast, curled up into itself and deeply breathing. It's big, occupying most of the space available, but not latched onto anything.

"Now imagine a box. It can be made of any material you want. You can use bricks like your mental shield, metal, glass, anything should work."

I start to see bricks creating a perimeter, but they morph into a swirling circle of water before my eyes, and I just go with it. Water is good—water I can control. Panting from the effort, I will it to move up and over the darkness.

"Seal the box with the darkness inside."

I feel sweat start to bead and run down my forehead as I fight to close the small gap at the top of my sphere. A drop runs down my nose, and it's enough to pull me from my concentration. The water sphere dissipates, and I physically drop to my hands and knees, chest heaving. Shield building was hard, but not *this* hard.

"Are you alright?" Mr. Simon asks, resting a gentle hand on my back.

I open my mouth to speak, but the darkness erupts. I instinctively know it's pissed off that I tried caging it.

"Go," I force out.

Instead of running, he instructs calmly, "Focus on your breathing. In and out."

The darkness latches onto me, pulling away the last of my control. I squeeze my eyes closed, trying to breathe, but I hear a loud grunt. I swivel my head around and, looking through a dark tunnel, see Mr. Simon on the ground, several paces away from me, soaked. My hand is outstretched toward him. *I did that.*

Panic creeps in, only giving the darkness more fuel.

"*Who do you love?!*" Coventina demands in my mind.

"What?" I ask out loud.

"*Who do you love?*" she repeats, and through the fog, her words slowly sink in.

"Greer! I love Greer!" The darkness's claws loosen, but it still maintains its hold on my muscles.

"*And?*"

"Ash! My parents!" I feel it release my arms altogether, and the one still outstretched toward Mr. Simon drops.

"*And?*"

"Mr. Simon! Everyone here in the community!" My vision starts to clear.

"*Your next answer better be me.*"

A small laugh escapes me, and I answer more calmly, "You and Draven."

"*Anyone else?*"

The picture of a tall blond who makes me warm and happy fills my mind, but I don't speak his name. The darkness returns to its quiet, curled-up form, allowing me to take a full breath. I drop to the ground entirely and roll to my back, looking up at the stars as I work to calm myself completely. A few heartbeats pass, and Mr. Simon stands over me, offering a hand.

"You should have run," I mutter as I let him help me up. My body feels exhausted, like all the energy has been sucked out of me.

"I love you, too," Mr. Simon replies gruffly.

"Sorry I hurt you."

"You didn't hurt me. The darkness did."

"But I *let it* hurt you."

"All I saw was you fighting it the best you could. You can't expect to be perfect at controlling it the first time you try. It will take time and practice."

I rub the back of my neck to work out the tight muscles. "Honestly, if it wasn't for Coventina, I would have been a goner." I look toward her, and she's in the same relaxed position she was in before, completely unfazed by what happened.

"*Not unfazed, just unconcerned. I'm a dragon. Worrying is not in my nature,*" she informs me.

I snort, knowing perfectly well that's not true.

"Then she is doing her job as your bonded," Mr. Simon replies.

Coventina chuffs at him, and the corner of his lips turns up a little.

"Is anything broken? Bruised? Let me check," I offer, sitting up.

"No, I'm fine—no need for all that."

"I feel like I just ran a marathon. Do you think gaining control will help with my energy level?" I ask.

He looks at me quizzically. "Using the darkness drains you much faster than using your abilities without it?"

"Yes. Even if I don't do much with it, like just now, I still feel weak."

"And when you do?"

"I usually get close to blacking out, like what happened on the Florida mission," I explain.

His expression reflects his displeasure at the idea. Ever since I've known Mr. Simon, he's preached to us about knowing your limits and never crossing them, so this bit of news likely isn't easy for him to hear. Eventually, he sighs and says, "The darkness is probably pulling on your magic at a fast rate to give you that boost in power. That's why you're getting depleted way too fast. But to answer your question, it seems reasonable to believe that once you can control how much magic the darkness pulls, you can control how much it depletes you. Goodness, you are lucky that your hair is as stubborn as you are. Otherwise, it would be turning white already."

I grimace. He's right, and I am not going to admit that I have found a few white strands in the last couple of years. Depleting yourself can age you if you're not careful. Gray or white hair is usually the first sign of using your magic too much. The strongest among us, and the ones who defend the community the most, tend to die younger than others, as well. That is, if they are blessed enough to reach old age.

"Do you need help getting home?" Mr. Simon asks.

"I'll be okay. My bonded can do her job and carry me." I laugh as I catch Coventina's very unimpressed expression. She gets up nonetheless and comes to my side, offering me her back. I climb up it and lovingly run my fingers through her hair.

"Get some rest, and I'll see you next week for more practice."

I nod and wave to Mr. Simon, then Coventina walks us slowly back to the house.

"Thank you for what you did, and for carrying me home. I could probably walk just fine."

"As much as it would amuse me to watch you fall on your face, that seems like more work than what it's worth," Coventina replies.

"Snarky dragon."

"Think of me first next time, and maybe I'll be less snarky."

"No, you'd still be snarky."

"Want to talk about the name you didn't say out loud?"

"Nope."

"Suit yourself."

She goes quiet, and so do I. I thought of Cas because he makes me happy, not for any other reason. I barely know him, and it would be ridiculous to have already developed such strong feelings for him.

Absolutely ridiculous.

CHAPTER 22

CASPIAN

"Now, if you reference back to chapter thirty-seven in your textbook, you'll see..." Professor Julian drones on, and my brain involuntarily shuts off.

It is a typical afternoon in the last class of the day, and, thankfully, it's Friday. I have only been attending college for two months, but I have learned that being a doctor is not for me. Or doing anything medical-related, for that matter. Why couldn't Talli be an art or business student? Those would be easier for me than this. My brain conjures the scenario of her volunteering to be the model for a painting, allowing me to capture her ivory curves and red-hued hair on canvas. Not that I am much of an artist either, but I have always enjoyed working with my hands.

I shake the images out of my head. I've never been much of a dreamer—well, not pleasant dreams, anyway—but ever since Sunday,

I can't help but wake up to the feel of her body pressed against mine, only to open my eyes and find my bed cold and empty. I wanted to keep her pinned to that wall while I ran my hand down her body, searching for every sensitive spot on her.

She is messing with my mind.

She started texting me last Sunday, and we haven't stopped since. Conversation is so easy with her. She is smart, sarcastic, funny, and dishes it out as easily as she takes it. We have also had lunch together in the cafeteria a few times. I have to admit to myself that things are going perfectly, quickly even, and I believe it's finally time to move to the next step.

A sigh of relief escapes me when the professor dismisses the class. I grab my books off my desk and look over to where she sat today, and find that she is being practically blocked from getting out of her seat by Jeffrey, a pompous ass who is here because both of his parents are doctors. A man who has never worked for anything a day in his life. I know because I looked him up the first time I saw him pestering Talli.

I can't hear the full extent of the conversation, but her back is straight, and I can see how uncomfortable she is from here. Suddenly, I remember that Jeffrey is the exception to Talli's no-hero rule. I have to hide the devilish grin behind my hand, then quickly adjust it to a casual one as I stroll up to them and unapologetically interrupt, "Ready to head out?" Pretending the ass isn't there, I force him back a few steps as I turn to face her directly.

She looks confused for a minute, and then I helpfully add, "Remember our movie date tonight? I look forward to making you watch *Lord of the Rings* with me."

Lord of the Rings? Of all the movies, that was the weirdest one I could have pulled out of my head. Talli obviously thinks so too, because her nose scrunches up, but she catches on and smiles back at me.

"I'm telling you, I don't think I'll like it, but a bet is a bet, and I'm a woman of my word." She quickly picks up her stuff and looks at Jeffrey. "Sorry, maybe another time. Cas is forcing me to be a nerd tonight."

Cas. This is the first time I have heard her use my nickname, and I have never enjoyed the sound of it more.

I feel daggers in the back of my head from Jeffrey's stare as she gets out of her chair. We leave the classroom together and stay quiet until we are outside, surrounded by a hundred other students ready to start their weekend.

"*Lord of the Rings*? Really?" Her tone is light and sarcastic.

"It was the first thing that came to my mind. Plus, Jeffrey is the exception to the rule."

She snorts and responds, "You're right, he is. So thank you, brave knight, for your gallant effort."

"You're welcome." I grin at her and give a slight nod. Her grip on her book tightens and loosens. She seems nervous about something.

"Well, have a good weekend," she says finally and turns around to walk off.

Oh no you don't.

"What about our movie date?" I call after her. To my satisfaction, she stops and turns back around to look at me.

"We never planned a movie date."

"Yes, we did. Just now."

Talli laughs, and I swear her eyes twinkle like the moon kissing the surface of the ocean. "Okay, but if you don't have *Lord of the Rings* readily available, I will deem it the worst movie date ever. I really have never seen it."

"And you call yourself a movie person," I scoff.

Talli follows me back to where my Jeep is parked, and I drive us to my apartment. After the first movie, we order pizza and eat in front of the TV. We talk on and off about random things, but for the most part, I can tell she is becoming very involved in the movies. From my distant observations of her and our recent in-person interactions, I know she is impatient, but she keeps asking me questions about the films, egging me on to give something away. I only respond, "Just watch the movie." Then she acts all frustrated and focuses again. I try my best to focus on the movie, too, but man, I keep finding myself looking at her. She is so fiercely adorable when she is focused on something.

When the second movie ends, I turn on the third one wordlessly, not paying any attention to the time. After about ten minutes, the biggest yawn I have ever had overtakes me. The timing could not be more inconvenient.

Her eyes turn sympathetic as she says, "It's getting late, and you're tired. I should go. We can finish this another time." She makes to get up, but I grab her hand before she can get far and pull her back down to the couch.

"No, you're invested, and I'm not turning it off. I'm just a little tired. No need to ruin your fun because of it."

"Well, how about this? Since I am the one keeping you up, I can at least offer you my lap as a pillow. Your couch isn't very big, and I don't mind if you want to doze off." She grabs the throw blanket she was using from where it's pooled at her feet and throws it at me.

I catch it. Maybe that yawn was just what I needed.

"No argument from me." Placing the blanket over myself, I lay my head in her lap. One of her hands settles on my shoulder, and she starts playing with my hair with the other. I have no idea if it is intentional or just an idle movement, but it's gentle and soothing. Her fingers run through my longer strands on top, and they make swirls at the nape of my neck, where my hair is trimmed only a little shorter.

Bless this tiny couch. I will never complain about it again.

"Cas?" Slight nudge. "Hey, Cas? I need you to wake up. I'm stuck." Another slight nudge on my arm.

I wake up slowly, surprisingly not startled by her waking me, but immediately alert. Without opening my eyes, I ask, "Yes?"

She lets out a little laugh at my evident lack of desire for moving. "The movie is over, and I'm stuck," a pause, "and I really have to pee." I open my eyes and realize I am holding onto her like a real pillow. My right arm is tucked under her legs, while my left is wrapped over and under them.

"Oh!" I quickly move off of her, and she springs up to her feet and runs to the bathroom. Running my hand over my face, I try rubbing away the last bit of sleep.

I can't believe I actually fell asleep! She must think I'm pathetic for falling asleep on her. I need to fix this. I need to fix this now.

Talli strolls out of the bathroom, looking a bit less tense. "So," she says. "It's late. I think I should get home. Thanks for the movie date. I hate admitting it, but I enjoyed the movies." One side of her mouth curves up.

Think, man, think.

"Let me drive you since we left your car at school."

"No, you're clearly exhausted. I wouldn't want you driving out like this. I can call Greer to pick me up. She'll be pissed, but she'll deal with it."

No, that won't do.

"I can't have you bothering your sister. Why don't you stay here? Promise no funny business." I fake seriousness with my tone before continuing normally. "I can sleep on the couch, and you can take the bed."

She bites her bottom lip, and her cheeks redden, thinking about it or thinking about said funny business. I am tucking that image away as one of the hottest things she has ever done.

"I don't have anything to wear."

"Easy. I have plenty of T-shirts and some gym shorts that should work."

Talli seems to think about this for another minute, looking around and assessing the situation. She then looks at the queen-sized bed through my open bedroom door. "Okay. But I can't let you sleep on the couch. Just stay on your side of the bed, and I'll stay on mine. We are adults and can share a bed without..." She laughs as she finishes, "funny business."

I flash her a grin, and without further comment, lest I say something to scare her away, I find her something to wear. She dutifully goes back into the bathroom to change and prepare for bed. I also use this time to grab an extra phone charger for her and get changed into shorts. I almost put on a T-shirt, but even putting on shorts is unusual for me.

When she emerges from the bathroom, we are both equally caught off guard, each of us stopping dead in our tracks when we lay eyes on each other. She is wearing the T-shirt I gave her, but there are no shorts in sight.

Fuck. I take back my earlier thought; this is way hotter than the lip-biting.

Talli is quite a bit shorter than I am, so thankfully, for the sake of my self-control, the T-shirt I gave her falls to just below the curve of her ass. It's baggy on her, too, but I can see the peaks of her nipples on her very full breasts pushing through the thin fabric. She obviously vetoed the bra. Hopefully, she still has some underwear on.

Hopefully? What is wrong with me? And what kind of game is she playing at? Hoping for said funny business tonight, maybe?

I pull my stare away from, well...all of her and take in her face. She is staring right back at me, following the lines of muscle on display.

"What happened to the shorts?" I finally ask.

"They kept sliding around on me. I figured the shirt covered me like a dress, so it was good enough."

Fucking short dress.

"Well, I guess we make up one whole outfit between us then."

She laughs, and that seems to dissipate the tension a little. Talli moves away from the door and hops into bed. I hand her the phone cord and take a turn in the bathroom myself. I throw cold water at my face from the sink, but nothing short of an ice bath is going to help me right now.

When I come back out, she looks like she has settled comfortably into a spot on one side of my bed, so I climb in on the other. The entire time, though, I am painfully aware of how many layers are likely on her body right now. Two, just two. Maybe one?

I swallow and shift to turn the lamp on my nightstand off when I feel the source of my curiosity growing even harder in between my legs. I grit my teeth now that it is dark and try to get comfortable. When it's been silent for a while, Talli asks, "I can hear your mind working from over here. Care to share with the class?"

I could lie, but decide instead that honesty might be perfect right now, giving me the opportunity to bring her attention to my attraction toward her. "I am trying to work out if you have one layer on or two," I say as seriously as possible.

"Two."

"Thank God." I sigh audibly, and then she laughs. Not the soft, sweet giggles I have been getting from her all week, but a hearty, infectious laugh.

"If you had said one, I don't think I would have slept tonight." This makes her laugh even harder.

"Hey, I am not the only one throwing punches. I think I am going to start calling you abs."

I feel my skin warm. "Please do. Maybe Jeffrey will leave you alone."

"Doubtful. That man is relentless."

"Yeah, he would just pull off his shirt and try to compare his to mine."

"That would be an interesting take on a measuring contest."

Said abs are starting to hurt from how much I am laughing, as I envision the situation in my head. I don't understand how this woman, my enemy, can make me feel so unburdened—so light. It's as if nothing else in this world matters aside from hearing her laugh and seeing her smile.

I will succeed in my mission, and she will fall in love with me, but how do I prevent myself from falling into the same trap?

CHAPTER 23

TALLIANA

My eyes open to the soft light from the window behind me. I am so warm and comfortable. I haven't been this comfortable in forever. Why am I...I lose my train of thought as I realize an arm is wrapped around my waist.

Cas's arm.

He's curled up behind me in the perfect big spoon position with his face nuzzled at the back of my neck. My shirt must have gotten hiked up in the middle of the night because I can feel his shorts on my nearly bare ass. I don't dare move for fear of waking him, and because I don't want to.

This feels right.

At some point in the night, I woke up to him having what I believe to be a bad dream. Greer used to have them when she first came to us after her parents died. Mom always told me never to try waking her, but just to let her know I was there in a very light, soothing way. So I did the same for Cas. Slowly moving my foot so it rested against one of his calves, I gently rubbed his leg until I heard his breathing slow again. It seems his body took this as an invitation to find the source of comfort and latch onto it.

After what could be two or twenty minutes of me lying there, motionless and thinking, Cas starts to stir. His grip tightens on my stomach and then freezes. He must have realized what position we were in. Slowly, he tries to remove his arm from around me. I debate for a minute, trying to decide if I should scare him half to death by alerting him to the fact that I am awake or save him the embarrassment and let him scoot himself to the other side of the bed before pretending to wake up myself for the first time. I choose the latter.

I stretch and turn to find him watching me with a smile on his face, not even trying to pretend like he isn't.

"How did you sleep?" he asks me softly, propping his head up with his arm while lying on his side.

"Good. I'm not used to waking up so warm and cozy. Based on how bright it is in here, I would say I slept in a bit too. How about you?"

He hesitates, then answers, "I normally don't sleep well—bad dreams. But last night, it was like they were there, then they vanished. I slept like a rock after that. You must have worked some kind of magic on me in my sleep." His tone goes from serious to teasing.

"Just call me a dream catcher. I catch all the bad dreams and make them go away."

He laughs but doesn't say more. I don't know why, but I have the urge to tell him exactly what I did for him. "I...I actually did notice you having a bad dream in the middle of the night. Greer used to have them when she was little, so I knew how to help."

His mouth drops open, and he looks at me with disbelief. Then he smiles almost sadly. "Thank you. I don't think I could express how much of a difference it made."

I think about his odd mix of gratitude and sadness as we take turns getting dressed and using the bathroom. Cas drives me back to my car, and once we arrive, I thank him for the movie night and the ride, then say, "See you on Monday," before getting out. Climbing into my car, I start the engine, but before I can leave, Cas has his window down and is waving to get my attention. I roll down my window and lift a brow at him, silently inviting him to speak.

"What are you doing today?" he asks with a corner of his mouth tilted up.

I laugh and respond, "A few errands, a swim, and maybe some downtime. Why?"

"The Fall Festival is going on this weekend downtown. There's going to be fair rides and games. Want to go with me tonight? I'll buy you popcorn and tickets for whatever you want to do." I can see in his eyes how hopeful he is.

"Depends. Is this a real date?"

"According to my math, this will be our third date."

"I think your math is flawed," I quip.

"The first was when we went for dessert, and the second was last night."

"What about the self-defense lesson?" I ask.

"I never bought you food, so it doesn't count."

I laugh and agree. "Okay, as long as you buy me cotton candy instead of popcorn."

His laugh is so wholesome, and his smile is genuine. "Pick you up at five?"

"That sounds good. I'll text you my address."

"See you then, Talli."

"See you then, Cas."

I roll up my window and drive myself home, feeling butterflies dance in my stomach.

Chapter 24

TALLIANA

Hearing the doorbell faintly from my bedroom, I look at the clock, and sure enough, it's five o'clock on the dot. I've been ready for thirty minutes, reading a book about medieval war strategies, and looking for anything that might spark an idea. I put the book down and open my bedroom door as I hear Dad call out, "Talli! Someone is here for you."

I rush down the stairs so that Dad has very little alone time with him. I'm relieved when everything seems civil, and Caspian looks completely at ease. Of course, because nothing seems to affect this man. Well, except for my stunt last night with his shirt. Reckless, but totally worth it. I had hoped it would lead to something, but Cas seems to truly be a man of his word, ensuring there really wasn't any funny business.

Cas locks eyes with me, and his smile is enough to melt my insides. Dad turns around to face me. "Ah, there she is. You two have fun on your date." He faces Cas and adds, "Bring me home a bag of cotton candy, and I don't care how late you have her out."

"Dad! Really?" I ask, feigning annoyance, but I'm really just surprised considering his previous *concerns* about me dating a human.

"Oh, and if you hurt my little girl, I won't be coming after you because she'll kill you long before I can."

"Dad!" I exclaim again, but I can't help but laugh. This is a side of him I haven't seen in a while. Not since before everything happened...

Dad shrugs at me, winks at Cas, then leaves the room. Cas has no sign of alarm or concern. Rather, he is eyeing me with approval. A look, I have no doubt, I'm reciprocating as I take him in. He's in a white T-shirt, brown leather jacket, dark-wash jeans, expensive-looking Nikes, and his wavy blond locks are a bit messy as usual, just how I like them. I could stand here and admire him for hours. But I pull myself from the daze. I walk up to him, breathing in his scent as I reach around him to open the front door. I mourned the loss of his smell on my hair when I had to shower earlier, so it's a relief to have it filling up my senses again—oak and sunshine.

He takes a step back, allowing me better access to walk out the door. I make my way to his Jeep parked on the street, but he manages to reach the door first to open it for me. It feels weird to think I woke up this morning wrapped in this man's arms, and now I'm on what feels like a first date. I have been excited all day to see him again.

"So...I have never been to a fair or anything like that before," he admits, shortly after we start the drive.

I laugh and reply, "Really? Not even when you were young?"

"Nope."

"Do they not have fairs or carnivals in Colorado?"

"They do," he laughs, "I've just never been to any. My father worked all the time and expected me to do the same, so I never had the time to go growing up."

The glimpses into his life growing up that I have gotten so far always leave me feeling sad, and something tells me I've only scratched the surface of the sad stories.

"We never went out much when I was young either, but I've at least been to a few fairs. I will make it my mission to ensure you get the full experience tonight. We are talking all sorts of greasy food, wasting way too much money to win stuffed animals at games, the Ferris wheel, all of it." I grin at him.

His lip kicks up in the corner when he glances over at me, then asks, "Are you sure you wouldn't rather do something more our age, like go to a nice dinner or something? I mean, if you would rather do that, I don't mind at all."

His confession to me and his offer are sweet, but I'm much more excited for the fair than a stuffy dinner anyway. "No, I really would rather go to the fair with you. Sounds like a lot more fun to me. I'm not a wine-and-dine kind of girl."

He grins. "Okay, greasy food it is."

We park in the grassy lot by the fair, and Cas cuts off the engine, flashing me an excited smile. It's chilly out tonight, but I put on my fleece jacket over my long-sleeve top, so I don't mind. My jacket, the millions of lights in front of me, and the prospect of spending time with Cas tonight warm me plenty.

"Ready?" I ask him as we start walking toward the ticket booth.

"I hope so."

I start him out on the carousel, each picking a worthy steed and spinning around, taking in all the lights. Then games. He is incredibly good at most of them, but so am I. He gives me the three stuffed animals he wins, including a giant purple dragon, which is now my absolute favorite for obvious reasons. I win two for him, a gorilla and an elephant. After he wins the fourth stuffed animal, the teenage boy at the booth shakes his head at our arms full of them and hands us a large plastic bag to help. We gratefully put all the stuffed animals in it, aside from my dragon, which is too big, and find food next.

After three hot dogs and a large basket of fries to share, our stomachs are full, and I am completely unaffected by the cold air. The chill that dances over my cheeks and nose is a welcome cooling effect from the warmth I feel inside. The night has been easy and full of uninterrupted conversation. No talks about weapons, which community was attacked last night, or people looking at me like I am a hero. For the first time in over two years, my shoulders feel unburdened, and my steps are easy. This is nice—*so* nice.

"Alright, what's next?" he asks.

I stop and look around at the options. Only the whirl-and-twirl spin ride and the Ferris wheel are left, but we just ate. I have a stomach of steel, but who knows how strong Cas's is. I don't want to find out tonight by doing the spin ride.

"Ferris wheel," I decide out loud.

"You got it." Cas shifts our stuffed animal bag into one hand and grabs mine with the other, interlocking our fingers. It's such a simple gesture, but one that makes my stomach tumble with happiness as we head toward the tall wheel.

The Ferris wheel goes around once, and I feel his eyes on me the whole time. I build up the courage, then turn to him and confirm my suspicions. My face heats, and the way his eyes move from my hair to my cheeks, I know he sees it.

"Tell me something about you. Something not many others know or could guess," he says. His tone is serious and alluring, unlike his usual lightness.

Good question. I think for a minute, and noticing my contemplation, he adds lightly, "Aside from being an assassin, of course."

My heart stops. Then I remember the conversation when he picked me up. I breathe easier again.

"I like to do puzzles," I offer.

"Puzzles? Like game puzzles on your phone or actual puzzles?"

"Actual puzzles. A thousand-piece, takes you half a year to complete, don't-breathe-on-it-funny-or-you-might-lose-a-piece puzzle."

His eyes crinkle in amusement. "I like that. It feels random yet perfect for you."

"And you?"

"I'm afraid of heights," he admits in a nervous laugh.

Immediately, I realize that the entire time we have been up here, he has kept his eyes trained either on me or on our laps, where our hands are still clasped together. My mouth drops open in horror. "Why didn't you tell me before we got on the Ferris wheel? I would have understood." I really would have, even if heights are something I love.

"Because I wanted to experience my first Ferris wheel ride with you. I like experiencing new things with you, because you make my fears seem so much smaller." His hazel eyes, looking very brown at the moment, lock onto mine, and I can see how vulnerable he's allowing himself to be right now. My heart immediately warms to it. There's this pervasive stereotype that women want a man who is dark and mysterious, even slightly dangerous. I mean, I get it. I see the appeal, but what's in front of me right now—a man who is open, honest, kind, and even vulnerable at times—this is real. This is what a true knight in shining armor should look like.

I squeeze his hand and ask, "Is your fear from childhood trauma, or did it just appear one day?"

He chuckles softly. "Childhood trauma."

"Will you tell me what happened?"

He sighs and runs his hand through his hair, something I've noticed is a nervous habit of his. "When I was a kid, my father didn't let me spend much time after school with friends. On occasion, though, I would bust my ass to get ahead on all my studies, and he would say yes to an afternoon with my best friend, Dylan. So this one time, I was at his house. It was the middle of winter, and we had gotten hammered by a ton of snow the night before. Their detached garage had a low roof that they would sled off of into a giant snow pile. It looked like so much fun. When it was my turn, though, I climbed over a patch of ice and slipped." Reflexively, I cover my mouth with my free hand. He continues, "I slid down the roof and tried grabbing the metal gutter, but ended up slicing my hand open, and falling anyway. I didn't hit the big pile of snow, though. I ended up falling onto the cleared path of cement that skirted the garage. I broke my arm, had to get stitches in my hand, and then got a firm lecture from my father on being reckless."

His empty hand opens to show a faint scar spanning the entire length of his palm. I trace it with my finger and he shivers.

"How old were you?"

"Eight. I've been afraid of heights ever since. It makes me feel out of control whenever I'm too high up."

Nodding, I swallow hard. I know exactly what that feels like. He must read my expression, because he asks, "You've been through something similar?"

I can feel that my smile is small and sad, and I don't know why I admit this to him because I haven't revealed this to anyone, but I reply, "Not exactly. But yeah, I feel like I have no control most of the time. I'm working on fixing that, but sometimes…sometimes I wonder if it's just easier that way so that I can place the blame on something other than myself and my own poor decisions." I look up to find him studying me closely, his expression one of understanding. People often look at me that way, but it's always a lie. No one understands me, and no one truly could. But for some reason, I feel like Cas just might, even though I know that's impossible. I add, looking away, "I sound like a coward, don't I?"

His hand reaches over and tilts my chin up so that I'm looking at him again. "Not at all. I think you sound like a human just trying her best to do the right thing. And admitting that, how you truly feel, out loud, makes you incredibly brave. You're brave and beautiful, Talliana. Inside and out. You should be told that every day for the rest of your life, so that you never have an opportunity to forget it."

My heart swells, and I feel like I'm flying again for the first time. His thumb gently moves to caress my cheek. I'm being touched by the sun even though the sky is dark. His molten eyes drop to my lips, and I know what will come next…

"Please disembark." The bored tone of the Ferris wheel operator suddenly pulls me out of my trance. I look past Cas and see him waiting for us to exit the ride.

Cas pulls his hand away from my face and turns around to exit. He keeps his fingers interlocked with mine, though, and I'm surprised at how grateful I am for it. I'm afraid losing contact with his skin altogether might leave me shivering.

We walk back to his Jeep, and in what I now know as normal Cas fashion, he follows me to the passenger side, presumably to grab the door for me. To my surprise, though, as soon as we get to the door, he doesn't open it. Instead, he stops and turns to look at me.

One heartbeat. Two heartbeats. I'm about to ask what's wrong when his mouth crashes onto mine and he pushes me up against the side of his Jeep, placing his hand behind my head to soften the impact.

Surprise quickly morphs into a hungry current racing through my body, and I throw my arms around his neck, stuffed dragon still in one hand as I hold onto him. I open my mouth for him, and his tongue sweeps in while mine greets him there. His groan of approval sends goosebumps all over my skin. The plastic bags he is carrying fall to the ground beside us, and he grabs my waist, right above my hip bone.

My entire body responds to his as if my very survival relies on it, and that initial current of energy starts to feel like a tangible thing as I lose myself in his touch. I haven't felt a spark, a need like this since...well, honestly, I don't think I've ever felt this. God, this is beyond shared attraction. It's so much more than that in ways I can't explain or decipher right now. All I know is that I need him, and I feel it in my gut that he needs me too.

After a few more moments, though, he gently pulls away, looking as breathless as I feel. "I really like you, Talli." His tone is soft, and I feel his words dance along my skin.

"I really like you too," I respond breathlessly. His mouth curves into a wide grin. Without looking away and still caging me against the Jeep, he reaches over and opens my door. Then, he takes two steps back, allowing me space to get in.

I feel reluctant as I climb into my seat, and he closes the door. I will my heartbeat to slow as he first opens the back door to store our precious stuffed cargo, then climbs into his seat and starts driving me home. I still haven't let go of my stuffed dragon, which rests on my lap.

"*That stuffed toy looks nothing like me,*" Coventina chimes in my head.

"*You don't look like most dragons,*" I counter.

"*True. I'm much more magnificent than my brothers and sisters,*" she declares, full of pride.

I snort, and I notice Cas glancing at me. "What's so funny?" His tone is light, as if he is waiting for a joke.

"Oh, nothing. I was just thinking about how we forgot my dad's cotton candy," I lie smoothly. We shared some freshly spun cotton candy earlier, and I meant to grab a bag of it on our way out for Dad.

"No, we didn't. Look in the back seat."

I twist around and see a second plastic bag with cotton candy peeking out. I hadn't even noticed it.

"When did you manage that?" I ask.

"When you went to wash your hands on our way out."

"Well, aren't you on top of it?" I tease.

"I do like being on top, but I am always happy to let a lady choose." His tone is equally teasing.

I snort at his bad joke. "Is that so?"

He flashes a wicked grin and reaches across the center console to grab my hand again.

Warm. I feel warm inside. If I am the layer of ice over the lake in the winter, he is the sun rising on the first day of spring.

Chapter 25

CASPIAN

We walk up the steps to her house, her arms full of stuffed animals and cotton candy. Talli opens the front door, but turns at the last moment to kiss me again before closing it. I climb back into my Jeep and try not to look desperate as I haul ass out of this community.

I know being here is good for my mission. It never hurts to gain as much perspective on this place and these people as possible, but it makes me uneasy. As if, at any moment, someone will find me out and ruin everything. I'm in enemy territory, which would make any logical person uncomfortable, but I need to get used to it if I intend to learn everything there is to know about this place. It appears so normal on this starry night, but I know it is far from it.

The gate in front of my Jeep lifts, and I nod at the guard as I pass him. As soon as the community becomes consumed by the night in my rearview mirror, I release a breath.

Talli is officially *mine*.

Everything is going so smoothly. At this rate, I'll have her spilling all her secrets to me by New Year's. Okay, maybe Valentine's. I don't want to push this too hard.

I've given this next phase a lot of thought, and I need to play it carefully. The amount of self-control I am going to have to exhibit might kill me, but it will be crucial to make sure she doesn't just use me and run. I must ensure that she will keep coming back to me.

She has to fall in love.

I hate to be cocky, but by the way she looked at me tonight, I'd say she is well on her way to that already. Her body melted in my arms when I kissed her lips, lips that taste like sugar and a mouth that feels as deadly as the rest of her. The thought alone of what she could do with it...

I adjust myself in the driver's seat, my skin feeling hot from the images that just flashed through my mind. Fuck me, I shouldn't want this—want her—as much as I do right now.

It's confusing how she feels so genuine and innocent when I know her body count far surpasses my own. Does she even feel the deaths on her conscience like I do? Do they keep her up at night, too? She seemed to sleep pretty well last night, and what she did for me had to be magic. There are very few nights that nightmares don't plague me. They started the night I made my first kill. How can someone truly evil provide so much comfort?

Waking up to her this morning was like waking up to the most pleasant dream. My shirt draping over her body, her round ass pressed right up against me and her lace underwear doing not much to cover it. Why does she feel so perfect? I've had sex with plenty of women, but none have ever felt as right as she does. I haven't even had sex with her yet, and I already feel this way. It's my imagination. It has to be, because I can't allow any other explanation for it.

I enter my apartment and pull out my phone to send a carefully crafted text to my father.

Me: *Hello, Father. Everything is going great here. Classes and work are good. I met a girl. I think falling in love will be easy. Everything is going as planned.*

Father: *That's good to hear. I trust I won't be disappointed in you this time.*

Sighing, I collapse on the couch. How would a normal father respond to a text like that? I wouldn't know. I do know, however, that a guy should text his girl after a great night. Picking up my phone again, I carefully craft another text.

Me: *I had a great time tonight. Thank you for helping me with my fear of heights.*

Talliana: *Me too. Thank you for my small army.*

A picture loads, showing all of the stuffed animals I won for her tonight lined up on a pillow on her bed.

Me: *By far the most terrifying army I have seen. Mine look as if they are going a bit soft. I need to whip them into shape.*

I line them up on the couch beside me and take a picture of myself looking at them disapprovingly.

Talliana: *That is a problem. Maybe you should start by giving them some self-defense classes.*

Me: *No. Those classes are reserved just for you. Now that you bring it up, though, I think we should pick up where we left off last session.*

Talliana: *How about someplace where no one can interrupt such an important lesson?*

Me: *Agreed. My apartment. Next week?*

Talliana: *It's a date! Goodnight Cas*

Me: *Goodnight*

Me: *Hey Talli?*

Talliana: *Yes?*

Me: *I'm looking forward to seeing you again.*

Talliana: *Me too. :)*

I toss my phone back down on the couch and go to the bathroom to turn on the shower.

Catching my reflection in the mirror, I see a smile spread across my face—a smile because, clearly, my plan is working.

I disappointed him again. I always disappoint him. He caught me using my water ability without permission. He moved to punish me, but something inside of me made me move faster. It made me fight back. It felt like being aware of my body without being able to control it. My water wrapped around his neck, and i felt it squeeze. I saw his face turn red and his eyes bulge. I never felt more powerful, even if i had no control. Eventually, it let go, and i knew i would be held responsible for the actions of my water, which had acted on its own. But i took the beating and did not try to explain. He wouldn't believe me if i did, and if my water chose to protect me in that moment, i could only hope it would do so again the next time.

- Journal of Katarina Lehmann

CHAPTER 26

TALLIANA

November

I TAKE THE STEPS two at a time, going down, down, down to the lab. I love Ash's parents, and I have even made an effort to learn some American Sign Language so I can communicate with Mrs. Hansen better, since she can no longer speak. But I *hate* visiting them at the lab because it means they are putting me through more tests.

"Talliana, thank you for coming today. We know you probably have other things you'd rather be doing, so as always, we promise not to take up too much of your time," Mr. Hansen says in greeting.

"Anything to help the war effort," I sigh and take a seat on the exam table.

Mrs. Hansen greets me with a soft smile and a reassuring squeeze on my shoulder, then she begins placing the neurofeedback machine on my head. It monitors my brain wave activity as I use my memory-seeing ability. I consider myself fairly knowledgeable about the way many things in the medical field work, but I won't pretend to ever understand what they are looking for when they hook me up to this machine.

Ash walks through the lab doors and takes a seat on the other side of the exam table. He is usually the one to help during these tests.

"What memory are we watching today?" he asks the room casually.

"We are actually going to try something new today," Mr. Hansen answers from his station in front of the computer.

Mrs. Hansen steps back from me and moves to stand beside her husband. She pulls her brown curly hair away from her face with a clip and slides on her blue-framed glasses.

"Like what?" I ask.

No one answers me for a few moments, until finally, Mr. Hansen explains, "We want you to find a memory and see if you can manipulate it in some way. Any way you can will do, but might I suggest finding something simple, such as what Asher ate for breakfast this morning."

"I—I can't change memories. That would be..."

"We have reason to believe you might be able to."

"No pressure, but let's try it and see what happens," Mrs. Hansen signs.

I look over to Ash to find his face scrunched in his thinking mode. He's not too sure about this either. But eventually, he turns to me and nods, giving me permission.

Hesitantly, I reach out my fingers to his temples and close my eyes. I mentally leap into his mind and open my inner eye to come face-to-face with the familiar rows of bookshelves. I've come to learn that, like mental shields, memory organization can come in different forms depending on the person. Ash, for example, stores each memory in books that are lined up in order on bookshelves. Each bookshelf represents a year, each row represents a month, and each book represents a day. Ash easily has the most organized mind that I have ever seen.

I slowly move to the closest bookshelf and grab the last book on the shelf. I flip through the first couple of pages until I see a picture of a cereal bowl and two slices of toast. The image moves, and I watch as Ash looks up at his mom, who is handing him a glass of orange juice. Staring at the memory, watching it replay over and over again, I decide to change the orange juice to apple juice. But how? How am I supposed to change his memory? I try willing the drink to change. I try picturing it as apple juice instead. I even try touching the image and then willing, but nothing works. So I shut the book, place it back on the shelf, and leap back out of Ash's mind. Ash lets out an audible gasp of relief, and I let go of his temples quickly.

"How did it go?" My eyes pop open in surprise at hearing my dad's voice instead of Mr. Hansen's. I find him standing a couple of feet away from me, studying me.

"I tried but couldn't figure out how to change it. This would be a lot easier if I had an instruction manual."

Dad sighs, and the sound immediately makes me feel like a disappointment. Like I am not enough.

"There isn't a manual or a teacher for memory-seeing, but maybe it works similarly to dream-walking and how they can impact a dream?" Ash suggests.

Mrs. Hansen shakes her head up and down and smiles at her son. "Brilliant thinking, Ash," she signs.

"Yes," Dad agrees. "Worst case that might at least spark some ideas. Talli, Ash, I'll set up a meeting with Theo Matisse for tonight. I'll go talk to him now and text you both the time." Dad doesn't wait for a response, leaving as swiftly as he came in. Mr. Matisse is our most senior Dream-walker in the community. He is the one who taught Trey when his ability manifested.

Mr. Hansen runs through some questions about what I tried, while Mrs. Hansen removes the neurofeedback machine from my head. Ash and I walk out of the lab together, but stop short when we hear Dad's rough whispering. Ash pulls me to the corner ahead of us and presses himself against the wall, straining to listen.

Why is Ash eavesdropping? I am about to ask, but I sense Ash's accelerated heartbeat, and his worry hits me next when I tune into him briefly. Something is going on. I trust Ash, so I take up a place beside him and try to hear Dad's words.

"I know they are strong enough, but I won't risk them. If something happens to my girls, then we are all dead. We have to keep them benched while we work on plan B."

"Are you planning on telling them? Or are you going to continue to coddle them?" Chief Lu asks. Ash tenses next to me, but we both continue to listen.

"It's not coddling, Kasumi. It's a matter of convincing. Greer will be the soldier I raised her to be, and she will fall in line. But Talli will not be so easy, and if we can't convince Talli, then we won't have Greer either. Just let me focus on my girls' part of it, and you focus on your own girl's part of it."

Their footsteps echo down the hall as they move away from us. Once I hear the elevator *ding*, I whirl on Ash. "What is going on?"

Ash shakes his head. "Not here." He doesn't say a word to me until we are all the way to the lake and Greer has managed to get away from work long enough to meet us here.

"Well?" I ask, annoyed that they have been keeping anything about plans for the war from me.

They both exchange glances, then look at me. Ash starts. "I came across something interesting on my father's desk a few weeks ago. It was research on the gas used during the Holocaust. I was confused why he would have something like that, so I looked at some of the other paperwork on his desk, and everything had something to do with the use of gas, whether in times of war or for medical practice. Then I found a chemical breakdown of Greer's shadows, alongside the chemical breakdown of various gases."

"I'm not following," I admit.

"We think they are trying to find a way to fuse the memory elixir into my shadows," Greer clarifies.

"I don't understand how that's a bad thing. Seems much more efficient when distributing the memory elixir." But as I say it, an uneasy feeling settles inside of me.

"Not when they want to use it on entire areas where we only *suspect* the Brethren to be."

I stare at Greer in horror. No. The Brethren live among innocent humans; they don't separate themselves like we do. Aside from the creepy cabins in the woods they use before they attack, they are never truly away from people who have no idea this war exists.

"Even if all their exact homes could be pinpointed, they have families, kids— people that are as innocent as the clueless humans next door," Ash adds to my train of thought.

"That can't be right. We don't hurt innocents. No one would ever agree to this. How would they even explain it? Are they considering a total wipe? Or...maybe a partial?" I shake my head, unable to stop my racing thoughts.

"A partial wipe of their memories wouldn't be good enough. Who knows when these people are indoctrinated, so it would be too great a risk to try taking away just a few years. As far as how to explain entire areas waking up to no memories? We have no idea," Greer answers.

"The most logical path would be to blame it on a virus," Ash replies.

"Well, you will tell them no. You won't do it," I say to Greer.

"It's not just Greer. Last week, I found my dad talking about making the elixir potent enough to be delivered through water. Through a mist, specifically. My guess is that the shadows would be used to get people inside, while the mist would cover everyone outside," Ash explains.

"So that's what Dad meant about convincing both of us. What is Mei-Lien's part in all this?" I ask.

Greer looks at me sharply, and Ash gives her the rundown of what we heard in the hallway between Dad and Chief Lu. She frowns deeply, but replies, "I'll talk to her. See what she knows."

"I still don't understand. We can tell them no. We can march over there, tell them we know what they are up to, and tell them we won't do it," I try again, but Ash and Greer look very unsure.

"Shadow-wielders are sparse, yes, but not extinct. And there are plenty of Water Elementals to go around. The only trick is getting them into the sky to distribute the mist. So they will want us on their side, but they can do this without us if necessary."

"You think the Russians would agree to help?"

"I don't know," Greer admits. "But I do know they are desperate for an allied community to help them with supplies. Alaska does what it can for them, but Massachusetts is the one with all the resources. They're also running out of people. They need Florida to get them more placements to help keep their bloodlines alive. Dad could offer them everything they need, like supplies and Hawks at a prime child-bearing age."

My nose wrinkles at the last part, but before I can comment, Greer's phone rings, and she pulls it out of one of the many pockets she has in her police uniform. "I've got to go. Talli, don't do anything. Just let Ash and me continue looking into this situation. We'll let you know if we learn more. Sorry, that we..."

"Kept this from me?" I finish for her. "I guess you both figured it was too risky to let the uncontrollable one in on a secret like this."

"Talli, it's not like that. Really, it's just..." Ash tries.

"No, it's fine. I'm going to go." Coventina climbs up the bank from the water, and I climb onto her back, asking her to take off before the first tear can fall.

CHAPTER 27

CASPIAN

I LOVE DAYS LIKE this when I can convince Talli to come back to my apartment after classes. Sometimes we watch a movie, sometimes we chat, and sometimes, I get her *full* attention.

My tongue has memorized every inch of her mouth, but I still can't get enough of her taste. She wants to progress further than just kissing. I can feel it in the way she moves against me and tries to egg me on to touch her. But this is a vital part of my plan. I have to keep everything at kissing, nothing more. It's agonizing for both of us, but I know this is the right move, even if my body is in a constant state of protest.

"Cas...I want you..." she moans between kisses.

"You have me," I reply, also between kisses.

"No, I want you. All of you." Her kisses are turning desperate now.

Oh, she's finally cracked. I'm going to regret what I'm about to do.

"Is that so?" I reply with teasing in my tone.

Her kisses abruptly stop, and using her arm against my chest, she props herself up to look at me. Her eyes are daggers, with every intent of trying to cut me. "I'm being serious. I've tried dropping hints that I'm open to you asking, but I'm done with your obliviousness. Now I'm asking."

I'd better get right to it, then. Trying to keep my voice as light as possible, I say, "I think we should wait a bit longer."

There's the disbelief, and, oh no, hurt flashes behind her eyes. She opens her mouth, then closes it. Before I can get any words out to explain, she scrambles from my bed and starts grabbing her stuff.

"Talli, whatever you're thinking, it's not that," I tell her quickly. I'm not sure what she could be thinking, but it's not good, considering her reaction.

She almost whispers as she replies, "Then tell me what to think." Her body language is rigid, and she won't look at me, but to my relief, she stops collecting her things.

Crossing the room to her, I reach for her hand. She doesn't resist, but keeps her head down. "Look at me. Please," I beg.

That seems to get her attention, because her eyes meet mine, and I want to throw myself down a hole for the pain I find there. "Please come sit down and let me explain." She nods and lets me lead her back to the edge of the bed.

"You are the most beautiful woman I have ever known. Every time I learn something new about you, it's like a knife to the chest because it's just another reason why I am unworthy of you." I have no idea where these words are coming from, but I can't stop. *This shit is good*. "I've slept with a few women, happy to take whatever they were offering." Her eyes, which were starting to soften, turned cold again. "But you're different. You deserve more than sex in the heat of a moment. You deserve to have someone who will make love to you and worship every inch of you." I swallow hard, a lump suddenly in my throat. I continue, "I want to be that man who will give you what you deserve. I want to love you with everything I have before I ask you to give me every part of you. I just need a little more time to get to know you."

A tear rolls down her cheek, and I brush it away with my thumb. There is a distinct ache in my chest at the sight of it, but I ignore it as best as I can.

Get it together, man.

"I'm sorry for being stupid," she says quietly. Despite her tone being soft, her face looks grave.

"You're not stupid. I'm the idiot for not bringing this up to you first. I just wasn't sure how to say it." She nods, but I can sense her withdrawing further into herself. "What's wrong? Are you upset with me?"

"No, I just...If you are truly committed to this, to us, you should know something about me."

My heartbeat quickens as anticipation courses through me. Is this really it? Is she going to tell me this quickly? I didn't think it would happen so soon. My father will finally have to respect me after this, but at the same time, I'm feeling mournful over losing more time with her. I get a grip on my rivaling emotions. "Tell me. There is nothing you can say that will scare me off."

She hesitates and then answers, "I'm broken, Cas. Like, really broken."

I'm surprised by her words, but she still might reveal more, so I let her continue.

"You say that I am beautiful inside, but I'm not. I'm a raging storm. I have been for a long time. Ever since..." she trails off, and I squeeze her hand to encourage her to continue. "A couple of years ago, my boyfriend died in a bad accident. A tragic accident. We had plans for a future, and I loved him with everything I had. Afterward, I wasn't myself. I'm still not, and I don't know if it's possible to be who I was again. I've been trying to get as close to her—the old me—as I can, but I'll never be the same. I'm afraid my heart is too shattered for the pieces to fit back together again and love you the way you truly deserve."

Her tears fall in a steady stream now, and I gather her into my arms. This is about Treyton. I never learned what happened to him, but by the sounds of it, the Brethren were responsible. Given her "couple of years" remark, I have little doubt he died during the slaughtering we brought to their community door.

After a moment of letting her cry, I whisper into her hair, "You're wrong." She pulls back and looks at me. Her face is blotchy but still incredibly perfect as she studies me. I tell her again fiercely, "You're wrong."

Gently, I place my hand over her heart. "Your heart isn't broken beyond repair. It's right here, just under your skin. It's beating, and it's strong. Part of it may be lost with him, but the rest is still here. Beating for everyone else you love, your parents, your friends, Greer, Ash. And one day," my hand moves from her chest to lightly cupping her cheek, "it will beat for me, too, even if I have to spend every day convincing you that it should. Because Talli, we're all broken and flawed in one way or another, but I refuse to believe that either of us is beyond repair."

"I want to believe that, but I don't know if I can."

"I can't force you to believe it, but all I ask is that you don't overthink it right now. Deal?"

Her eyes flutter closed, and she leans into my hand. After a moment, those beautiful eyes reopen, and she answers, "Deal."

Pulling her toward me, I kiss her as softly as I can manage. She returns the kiss with one of her own, and before I know it, we are right back where we left off before this conversation and whirlwind of emotions swept us away. But all the playfulness we had before is gone, replaced with tenderness. Like the healing of one another has already begun.

I'm a fucking fraud.

What I am doing is worse than anything else I have ever done. Talli is opening herself up to me in such a vulnerable way, showing me exactly who she is inside, just for me to slide into her already broken heart and do more damage. She must have gone through unimaginable tragedies that my people caused, turning her into what she is now. Does anyone ever truly want to deal out death the way she has? Or is this something she feels like she needs to do for the people she cares about? I have been doubting my beliefs on exactly who and what Talliana is for a while, but now I know with absolute certainty she isn't a monster.

That only makes everything so much more challenging. What I have to do to her might be what breaks me. Because even though I don't want to, I still have a mission to complete and a duty to my own people.

Chapter 28

TALLIANA

A scream tears through my throat as I try to force the darkness into its cage. What originally started as a cage made of raging water is now made entirely of ice.

"Keep pushing, Talli! You're in control!" Mr. Simon shouts from somewhere next to me.

I dig my nails into the dirt and try to will it further in. Almost there...almost...The darkness slams against the ice, and it cracks, then shatters, allowing it to spring free from its cage entirely.

Magic surges out of me, all around me, and I hear Mr. Simon let out a gasp. I want to open my eyes, I want to make sure he is okay, but the darkness is forcing them to stay closed.

"No! Stop this!" I scream at the darkness, but it only digs its claws in deeper.

Greer. Ash. Covey. Draven. Mr. Simon. Mom. Dad. Cas.

The darkness shrieks as if hit by a physical blow and lets go of me. With my control back, my eyes spring open, and I find a layer of ice instead of dirt under my hands. I get to my feet and realize I am surrounded by ice, a flat sheet under my feet that shifts into spears at the edges, completely surrounding me.

"Mr. Simon!" I call out, terrified that he got hurt.

I catch sight of him getting back to his feet on the other side of the ice. "I'm alright," he says, cupping his face. He slowly pulls his hand away, and I see blood smeared all over his left cheek.

Ignoring how bone-deep tired I am from that fight with the darkness, I move my hands over a section of ice, willing it into water and using it to cover Mr. Simon's cheek and heal the gash. The moment it's sealed, I drop to my knees back on the ice. He reaches me in the next moment, helping me off the ice and onto a patch of soft grass.

"Maybe we need to stop meeting on damp nights. But good news is that we are really pissing it off now, so we must be close," Mr. Simon muses, almost as if it's funny. But I know better. Mr. Simon doesn't joke around; he's being serious.

My ice ability needs water to form, so without water, neither I nor the darkness can make ice. But on nights when there is moisture in the air, even a little, I can pull it out of the atmosphere. On my own, I can use it in small ways, but the darkness can use it to a catastrophic level.

"It's going to make me kill you one of these days." I can't believe I'm about to say it, but I do. "Maybe we need to bring Greer in on this, if only for backup. She can contain me or stop me if needed."

"Talli, I don't mean to alarm you, but even Greer couldn't stop the darkness if it decided to go on a rampage through the community. It would take a killing shot to stop it, and she would never be strong enough to do it."

"Then you have to be. Someone around here needs to be strong enough to kill me if necessary."

"It won't come to that, because you are strong and you will gain control. Consider how far you've come. I can actually see *you* again, and I won't let the darkness take you away for good. I promise you."

I let his words sink in. I really have been more myself lately than any time in the past few years. There are so many reasons why that could be, but I do feel like Cas is a significant contributor. However scared that makes me feel.

"Can I ask you something?" I wrap my arms around my knees and look over at Mr. Simon sitting on the ground across from me. Seth is lying right next to him, watching me just like his bonded Hawk. "Do you think I'm at risk of the darkness trying to seize control even when it's not provoked? I...I'm worried it might try when I am unprepared to deal with it, when it could harm someone who can't fight back."

"No," he answers without hesitation. "The darkness only seems to lash out when it perceives some kind of threat toward itself or you. It doesn't appear to be violent for the sake of being violent."

I nod. That makes sense, but I can't help but worry about Cas. He has no idea about the monster inside of me, and that he could be in serious danger if it decides he is a threat.

"You deserve to be happy, Talli," Mr. Simon tells me out of nowhere.

"What?"

"The guy you're dating, his name is Caspian?" I nod again, and he continues, "Don't give him up to try to keep him safe. You're stronger than the darkness, and if you care about him, you won't let it touch him."

"You don't think I'm being reckless, dating a human? Dating someone who doesn't understand any of this? Dad and Mom certainly don't approve of it. I think they're worried about what might happen if my heart breaks again."

"I think it's up to you to decide what's reckless for your life. It's not up to them or anyone else to approve of what makes you happy. You spend a lot of time taking risks for everyone else. Maybe you should start taking risks for yourself."

My heart swells. There is nothing like some Mr. Simon wisdom to make me feel better. He always has my back and always speaks the truth to me when I need it the most. It's times like these that I envision movies where the old man trains the hero with random exercises that don't make sense or poses philosophical riddles that you puzzle over for the entire movie, only to have everything fall into place in the last five minutes. But that is not Mr. Simon. He may force me to stay at an easy step for much longer than I think is necessary, but there is nothing cryptic about him. He is straightforward and tries to explain things as simply as possible, qualities that make me appreciate the fact that my life isn't some chosen-one movie. Plus, Coventina is cryptic enough for everyone.

"Did you take a lot of risks in your life?" I ask, wanting to truly know more about the man who never talks about himself.

He huffs out a laugh—a rare display for him. "I didn't take nearly as many risks as I should have. Still don't."

"Why?"

"Being a human lie detector makes it hard to trust people, even people with good intentions," he answers.

"What made you trust Ms. Trisha?"

"I decided that being happy was a big enough prize to risk being hurt."

Chapter 31

TALLIANA

December

Christmas Eve has approached quickly, and I've been running around all day, stacking board games and triple-checking the pizza supplies to ensure we have everything we need.

"Talli, is there any particular reason that you're freaking out about tonight being perfect?" Ash asks as he watches me pull out more games from the closet. He takes them from me and dutifully brings them to the stack already in the living room while I follow him.

"I just want you all to like each other. He's really important to me, and if he can't fit into our group, then I don't know what that could mean for Cas and me." I invited Cas to our annual Christmas Eve game night on a whim last month.

"We've already met him a couple of times and like him."

"Yes, but you two haven't spent time with him. Tonight will be the first time you can really get to know him. What if you both decide you hate him?" I rearrange the boxes from "most likely to play" at the top to "least likely to play" at the bottom.

"I don't think there is a chance of changing Greer's mind about him, and as for me, well, I trust both you and Greer to be good judges of character."

Stopping my frantic rearranging, I look to Ash. We have spent so little time together lately, especially just the two of us. Greer and I talked about what they were going through a few months ago, but I haven't had a chance to talk to Ash about it. We likely only have a few minutes before Greer is home from her shift.

"Ash, are things good between you two?"

His face shifts into a grimace. "We're fine. I think Greer is just really wound up tight over what the future looks like. She's worried about you and about being there when you are ready to end the war. Once everything is over, she'll let herself plan for a future with me. I'm sure of it. I just had to resign myself to waiting in the meantime."

Guilt twists inside of me. I don't control what Greer does, but she is waiting for me. She is putting her relationship and future plans on hold for me. And here I am, worried about selfish things like my sister and best friend liking my boyfriend.

"I'm trying, Ash. It may not appear that way, but I really am trying to solve the puzzle. I thought that Dad's plan to take out Brethren leadership was going to be the best way, but with us staying low and whatever he is planning now, I'm afraid I should go back to the drawing board and figure this out myself."

Ash's face softens, and he says, "We are in this together, remember? Greer and I aren't sitting around waiting for you to solve all our problems. The three of us will figure this out, and then you will be free to ride off into the sunset with Prince Charming."

We are in this together. I know that. Ash is always researching ways to end the war between projects, and Greer is always bouncing different strategies off of me. And I'm working alongside them both during every bit of free time I have. I've never been alone in this, even if the darkness wants to make me feel that way.

Before I can respond, I hear the door open, and Greer calls out, "Don't worry! I'm home!"

Ash and I laugh. She emerges from the corner in her black police uniform. "I need to change, and I'll be ready." She kisses Ash quickly, and he says, "Don't change on my account." Her answering smile is mischievous, and I internally gag as she races up the stairs to change anyway.

A knock at the door sounds, and my head immediately perks up.

"Want me to get it?" Ash teases, a grin lighting up his face.

"I got it, thank you very much."

I hop to my feet and head to the door. When I open it, I am greeted with a large pot full of poinsettias. I look up and Cas smiling at me.

"Before you get the wrong impression, they are for your mom," he says.

I fake a frown and then laugh. "She'll love them. She and my dad will be on their way out soon. They have their own plans tonight."

He lets out a visible breath.

"What? Are you afraid of my parents?"

"Not at all. It just relieves some pressure a bit to want to impress them."

"The only one you need to impress is me." I grin at him.

He leans down and kisses me gently, then says, "Good thing I brought you this." With his other hand, he produces a large cake box.

"You didn't," I respond as I take the box from him. I open it up and see Gus's Cinnamon Roll Cheesecake. "You did! You are such a beautiful, perfect man!" I let Cas actually in the door now as he laughs at my response.

Mom comes breezing into the entryway, looking spectacular in her red Christmas dress.

"Oh, Cas! Nice to see you again! By the look on my daughter's face, you brought her something sweet, didn't you?" Mom asks.

Cas smiles and answers, "I also brought you these as a small Christmas present." He hands her the flowers, and her eyes light up.

"How very thoughtful! Thank you!" Mom exclaims. Then she adds, "I'm sorry we won't be around tonight to get to know you better, Cas. Talli needs to bring you by again soon so that we can."

"I'd love that," Cas replies, and I have to restrain myself from laughing at the lie.

Dad makes his appearance, coming around the corner from his office. "Ah, Caspian. Talli told me you were joining the traditional game night tonight."

"Yes, sir. I am honored to have been asked."

I smile up at Cas and lean into him slightly, holding the cheesecake to my chest. Dad tracks my movement, but then he looks back to Cas and says, "Word of advice: watch out for Greer. She's a sore loser."

Cas flashes him a grin. "Noted. Thank you for the heads-up."

Dad claps a hand on Cas's shoulder as he and Mom walk out the door, shutting it behind them. I watch Cas visibly relax, and I go up on my tippy-toes to plant a quick kiss on his lips.

"Thank you for the cheesecake."

He gently grabs my chin and brings my lips back to his, taking his time to taste me completely, then pulls away again and replies, "Anything for you."

I feel my cheeks heat, and I open my mouth to respond, but Greer's snort from behind me stops me. I turn, finding her leaning against the wall across from the front door, arms crossed, with a smug expression on her face.

"Yes, Greer?" I ask.

"Oh, nothing." She pushes off the wall and strides into the living room.

"Sorry about Greer. She umm...can be weird," I explain to Cas.

"I heard that!" Greer calls out from the other side of the wall.

"Let's get dessert into the fridge, and then I'll give you the tour before we start the pizza." I grab his hand and pull him into the kitchen where I deposit the cheesecake. Then, I proceed to show him around the house.

When we reach Greer's and my room, I awkwardly stand in the doorway and watch him look around the space. His face warms when he sees my tiny stuffed animal army at the end of my bed, then he moves to my desk and analyzes my photo collection on the wall above it. My breath catches when I see his face tense and his eyes close for a minute. They open and find mine.

"This is him?" He nods his head toward the center of the collage. I don't have to check to know he is looking at the right photo—the one I took of Trey and me a week before the March on Massachusetts.

"Yeah." I bite my lip, unsure of what to do.

He takes a few steps toward me and pulls me to his chest, cradling my head to him as he kisses the top of it. It feels so crazy, but the urge to cry overwhelms me. His gentleness, his sensitivity, his hug that tells me he wants to take all the pain away even though he hasn't said a thing. After I moment, he releases me and I pull away enough to look up at him. Clearing my throat, I say, "As silly as this may sound, I would really like it if we could take some pictures of us for me to add to the wall."

He smiles. "Not silly. I would love that, as long as you promise that you never feel the need to take down or move his pictures. Those should stay right where they are."

I reflect his smile back at him. "Promise."

He runs his hand down my back. "Let's go make some pizza. I'm starving."

The night passes in laughter. Laughter and, between Cas and I, looks of desperate desire.

God, I need him.

I keep finding my thoughts wandering to mental images of him dragging me up the stairs, throwing me onto my bed, and having his way with me. To put it as eloquently as possible. I am not a Thought-reader, but I don't think his thoughts are much different from my own.

He wants me as much as I want him. It's obvious in how his gaze is always skating over my body, how he intertwines his fingers with mine every time he has the chance, and how his lips always linger a moment longer than necessary before moving away.

But the rule we made for ourselves and each other still stands, as much as I hate it. I feel myself wanting to voice those words, but I'm not positive yet. I'm afraid of being positive that that is how I feel, because love...it changes everything. Not just what's between thw two of us, but it changes *me*. It has already been chipping away at the darkness, which is a good thing, but what if love chips away too much and I lose my strength—the ruthlessness that I need to end this war?

Maybe I jumped into this relationship too fast, not realizing what the consequences really could be. Like what Ash said earlier about his relationship with Greer being practically on hold until I finish this. The longer I take, the more my people will suffer because of it, killed because of it.

I need my inner ice bitch back. Cas has warmed her up so much that she has turned into a silly little girl. Dad needs to let us back into the field. I need to go on another mission. I need the monstrous act of eliminating more Brethren to freeze me over again. I need—

"Talli?"

Cas's voice forces life back into me, and all my thoughts scatter. My attention turns to him standing in front of me. My chair is pulled out from the table. That's strange. I was just pushed into the table a minute ago. Was I that far into my mind that I didn't notice Cas pulling my chair out?

I look across the table and see Greer and Ash watching me with questioning eyes. I nod slightly, giving them the indication that I am okay, and turn back to Cas.

"I'm sorry. I'm a bit tired, and I guess I zoned out for a moment."

His expression changes from concerned to soft as he studies my face. "It's late, and I should get going so you can get some rest."

"I'd rest better if I were in your arms." The words tumble out of my mouth without a thought. In the corner of my eye, I see Greer and Ash quietly get up from their seats and leave the room, clearly not wanting to intrude on our goodbye for the night.

"My bed and my arms are available anytime you want to make use of them. I think tonight you should be with your family, though," he reassures me.

A sigh escapes me, and I realize I really am tired. "Yes, you're right. Are you sure you're going to be okay tomorrow? No one should be alone on Christmas."

"Yeah. My father is going to call me, and I think I will just sleep in and watch movies all day. I don't mind a quiet holiday. It's what I have been used to since my mother died. I guess it's like my tradition."

I nod, though my heart aches with sorrow for him. "If you change your mind, call me."

"I will." He bends down on his knees in front of me and pulls my face toward his, giving me a kiss that is full of so many promises—promises that I want more than anything for him to say aloud so I can promise them back.

Too quickly, he's standing up and moving toward the door. I get up and follow him out. Watching him descend the front steps toward his Jeep, I feel like there is something I should say or do, but I don't move. He turns toward me again after opening up his driver's side door and calls out, "Merry Christmas, Talli."

"Merry Christmas, Cas." I give him a half-hearted smile and watch him drive away.

What the hell is wrong with me? Why can't I just be happy without feeling guilty every time? Why can't I just let myself admit...

"You really love him, don't you?"

Ash's question makes me jump, and I turn around to see both him and Greer standing inside the door. I move past them and up the stairs without answering the question.

CHAPTER 30

CASPIAN

CHRISTMAS IS MY LEAST favorite day of the year.

It's a holiday people usually spend with their families, but I have never had one. Not really. Not after my mother was killed.

I had her for four years, and then the Hawks took her from me. They came like death in the night and killed her just for being married to a captain in the Brethren—a captain who was rising quickly for his cleverness. They couldn't get to him, so they took out an innocent instead. But that's what they do. They wreak havoc on the innocent.

The founding father of the Brethren was deceived by his own wife. He was an innocent man until he discovered her using magic to hurt people in their village. He saw her for what she was: an evil witch. So he started an organization to eradicate them all so they could no longer hurt the innocent.

But...are they truly still evil? I have only seen kindness from Talli and her family. They are so normal, as if they are human. I can't imagine a single one running out in the middle of the night to kill innocent people.

I shake my head violently. I know better. *I do know better.* It's all an act. These witches— *her*—they have slaughtered many of the Brethren. They slaughtered my mother. They are the reason why I prefer to spend Christmas alone every year.

I should have taken Talli up on her offer to spend Christmas with them. It would have only benefited my mission, getting closer to everyone. But I needed a day, one day to get my head back on straight. Because fuck, has it been messed with.

She has been messing with it.

It has to be some kind of magic, because the idea of not constantly being around her, touching her...I feel like I'm going out of my mind. I have never felt so connected to someone in my life, and if something happened to her, if *I* had to do something to her...

I need to refocus on my mission. Make her fall in love with me. Make her tell me everything. Make her fall to her knees before me and remove her as a threat. The assassin of the Order. A woman who has dealt out so much death. The woman I...

Jumping to my feet, I start to pace around the couch, running my hands through my hair repeatedly in the nervous habit I have had since I was a boy. Anxiety is what the doctor called it. They tried to give my father pills to help manage it, but my father had another way of managing it. No son of his, of the mighty General Campbell, would be weak or flawed in any way.

What am I going to do? Maybe I should tell her. Let her kill me now before this goes too far, and continue to be the disappointment I have always been for my father. Maybe I should see this through, then tell her to run and hide, leave it all behind so he can't hurt her. Maybe I should go with her.

A knock on my door lights up my nervous system, and I jolt mid-step, nearly tripping and falling on my face. I quietly walk to the door, so as not to be heard, and peer out the peephole.

Talli.

She has a wrapped box in her hands, and is biting her lip in her own nervous habit, one I have come to adore. I take a deep breath to soothe the inner debate raging inside of me, making me feel like a caged animal. Opening the door, I don't have to force the smile that fills my face. I truly am happy to see her if the way my heart leaps in my chest is any indication.

"Why, Mrs. Claus, does your husband know you're here?"

Her face brightens, and a fiendish grin spreads across it. "Oh yes, your present requires personal delivery."

"Hmm...is that so?" I pull her through the door, shut it, and put her back against it. Lowering my voice an octave, I ask her, "So, I've been good?" I lean into her space and press my lips to her neck.

She squirms underneath me in such a delicious way, but I hear her gasp out, "If you keep this up, our rule will be broken."

My cock hardens. "Who says it would be broken?" Not the words I meant to say, but I am rewarded when I see her neck flush under my kisses. I pull back, giving her space. When she doesn't answer, I ask the obvious, "Shouldn't you be with your family?"

Her throat clears. "I was, but we were pretty much done with Christmas, and no one objected when I decided to leave. I really didn't like the idea of you sitting here alone, despite your reassurance that you were okay."

I shift slightly, uncomfortable. I don't know what to say, and I *always* know what to say, but this woman has left me speechless with her thoughtfulness.

She notices and adds, "I'm not entirely selfless, though. I was hoping to take you up on your offer yesterday for warm arms and a bed. But now that I am thinking about it, I'm not entirely sure that is the best idea."

"Why?"

"Your welcome has made me feel a bit…"

"Yes?" I egg her on, getting closer to her again.

She hesitates, then settles on, "Needy."

"I'm not sure that's the word you were going to say."

"Maybe not, but I think it works well enough."

"I disagree."

I find myself getting lost in her eyes as she stares back at me. Two dark-blue orbs, as endless as the ocean, and I'm a fisherman lost at sea. I thought I had a map, navigation, and I knew where I was going, but all that got thrown out the moment she locked eyes with me, which feels like so long ago now.

Pushing everything away, my conflicting thoughts, my worry, my desire to bring this war to an end, I open my mouth to voice exactly what I really want to say to her in this moment, but she stops me by extending the wrapped box toward me.

"I got you something," she says quickly.

I take the offered present and am surprised at how heavy it is. I give her a curious look, but she doesn't say anything, just presses her lips together, trying to hide a smile.

I carefully open it and find a rock about the size of my hand inside. I laugh and admit, "I'm afraid I don't understand."

"Someone once gave me a moonstone when I was fighting a bad dream." She absently grabs the necklace around her neck, something I've watched her do a hundred times. She continues, "It helped a lot. I thought maybe a moonstone could help you, too."

My jaw drops, and I look between the small white stone resting against her chest and the much larger one in my hand.

"Talli, I..." I start, but stop myself.

It's time to make a decision. Everything has led to this moment, this decision I was always meant to make. It's time to stop pretending that I'll end up making the smart choice, the choice that is demanded of me. No, it's finally time to choose what I want, what I need. If it gets me killed, so be it. I choose...

I choose her.

I put the stone down on the counter to the left of me and reach for her all in a span of a second. My mouth is on hers, and my hands are tangled in her hair. I feel the chill of her hands resting on the back of my neck, pulling our bodies closer together. Shifting my hands to her ass, I lift her into my arms and carry her to my bed. I set her down on it like she is as fragile as the stone she gifted me tonight, then I pull away from her lips so that I can kneel on the floor in front of her.

"I love you, Talliana." Her eyes widen, and I decide to push through it—the baring of my heart and soul to her—before I lose my nerve. "The first day I met you, I knew then that falling in love with you would be easy. But shit..." I run my fingers through my hair and, finding her eyes again, I continue, "I fell right off a cliff, head first into a raging river. Even if I could get my head above water, I don't want to. I never want to. I have never been happier in my life, riding every current and drowning in how I feel for you."

With that full admission to both her and myself, the urge to tell her everything, the entire truth rises hard and fast. She has to know. I have to tell her, whether she kills me right here or hates me for the rest of our lives, at least I will have died an honest man.

"Talli, I need to—oh no, please don't cry." It is right at the tip of my tongue when she starts crying, sobbing really, into her hands. I move to her side, sitting on the edge of the bed, and lift her onto my lap, holding her as close as I can. I rub circles on her back, trying to comfort her. She lets me for a few moments before standing up and choking out, "I have to go," and then she runs for the door.

I stare after her, shocked and confused. But I don't move. I can't move.

What just happened?

Love is something i have never known until now. My child, who came from within me, who is a part of me in ways no other could be, is finally here. My son. My perfect baby boy. When i held him in my arms for the first time and heard the joyous sound of his cries, i knew i couldn't let anyone harm him. Not the hypocritical elders who have sworn to protect us, unless they want to use us. Not the man who sired him, right after forcing me to heal the bruises he left behind on my flesh. Not my mother, who has done nothing but deliver me to any man who wishes to harm me. No, my son, i will be better than all of them, and i will keep you safe. This i swear to you.

- Journal of Katarina Lehmann

CHAPTER 31

TALLIANA

I CAN'T EAT. I can't sleep. I can't do anything past seeing Cas on his knees in front of me, saying words I didn't realize would equally destroy and rebuild me.

School is on holiday break, so I haven't seen him at all. He texted me once asking if I was okay, and I told him I needed some time to think. The truth is, I'm terrified. I started this relationship only wanting it to be a fling, something that didn't go this far...but what he had told me last month about wanting to be in love with me...all I've done is think about it. I thought maybe I would be ready for it when it came, and that maybe Greer was right about him being something special. But the war and my role in ending it aside, thinking about all the real implications of love and what it could mean if I lost Cas, like how I lost Trey...could I survive it?

No, I really don't think I could. I have been fighting week after week to get control of the darkness, but if I lost Cas, I wouldn't just be controlled by the darkness. Darkness would be all that was left of me.

A few tears fall, but they are quickly whisked away by the wind blowing in my face. Coventina and I are out flying. Aside from the water, the open sky is my favorite place to be, because there are no expectant stares turned my way up here.

"*He's not Treyton,*" Coventina reminds me.

I know he isn't. He isn't in this fight like Trey was. But who's to say he won't be a target because of me, or won't try to save me when I'm in danger? Even if I told him everything and he accepted me, he might still not understand how much danger he or I could be in because of who I am.

"*I can't lose him, too, Covey. I...I love him too much.*"

"*I know. You don't understand this now, but falling in love with him is the first step of many that will change your life and his.*"

Great. More cryptic dragon nonsense. "*Care to elaborate? Like, change my life for the better or worse?*"

"*You have to allow yourself to live it to find out.*"

"*You're so unhelpful,*" I mutter into my mind.

"*Talliana, trust your intuition. It will never lead you astray.*"

The feeling of déjà vu hits me, and I feel unsettled, like there is a piece to the puzzle here that I am missing.

"*My intuition or the darkness?*"

"*They aren't the same,*" she retorts. It wasn't long ago that I thought they were. But they are different. My intuition is my gut feeling, but the darkness is like a little voice.

"*I'm pretty sure my intuition is linked to yours.*"

"*Exactly, and I'm never wrong.*"

We both laugh, then Coventina clarifies more seriously, *"Your intuition is not linked to mine, not really. Yours has always been yours. I am more like a guide who helps you follow it."*

"And you, as my guide, are telling me that I should let myself fall in love with him?"

"We both know you are far past that point."

Sighing, I know she's right, and like it or not, I am in love with him. I can try to fight it all I want, but it will get me nowhere. He consumes my every thought, and he's the only thing my body craves. He is everything I have ever needed and more. He is my hope and my *light*. And now that I have him, I'd give anything to keep him.

"Alright, take us down. I have someone to go see."

Coventina obliges me and flies back home. When she lands, I take care of her saddle and watch her head to the lake, tail swishing. I pull out my phone and am about to text Cas when I realize what day it is. It is New Year's Eve. He told me he would be working all day at the club, preparing for the party tonight. I slide my phone back into my pocket, then turn and almost run into Greer.

"Damn it, Greer! I almost peed myself!" I scream.

Her face remains straight as she asks, "What just stopped you from texting him?"

For fuck's sake.

"It's New Year's Eve. He is working all day. I'll text him tomorrow."

"Nope. You are going to put on a dress and..." A wicked grin spreads wide on her face. "Cause a scene."

"Now is not the time for payback, Greer," I scold, referring to two years ago, when I made her put on a dress and *cause a scene* at prom to finally admit her feelings for Ash. But then *I* ended up causing a bigger scene than she did when I had a stare-down with Mei-Lien.

She only grins wider in response.

"I know exactly what you are thinking, and this is already hard enough for me. I don't need to do it in front of a hundred strangers," I argue further.

"That's exactly what you need to do. Now come on, let's find a dress and get you to the ball before midnight."

Pushing my way through the crowded space, there are only a few minutes to spare until midnight. How am I going to find him in this mess?

I hear Ash offering apologies as Greer shoves her way through people to stand beside me. "Divide and conquer," she says as she heads to the left. Ash goes right, so that leaves me to go straight in the direction of the bar.

I duck, swerve, gently push, politely yell for someone to move, and finally, the bar is in sight. Going onto my tippy-toes, I see golden waves between the people crowding it.

A giddy lightness fills my chest. I love him. I love Caspian. I have no doubt in my mind or heart now that I have pushed out all the worry, thanks to Coventina's pep talk. Who knew a dragon would be a great source of girl talk?

"*I knew,*" she chimes in.

"*Yeah, yeah. Go back to eating your fish.*"

"*Gladly.*"

"Cas!" I call out over the noise.

"Talli?" I hear, and then his head lifts above the people blocking my view of him.

I work my way closer to him and see him trying to do the same. Once he reaches me, I quickly say, "I need to talk to you."

"Does this mean you're not avoiding me anymore?" he asks, looking anything but pleased. I hurt him. I *really* hurt him. I open my mouth to refute, but he cuts me off, "Don't act dumb. It doesn't suit you."

I close it, then try again. "I'm sorry I haven't reached out sooner. I needed some space to think this week."

"This week has been absolute shit for me. I thought you were running away from me right after I laid myself bare before you."

"No!" I practically yell and wince at how desperate it sounds. I take a deep breath, trying to regain my composure. "No, that's not it."

He nods and lets out a deep breath. "Good. Let's talk in the morning. I'm really busy right now."

"Ten...Nine..." The crowd starts to count, and Cas turns away to go back to work.

Panicking, I yell, "Wait!"

"Eight...Seven..."

"We'll talk tomorrow, promise." Cas moves even farther away from me, and I scramble toward him, grabbing his hand.

"Six...Five..."

He turns, and I pull him toward me. Like gravity, his body collides with mine, nearly toppling me, but his arm wraps around my waist and holds me steady.

"Four..."

"Not tomorrow. Now."

"Three...Two..."

"Cas...I..."

"One..."

"I love you!"

The crowd erupts, and everyone grabs a partner, kissing and cheering the start of the new year. But Cas and I just stare at each other. Nothing else happening around us matters, the bodies near us turning into a blur of colors.

"I have for a long time, I think. God, it feels like I have loved you my entire life, like there was never a moment that I didn't love you. But I'm terrified! If something happens, losing you will have consequences that will impact more people than just us. I am not who you think—"

The force of his kiss knocks the breath out of me, and I love every second of being breathless for him. He places a hand on my neck, his thumb stroking my cheek as our lips collide and our tongues tangle.

Pulling away panting, he rests his forehead against mine and says, "If our love will shatter the world, then let it shatter."

My heart starts to race as I look into his eyes, and without an ounce of hesitation, I nod. Cas's lips find mine again, and he kisses me so deeply, so thoroughly, that I feel as though he is physically touching every part of my heart and soul.

He slowly pulls away, this time like he has to fight every ounce of himself to do it, and then he rests his head against mine again. "I have to get back to work. But we should continue this conversation the moment my shift ends. Will you wait for me? You don't have to do it here. You can go to my apartment if you'd like. It'll be a couple of hours before I'm done."

"I'd like to wait for you here. Watch you work, flash you some suggestive looks, distract you thoroughly," I respond.

He steps back and looks down my body, as if he is just now noticing the little black dress I am wearing. His eyes darken, and the muscle in his jaw flexes, but his words are smooth as he says, "All you're going to do is convince me to quit on the spot so I can have you all to myself sooner."

"Caspian?" A male voice calls out.

Cas groans. "That's my boss." He kisses me quickly and continues, "Find a seat, and I'll send you over something to drink and snack on."

Nodding, I watch as he turns and leaves. As soon as he is out of sight again, Ash and Greer appear beside me.

"A perfect romance movie moment." Ash grins at me. That is something I would have said if I had witnessed the same thing.

"I think I can count on both hands how many times I have watched the scene in a movie where one person interrupts the other with a kiss during a speech about how being in love is a bad idea," Greer comments.

"What I think is that we have watched way too many movies in our lives, and we should consider finding something else to do in our free time," I say to them both.

But I know they're just teasing me because I'm actually the one who has always been enthralled by movies and fiction books, not them. They just joined in to make me happy. These two really are amazing, and I'm so grateful to have them in my life.

"I love you both so much," I tell them, throwing my arms around their necks.

Greer wipes at her eyes, and I laugh at how perfect this moment is—perfect enough to bring her to tears. She sniffs slightly and suggests, "Let's find a table. We'll wait with you."

Cas opens the door to his apartment and holds out a hand, allowing me to walk in first. I do, and he follows me in, shutting his front door and throwing his keys onto the kitchen counter where he always keeps them.

"I smell like sweat and alcohol. Do you mind giving me five minutes to shower?" Cas asks.

"I could join you if you'd like," I offer.

He groans like he is in pain. "Next time. This time, I want you in my bed. Three minutes, promise!"

I laugh and wave him off, taking a seat on the couch in the small living room. I nervously adjust the lacy things under my dress. Yes, I had hoped that once I told him I loved him too, this night would end on a very good note. Despite it being past two in the morning, I am wide awake.

The butterflies in my stomach are making a mess of me, causing my hands to fidget and my legs to bounce. I don't think I've had butterflies since the first time, which was close to three years ago. This is what this man does to me. He has awakened all the feelings I didn't know I could feel again.

Three minutes later exactly, just like he promised, Cas walks into the bedroom and places his hands on the top of the inside of the doorframe across from the couch. He leans forward onto his toes, his shirt lifting enough to give me a show of his lower abs, and then he caresses me with his eyes. I flush with heat, my core throbbing in anticipation between my legs.

"I did want to talk for a couple of minutes first, if that's okay," I force out. I am physically restraining myself to the couch, when all I want to do is launch myself at him.

"Of course. We can talk for as long as you want. I really do mean that, too. I will never pressure you," he replies with a smile. He straightens and comes to sit next to me on the couch.

I take a deep breath and say what needs to be said.

CHAPTER 32

CASPIAN

"I need you to promise me something."

I take her hand in mine, brush a gentle kiss to the top of her knuckles, and I am rewarded with her squeezing her thighs closer together. "What is it?"

She hesitates for a minute, looking as though she is trying to build courage, "Promise me that you won't ever try to be my hero. Don't ever try to save me or sacrifice yourself if I am in danger."

I frown. "I won't promise you that." Why would she even ask this of me? I would never stand by and watch her be hurt. Not now, not ever. The idea of it makes my stomach knot up.

"I mean it, Caspian. Even if it seems like I need saving, I won't. You have to trust me to handle what is happening. I cannot watch you get hurt in an attempt to save me. Death follows me and...I can't go through that. Not again." There is pleading in her voice that makes my heart ache for her. Her last words, "not again," ring through my head like bells in a tower. This is about him again. Treyton. So, I was right. He must have died during the Cleansing of Massachusetts, and while saving her, no less.

I squeeze her hand while lifting her chin so we can look at one another straight in the eyes. "I do trust you. I trust that you know what you're doing and can handle yourself. The thing is, though, to me, loving someone means fighting every battle together. So I will never step back or walk away while you fight. Instead, I promise to always stand by your side, whether you need me there or not."

God, I wish more than anything that we were talking about normal people stuff. Everyday battles like trouble at work, arguments with family, or finding the perfect place to vacation. She probably believes that's what I'm thinking, but I know exactly what she's talking about. She's asking me not to take a bullet, a sword, or an arrow for her. But I would. I would take a death blow in her stead. I would lay down my life for her without a moment's hesitation.

I want to scream at myself for letting this happen. I have been doing just that this week while she went quiet on me. I should be thinking about how to deal a deadly blow to her, not about how to save her from one.

I almost don't hear her when she quietly replies, "Cas, I don't know how, but you have managed to glue my broken heart back together. If something happens to you..."

"I can't promise you nothing will happen to me, like you can't promise me that nothing will happen to you. That's just the risk we have to take."

Her face falls slightly, and I can see the stress plaguing her body. I want to take it all away. I want to make her happy more than anything in this world, so I let my heart dictate my next words. "I've never had the privilege of truly loving someone before you, so I can't imagine how it would feel to lose them. I can't imagine what you've been through, but I promise to do everything I can to be worth the risk. Because you definitely are."

Guilt racks through me, and I want to break from the way everything inside of me is divided. I can't do this to her. I can't break her heart, not when she is so freely giving it to me.

Before I can give in to my conscience and tell her everything, the breath is stolen away from me as she presses her lips to mine. Her arms wrap around my neck as I deepen the kiss, and she climbs into my lap, straddling me. My arms snake around her lower back, pulling her in closer until there is no space between our chests. I feel her hands reach down and tug at the bottom of my shirt. I let her pull it over my head, only breaking our kiss for a second. Her fingers start to explore every ridge and line of my torso, and I shiver from the electricity of her touch. My hands work their way down the curve of her hip and thighs, then back up to where her dress is hiked up almost to her waist. I don't feel a zipper on it, so I slide it up and off of her, tossing it to the floor. Then I lunge back for her mouth, desperate to feel her skin pressed up against mine again.

I should stop this. Make sure she knows the truth before we cross this line. She'll hate me once she finds out, but she needs to know who she is getting into bed with. I'm not the nice, studying-to-be-a-doctor guy, with simple hopes and dreams from a relationship that I've pretended to be. I wish nothing more right now than to be that guy for her, the guy she truly desires.

Talli starts grinding into me, and I can feel how wet she is through my pants. Oh God...damn the right thing.

I want this. I need this.

I need *her*.

CHAPTER 33

TALLIANA

I NEED HIM.

I need him more than air at this moment, which really I am not getting much of during our mouths' embrace that seems never to end. I am grinding myself against him, desperate to feel him against my sensitive flesh. The deep noises from him only encourage me to move faster and harder.

His hands move to my back, and with a flick of the wrist, I feel my bra loosen and fall between us. I move my arms to pull them out of the straps and discard my bra somewhere on the floor with my dress.

Before I know it, my breasts press up against his warm chest, and I about split in two from the brush of his skin against my hard nipples. Cas's right hand slides in between us, and I feel him cup my breast, giving it a gentle squeeze. His fingers splay, catching my nipple with two fingers, rolling it around between them.

My breathing hitches, and suddenly his left hand starts doing the same thing to my other breast. He is working both so deliciously that I can't help but let my lips leave his as my head falls back, pushing myself further into his touch.

His lips graze my neck, soft at first, then sucking. He leaves a trail of pulsing kisses until I feel his tongue flick one very sensitive nipple. I groan loudly, giving him clear permission to do it again. He does it a few more times until he clamps down and starts to suck.

"Oh God...Cas..."

He drags his teeth against it, causing me to lose my balance on his lap, but one of his hands grabs my lower back, catching me from falling. I allow myself to rest against his steady hold while he takes his sweet time exploring every dip and curve of my chest.

Once I am completely sure every bit of fabric still between us is soaked from my arousal, he stands, taking me with him as he walks into his bedroom and lays me gently on the bed. He takes his time looking down at me, eyes full of so much hunger that I start to squirm in an attempt to feel something move against my skin. He smirks, knowing what he's doing to me, then he removes his pants.

Fuck...he is so beautiful. Someone should sculpt him and put the statue in a museum. I would gladly go sit in front of it and admire it all day.

He lets me have my look, the smirk playing on his lips just moments ago growing into that cocky smile he wears so well. Finally, he gets on the bed and crawls up the length of me. He reaches toward my hips and gently shimmies my underwear off. Hovering over me, eyes roaming over my body, he says, "I have never seen a more beautiful woman. I want to worship every inch of your body and claim it as mine."

Goosebumps rush over my skin. If he had said that to me when we first met, I would have run for the hills. I have never wanted someone to claim me. It's the exact thing I have been avoiding, but coming from Cas's lips now with the beat of his heart echoing inside of my own, there is not a single thing I want more.

He doesn't give me time to respond. His lips are on mine while his fingers run the length of my body, leaving a trail of fire along my skin until he reaches the one place I have wanted him since this started. His finger presses into the sensitive bundle of nerves, and my hips buck, lifting off the bed in a severe arch. He strokes me in long, slow movements as I squirm underneath him. He stops kissing me and watches my body react to everything he does.

Once I am at the point of nearly coming from his stroking alone, he teases my entrance for only a second before sliding a finger in, working me and stretching me, then he slips in a second finger. My hips move in beat with his fingers until I am breathing hard, moaning at every thrust.

"Cas..." I plead.

"No. I am going to make this last as long as possible." He flashes me that cocky grin again, then adds, "And I have been dying to know what you taste like."

My cheeks heat, and he slides down my body until his face is between my thighs. He pushes my legs into a bent position and opens them up completely, baring me to him.

"I have been dreaming about doing this since the first time I was between your legs at the gym," he admits.

I want so badly to reply, to say something snarky or teasing, but I feel the press of his tongue against my clit, and I completely lose all thoughts.

Oh, he tastes me, alright.

Cas licks me from my entrance to my clit, taking in every bit of me that he can. He dips his tongue inside of me, causing my body to shake and my lips to part in a loud moan, one I have no doubt his neighbors can hear. He sucks my clit hard between his teeth, then plunges a finger into me, curling at just the right spot.

My body breaks apart, and his finger and tongue work together to ride me through the orgasm. Once my limbs are limp with pleasure, he moves back up my body until his face is level with mine once more.

"You taste perfect. You are perfect."

His words cause a surge of arousal to rush through me once more, my body still throbbing with the need to be filled.

"Cas?" I ask sweetly.

"Yes, my heart?"

My heart. The name makes me feel dizzy with love.

"Fuck me. Now."

I feel his chuckle everywhere our bodies meet, only making me more sensitive. His lips briefly brush mine, and then, without warning, he slowly pushes his cock into me until he presses up against my inner wall. I gasp at the unexpected stretching and then release a contented sigh when I feel myself relax around him. His fingers brush the hair away from my face, and I open my eyes to find him looking down at me. His face is completely at ease, telling me that he is as content as I am in this position.

We are connected as one. He is mine, and I am his. And God, does this feel right. Like I have finally been deemed worthy enough by the Great Hawk to have the exact thing I could ever need in my life. *Him.* If I have to sacrifice everything else for my people, including my life, that's fine. As long as I get this bit of time with him, I'll die knowing I truly lived.

Cas's eyes dart around my face, as if he, too, knows our time is limited and he wants to ensure he remembers every second of this moment. Then he reaches down, kissing me again, and I feel him shift his body weight so that his arms, on either side of my head, are holding him up. He releases my lips and, never moving his eyes away from mine, he pulls out right to the tip of his cock and then thrusts himself right back in.

"Oh..." I moan. My hands grab onto his biceps so that I have something to hold onto while he pulls out and thrusts again, faster and harder this time. I don't just feel his cock inside of me, I feel *him* inside of me. His mind, his heart, his soul. I have never felt closer to any person in my life. He is *everything*.

My pleasure coils up tight inside of me as he works out every sound possible from my lips. When I get close to climaxing, my moan reaches a high pitch, and I feel his body tremble and his thrusts become frantic in response to it. I scream his name as I orgasm again, my body shattering into a million pieces underneath him. He thrusts one last time, and with a loud "Fuck!" he comes inside of me.

We hold onto each other, him still buried deep, as we come down together from the intense moment. He slowly pulls out of me and moves to rest on his side next to me. His hand reaches over and he cups my face, turning it toward him. I notice his eyes are glazed, and there is a little bit of sweat on his forehead.

I try to clear my parched throat, then say to him, "I have had sex before, but that..."

"That was different," he agrees.

"I don't understand why," I admit.

"Because our love is meant to shatter the world."

Chapter 34

CASPIAN

IF WATCHING HER WHILE she sleeps is considered creepy, then that's fine. I'm a creep.

This woman. So beautiful, so caring, so wild, so vulnerable. She's going to be the death of me. I've been going out of my mind this week, thinking I had scared her away, and I would never get to hold her again. Then seeing her tonight at the club, looking for me, I felt like I could breathe again for the first time.

I. Am. Fucked.

Forcing myself out of bed, if only to gain some space to think for a moment, I get to my feet, careful not to wake her up. But before I can move to the bathroom, I hear a dripping noise. I instinctively look up, but I don't find a leak in my ceiling. At least not a normal leak. I stare in confusion at the icicles in two clusters on either side of the bed until I realize...

Talli.

Looking back at her, peacefully sleeping, I realize that had to have been her. Her magic. I refocus on my target of the bathroom and shut the door behind me. Pressing my back against the door, I try to wrap my mind around everything.

Her. Us. The ice on my ceiling. I have no idea what I am going to do. But after what happened between us only a few hours ago? I meant what I had said to her. That was different. There is something between us that goes beyond any normal human connection. Even though I was the one physically inside of her, I felt *her* inside of me, like her magic was attaching itself to me. Claiming me. Just as I was claiming her.

I have to keep her at all costs.

I want to tell her the truth. I want to prove to her that I chose her over my father and all of my loyalty to the Brethren. But I will lose her if I do. So, no, I can't tell her the truth. I need to find a way to leave everything behind and take her with me. This is our fathers' war, but it no longer has to be ours. Let them kill each other for all that I care. It doesn't matter to me, even if we have to live the rest of our lives looking over our shoulders.

As long as I can keep her.

Because there is no doubt in my mind that she is more precious than anything or anyone else in existence. It's truly as if I have been living my life without a heart all along, but now I have found it.

She is my heart.

And I'll be damned if I let anyone take her away from me.

A new sense of resolve replaces my worry, and I leave the bathroom. But when I look up at the ceiling again to figure out what to do about the ice, it's gone.

Maybe my mind is playing tricks on me.

When I am caring for my son and Klaus is not around, I read. I read everything I can get my hands on. When my son is in bed asleep and Klaus is warming another woman's bed, I practice fighting with my water. I need to be as strong as I can be for my son, so I can take him away from the monsters here.

In my reading today, I learned a term I realized I already knew. Darkness. That is what is inside of me and what controlled the water that day. That is what makes my magic strong when I am angry. That is what will help me escape with my son. I just have to learn how to use it.

- Journal of Katarina Lehmann

Chapter 35

TALLIANA

February

Ah, Friday. Finally.

I have plans to spend the weekend with Cas, and then we will both spend Sunday with everyone for my birthday. This is the first time I have actually been excited about my birthday in a few years. I'll be surrounded by the ones I love, and there will be cake. I love cake.

Cas brushes his hand along the inside of my leg, sending a shiver rolling over my skin. He does that every time I seem to lose focus in class. This particular class is held in a large auditorium with long benches and desks, meaning Cas can press his side right up next to mine. I love this class for the simple fact that he can keep me warm in the normally chilly space.

These last couple of months have felt like floating. Is this how normal college students live? Just go to classes, occasionally work a job after, study, have life-changing sex with your boyfriend, and then do it all over again the next day? If so, I want nothing more than to be normal.

As if the universe were determined to remind me that I am not normal, my phone buzzes next to me. I discreetly grab it and look at the text under the desk.

Dad: *You got your wish. As soon as class ends, I need you in my office.*

I spoke too soon. This kind of text only means one thing: Dad has a mission for us. Part of me feels disappointed because my plans with Cas will change, but I'm ready to get back in the field. I've been bugging him since Christmas to let us back out. We have been benched for too long due to our identities being compromised. I need this to be over already.

I made myself a promise after New Year's that I will end this war, and once I do, I will walk away from everything to be with Caspian. I want a normal life with him more than anything else. I want to live past the end of this war for the first time since I found out my true role in it.

I know I should tell him the truth. He has a right to know who I am and what I've done. But he could turn his back on me and run for the hills. I wouldn't blame him for it at all, but I can't risk it. I will end this war, leave the Order, and become a normal human woman.

"A normal human woman with a dragon in the backyard," Coventina points out.

"Lizards are very normal pets to have," I reply.

"If you think you can put me in a glass box, I—"

"Relax. I'm kidding."

She grumbles in my mind, but I pay her no heed. We'll figure that all out when the time comes.

Class ends fifteen minutes later, and Cas turns to me. "Ready to start the birthday celebrations?" His grin is devilish, and I groan. Why this weekend? Why couldn't the mission be next weekend?

He must read my expression because he asks, "What's wrong?"

"Dad texted me. Family emergency. I have to run home and see what's wrong. Maybe it'll be something quick, and you'll see me tonight." I highly doubt it, but this is a sacrifice I have to make if I want forever with him.

I give him a quick kiss and collect my book and notebook. His face turns into a frown. "I hope everything is okay with your family."

"I'll let you know as soon as I find out, promise," I reply.

I let him walk me out to my car, and before I can get into the driver's seat, he pulls me to him. He gives me a long, sweet hug, and follows it up with a feverish kiss.

"Be safe, please," he whispers against my lips before stepping back.

I laugh, though his sentiment is sweet. "Well, it wasn't on my agenda to get in a fight with a bear today, so I think I'll be alright."

The corner of his lip tugs up, but his eyes still look worried. I place a hand on his chest. "Cas, I really have to go, but are *you* okay?" The urge to tune into him is there, but I squash it. I swore to myself that I would never try to read his emotions, not once, not ever. I will not break that promise now over something that's probably nothing.

His features smooth out, and he answers, "Of course. Sorry. I just worry sometimes. It's not a big deal."

"Everything you feel is a big deal to me." I lean in, going on my tippy toes to kiss him one last time. "I'll be okay, promise."

He nods and lets me climb into the car. Giving him a wave as he steps away, I drive off, heading home.

I do my best not to wonder why Cas is so worried about me, but I spend the entire drive home doing just that. I pull up to the community building and find Greer leaning against the exterior wall, waiting for me. She is still in her police uniform, and Draven is perched on her shoulder in lizard form. It's nearly impossible to see him since he is only a shade lighter than her uniform, but the sun's rays bounce against his shimmering scales enough to catch my eye.

"Do you know what this is all about?" I ask her as we head inside together.

"Yeah, we have been cleared to start doing missions again," she answers in a bland tone.

"Not thrilled?"

"I'm glad to not feel like a sitting duck anymore, but I feel like this is just a way to keep us busy while Dad plots behind our backs," she quietly admits.

Greer and Ash are still keeping a close eye on Dad, Chief Lu, and the Hansens to see if they can learn anything else about this "Plan B," but they haven't been able to figure anything out. Greer had a conversation with Mei-Lien, and she seems as in the dark about it as we are, but she has promised to watch her mother for us. Considering the gravity of what we believe this plan is, infusing the memory elixir into Greer's shadows and my water to use on whole areas full of innocent people, it makes sense why they are being as secretive as possible about it.

I turn to her before entering Dad's office. "Maybe this plan can still work. If we fight hard enough, take out the big guys, Plan B will no longer be needed."

Sure, Ash and I have been researching our asses off and Greer's always trying to think through different strategies to end the war, but ultimately, Dad's plan is what we had hoped would work. The plan was to kill all the military officers leading the Brethren, causing enough chaos for us to easily memory-wipe all of the soldiers as they come.

Even if we missed a few, it wouldn't be enough to ever cause a serious threat to us again. I have to hope it will still work, because it's the best we've got.

"I wish it were that simple, but I don't think it is."

Greer's response jars me, but she knocks on Dad's door before I can ask her to elaborate. He opens it a moment later and asks us to sit.

"I hate doing this right before your birthday, Talli. But an opportunity has presented itself, and we can't push it off," Dad starts.

"My birthday is just a day. Missions are more important," I reply.

Dad appears regretful, but he nods. "General Campbell has been spotted."

My body freezes up, and the darkness starts churning inside of me.

"There's no way. No one has laid real eyes on him in over fifteen years. The only reason we know he's still alive is because Talli has been able to find images of him inside of random soldiers' minds," Greer responds.

She's right. Mei-Lien does most of the interrogating when we capture soldiers, but a few months before we went after Mackay, Dad asked me to do a little memory-seeing to try and find any useful information, and I saw the General in three different minds.

We were definitely winning the war until Campbell came on the scene, then the tables drastically turned. He organized the Brethren like no one had before him. Up until then, they were brutes who wildly attacked us, but after, they became well-organized soldiers. Killing him could be the key to giving us the upper hand again.

Dad turns on the monitor above the table, and there he is. The picture is a bit grainy, but I can see his face well enough.

"Where was this taken?" Greer asks.

"Boston."

My eyes widen. He is close. I could have an arrow through his chest in a matter of hours. "When?" I ask.

"Four hours ago. I want you girls in the air within the hour. Chief Lu, along with five others, will meet you there to explain the plan and act as backup."

Greer's whole body goes rigid beside me, and I grab her arm out of reflex. Her eyes are squeezed shut for a moment, and then they pop open widely. Her alarm is palpable as she says stiffly, "It's another trap. He's looking for Talli."

Both Dad and Greer look at me, waiting for my reaction to Greer's vision. Are they expecting me to look afraid? Or worried? Because I'm neither. I just want to get this bastard. "I don't care if it's another trap. They are going to keep coming after me, so let them come."

A knock sounds at the door. Dad calls out, "Come in, Reef."

Reef walks through the door, dressed in a standard Hawk mission uniform—black pants and a black leather jacket. Odel is on his shoulder, looking a bit fierce for an adorable otter. Dad must see the face I make, because he says, "Reef is going on this mission, as well. I expect everyone to play nice and focus on the task at hand."

I purse my lips, but nod in understanding.

"This is a team mission, but if one of you has a chance for a shot...take it, no matter the casualties."

Greer tenses at my side, but she nods and responds, "Yes, sir." I do the same, and Reef echoes me. I'm not comfortable with any casualties, Hawk or human, but that would be a small price to pay to get Campbell.

Wouldn't it be?

CHAPTER 36

CASPIAN

TALLI'S TEXT DOES NOT come as a surprise.

Talliana: Hey, this is going to be an all-night thing, but I will be in your bed the moment I am free.

Me: I hope everyone is okay?

Talliana: Yes. It's just family drama. No one's dead...yet. Haha jk

Me: Good to hear. I think... Love you. Text me if you need me.

Talliana: Of course. Love you too.

I set my phone down, feeling uneasy. Talli has been surprisingly available the last few months. So much so that it's easy to forget who she is, but I have little doubt that whatever it is that's keeping her, it's Order business. She is going to go after someone tonight. Who? I couldn't even try to guess. All I can do is sit here and hope she returns to me tomorrow.

I know she can take care of herself, and none of our men are a match for her, but I can't help but stress about not being there with her. What if someone else gets the dumb idea to try grabbing her for themselves like Mackay did?

My phone rings, and I pick it up to see it's from a familiar number. My father. I clear my throat and answer, "Yes, sir?"

"Ah, Caspian. I'm in Boston tonight. I would like you to meet me for dinner."

I feel the blood drain from my face. This is not what I need. My father is especially good at seeing through my lies. If he questions me tonight when I'm already worried about Talli, he might see right through me.

"Is that wise to meet in person so close to my mission? Someone could see," I suggest, hoping he will change his mind.

"It's not a request. I want to be briefed on your progress in person."

His tone suggests no room for argument, but I try one last time. "She's supposed to be here any minute," I lie.

"I think your little whore can go without you for one night. Or are you unable to go one night without getting your dick wet? Tell me, Caspian, are you getting used to having her in your bed?"

My fist clenches involuntarily at my side, but I force my voice to come out even as I answer, "Of course not, Father. I will cancel."

"Good. I'll have someone text you the information."

He hangs up the phone, and I let out a deep breath.

Fuck. Fuck. Fuck.

This perfect weekend that I worked hard to plan out meticulously for Talli's birthday has completely gone to shit.

My father's men lead me into a hotel service elevator, which I quickly note has no cameras or staff around. Out of all the men in the Brethren, my father has always kept the best as his personal bodyguards. Standing behind them in the back of the elevator, I can see how rigid their backs are in their military stance. He's had these two for a while, so I know their backgrounds are U.S. Marines.

The elevator opens, and they lead me like a prisoner to my father's room, one man in front of me and one behind. I pass four more guards in the hall who don't even acknowledge me until the one guarding my father's door looks me over carefully before letting me inside. They either suspect witchcraft could be at play, or they just distrust me. Or possibly both. Very few of my father's men like me. My own father doesn't even like me, so why would his men? But frankly, I couldn't give a shit about any of them liking me.

"Caspian. Sit. I want a full report," my father greets, if you can even call that a greeting. He is sitting at a small round dining table, which is empty save for a bottle of scotch and two small glasses. His glass is already filled, and he is idly tapping the side of it as he waits for me to remove my leather jacket, take a seat, and pour myself a glass. I have never had a taste for scotch, but I know what's expected of me. As soon as I finish pouring an appropriate amount, two young girls, maybe sixteen years old, come forward with plates overflowing with seafood and place them in front of us. My father immediately dismisses them and begins cracking open the bright red lobster in the center of his plate.

I hesitate, my stomach churning at the idea of eating right now when I'm so stressed about everything. Of course, he notices and asks, "Has she turned you into a grass-eater?"

"Not at all. It's just late for dinner by Eastern Standard Time," I answer coolly, since it is ten o'clock, and then start picking at my food to appease him. If I'm lucky, he will dismiss me before I can eat much more.

He seems to accept that answer and continues working on his food while he says, "Report. I want to know how close you are."

I swallow the small bite of food and straighten my back, trying to make it as rigid as my father's men. "She's in love with me. I've been strategically trying to spend more time with her family and putting pressure on her about being honest and open. I know it's affecting her, and she will tell me soon, I'm sure of it."

He doesn't look at me, but replies, "Family time, pressuring her to be honest, and what? A whole lot of charm and sweet-talking?" He looks up at me, and his dark-green eyes pin me to my spot as he continues, "Do tell, what amount of time do you classify as 'soon'?"

"It's impossible to put an exact time on it. It's only been..." I start.

"Six months. I gave you nine before I expected you to start feeding me information."

"Then I have three more months."

The annoyance and impatience radiating off of him are palpable. He is a man often quick to anger, so I'm surprised when he doesn't say anything else, but instead, eats more of his dinner.

Minutes pass of quiet eating, and my anxiety is spiking to an all-new level. Finally, he says casually, "I assume you have met Aaron Hoffman already."

"I have," I answer.

"Tell me anything you know about him."

I almost shrug, but stop myself. My father hates the gesture. "He seems like a normal human dad. He cares greatly for his daughters, tries to be funny to embarrass them, and appears to adore his wife." What I don't say is how he always looks like he is calculating every single word and action of everyone around him. He is clever. Maybe even clever enough to rival my own father, who seems disappointed in my answer.

"If you learn anything more about him, contact me immediately. Despite the Hawks' claim of not having a singular leader, I believe that is exactly what Hoffman is."

"Yes, sir."

The man standing at my father's right leans over and says something into his ear, too low for me to make out.

"Well, Caspian, it's time for you to go. Your little witch will be here in less than five minutes, and I don't think you're prepared to explain to her why you are here," my father says, standing from his chair and dropping his napkin on his mostly eaten plate.

My entire body stiffens, nearly snapping against the strain as his words sink in. Talliana did go on a mission tonight...a mission to kill my father.

"You knew she was coming? This entire time?" I get up from my chair and put on my jacket as fast as my half-frozen arms allow.

"Of course. I set this trap."

I gape at him. "Why?"

"I thought it was time I officially met my son's girlfriend."

I choke out a laugh. "She is not someone any Brethren should want to meet in person."

"That may be true for many, but I'm the General. She can't touch me."

His cockiness is so much like my own that I want to find a way to rid myself of the quality altogether. I despise the idea of being anything like him.

"Two minutes," my father announces. One of his men grabs my arm and starts to lead me to an adjoining room door when I ask quickly, "Are you going to hurt her?"

A mistake. I shouldn't have shown my hand like that. My father assesses me and it takes all of my self-control to not further react or show concern.

"You will get her back in one piece."

That is not the answer I want, but it will have to do. If I don't leave now, she will find me, and this will all be over. I turn to leave when my father calls, "And Caspian?" I face him again. "If you lie to me again, I will consider this mission a failure, and I will come for both of you."

I feel like the wind has been knocked out of me, but I keep my expression indifferent as I let my father's man lead me out of the room, securing the door behind us. We move to the main door when the lights in the hotel flicker off, plunging us into almost complete darkness. The only light remaining is the glow of the moonlight coming in from the window. The man goes to open the door, but I catch his wrist, stopping him. I run for the bed and drop to the floor, sliding myself under it.

The moment I pull my head under, the door slams open. I hear a grunt, and then my father's man falls to the floor, lifeless, with his neck sliced open. Several pairs of feet shuffle into the room. I watch as they walk around, probably searching for anyone else, and then they take a position at the adjoining door. The one I just walked through.

The moonlight catches something next to a pair of boots, and I squint my eyes to try to see what it is. Is it some kind of sword? No, spear. One of the boots next to it starts bouncing in a nervous gesture

I know well. I almost gasp, but stop myself before I can make a noise. The boot halts.

"Talli, what is it?" I hear a low whisper, a voice I also know well.

"I thought I smelled…"

"What?"

"Oak and sunshine."

"I don't smell anything. You're probably smelling him on your hair. He's home safe."

Another pair of boots steps up too close to hers, and I hear a man's voice whisper, "Missing your human, princess?"

My body suddenly constricts with…shit, I don't know what. Anger? Jealousy? Some instinct to protect what's mine? I wait for Talli to respond with something snarky, stomp on his foot, hit him, something! But she doesn't, and the adjoining door opens, and her boots shuffle through it.

"Talliana Hoffman. It is an absolute pleasure," my father drawls.

Chapter 37

TALLIANA

I DON'T HESITATE. I send my ice spear spiraling toward General Campbell's heart. In the blink of an eye, it shatters a foot away from him. Our entire team stands in shock for only a split second, and then everything is hurled at Campbell: shadow, fire, water, and knives. Everything seems to hit an invisible shield.

The sound of hearty laughter reaches my ears as we all stop our assault. Campbell's shoulders are bouncing from his laughter. Both he and the two men standing on either side of him are completely unharmed.

"Hawks, Hawks, I don't want a fight. I only want to chat with Ms. Hoffman. It's time we came to an understanding."

I form ice daggers in each palm from the water in the open canteen I have strapped to my side, as I step forward. Chief Lu steps in front of me, sword still raised high in front of her, and says, "I am Kasumi

Lu, Elder of the Massachusetts Community. If you want to chat, you speak with me."

"I didn't say your name, now did I? I only speak to the most powerful, and in this case, that is Ms. Hoffman," Campbell sneers at her.

Her shoulders go rigid, and I push her out of the way, walking right up to the invisible shield. He smiles widely at me. It is a smile that I am sure was once charming and would draw anyone to him, but now it looks wrong.

"Are you impressed with my shield? It is courtesy of Killian Hansen. He built it for me right after I had his loud-mouthed wife's tongue cut out. Honestly, I really should have done that sooner," he muses.

The darkness starts to fight me for control, ready to take over. But I need to keep my head on straight for this.

"It's too bad you let your grip on them slip. You should see what they are capable of when they are treated with things such as gratitude, friendship, and common decency," I reply.

"*Keep him talking. My shadows are trying to find a device for this shield,*" Greer says down our mental connection.

"Common decency? You Hawks are all the same. Believe you are so much better than everyone else, but really, you are an abomination that needs to be eradicated—an evil that has plagued this earth for long enough."

"Coming from the monster who is responsible for thousands of deaths," I retort.

"It takes a monster to kill a monster."

"Well, it's a good thing I have very sharp teeth, then."

His lips purse. "Ms. Hoffman, I want to be clear about something. I have an army at my disposal, as you very well know. For every man you kill, I have another lined up to take their place. You will not win this war. So, let's save ourselves some time and paperwork, shall we? Surrender yourself now, and I'll give your people a year's head start to flee the country before I hunt them all down one by one. A generous offer, really."

I huff out a laugh. "Let me make something clear to you, General Dickhead. This war ends the moment I kill you, which is in the very near future."

"Got it. I'll smash it in five seconds. Get ready."

"So be it. The ones you love will all die as you watch. Good evening, Ms. Hoffman."

Campbell turns toward the window behind him as it opens. Sparks fly in the room, and his men frantically rush to cover him. My ice dagger is faster, and I catch his leg as he climbs out of the window and jumps.

Damn it!

Racing forward, I will another one to form, and I...

BANG.

Searing pain cuts through my right forearm. I scream, looking down to see the flesh torn into a wide hole. I fall back from shock, but Reef catches me before I hit the ground. A loud roar shakes the whole room, and I look up through bleary eyes to see Coventina hovering by the window. Campbell is gone, and his men are both dead in front of the window.

Reef carries me up and onto Coventina's back. Greer gets on right behind me, and we fly.

God, I'm in so much pain.

"Covey, I need healing water now," I tell her urgently.

"This is going to sting."

I look down below us to see the ocean.

"*Oh no, no, no. Find us a lake or a pond or something else,*" I plead.

Coventina does a spin, dropping both Greer and me into the pitch-black North Atlantic Ocean.

Icy water closes over my head, and my arm feels like it is being burned with fire. I can't see anything aside from the dull blue glow coming from my arm, telling me that I am healing. I scream from the pain and shock, and salty water tries filling up my lungs. Quickly closing my mouth and dispelling the water from inside me, I lift up my arm the best I can, trying to search for Greer using the slight glow to see. I spin, but I can't find her anywhere.

Kicking hard, I break through the surface and suck in a breath.

"Greer!" I shout. Waves keep crashing into me, knocking me around.

"*She's sinking*!" Draven screams in a panic.

"*How was I to know she was a bad swimmer*?" Coventina asks incredulously.

There is a loud splash a few yards away, and I manage to catch sight of the edge of Coventina's split tail. Panic surges through me, and it's enough for the darkness to break free. The corners of my stinging eyes darken, and all I know is that I must help Greer.

The darkness forces me to take a deep breath, and I sink under the surface of the water again. My eyes close, and my healing instincts mentally search for Greer's heartbeat in the water. After a moment, the darkness locks onto Coventina furiously swimming down, and I feel the faint echo of a human heartbeat a few yards below her.

The darkness uses my water ability, willing the water around her wrists to freeze into cuffs with a chain in between them. It lassos a rope of water around the chain and pulls with all its might. Her descent starts to slow. It senses Coventina reach her, and it lets go as she brings Greer the rest of the way up. I break the surface again myself a moment before Coventina does, with Greer unconscious on her back and the ice chain around Coventina's neck. I will the water to surge me forward to them and I climb up Coventina's back leg when I get close enough. The darkness focuses on Greer in the next instant and immediately pulls the excess water from her body. She chokes and gasps, trying to dispel the last of it and catch a breath. It swiftly wills the ice chains to disintegrate so she can use her hands again.

Greer pushes herself up and eventually, after a lot of coughing and hacking, moves to a sitting position on Coventina's back. I feel the darkness subside, but only slightly, so that I regain some control.

Greer slowly looks over to me and, with her teeth chattering, says, "I hate your dragon."

Coventina chuffs, but she doesn't argue. She messed up, and she knows it. Though I doubt she'll ever admit it.

I sense Greer's heartbeat, and it is pumping way too hard. Grabbing what I believe to be her hand, I feel how icy it is. She's hypothermic.

"*Covey, get us skyward. Greer needs to be warmed up. Now!*"

Coventina jumps from the water, catching air under her wings, and she flies us up again. I catch the faint shimmer of Draven's charcoal-colored scales as we fly by him.

"*Drop us off in an alley behind a hotel. The first one you see,*" I direct her.

She swoops down and does as I ask. I help Greer dismount and sling her arm over my shoulder as I try to walk us as fast as possible to the entrance of the hotel. I almost slip on the icy sidewalk twice, but I drag us both around the final bank of snow and into the warm hotel.

This hotel is *nice*, but most of the hotels on the ocean are. Thankfully, there are not many people in the lobby due to the late hour. I half-drag Greer's shivering form up to the front counter, and the woman at the front desk gasps at the sight of us. Dripping wet and no doubt looking frosted over.

"We need a room—the closest one you can get us. I don't have a card on me, but I promise to have someone call you in ten minutes to pay over the phone," I explain quickly enough that I immediately feel out of breath.

"You need a hospital," the woman argues.

"Now, please! There isn't time. I need to get her warm."

The woman gapes at me a moment longer, then scrambles around her desk to get us a keycard. "Room 103. Down the hall, second door on the right," she directs.

I nod my thanks and get Greer to the room. Placing her into a seated position on the tiled shower floor, I turn on the cool water and direct it right at her. I step in behind her, then get to work removing all her clothes and slowly warming up the water. Under the light of the bathroom, I can see that her alabaster skin is blue. A minute longer, and she could have died. I would have been useless to help her. My ability can heal most ailments, but it can't warm someone up or save them from hypothermia.

My eyes start to burn again, not from the leftover saltwater clinging to my lashes but from being so close to losing Greer. Over a stupid mistake, no less. Coventina was so worried about me that she didn't think about the danger she was putting Greer in.

I reach over to the temperature handle and turn it up some more. Greer has her arms wrapped around her bent knees, still shivering, but the blue is slowly fading. I step out of the shower and lean against the sink, letting my head fall into my hands.

"Was it you or her that saved me?" Greer's shattered voice asks.

"It was more of a group effort. All three of us got you out," I respond.

"Three? But Draven can't go in the water."

My laugh in response is slightly deranged, and I probably shouldn't admit the full truth to her, but she almost died, for fuck's sake. I'm tired of dancing around it. "The darkness. It took over and helped us save you."

She looks at me, studying my face, but only swallows hard and nods in response.

"I'm going to call Dad real quick, and then I'll be back to check on you." I turn to leave, but Greer says, "It's no one's fault what happened—not Covey's and not yours. Okay?"

"If I hadn't gotten shot..." I start.

"No one's fault. I don't want to hear another word about it. Now get yourself under control."

Her voice is getting stronger, so I decide not to argue. I leave the bathroom and focus on calming down. I hadn't even realized the darkness still had a hold on me, but it's there, lingering just underneath my skin, keeping me strong enough to make sure Greer is safe.

Breathe.

Think of someone you love...Cas.

The darkness settles, content to completely let go of me. My body feels like a weight is suddenly pressed upon it, and my legs no longer feel solid beneath me, but I'm okay. All the work with Mr. Simon has made me stronger, more capable of handling the magic depletion.

I take one more deep breath and call Dad to explain what happened, then ask him to pay for the room for the night. He's not happy, but not surprised since Chief Lu already reported back to him.

I head to the bathroom again to check on Greer, when I hear a very angry Draven in my head. *"Let me in before I shift and push down the door."*

Rushing to the room's door, I open it, and Draven and Coventina scurry in. Draven goes right to the bathroom, and I can hardly blame him for it. I'll give the two of them a minute.

"Just because your body isn't impacted by the cold water like hers is doesn't mean you don't still need to warm up, or finish healing."

Pulling off my stiff leather jacket, I find an angry-looking scar where I was shot on my right forearm. I twist my wrist and see another scar where the bullet exited. But my shattered bones are healed, and my muscles are in working order.

"I'm fine," I reply.

"If you don't finish healing in the next few minutes, that scar will remain."

"I don't care about a scar!" I snap. *"If anything, it will serve as a reminder of how even a tiny mistake could cost us those we love."*

Her small lizard mouth closes, and she swivels her head away from me.

Good.

I take a seat on one of the queen-sized beds and try to run through everything that happened tonight. Campbell clearly set up a trap for us, like Greer's vision warned. But for what? Just to offer me a deal he knew I would never take? It doesn't make sense. Why risk his life for something so pointless? Maybe it was some show of power he wanted to flaunt in my face. Maybe it was more than that. I truly believe he would have tried harder to kill me if that was the goal. From what Dad confirmed over the phone, I was the only one who got hurt during the skirmish. That is a relief, at least.

Greer exits the bathroom with a towel wrapped around her. Her face looks puzzled as she studies me. "Why didn't the cold water affect you?" she asks.

I shrug. "The water ability that flows through my veins is already icy. You can't freeze what's already frozen."

The crease between her eyebrows deepens. "Your ice ability is not surface-level? It comes from inside you?"

"Yeah. Sometimes I call her my ice bitch."

Greer's serious expression breaks, and she starts laughing. Like *laughing*, laughing. Like she has just heard the funniest joke on the planet.

When it finally subsides, and I'm just as annoyed as I am cold, I tell her, "Get in bed and rest. I'm going to shower the salt off my skin and then find the laundry room to get our clothes clean."

She climbs into one of the beds with the towel still wrapped around her. She grabs a piece of laminated paper on her way and says, "I'm going to order us some warm food."

I look at the clock on the nightstand. It's almost midnight, but I guess it's worth a shot. I nod and head to the bathroom to try to get rid of the shakiness in my bones.

CHAPTER 38

CASPIAN

I CANNOT UNHEAR HER scream. It has been echoing inside my head for the last couple of hours as I've forced myself to drive home.

First there was a loud bang, and then when she screamed I felt like my heart was being ripped from my body. I didn't think about the consequences when I heard it. I just clawed my way out from under the bed, but by the time I got out, everyone was gone. She was gone.

Once I got to my car, I tried calling her, desperate to know she was okay, but there was no answer. I tried calling Greer next, but there was no answer from her either. I tried each of them again about halfway home with the same result.

Walking into my apartment now, I feel so on edge, I don't know what to do with myself. I pace around the couch until it comes to me. Asher. Grabbing my phone, I dial his number, and to my relief, he answers immediately.

"Hey, Cas."

"I can't get a hold of Talli. Greer is also not answering. Is she okay?" I meant to hide my fear and desperation, but it came out in such a rush.

"She's fine. It's just family stuff. I think they both had to turn off their phones for a bit."

"Are you sure?"

"Yeah, I talked to Greer about thirty minutes ago. They were about to go to bed, but I'm sure Talli will call you in the morning."

I let myself take a breath in relief. She's okay. Ash wouldn't lie to me if she were on death's door. It must have been just a graze, but enough to hurt her.

My father did this. He hurt her, and I want to kill him for it.

"Thanks, Ash. I'm sorry if I bothered you. I worry sometimes, but it's probably stupid." I try brush the whole thing off, but Ash goes quiet for a while, and my anxiety spikes again. Just when I'm about to ask if he's still there, he responds, "It's not stupid. It's love, and I hope that you never stop worrying about her. She needs your worry."

"I couldn't stop if I tried," I reply simply.

"Good. And I don't know if you have made many friends since moving to Massachusetts, but if you need one, I'm here. If you want, of course. I've really only been friends with Greer and Talli, so I may completely suck at being a friend to a guy, but I can try my best."

"Ash?"

"Yes?"

"Thank you. I do consider you my friend."

I can feel his smile through the phone. I really do like Ash. I'm not sure exactly what it is specifically about him. At first I thought it was because he's human, and that puts me a bit more at ease around him, but I just genuinely like him. He's a kind person and a lot like his mother.

"Good. I mean, the same. I consider you a friend too." His awkwardness makes me chuckle, and I tell him thank you one last time before hanging up the phone. Sinking into the couch, I force my body to relax.

She's okay. She's okay. *She's okay.*

Tonight was a test, and I failed. My father is losing patience and pushing me to work faster. But I don't have a plan yet. I have no idea how to pull Talli away from this and make her walk away from the fight. And I can't help but wonder, if I pull her away, would I be tipping the scales in the Brethren's favor? She is an assassin. Her magic has to be powerful, and in a war like this, every bit of power makes a difference. I'd also be dooming her to a life of feeling guilty for leaving her people. Because Talli would. She would let guilt eat her up inside, and I can't watch her do that to herself either. I want her to live, but not as half a person.

I need her to tell me everything, and then from there, I can come up with a plan. It's time to break out *the gift* and see what happens.

CHAPTER 39

TALLIANA

As soon as we got home, I changed, packed a bag, and headed straight to Cas's. There is something about being shot that makes you want to be close to the people you love. And God, I love him.

I knock on his door with my small bag slung over my good arm. It really only contains a change of clothes. Everything else I need is already here. I am very pleased that I didn't have to be the kind of woman who just slowly started leaving things at his place. Instead, Cas got tired of seeing me carry a large bag every time I came over, so he took note of everything I used and liked, then bought it all for me to have here, too, since I'm here almost every weekend.

The door swings open, and I'm immediately pulled into strong arms. Cas's warmth envelopes me, and I let out a sigh of relief as I breathe in his scent of oak and sunshine. He pulls me away from him, holding me at arm's length while he scans me from head to toe.

"Cas?"

He doesn't answer, just continues his scan while I stand in the doorway to his apartment. Then he pulls my right arm toward him and instantly locks onto my scar.

Why did I already take off my jacket in the hallway? I internally curse myself for it, but he seriously has never greeted me like this before. The scars did heal somewhat more in the shower, thanks to my healing ability, but they did not disappear altogether.

Cas's jaw clenches as he runs his thumb over it, then twists my arm to examine the other scar. His eyes lift to mine. "What happened?"

I swallow and carefully pull my arm away. "It's been there. I usually cover it with makeup since it's not particularly attractive to look at. I was just in such a rush today to see you, I forgot." The excuse is weak, but I literally have no other way of explaining it to him. I can't tell him I just got hurt, because there is no way it would have healed like this in less than twenty-four hours. Not by human standards anyway.

"Talli, I've had my hands and mouth on every inch of your body. I'd know if you had a scar like that on your arm, makeup or no."

Shit. Time to try to distract him instead.

"Cas, are you okay? Ash told me you called him in kind of a panic last night, thinking I was hurt."

He runs his hand through his hair, sweeping the wavy golden strands aside. "I...I got a feeling. Like something inside was telling me you were hurt. It's silly, but I called you to make sure you were okay, but you didn't answer. Then Greer didn't answer, so I called Ash."

He couldn't reach us because both of our phones were destroyed in the ocean. Somehow, the waterproof zipper pouch on my pants, where I keep my phone, got damaged and saltwater got into it. No amount of rice in a small baggy could save it. Granted, I also wasn't willing to wait a few hours either like Ash suggested.

"I'm sorry, we had our phones turned off. It was a long day," I reply.

Cas looks me over again and then asks, "Are you sure you're okay? You know you can tell me anything, right? I want only honesty between us."

His eyes meet mine, and I feel like he is looking into my very soul. Guilt threatens to swallow me whole. I want to tell him. I want to share my entire life with him and have only honesty between us, but how could he love a monster? Because Campbell might be wrong about everything else, but he isn't wrong about me being a monster. That is exactly what I am.

Shoving all the guilt and self-loathing into the deepest corner inside of me, I close the distance between us. I wrap my arms around his neck and, shifting to my tippy-toes, reach his lips and show him just how okay I really am.

His moan is deep and rumbles through our mouths and right to my core. I thread my fingers through the hair at the back of his head and pull his mouth closer to mine. He spins us in the next moment, actually putting me inside his apartment, and I feel the breeze of the door close shut. Apparently, he did not want to risk putting on a show for his neighbors.

Cas kisses me a few moments longer, then pulls away, panting hard. He pulls me to his chest again, though, and I nestle my head into it as I listen to his rapid heartbeat start to slow.

"I know your birthday is tomorrow, but can I give you your present now?" he asks.

I laugh and pull away. "Of course."

His smile is wide as he kisses me again, then he turns and heads into his bedroom.

I take a seat on the couch, unable to wipe the grin off my face. He only makes me wait a second before he sits next to me and turns so that our knees touch. He fiddles with the wide black suede jewelry box as he looks up at me.

"In the spirit of only wanting honesty between us, I do have something to tell you. I have been wanting to give this to you for a while and explain, but I kept pushing it off, and then it got to a point where it felt like too much time had passed, and now it feels even more weird that I haven't brought it up. And if it's all too weird, I can buy you something else." He extends the box to me and I take it hesitantly.

"In the spirit of honesty, you have me nervous about what could possibly be in this jewelry box."

Cas has been acting weird since I told him about the family emergency, like he knows I am lying to him. It's either that or something else has him wound up tight. Whatever it is, maybe this present will give me a clue.

"Just open it and I'll explain."

I look down at the box and slowly open it. Inside is a beautiful heart necklace. It is open in the middle, and the shape of the heart is made up of tiny hearts with small diamonds in the center of each one.

"It's beautiful, Cas. Thank you. It almost seems familiar..." I start, and then my breath catches.

It is familiar.

I look at him, back at the necklace, and then at him. Shock hits me like a wave, and I press my hand against my mouth.

"I admit, someone helped me pick it out. A long time ago," he says quietly, searching my eyes.

How could I forget? How did I not remember him? Almost two and a half years ago, at the mall, a man asked me to help him pick out a necklace for his girlfriend—the exact necklace that is in my hands.

"You remembered me, and you didn't say anything?" I ask, not quite upset but confused as to why he didn't bring it up sooner.

He hesitates but answers, "Yes. I recognized you on that first day. I was just afraid to freak you out by mentioning it right away. Didn't want you to think I was some kind of weirdo. I thought maybe you would recognize me after some time, but it turns out I'm not very memorable." He half-laughs, playing it off as a joke, but I only feel sad at not remembering him. Now that I pull the memory out, it is playing plain as day in my head: those same beautiful hazel eyes that I always get lost in, and the warm smile.

"No, please don't say that. I remember that day perfectly, it was kind of a crazy day for me, and meeting you almost felt like a dream that I wasn't sure actually happened. Your hair is much more golden now, and your skin is tanner, too." I point out, but I'm unsure of the real point I'm trying to make.

His lips quirk, "A good dream?"

I laugh as my shock finally wears off and I feel like I can effectively use my brain again. "I'm so sorry I didn't remember you. You did leave an impression on me, very much so. An embarrassing amount, in the spirit of honesty. At the time, my boyfriend and I were...separated, but it still felt a bit like a betrayal, how much I felt toward you in that short moment. I didn't even tell Greer about it, because I was afraid of how it would sound if I said it aloud. God, now I sound super weird."

His face warms in the same way it did way back then, and I mentally slap myself for not seeing it sooner. Did he really think I was going to be weirded out that he didn't bring it up? I guess I do wish he had said something sooner, but I get it. I understand why he might be worried about how I could react.

"No, not weird at all. I...well, I actually felt the same. Like maybe I was shopping for the wrong person."

"Wait. Wasn't this necklace meant for her? What happened?"

"I never gave it to her. It didn't feel like it belonged to her, and we broke up a couple of weeks later anyway. I meant to return it, but when I got to the store, I decided the rightful owner was out there somewhere, and I would find her. I never thought...I never thought I would see you again—the girl with eyes that remind me of the deepest part of the ocean. But then I saw you that day in the Registrar's Office before classes started, and I knew I needed to find out if the necklace belonged to you."

"So, at the beginning..."

"Yeah, I didn't even try to stay away from you, but I didn't want to just blatantly ask you out either. I had seen, what, like five other guys do exactly that and get brushed off by you? I knew I had to connect with you first." His gaze drops to our legs, now interlocked, with one of my legs between his and one of his between mine.

It all makes sense now. The games I felt like he was playing, always being there but not obvious about his intentions until the first official date at the fair. After that, his intentions have never been unclear. I've always known how much he wants me, even during the whole wait-for-sex miscommunication.

I truly understand Cas now. He is just a guy with a ton of anxiety, always worried about messing things up. I could psychoanalyze why he's like this without any trouble. His mother died when he was a young boy, and he was raised by a father who only expected perfection from him and never showed him love. Of course he would be afraid of losing someone he loves, and of course, he would worry about falling short and ruining things.

Using a play from his book, I grab his chin and lift his face to meet my gaze again. I don't let go of him as I tell him very clearly, "I love you. I don't want you to feel an ounce of remorse for how we ended up here. I knew you were playing games, and I played them right back. I'm so grateful that you remembered me and sought me out." Tears well up in my eyes, and my throat starts to constrict, but I force myself to continue through the emotions. "You have made me so happy, Caspian Stewart. Maybe in this fucked up world, there is such a thing as fate and we were fated to find each other, fated to be together."

His hand closes over mine, and he moves it until it is pressed between his hand and cheek. He leans his face into it and closes his eyes as if my words are almost too much.

"Hey, help me put it on?" I ask, pulling him back to me.

He opens his eyes again, his smile soft as he reaches for the jewelry box. I let him take it and reach to remove the moonstone necklace Trey gave me, but he stops me by saying, "Don't. I have no intention of replacing him. All I am asking for is to share some space."

He extends the new necklace around my neck and clasps it, but he doesn't let it fall to my chest. He guides the heart pendant down and positions it so that it rests just below my collarbone and a couple of inches above the moonstone.

"You're my heart, Talliana Hoffman. I will give you everything I am capable of giving you, so long as you're willing to be mine."

"All I want is you. Your love and your trust. I..." I hesitate, unsure how to word what I need to say without ruining this moment. "I know how this is going to sound, but there is some stuff in my life that doesn't make sense to most people, and I can't quite explain it to you right now. But one day, I will tell you everything. I just need you to trust me in the meantime."

The light in his face dims slightly, and I know I've hurt him. I open my mouth to speak, but he says, "I trust you. You'll tell me when you're ready." He reaches his arms around my waist and pulls me onto his lap so that I straddle him—one of our favorite positions.

"You're really not weirded out?" he asks.

I nuzzle his nose playfully with mine and answer, "No, I am honored. How could I not be? You're the most thoughtful, understanding, handsome, generous, and all-around perfect man for me. And if I am your heart, then you are my light."

Cas captures my lips with his, and he kisses me until we are once again breathless.

"You know, I was jealous of your girlfriend back then. All I could think about was how lucky she was to be with you."

He grips my ass still in his lap, and his eyes go molten. "Did you now?"

"I did. I also thought about how she had to be with you for your looks and not for how observant you were," I tease him.

His laugh echoes through me, warming me up from the inside out.

"Coming from the woman who swears to have had an instant crush on me the moment you saw me, then didn't recognize me a mere two years later."

"Almost three!" I correct.

"Almost three years later."

I run my fingers through his hair, studying it. "I really like it better as this shade. The tanned skin, too. Did you spend serious time in the sun in the last few years? Wait, why were you in Massachusetts at a tiny mall looking for a present for your girlfriend?"

"We were long-distance. She actually used to go here for college, and I was visiting her when I went to the mall. She's the reason why I moved here. Not for her, obviously, but because she had convinced me this college was better than the one I was looking at in Colorado," he explains, wincing slightly, then continues, "And to answer your first question, yeah. I spent a lot of time during those years working on my fighting skills, and I did it mostly outside in the sun."

"So you're a masochist?" The idea of sparring with Greer in the hot sun sounds like a nightmare for both of us. I'd give her five minutes before she would create an umbrella of shadow to cover herself.

Cas laughs. "There is nothing wrong with getting a nice tan while working out."

"Coming from someone who actually tans. I burn, then freckle."

He yanks off my shirt and then pulls my upper arm out to examine all the little dots. He traces them all up my arm, over my shoulder, across my collarbone, over my other shoulder, and then back down the other arm. I'm covered in goosebumps by the time he is done. He brushes a thumb across my cheekbones and then boops my nose, causing me to giggle.

"I love all of your freckles. They are like a constellation of stars on your skin," he replies.

I smile at him, utterly entranced by how he always knows the right thing to say. "Take me to bed, Cas."

"It's almost lunch time," he points out, but his voice is low and husky. I can tell he needs me as much as I need him right now.

"Order us some delivery then. It'll get here right when we finish round one."

His eyebrows rise. "Round one?"

"I plan to wear either no clothes at all or only your T-shirt for the rest of the day. It's my birthday wish."

His grin is fiendish as he asks, "Pizza or Mexican, my birthday girl?"

Blindly thinking is a dangerous practice. Elder Ludwig can read my every thought, and I would never know if the claws of his mind invade my own. If he catches my thoughts about the darkness, I could lose the only thing I care about.

- Journal of Katarina Lehmann

CHAPTER 40

TALLIANA

March

I SHOVE HARDER THAN I have ever shoved before. But it still doesn't feel like enough.

Please. I whisper to the darkness, but it only pushes back.

"Show it your teeth! Fight! You are the master of your body, not the darkness! Take back your control! Give it no other option than to obey you!" Mr. Simon yells at me.

My skin prickles, and I feel a chill seeping into my bones. I'm done being nice. I'm done letting it push me around. The darkness is just another bully, and I know how to deal with bullies.

Instead of trying to push it into my ice cage, which is waiting for it, I wrap ice around it, creating a cage where it currently sits inside me. I don't give it a chance to escape by creating a door that needs to be shut; I surround it with a thick layer of ice with no beginning or end.

I collapse suddenly, like I have been literally released from the darkness's grasp, and tears immediately fall from my eyes from the immense relief I feel. I did it? I did it!

"Talli?" Mr. Simon asks, tentatively.

"I did it! It's contained!" I want to leap to my feet, but I'm exhausted from that internal battle I just won.

Seth trots toward me and starts licking my face, his tail wagging furiously.

"Seth!" I giggle and force myself to sit up.

"Well done, Talli. You can now cage the darkness when you need to. You'll still need to work at it, learn how to cage it without draining your energy, especially in high-stress situations, but you've done it," Mr. Simon praises.

It feels like it has taken forever to complete this step, but I've finally done it, and it feels so amazing. "Does this mean I'm ready for the next step?" I ask hopefully. He hesitates, but I push. "At least tell me what it is."

He sighs. "Ready is not quite the right word. You need to learn it so that once you are ready for it, you'll be able to use it. However, it will be complicated, and Katarina's journal doesn't supply many answers as to how she achieved it, but I trust we can figure it out together."

"Okay..." I hesitate. I have been wondering what this next step would be for months, but now I'm nervous to find out.

"This next step is also where Katarina stopped. There is nothing more after that. So I believe this will be the last step for you as well," he explains.

Excitement fills me, and I can't believe we have reached this point. I find the strength to stand, but I put my back to the table to help steady myself. "Alright. Lay it on me."

"In order to have complete control, you need to fill yourself with equal parts light and dark. From what I can tell, once you do that, you will have access to the power of the darkness without risking losing control. She stresses that perfect balance is the key. If the darkness takes up more space, then you can lose control, but if the light takes up more space, then you will lose the power the darkness affords you."

I slump back against the table, needing it sooner than I would have liked. "And this is where I won't be able to progress," I admit in defeat.

Mr. Simon studies me closely, then asks, "Why not?"

"I'm afraid the light hasn't been my friend for a long time. There is a tiny bit that coats my heart, but that's it. The rest left me the moment I made the decision to let the darkness consume me."

"Have you ever tried filling yourself with more light?"

I shake my head. "I haven't tried, because I always knew I needed the darkness more."

He frowns. "I'm sorry I have withheld the journal from you, but I believed you needed to focus on control first, then learn everything else she has to teach you. Maybe I was wrong."

"There is more to learn?" I ask.

"Yes. But not about controlling the darkness. Rather, about controlling yourself. But Katarina's story is not pleasant, to put it mildly."

"How so?"

"Do you trust me to give it to you when the time is right?" Mr. Simon asks.

I hesitate again. I really want to read it and find out everything I can about the woman who came before, but his initial decision to not share it with me right away gives me pause. Mr. Simon has always been the first one to provide me with the truth and treat me like an adult. So if he doesn't think it is healthy to have all the information now, then I trust his judgment. I have to.

"I do trust you. Completely."

He bows his head slightly. "Filling yourself with light can look different for everyone. But I don't think it's much different than thinking about the ones you love. You have to fill yourself with good things. Love, hope, forgiveness, kindness, and so on."

"Equal parts light and dark," I say to myself. "So like doing the wrong things for the right reasons type of thing?"

Mr. Simon seems to think about this, then admits, "I don't know, but I believe that's what Katarina was likely thinking at the end."

"She didn't die in a natural, old age kind of way, did she?"

"Far from it."

I almost ask how, but decide I do trust Mr. Simon and I'll find out when I'm meant to.

I feel like I am in an art museum. Greer's most important memories are playing out on large canvases surrounding me. I step closer to one, a memory from when we were kids, but hear the crunch of paper under my feet and stop. Lifting my foot, I pick up a sketchpad full of mundane moments, like her getting dressed, walking to work, and so on.

This part of Greer's mind is a mess. It's so different from Ash's pristinely organized library. It would be funny if I didn't sometimes have the chore of rifling through it to find something. Her memories are either on canvases, sketch pads, random pieces of paper, or graffitied on the white walls. Flipping through the sketch pad in my hand, I find something meaningless to try to manipulate.

I focus on Ash's blue shirt from yesterday and try to change it into a green one. Using a technique that Mr. Matisse, our senior Dream-walker, suggested, I close my eyes and imagine a green marker in my hand. When I open them, I find that a marker is in fact in my hand now, surprising me. I have tried this five different times, and nothing has happened until now.

Moving quickly before the marker disappears, I run it over Ash's shirt in the memory and hold my breath. A few moments pass, and his shirt seems to stay green, so I drop the sketchpad and leap out of Greer's memories.

After Greer catches her breath from having me mess with her memories, I ask, "What color shirt was Ash wearing yesterday?"

Her face twists, then her nose wrinkles. "Uh...I can see him clearly. Like, I know I saw him yesterday, but I can't make my brain conjure what he was wearing."

Mr. Hansen scribbles something on his notepad, giving no reaction, but Mrs. Hansen smiles at me. "Not the results we were expecting, but well done, Talli. Greer's memory was affected by whatever you did, and that is progress!" she signs.

"No offense, but I hate having you in my mind. It's like I'm being forced to relive the memories you look at. It's weird," Greer tells me, scratching her head.

Mr. Hansen's head perks up from behind his computer. "What did you say?"

"I can see the memories she looks through in my mind."

"Has this happened every time Talliana has entered your mind?" he asks, his eyes alight with curiosity. Mrs. Hansen comes around to stand next to him, looking confused.

Greer slowly answers, "Yeah...I thought that was what was supposed to happen."

"Asher can't see what she looks through. Talli, are you doing any-thing different with Greer?" Mr. Hansen asks. I shake my head.

"Do you think that's a limitation, Killian? One that protects the other Hawks?" Mrs. Hansen signs to him.

He signs back, "Yes, it must be. Humans can't tell what memories she looks through, but Hawks can. We need more test subjects to be sure." He turns back to us then. "Thank you both for your time, you can go. Talli, we'll give you a call when we're ready for another test."

Greer and I don't hesitate. We leave the lab as quickly as possible. On the way up the stairs, I comment, "Well, at least you'll never have to worry about losing or forgetting anything. If you do, I can just pop into your mind and find it for you."

She snorts, then points out, "That's great, but I'm not the sister who forgets things."

She has a point, and I can't use my ability to search my own mind. "I guess I'm just destined to forget where I put my phone for the rest of my life."

"Funny, I don't remember you losing your phone once since you met a particular tall blond."

I shove her playfully with my shoulder. Then ask, I bit more somber, "Did Ash find anything else out about my ability?"

Ever since the Hansens mentioned that I may be able to manipulate memories, Ash has been working day and night to find anything he can on it, but he has been coming up empty. He was able to confirm their theory by finding one mention of a Memory-seer being used to take away someone's memories completely, but that was all.

"No, but he's still trying. The Hansens, or Dad, had to have gotten the belief from somewhere, and if anyone can find it, it'll be Ash."

We climb the rest of the stairs, and I decide I'm not quite ready to be alone, so I ask, "Do you have time for a quick session on the mat?"

Her answering smile makes me happy. I really feel like I have my sister back. Things aren't perfect between us, but they have definitely gotten so much better over the last month.

"Yeah. Let's do it."

CHAPTER 41

TALLIANA

May

It's been a long day—two tests and three papers due for finals. But classes are over for the summer, and I am so relieved. I was going to keep pushing through with summer classes, but I decided to focus on ending this war instead. Because ending the war means I can have my happily ever after with Cas, and I am desperate for it.

I'm tired of lying to him whenever we go on a mission. Thankfully, Greer has managed on her own the two times we had an alarm go off while I was at Cas's over a weekend. But it's not fair for that responsibility to fall on her. We are a team, and I've been a shitty partner lately. It's time to get my head out of the clouds and get to work.

I walk through the front door of the house, and before I can even shut it behind me, Mom and Dad are standing there, clearly waiting for me.

"What? Did something happen?" My body immediately switches into alert-mode.

"No, nothing happened. But your dad and I want to talk to you," Mom answers in the voice I've heard her use a hundred times. She primarily uses it on patients, and it's the kind of voice that says, "You'll live, but you'll lose your arm."

I groan, knowing this cannot possibly be good, then I toss my backpack on the ground and kick my shoes off. I feel like a teenager again, about to get in trouble. I follow them to the living room and curl up on the couch. "Alright, what is it?"

"Talliana, your father and I are concerned—" Mom starts, but Dad interrupts her. "How much longer do you plan on messing around with this human?"

Shock hits me like a slap to the face. I thought they were used to the idea, okay with it even, since they haven't said a thing about it since meeting Cas. Apparently not. "Excuse me? He's not a toy that I'm just going to get tired of and throw away," I respond incredulously.

"Talliana, it's time to get realistic. You can't marry him. You are the only one left in the Hoffman bloodline, and it's your duty to keep it strong. You know that, and you also know having a relationship with a human isn't realistic long term."

Anger boils inside me, and I open my mouth, but Dad holds up his hand, indicating he isn't done. "Look, we know you like him, and he seems like a nice man, but you have a responsibility to your people. This will end in heartbreak, and you can't afford that setback. We need you to focus on your destiny."

My anger is now a quiet rage. I feel the ice rising under my skin and the darkness pressing against the walls of its cage. But I can't lash out against my parents. They can't see my monster.

"Honey, choosing a human is a hard life. I mean, look at Greer's parents and the life they had to lead, hiding all alone with no community protection," Mom reasons.

"Right, Greer's mom wasn't a Hawk, and yet Greer still turned out to match me in magical strength before my destiny unraveled," I argue.

"Because her father's bloodline was the purest in current times until her. Now it will be even more watered down when she marries Asher. If her father had married a Hawk, that child would have been much stronger," Mom explains.

This is bullshit. They can try to reason with me all they want, but they don't own me. I am an adult, and I make my own choices. You would think being the most powerful Hawk would earn me some rights and respect, but I'm still just a rebellious child in their eyes.

I take a deep breath, trying to calm all the raging emotions inside of me. I stand up and look at them both with the most civil expression I can muster, but say carefully, lethally, "Your concerns are heard, but disregarded. Caspian isn't a human distraction. It may have started that way, but he is the man that I love with everything I have inside of me. He is here to stay, and if anything happens to him because of your interference, I will burn this community to the ground myself. Do you both understand me?"

Dad looks like he is about to explode, and Mom seems tired. I turn on my heel and walk right back out the front door, grabbing my shoes and purse on the way out. Before I can shut the door behind me, I hear Dad shout, "If you love him so much, tell him the truth. See if he sticks around."

I slam the door, and with eyes burning, I run back to the car.

"Talli? Are you okay?"

I look and see Reef walking down the street toward me, genuine concern etching his face, but I don't stop my escape. "I'm fine!" I shout at him and get into the car.

My rage must have transferred to my driving because before I know it, I'm parking the car at Caspian's apartment complex and running up the stairs to him. I knock on his door, and he opens it, looking surprised—if not slightly pleased—to see me.

"Are you busy?" I ask before he can say anything.

"Laundry can wait. What's wrong?" he moves over, allowing me to walk in. He does indeed have a laundry basket set by the door.

He shuts the door behind me, and I spin, crashing my mouth to his. He catches me as I jump into his arms, wrapping my legs around him and deepening our kiss. He groans, and his grip is tight around me as he kisses me back.

"You going to tell me what happened?" he asks in between kisses.

"After."

He doesn't protest as he walks me into his bedroom and places me onto his bed. At first, his movements match my own frenzied tempo and speed, but he eventually slows down, turning my rough need into lazy touches. He can tell that I'm upset, and he knows how to calm me without denying me what I need. This man couldn't get any more perfect for me if he tried.

"I have a few minutes to shower and head to work. Do you want to tell me what's wrong now?" His voice is calm as if he's trying not to spook me.

I open my mouth and close it. There really isn't much I can tell him about the conversation I had with my parents. Dad's parting words haunt me. I believe he wouldn't leave if he found out who I was, but I don't know for sure. We love each other, I know that, but we need more time for it to be strong enough to overcome that hurdle. Don't we?

"I had a fight with my parents," I answer.

He lifts an eyebrow, indicating that I should elaborate. I swallow and go on, thinking about my words carefully. "It was about you. They don't think we are serious, and I'm wasting my time."

"I don't understand. I thought your parents liked me. Plus, how are we not serious?" His brows furrow in confusion. I usually admire how cute he is when confused, but I can't this time.

"They do like you. They just are snobbish, I guess, and always expected me to marry a son from their circle of friends."

"Don't parents normally want their daughters to marry a doctor? Are they afraid their grandkids will be blond?" He chuckles lightly.

I can't help but laugh, too. "What? Is that a thing? People being judgmental toward hair color?"

"You'd be amazed at what people will judge," he replies.

God, there is no way to explain this to him. I hate that I opened my mouth. Why did I rush over here? He doesn't truly understand anything about me. I want to cry from frustration. I can't lose him. Not yet.

"It's impossible to explain. I'm sorry I said anything. I just...They bombarded me when I got home, and I just went to the one place where I knew I would feel better." I snuggle into his chest and state the obvious, "Your arms always do the trick."

I feel his smile. "Don't be sorry. I want you to confide in me about everything. Is there anything I can do? I want your parents to know I'm serious about you and not going anywhere."

Now it's my turn to smile. "Just keep being yourself. They'll deal because when it comes down to it, you're mine to choose, not theirs."

He places a gentle kiss on my forehead and gives me one last squeeze before reluctantly getting up and heading to the bathroom. I hear him turn on the shower, and the temptation to get in with him is strong, but I push it down. He will be late to work if I do, and I have already messed up his laundry. I stay put and let myself idly think about what a future with Cas would look like. Could he be happy living in the community with me? How would he respond to a dragon living in the backyard? Would our kids have his blond hair or my auburn hair?

Before I can go too far down that line of thinking, he emerges from the bathroom with a towel wrapped around his waist, steam coming off of his wet, muscular body in waves. My mind immediately goes blank as I ogle him. I watch him like a predator stalking prey as he moves around the room, grabbing clothes from drawers. I track every water droplet that rolls down his abs until they hit the towel that sits just below the V-shape that the lines of his body make.

"Do you really only work out a couple of times a week? You look as though your job is the gym."

He stops and lifts a golden eyebrow at me. "Sometimes it's three or four if you're busy that week. I work out when I'm bored." He shrugs and starts pulling on his jeans, much to my dismay.

"I must leave you bored a lot."

He laughs and agrees, "Yes, I guess you do." He eyes me critically then. I'm stomach down on top of his comforter, head at the foot of the bed, pillow underneath my folded arms, legs bent and crossed, with my ass on full display. After taking me in, he adds, "You leave me bored a lot to work out yourself, it seems. Perhaps we should do it together sometime. Compare notes and share techniques. Have another self-defense lesson." His grin is boyish and teasing, causing my very naked body to ache for him again.

"Hmmm...maybe we should. See which one of us breaks first."

His smile widens, and he bends down to give me a quick kiss. "Promise you'll be naked in my bed when I get back tonight?"

"I'm not going anywhere," I state, snuggling my face into the pillow. Cas gives me one last longing look and heads out the door.

Thirty minutes pass, and my brain will not shut off. I keep switching between picturing Cas in my Hawk life and seeing him leaving me when I tell him. Both images are tormenting.

Once I start contemplating how the meeting with Coventina might go, I get up. After getting his laundry going downstairs, I return to the apartment, order pizza, and get to work.

Chapter 42

CASPIAN

I walk through the door to my apartment. It's dark except for the small light over the oven. Talli must be asleep. That's good. I had hoped she would get some rest while I was working.

I know that her conversation with her parents must be about the fact that I am not a Hawk. They probably think I am just a toy for her to play with for a while and eventually tire of. I'm not sorry to disappoint them. I hated leaving her tonight, but if I always dropped everything and skipped work to be with her instead, that would look suspicious or obsessive. Neither is suitable for a real relationship.

Real. That word always cuts me deep when I think of it. Someone in a real relationship wouldn't lie about who they are. Yet here we both are.

I step around where I left my laundry basket earlier, but notice it's not there anymore. She must have moved it so I wouldn't trip. Walking farther into the apartment, ready to crawl into bed with her, I realize something feels off. I look around, trying to figure out what's got me on edge, and slowly realize everything is *extremely* clean. Quietly opening the cracked door to my bedroom, I see Talli curled up on my bed, covers tucked under her chin. She looks peaceful. I wonder if she has any other place where she feels truly at peace. Something tells me that she doesn't.

On my way to bed, I notice one of my dresser drawers is slightly open, so I go to push it back into place, but find neatly folded shirts staring back at me. I'm astonished. This woman did my laundry and scrubbed my apartment while I was working.

Is this what it's like to be in a long-term relationship? Rushing to the other when you're upset by something your parents said? Helping each other simply because you want to help? Leaving work knowing that you'll find a warm, gorgeous body in your bed?

I dispel those thoughts as soon as they come. A life with this woman, even if she didn't tell me the truth eventually about who she really is, would not look like this. It would be a lot of her randomly running off, having responsibilities she couldn't quite explain, and mysterious scars that appear. That is exactly what these last few months have been filled with. I know, because Matthew has informed me of every kill she has made. I have only received one text from my father in response: "Control her." But there is nothing I can do to keep her away from it.

What am I going to do? I have one more week left to start feeding my father real information, or he promised to come for both of us. I can't let that happen. He can do whatever he wants to me, but he won't get his hands on her. I rub my face with my hands and take a deep breath. I have no other choice but to tell her. She has to know that he is coming for her, and she has to run.

Tomorrow. I'll enjoy one last night with her, then I'll tell her tomorrow.

Getting out of my clothes, I climb into bed with Talli. She unfurls from her balled up position and reaches out to me, turning to face my chest. "You're home," she whispers.

"Yeah, I'm home, my heart," I reply, wrapping my arms around her as tightly as possible without disturbing her rest any more than I already have. She starts softly breathing again, and I know she's asleep. "Please, please hear me out tomorrow. I can't bear to lose you," I plead into her hair.

Hair tickles my nose, and I crack an eye open to see Talli's auburn strands streaked across my face, the smell of my shampoo wafting off of them. I gently move the hair out of my face and, turning to face her, I see the back of Talli's head, her breathing still soft and steady. I glance out the window, and the sun is high. I turn onto my side and wrap my arm around her stomach, tucking her up against me.

Her breathing shifts, and I know she is awake. She's awake and still very naked. She turns in my arms and looks at me. "Good morning," she says, a sleepy smile lighting her face.

"Good morning. Did you have a good, relaxing night last night?" I ask, not able to stop myself from bringing up what I found when I got home.

Her sleepy smile turns sheepish. "You noticed?"

"Yep."

"Even in the dark?"

"Even in the dark. You folded all my clothes in the drawers and cleaned my entire apartment."

"And color coordinated your shirts," she points out.

I laugh. "I should leave you alone in my apartment more often."

"You're not weirded out? Or bothered? I promise I didn't do it to snoop or anything. I just wanted to help."

"Why would that bother me? Now granted, I had hoped you would rest while I was gone, maybe watched a movie or something, but I can't say it wasn't a nice surprise coming home to a clean apartment and a naked you in my bed. A man could get used to such things," I tease, running my hand up and down her stomach and side. I let my hand gently brush up against her breast, but don't linger too long. That is also a tease I feel like inflicting at the moment.

Her eyes sparkle. "It may not have been resting, but it was therapeutic to clean and do your laundry. It helped me clear my head."

"Well, in that case, I'm glad I could help by having dirty laundry. You're welcome to do it anytime your head needs clearing in the future."

"I'll keep that in mind."

"Good. Now is the question of payment for all your hard work." I continue touching and teasing her, making her squirm. But her response catches me by surprise. "Help me avoid my parents for the next couple of days. Monday, I'm sure my dad will be expecting me home to start helping with the summer projects, but this weekend is mine and I don't intend to deal with them if I don't have to."

Summer projects. That is what she gave me as her reasoning for not taking classes this summer, as she had planned. But I know better.

Tell her today. My mind reminds me of the promise I made to myself before climbing into bed with her.

"I can do that. I have a few days off from work. What do you have in mind?" I ask, although my mind visualizes a prison cell or a knife to my throat.

"I don't know, but I want to do something different. Have some freedom," she explains with her nose scrunched in thought.

"Want to get out of town? We can go somewhere new. Get a nice hotel, eat some food, and do some exploring. I'm sure we don't have to drive too far to find a good spot." Somewhere just far away from other Hawks who will line up to watch my execution once I tell her. If I live that long.

Talli's eyes light up, and I know I made the right suggestion. I wonder if she ever leaves town for the fun of it, rather than obligation. Maybe I'll give her a day of fun, then break her heart.

"That would be perfect. I don't even care where we go, but let's go." Her smile is enough to shatter me. I love making her happy, and all I want to do is make her as happy as possible for as long as I can.

I cup her breast fully with my hand, and her eyes go from happy to sparkling. Her finger runs up my length, and I harden even more in response. Bringing my face close to hers, I announce, "I'm going to fuck you, then we can pack up my Jeep and you can pick anywhere on the map you want to go. As long as we can be there by tonight, so I can fuck you again on fancy hotel sheets."

She closes the remaining distance between our mouths and grabs hold of my cock, then says, "Deal" against my lips.

I don't need any further permission as I take her mouth in mine and say thank you for my color-coordinated shirts in many, many delicious ways. The last thank you I'll ever be able to say to her.

CHAPTER 43

TALLIANA

I DECIDED THAT I wanted to go to Acadia National Park. I've never been, and it seems like a perfect place to go to find some peace with Cas for just a couple more days before we have to face reality again.

Greer helped me sneak into the house unseen so I could pack a bag, and I promised her this would be the last time I would ask her to handle any triggered alarms by herself. While I did that, Cas sat in the car and booked us a place to stay, but he wouldn't tell me exactly where it was. The drive there is a few hours long, though, and despite my reassurances that I'd be fine, I can sense Coventina lazily flying far above us, unwilling to let me too far out of her sight.

"Can't that machine go any faster? This is boring, having to loop around because I cannot physically fly that slowly," she gripes in my mind.

"This vehicle can go faster, but not much, and if it did, Cas would be breaking the law. Can't you fly ahead and wait for us there?"

"No."

"Alright then, mother hen, stop complaining. This is vacation for me and I want to enjoy myself."

I faintly realize Cas is talking to me, so I shut Coventina out the best I can and ask him, "I'm sorry, what did you say?"

He lets out a little laugh and asks, "Where do you go when you do that?"

"Do what?"

He gives me a brief, pointed look, indicating that he is not oblivious, but answers, "Zone out."

"I'm sorry. I try not to, especially when I'm with you. It's just hard to get out of my mind sometimes."

"Are you still thinking about your parents?"

I internally cringe at the thought. "No, actually." I smile at him, then continue, "Thinking about how excited I am to get away with you. How this is a vacation for me, my first one in a really long time."

"Be careful, say stuff like that and I'll start trying to pull you away every chance I get to run away for a weekend."

"You can't, though. If you do, I'll become spoiled and lazy, then you won't love me anymore," I fake-whine at him.

"It's not possible," he responds plainly.

"Which one? Me becoming lazy, or you no longer loving me?"

"Both. You have the energy level of a bunny rabbit, and I...well, I just can't get enough of your white cotton tail."

Giggling uncontrollably, my smile brightens when his warm hazel eyes meet mine. Too quickly, though, they turn back toward the road. This man could make me lose my mind with the things he says, the way he makes me feel, and how he makes me laugh.

"Hmm...a big tasty carrot does sound real good right about now," I muse right as he takes a sip of water. He spits it out all over his steering wheel, as laughter rumbles out of him.

He wipes the water off his face with the back of his hand, then he takes the napkins I offer to wipe off the steering wheel. "You are going to pay for that," he warns, and I can't help but laugh harder.

We arrive at our destination a short while later. I'm surprised to find that the hotel is not just a hotel but a resort. A very nice resort that looks like it was once a large manor. Cas parks the car in the front and doesn't hesitate as he hands his key to the valet before grabbing our bags from the back.

Stunned into silence—not a frequent occurrence for me—I follow his lead as he politely declines the bellhop's offer to take our two duffle bags from us, then heads into the lobby. The resort is not over the top, per se, but it's certainly the nicest place I've ever stepped foot in. My eyes can't help but take in all the different elements as we make our way to the front desk. It was definitely once a home for a very wealthy family; there are still some old touches that appear original, like beautifully crafted crown molding and thin-planked wood floors. Whoever turned this place into a resort did a great job furnishing it too, with furniture that matches the time period of the home, but reupholstered in soft blues and creams to feel fresh and clean instead of dark and old.

The woman at the front desk smiles at Cas much too brightly for my taste, as she hands him two room keys. Actual keys instead of keycards. Her small nose is barely holding up the glasses that are perched at the edge of it. Her obnoxious giggle at Cas's simple "thank you" makes them tumble off her face, and I have to suppress a laugh as she scrambles to catch them before they fall to the ground.

Cas leads me up a winding staircase to our room. As if this situation couldn't get any crazier, he takes me to a suite on the top floor. He opens the door, and we walk into a room bigger than his apartment. There is a large living space, dining area, kitchenette, bedroom with a private balcony overlooking the ocean, and, to my absolute glee, a bathroom with a huge jetted tub. I walk out of the bathroom and back into the bedroom where he is standing at the end of the king-size bed, waiting for me, arms folded across his chest.

"You haven't said a word since we got here. I'm not sure if I should be worried or pleased." He lifts an eyebrow at me, waiting for my response.

"How did you afford this?" I ask, sweeping my arms around.

Cas unfolds his arms and quietly laughs. "There it is." He shrugs and answers, "I make a lot of good tips, and I have nothing better to spend the money on."

I snort. I have little doubt that all the single women at the club tip him very well. "This much money though? It had to cost a fortune for this room," I argue.

"Actually, it's not quite busy season here yet, and I might have used my father's business connections to get a good deal."

"Is he in the hospitality business?" I ask. Cas has never gone into detail about what his father does, just that he is a businessman.

He drops down onto the bed, sinking right into the massive white comforter. Then, looking at the ceiling, he explains, "He does real estate. He buys property and rents or sells it at a grossly high rate. He's friends with the man who owns this place, and my name is on a special guest list at all the hotels he owns. I didn't even ask for a suite, they just gave it to me."

I can feel Cas's discomfort from where I stand without any effort on my part. He doesn't like talking about his father, and from what little I know of the man, it seems to me that he is the exact opposite of Caspian. I plop down on the bed next to him, landing on my stomach. He looks over at me, and I make a decision. "Enough about parents. The room doesn't matter. The only thing that matters is the person I'm in it with."

He grins. "And that tub."

"And that tub," I agree.

He throws his arm around my waist and grabs me, pulling me on top of him, both our feet dangling over the edge of the bed. He kisses me once, then twice, then asks, "What do you want to do first?"

I think for a moment and look out the balcony doors. It's midafternoon and the weather is actually warm today, but I know the ocean will be freezing, like it typically is in New England. I'm also not in a rush to get back into the ocean after what happened to Greer a few months ago. I want to be in the water, though. "Is there a pool here?"

"Yes, and it's heated. Want to go for a swim?"

"Absolutely, and you're in luck: I brought my sexy swimsuit with me." I smirk at him.

His dimpled cheeks turn a little pink, but as cool as ever, he replies, "Let's hope there are no kids here this weekend."

We had the heated outdoor pool to ourselves and I felt entirely satisfied with my sexy swimsuit choice, because Cas looked hungry for me the entire time we were there. After a while, though, we headed back to the room to shower off and get ready for the dinner reservations Cas made for us. Dinner was delicious, but the walk on the moonlit rocky beach after it was perfect. With my sandals in one hand, Cas holding the other, the chilly water at my toes, and the moon feeling like a power source charging me up and soothing my soul all at the same time, nothing felt more right.

I could sense Coventina in the ocean close by, enjoying the change in food options. At one point, she leaped out of the water like a fucking dolphin, making Cas jump out of his skin. Thankfully, she was far enough away that I was able to convince him that it had to be a whale. It wasn't hard forcing a look of enchantment upon my face at the thought of a whale being close by, and he went along with it. I swore at her, though, for not using her glamour and forcing me to lie, but I clearly couldn't tell him that it was just a water dragon—a dragon I talk to, ride on, and who amplifies my magic. Magic he doesn't know I have. I feel like I'm digging a hole deeper every day. Maybe once I tell him the truth, I can bury myself in it.

When we get back to the room, Cas excuses himself to use the bathroom, and I can't help but open the balcony doors and lean against the handrail to soak in more of the moonlight. Closing my eyes and listening to the crash of the waves, I breathe deep, and when I open my eyes again, a star shining brighter than all the others catches my eye. It's as if it's sitting right there just for me, like a firefly once did long ago...

Closing my eyes once more, focusing on the star, I whisper softly, "Please, let me keep him." It's a silly, selfish wish, but I have to try. I want him to choose me, the real me, once he learns the truth. Before I can open my eyes again, arms snake around my waist. I feel Cas's lips press into my hair. "God, I think you were made to be in the moonlight. You are breathtaking in it."

I lean my head back to rest on his shoulder, and he pulls me wholly against him, supporting my weight as I let him take control. I decide to ask cautiously, "Do you believe in magic?"

His body goes rigid for a flicker of a moment, and then it relaxes again. "I believe there is magic in love. Love bewitches you, holds you captive, and makes you do impossible things. I believe that when I touch you or hear your laugh, I can fly on that love alone."

Turning in his arms, I wrap my arms around his neck. "Do you believe love can overcome any obstacle?"

"Absolutely."

There is no hesitation. The truth bubbles up on my tongue, and I want to say it, to confess everything right here and now. His warm eyes seem to be begging me to give in, give in to the urge. So much patience and understanding waiting right there, willing to accept me. I open my mouth, but he speaks before I get the chance to.

"You're cold," he observes, pulling back to rub some warmth into my arms. "It's really starting to cool down outside. Why don't we go in and start a bath?"

With both the moment and my nerve gone, I simply nod and let him lead me inside.

CHAPTER 44

TALLIANA

"*TALLIANA!*" THE SCREAM IN my mind wakes me up, and I jolt upright in bed. The resort bed. It's our second night here.

"*The community is under attack. Balcony now!*" Coventina yells.

I feel utter dread surge through my veins, and I scramble out of bed, grasping around in the dark for my clothes. I stub my pinky toe on the reading chair in the corner of the room and curse under my breath.

"Talli? What's going on?" Cas's voice is frantic, confused.

"I have to go. I'll explain later."

"What? Where? Let me go with you." He gets out of bed and turns the nightstand light on.

"There's no time. This is a family matter, and I need to go. I'll explain later." I plant a quick kiss on his lips and run out the balcony door. I climb over the rail and jump. Coventina isn't wearing her saddle, so I squeeze my legs tight around her as she flies off into the night toward home.

Damn it! There is no getting around this now. I'll have to tell him everything. That knowledge fills me with a mix of immense relief and undeniable terror.

I feel a buzz in my head, and I know Coventina has connected me to Greer and Draven. *"Greer! Draven! I'm on my way. What's going on?"* I ask down the connection.

No answer.

"Hello?!" I try again.

"We're busy," Draven grounds out.

Coventina speeds up, and I nearly tumble off her back. I lean my body down along hers, grasping the bottom horns, trying to make myself as small as possible so the wind doesn't catch me again. Twenty agonizing minutes pass before I see the smoke. I raise my hands high and form rain, and as soon as we get close enough to the engulfed house, I send it down in a rush. Once all the flames have vanished, we descend to the street where Greer and Draven are, along with a small crowd of emergency officers.

Pale blonde hair catches my eye, and I realize Ms. Trisha is kneeling on the ground, back toward me, with someone lying in front of her. Seth is beside her, head hanging. In my haste to put out the fire, I didn't realize which house it was.

No. No. NO.

Running as fast as I can, I reach them and see it's Mr. Simon on the ground. He's covered in black soot and badly burned...everywhere. I check for a pulse with my senses, but there's nothing there. I drop to my knees on the other side of his body and scream, "Water!"

Ms. Trisha looks up at me, soot smeared on her face and clothes, but otherwise unharmed, and says with a strained voice, "Talliana. He's gone."

"Just let me try!" Tears start streaming down my face as I feel my heart crack.

A bucket of water appears next to me, and I don't hesitate. I push the water into his chest and focus it over his lungs, clearing out all the smoke inside. I pull another ball of water from the bucket and work it over the burns, willing his skin to regenerate. When nothing seems to work, desperation tears at me, and the darkness rises to the surface. I push more water into his body using the boost in power the darkness is giving me, searching for somewhere that needs healing, something that I overlooked, something that is preventing him from being okay. My body shakes violently, causing me to lose control of the water I currently have under my grasp. I turn back to the bucket, but it's empty.

"No...not him." I turn my face up toward the sky and scream to the Great Hawk, wherever he is, "NOT HIM!"

A hand covers my shoulder and I sense Reef, of all people, behind me. "Talli," he calls softly.

Placing my hands over my face, I sob into them. *This is my fault*. I wasn't here. I should have been here.

Reef's arms wrap around me, and he pulls me to his chest. I have no fight left to refuse or to pull away from him. I let him hold my body together, while grief destroys me from the inside.

Why him? Why this sacrifice? Who's next? My parents? Greer? Ash? Cas?!

No. *They can't have him.*

I feel soft fur against my leg, and I look up to see Seth lying against me. Ms. Trisha is now gone, and so is Mr. Simon's body. Very few people are left around us. Greer and Ash are sitting together on the street a few feet away, both of their eyes glassy, with Draven and Coventina standing next to them. Dad and Mr. Waterstone are murmuring to each other a little ways away.

Remembering myself, I pull away from Reef and stand to my feet, wiping away as many tears as possible. Everyone seems to follow suit, standing as well. They were all waiting for me. Dad approaches, but doesn't pull me into his arms like I expect. Instead, disappointment hardens the lines of his face, and he scolds, "You should have been here."

Feeling as though I have been slapped, I stumble back, but Seth is right there on one side, and then I feel Reef catch my arm on the other. Once I am steady, Seth growls at Dad, and Reef says, "It's not fair to put this on her."

Coventina is behind Dad in an instant, lowering her head and growling too. Greer and Ash, reading the scene, move to my side as well. Dad's frown deepens as he realizes he is surrounded, but before he can say more, Mom enters the scene. "That's enough, Aaron." She pushes him away and out of the dangerous situation he put himself in.

Everyone seems to relax, and Mr. Waterstone approaches Seth from the side. "Seth, why don't you come home with me for a while? Lemon will be happy to let you borrow one of her dog beds for as long as you need," he says to the German shepherd.

Seth sits down in front of me and shakes his head. I move toward him, and he nuzzles his snout into my hand. "Do you want to come home with me?" I ask.

He swings his gaze to Coventina, and she answers for him, "*Yes. He believes his place is with you now.*"

Lowering myself to the ground again in front of him, I stroke his head. "I promise to take care of you for as long as you want me to." He puts his head on my shoulder, and a few more tears slip out from my eyes. I stand again and announce to everyone, "Seth will stay with me. There is no need to find him a new home. I'll take care of him."

No one questions the decision, at least not tonight. Mr. Waterstone responds, "I'll grab some dog food from the house and bring it over for you."

I nod in thanks, and he quickly departs. Then I turn to Reef, noticing he is covered in soot. "Are you hurt?"

"Don't worry about me, princess."

I want to argue, but instead, I utter words I never thought I would. "Thank you."

He bows his head slightly, not in a mocking gesture, but in a kind one. "I'm at your service. Anytime you need it."

"He's the one who pulled Mr. Simon out," Greer explains, coming up from behind me. I turn back around to watch Reef walk away, now noticing the angry red burn covering his left elbow. He's a Water Elemental, and he ran into a fire. Being surrounded by fire is the worst situation a Water Elemental could ever experience, because there is no water in the air. It's like being stripped of magic entirely. I immediately try to run after him, but Greer catches my arm and shakes her head.

I pull out of her grasp and run to him anyway. Reef turns at the last second in time to catch me in his arms. I hug him tightly, then pull away. "I will never forget tonight. You are a good man, Reef. You will always have my loyalty and friendship." Pulling the tears from my face, I grab his arm and will the water to heal the burn on his elbow.

Before he can say anything, I run back to Greer and Ash, and we all head back to the house. When it looks as if Ash might change directions to go to his house with his parents, I grab his hand and say,

"Please stay with us. I want everyone I love under the same roof for the night."

His smile is sad as he replies, "Aside from Cas."

"He is safer where he is right now." Ash puts his arm around me in response.

Greer and Ash climb into her bed, and Seth jumps in bed with me, curling up at my feet. Coventina and Draven find a spot on each of our nightstands. We turn off the lights, but I can't sleep. Too much grief fills my chest. No amount of ice can keep it at bay. And as much as Dad's words hurt, he was right. If I had just been here...

The next morning, we quietly sit around the dining room table, waiting for Mom to finish making breakfast. I offered to help, but she wouldn't let any of us do anything more than sit and wait. No one acknowledges what Dad said last night, or says anything about where I was instead of being here. We all just simply exist in mournful silence until Dad's phone buzzes. He checks it and looks up at me. "Caspian is here. They are sending him through the gates now."

My stomach flips, but I nod. I hadn't told anyone about how I jumped off a balcony right in front of Cas and promised to explain everything to him. It was reckless, so very reckless of me. But I couldn't think past getting to the community, and I didn't want him to think I had woken up and decided to jump to my death after having a perfect day with him, one that cost me greatly.

I need more time.

I want him to know, I really do, but what if the Brethren find out about him and go after him? Am I damning him to our fate by telling him about us? About me? I feel like I am stuck in a whirlpool, spinning and spinning around the same fears, changing my mind as frequently as my body is changing position.

A couple of minutes later, I hear a knock at the door. Standing up from my seat, I walk over to answer it. Cas is standing there looking disheveled and exhausted, my phone and bag in his hands.

"Hey." I shut the door behind me and lean back against it.

"Hey." He hesitates, looking me over for new scars and injuries, something he has done a lot lately. He eventually extends my stuff to me, and I gently take it from him.

"Thank you. I'm sorry about running out on you last night. I meant to call you right after breakfast using Greer's phone." I stuff my phone into the pocket of my fluffy bathrobe and toss the bag to the side.

Cas grabs my hands as soon as they are empty and pulls them up against his chest. He searches my eyes and asks, "Are you okay?"

"No."

He pulls me to him and wraps his arms around me. "I was so worried about you," he admits into my hair. "You jumped off a balcony, four stories off the ground. I flew down the stairs and searched for you outside. I was terrified I would find..."

Pulling away, I guide him to a wooden bench on our porch. We sit, and he retakes one of my hands. I look at them for a moment, then start, "A very close family friend passed away last night. I was in a rush to get home. I didn't mean to scare you."

His eyes fill with anguish and regret. "I'm so sorry, my heart. I understand your need to run home, but I don't understand anything else about what happened. I quickly packed our stuff, checked out, and drove straight here. But I didn't know if I would even find you here."

"I'm so sorry, Cas. There is so much you don't understand about me, and I want to tell you everything. I—"

His eyes find mine. "Then tell me. Let me understand you."

My entire self is conflicted. This beautiful, perfect man is in front of me, bearing his heart to me just for me to break it. Last night was a wake-up call. I have been so focused on falling in love that I wasn't where I should have been. I failed my people. I failed Mr. Simon, the man who has always been on my side and has spent so much of his time helping me become the person I am today. He was a second father to me.

Tears begin streaming down my face, and Cas instantly pulls me back into his arms. "I didn't mean to make you cry." His strong voice wavers.

I don't know how to do this. I can't do this. I take in another deep breath and push away. "Cas...I told you once that death follows me, and it comes for those I love. I don't know how to keep being selfish and keep you. I love you too much to let something bad happen to you because of me."

"No," he responds firmly.

"No?"

"No. You have tried pushing me away before over this belief. I won't let you do it again. I am a grown man who can choose for myself to take whatever risk you think there is in loving you."

He runs his hands through my hair and pulls my head close to his until I am staring into his eyes. "No," he repeats softly and pulls my lips to his. His warm mouth captures mine, giving me a hundred reasons not to push him away. With every slide of his tongue against mine, the little bit of strength I have buried inside of me deteriorates.

"Take some time to be with your family. Grieve, do whatever you need to do, then find me. I also need to tell you something, and there isn't much time left." He kisses me again and then walks back to his Jeep.

I bury my face in my hands.

Chapter 45

CASPIAN

I should have let her end things and walk away from me, but I panicked.

It would have been a clean break for both of us. She would have been able to leave with fond memories of me and the love we share, but I couldn't let her go.

When I saw the hesitation in her eyes and felt the slight tremble in her hand, I knew she was about to break both of our hearts. It was the worst feeling I've ever felt, but I know it will pale in comparison to the hatred and betrayal that I'll see in her eyes when I tell her the truth.

When she left last night in a panic, I knew something horrible had happened. The fear on her face told me that my people were responsible. I immediately called Matthew, and he informed me there was an attack on the Massachusetts Community, and none of the men made it out alive. I was so angry I wanted to lash out at him, but he had nothing to do with it. He is the only one willing to keep me informed about what is happening, so I forced myself to thank him and hang up.

What I can't figure out, though, is how she knew something had happened and how she got home without a car. I left maybe thirty minutes after she did, and yet she was in her pajamas and seemed foggy from a fitful sleep. I have never heard of an ability or magic making it so people could fly, but my mind keeps conjuring a broomstick, like that is the only plausible answer.

I'm facing my apartment door now, in the process of contemplating how I'm going to sleep at all the next week without Talli close when I realize my door is unlocked.

What the...?

I open the door and find Humphrey and Donald sitting on my couch, the two most idiotic men I have ever met. My eyes immediately zero in on Humphrey's finger, where he is twirling around a pair of Talli's underwear. It takes all my self-restraint not to snarl at the man. Instead, I shut the door behind me and demand, "What the hell are you two doing here? Do you want to compromise my mission?"

"Oh, you mean the mission where you play house with your little whore of a witch? I can't say that I blame you. I would hit that too before I tied her to a tree and lit her on fire," Humphrey drawls, and I contemplate killing them both right now, whatever consequences I face from my father be damned.

I march up to Humphrey instead, rip the underwear off his finger, and stuff it in my pocket where it can be kept safe.

"You're out of line, soldier. I am your commanding officer, and you will answer my question with respect, or I will stain this cheap carpet with your blood."

"You're dramatic, you know that?" Humphrey replies. He gets to his feet and walks around the other side of the couch. "Your father wants to see you. Now. We are here to escort you."

"Tell me where he is, and I will escort myself."

"Those weren't our orders."

"Fuck your orders."

Donald lifts the phone to his ear and says, "He's being difficult."

He pulls the phone away and touches the screen. I hear my father's low, dangerous voice say over the speaker, "Caspian, get in the fucking car and come see me now. Your time is up."

My jaw clenches. "Yes, sir." The phone disconnects, and I follow the two men to their car without a fight.

It's an uncomfortable flight to Colorado. My father owns four airplanes and a team of two pilots to fly them. The excessive number of planes allows them to be swapped out frequently, preventing the Hawks from easily tracking us. The pilots seem like good men who got offered too much money to turn down, but now that they are ours, there is no leaving. My father would kill them without hesitation if they tried to leave. That is the case with any Brethren, whether they came to us for the cause, the money, or a thirst to spill blood. Those who try to back out end up dead themselves, or their family is threatened if my father thinks they are valuable.

This is not going to be a friendly conversation. In my father's eyes, I have taken too long to get information from Talli. In my eyes, I've taken too long to tell her the truth and warn her about my father. I was going to tell her yesterday, as we sat atop that rocky overlook, taking in the sight of the trees and water below us. But I didn't want to ruin the perfect moment— that's what I told myself, anyway. The reality is, I'm a coward, and I am going to have to do everything I can to convince my father to give me more time—more time to warn her. If by some miracle I manage it, I'll run to her and tell her everything.

If my father doesn't like my excuse for not fully earning her trust yet, then he can pull the plug on all this and throw me in a cell to rot. But he has invested a lot into this, and I don't think he will give up that easily. No. He will force me to do something to push the situation. I have no doubt he sent these two idiots to drag me to him so he can share his new plan with me, then send me back to do his dirty work.

I can't show him how much she means to me. I need to lock everything down inside and play the role of a good son who is willing to do whatever his father asks. A son who didn't fail his mission. A son who isn't in love with the woman he swore to destroy. A son that is nothing like me.

I nervously run my fingers through my hair over and over as I wait outside my father's office for his meeting to adjourn. I have been here for thirty minutes already, and it takes another fifteen before the office door opens and the sound of laughter pours out along with the men. Perhaps this means my father is in a good mood.

Not for long, I think dryly.

I am standing with my hands now firmly clasped together behind my back, and I nod my acknowledgement to each of the men who are leaving the meeting. My father walks out, a slight limp in his step, speaking quietly to the last man to leave. He nods his farewell to him and looks up to see me. His face immediately hardens. Without a word, he motions me into his office and follows behind me, shutting the door before walking around and placing both hands on his desk. His eyes bore down into me before he asks, "How am I not surprised you missed your deadline?"

"Father, I'm close. Give me one more month. I promise I'll have information for you by then."

"Do you think you're clever enough to fool me? Do you think I haven't been watching you? You're stalling because you are in love with her," he accuses me, and I pray the look on my face isn't as terrified as I feel.

"Of course not, Father. You're just seeing my act," I try to explain.

"I am your general, boy. You don't deserve the right to be my son right now."

My body tenses, but I try to lie. "Yes, I've gotten caught up in how beautiful this witch is a handful of times, but I know it's just her evil magic messing with my mind. I still understand my mission and its importance. General, I am loyal to the Brethren. Tell me what you want me to do, and I will see it through." Each word tastes like dirt in my mouth, but the sharp edges in his features smooth out ever so slightly. I keep myself from breathing out a sigh of relief as he watches me for a moment with narrowed eyes.

"One more month. If I don't have information by then...well, you don't want to know the consequences," he warns.

"Thank you, General," I bow my head and turn to leave, but his voice stops me. "I'm not done with you." I turn back around and clench my fists to hide the shaking in my hands.

"I'm going to help you speed things along." I see him press the button on the edge of his desk, calling his guard in. I barely have a chance to turn around and take a step before I have four men surrounding me. I turn back around to my father, no longer able to hide my anger.

"What's the matter, Major? I am helping you. You will play damsel in distress, and she will come for you. After that, she will have no choice but to tell you everything. Easy." He turns his back on me, then says over his shoulder, "The time in the cell will also give you a chance to remember where your loyalty truly lies."

Talliana. My loyalty lies with her without a doubt.

Hands grip both of my arms and pull me toward the door. Managing to get one arm free, I punch one of the guards in the throat. He steps back, hunched over, half-gasping, half-gagging. "I can walk myself to the cells," I snarl at him, but more guards grab onto me, failing to drag me out of my father's office.

"Wait!" my father calls. "Give me his phone."

One of the guards reaches into my front pocket, pulls out my cell, and hands it to my father before he slams his door in my face.

I killed him. Klaus is dead, and my son is safe from his abuse. The darkness saw him push my son too hard this time, and it killed him in the blink of an eye with a sharp slice of water across his neck. It happened so fast, and I wasn't prepared to run. Panic overtook my senses, and I tried to leave anyway, but I was seen at the gates with blood on my face. Will this be the end to the horrors in my life, or just the beginning?

- Journal of Katarina Lehmann

CHAPTER 46

TALLIANA

IT HAS ONLY BEEN two days since I let Cas walk away to give me so-called time, but I already feel desperate for him. For his comfort and warm smile. I sit at the edge of the lake, letting my toes circle the water below me. My mind has been a slew of emotions. One minute, I'm sure I have made a decision, and then the next, I have made a completely different one. I've never felt more lost. I look up toward the moon, hoping it will provide answers, but of course, it doesn't do any more than light up the sky above me.

I sense Greer and Ash approaching behind me, and they both sit down on either side of me. Caging me in so I can't escape, I suspect.

"Trisha stopped by the house a few minutes ago looking for you. Gave me this." Greer flashes Katarina's journal at me. I figured it was lost in the fire, but I couldn't bring myself to care past that. Mr. Simon must have put it in his fireproof safe.

I'd rather have Mr. Simon than a journal any day.

"Thanks," I force myself to say, and watch as she hands it to Ash to put in his backpack for safekeeping.

"Want to tell me what it is? I know you have been training extra with Mr. Simon for the last few months. Is that what it's about?"

"He was helping me learn control over the darkness. That journal has answers on how to achieve it," I admit.

I feel Greer's arm flex where it is resting against mine, and as if he has no self-control, Ash pulls it back out of his backpack and starts looking at it closer.

"Without me? I should have been involved," Greer scolds.

"Greer, I don't want to talk about this right now. I just want to be alone," I tell her.

"That's not true. You want to be with him."

I get to my feet, forcing myself out from between them, and stomp off a few feet before whirling on her, letting all of my anger and self-hate find the target it was looking for. "He was meant to be a distraction—a temporary escape from the horrors, from the grief, from the guilt. Is that so wrong? To try to enjoy what little time I have left with someone I have fallen so deeply in love with that I can hardly breathe when he isn't close to me? I thought maybe I could have this one thing for a little while, but I can't even have that. I can't have him. If I don't end this now, he'll be another sacrifice on my growing list. I have given this war so much and won't stop until I have given it EVERYTHING. But not Cas. I'll give up my time with him if it means saving his life."

Greer's eyes widen, and I sense her heart starting to beat faster. Faster. Faster. She stands to her feet and breathes, "How did I not see it?"

I freeze, realizing too late that my words revealed the one thing that I hadn't planned on sharing with anyone, not even the most important people in my life. Ash stands, too, looking between us wildly.

"You don't plan to make it out of this war alive."

My silence continues to damn me, but I can't lie and tell her that she is wrong.

Her anger visibly rises. "No, Talli. You do not get off that easily! I'm your shadow, remember? It's my job to make sure you don't die."

"Dad should never have put that on you. That is not fair to you!" I scream back.

"It wasn't just Dad. That is *my* destiny. That is *my* role in all of this. It always has been. My father told me in that letter that I am meant to *help* end this war, and why else would I get a shadow ability unless it is to aid you? I'm not going to work so hard to keep you safe just to watch you die at the end. If you want to become a martyr so bad, then you'll have to do it knowing that I'll go down with you. If you fall, then I fall too, remember?"

"That's not what I want!"

"Then figure out what you want because I swear it changes every fucking day! Let me know what you decide so that I can break Ash's heart now and save him from feeling my death too deeply later."

"You both are breaking my heart right now! Quit arguing!" Ash hollers at us.

Ignoring him completely, I snarl back at Greer, "You're unbelievable. We just lost one of the most important people in our lives, and you're making this about me." My voice cracks, and tears start to flow freely down my face for the hundredth time today.

"Talli, everything has always been about you, whether you want it to be or not. That will never change. But stop making the mistake of thinking that you're the only one trapped here. I am just as trapped as you are. I am sacrificing just as much as you are. You may be responsible for everyone else's lives, but I'm responsible for yours."

"Well, you've done a shit job, because Cas has given me more reasons to live these past several months than you have." I regret the words the moment they fly past my lips. But instead of facing it, I stomp down the path. The darkness swirls restlessly inside of me, ready to explode. I'm trying to breathe and fill my heart with love like Mr. Simon taught me, but I have no strength to do either. I need to get away from Greer, before...

"Of course, do what you're best at. Run away and hope someone else solves your problems for you," Greer calls after me.

The darkness puts a vice grip on my heart, my very dim heart, and any control I have slips.

I want to hurt her. I want to hurt her for hurting me. I stop thinking.

Water from the lake surges toward me, then around me, making a whirlpool ready to destroy everything in its path. My hands are thrown in Greer's direction, and I watch as the water I hurtle at her splashes off the shadows she has surrounded herself and Ash with.

She bares her teeth at me and wraps a rope of shadow around Ash, pulling him away from us. More water surrounds me, and the darkness tries to pound her with it like a thrown fist. It gets a good hit to her chest, and she goes flying back into the lake. Ash is in front of me, saying something, but my darkened eyes only narrow on him.

"Ash! No!" Greer's voice breaks through the ringing in my ears. She sounds scared and desperate. Then I force my body to turn toward her to see her clawing through the water, trying to get back to land. I look back at Ash, who is standing his ground. "Talli, come back to us." His voice is like a faint whisper, but I hear it.

The darkness's grip on my heart loosens just enough for clarity to find me. I pull more water toward myself, careful to snake it around Ash and form a cocoon to lock myself inside. The coldness I feel in my chest is a sharp bite, and I will it into existence, turning the water around me into ice.

Now that Greer and Ash are safe from the darkness—from me—I slump to my knees and scream, dispelling as much rage and anguish as possible. Then I breathe. In and out. In and out. I focus on Cas. The unmistakable connection I feel toward him. The love that keeps trying to heal my broken heart. I think about Ash. My best friend, and someone with the purest intentions I have ever known. His bravery in standing between Greer and me, even though that is a trait that has never come naturally to him. Coventina. Draven. Mom. Dad, despite how pissed off I am at him right now. So many people whom I love. Greer. A girl who has lost so much in life, only to be faced with the idea of losing her sister, too. She must be terrified.

Just like I am.

The darkness completely lets go of its hold and I quickly create the cage around it again. I take my first deep breath and then assess my situation now that I am back in control. I'm trapped in the exact cage I use for the darkness when I am caging it inside of me. I don't know if I should feel relief that I managed to gain enough control to cage myself, or defeat that I even had to do it in the first place. And even though our fight only lasted a moment, it is clear that Mr. Simon was right. Greer can't stop the darkness. No one can except for me.

Something slams up against the dense ice.

"Talli! Are you okay? Talli, please answer me!" Greer is sobbing outside my cage. She rams it again.

I find my voice and answer shakily, "I'm okay."

"I'm so sorry, Talli. I shouldn't have pushed you like that. I didn't think...I didn't mean to push you to lose control." She's still sobbing.

"You're scared. I realize that now. I'm sorry for making you feel that way."

"I can't lose you, too. There has been too much loss, and I need you to live, Talli. I need you to want to live. If not for yourself, then for us."

"I want to live too," I quietly admit.

"Then fight like hell for it! There is nothing you can't do when you set your mind to it."

She's right. I decided a long time ago that I wanted to live, I wanted a life with Cas and my family after the war. But had I truly believed it was possible? No, I don't think I did. I've just always known that death would find me in the end. I *wanted* it to find me. But can I truly change my belief now? Is it possible that I can end this war without losing my life in the process?

"Can you get out?" It's Ash this time. I see the dark shape of his hand resting on the ice.

"I don't know. I have never made ice this thick before," I reply.

"Should I go get someone?" Ash asks.

"*You can get out of this. Focus,*" Coventina tells me.

"No, let me try to get myself out first. Back up, both of you. I don't want to accidentally hurt you."

I sense their heartbeats fading away until I can hardly sense them anymore. I stand on exhausted legs, do as my bonded says, and focus. I try to feel the water in the ice. I ask it to move. Slowly, cracks form in the thick walls, and the whole thing rotates around me until the ice eventually changes back to liquid. I drop it, letting it splash to the ground.

Greer and Ash approach me carefully, but before I can tell them that it's okay, I'm knocked over, flat on my back. I put a finger to my lip, expecting to find blood, but there is nothing there. I could have sworn something just struck me in the face.

I feel both of their hands help to pull me to my feet. "Talli, what happened?" Greer asks me frantically.

"I..." My knuckles sting, and I look down at them, but nothing is there. I stare out at the water while the wind starts blowing viciously around me. Coventina appears, swimming toward the shore fast.

"*Fuck you.*" Cas's voice fills my head, and the ice I just willed away chills my blood instead.

This can't be happening.

Not again. Not now. NOT HIM.

I turn immediately toward Greer's and Ash's bewildered expressions. Draven lands behind them. "It's Cas," I choke out. Coventina is behind me, and I reach back to her and climb on her back. She flies without hesitation. Knowing Greer and Draven are behind us, I try my best to focus on Cas, but I don't feel anything anymore.

In a few short minutes, we reach the roof of his apartment, and I run down the steps to his door. It's locked, which I find to be a mild comfort. Greer pushes in front of me and uses her shadows to unlock it. I burst in and find nothing—no Cas. Nothing is out of place. No signs of struggle. Maybe he is at the club? Maybe what I am sensing is a fight at the club, and not what I think.

I reach into my pocket and call his phone. The line connects, and relief floods my anxious veins. It must have all been a mistake. "Cas? Where are you?"

"Caspian is busy at the moment. Can I take a message?" A foreign voice asks.

My breath catches, and my hands start to shake. Not a fight at the club.

"That's right. I have your human. If you want him back in one piece, you must listen to me very carefully," the voice says.

"You don't know who you are messing with," I warn.

"I know exactly who you are, Ms. Hoffman. I wouldn't be surprised if your sister is also there with you as we speak. General Campbell sends his love, by the way." I look at Greer and put the phone on speaker.

I ground out between clenched teeth, "What do you want?"

"You, of course. Or rather, what you can tell us. You do as I say and answer my questions, then we'll let your human pet go."

"I will answer three questions, then you let him go. After I'm sure of his safety, then you can do what you want with me," I offer. Greer gives me an angry look, but she holds her tongue. She knows better than to argue.

"If you come without a fight and answer three questions for us honestly, then you have a deal, and we will let him go."

"Deal," I agree quickly.

"Perfect. I'll send the details to your phone."

The line cuts off, and I look to Greer, but neither of us says a word. This place could be bugged. We leave the apartment behind and climb to the roof. Once we reach the top, my phone receives a text.

Unknown Number: *Glenna Park. Midnight. Come alone, or he dies.*

Stuffing the phone back into my pocket, I climb onto Coventina and head back home. I have one hour.

"The attack on the community. It must have been meant as a distraction to grab Caspian. Only he wasn't at his apartment last night," Greer guesses through our connection.

She's probably right, and the idea that Mr. Simon died because the Brethren decided to try to trap me again makes me sick to my stomach. *This really is all my fault.*

"*What are you planning to do?*" Greer asks.

"*I'm going for a swim.*" The fact is, my magic is depleted quite a bit. I'm still not fully restored from trying to heal Mr. Simon, as I haven't been sleeping, and then there was that fight with Greer, the darkness, and the ice cocoon I made...it all adds up. A swim in the lake will help restore some energy, although not as much as I'd like. But some is better than nothing.

"*Shit. Are you that depleted from earlier?*"

"*Putting a gauge on it, I'm at about thirty percent. Post swim, I should be at forty.*"

"*That low?!*"

"*It doesn't matter. Saving Cas does,*" I nearly growl at her.

"*Okay, what's the plan after the swim?*"

"*I'm going to slice them all to shreds.*"

CHAPTER 47

CASPIAN

I KNEW BEING THROWN in a cell was a possibility, but this is so much worse than I could have imagined. My heart lurches at the knowledge that she will come for me. My father is right about that. It's the perfect plan. She won't have a choice but to tell me the truth. It's either that or wipe my memory with that potion they like to use on our men. Regardless of her choice, I will lose her in the end.

I hold a torn piece of my shirt to my bleeding lip, hoping it will stop soon. My father's men left a little while ago after trying to rough me up, claiming it was for the good of the act, but the assholes were happy to do it. I'm sure they enjoyed taking someone who has always bested them down a notch. I fought back, and even though I was outnumbered three to one, they look a lot worse than I do. If someone from outside the cell hadn't produced a gun, I would have killed all three of them. The Brethren are no longer my people.

A smug grin slides across my face as I think about the arm I snapped, but it disappears when, to my annoyance, I realize I'm not alone anymore. Standing in front of my cell with a broad smile plastered on his face is Sergeant McTavish. I fucking hate this guy. A complete kiss-ass to my father and someone who has always tried to make me fail.

"Ah, McTavy, how's the missus? Does she miss me in her bed?" I've never slept with his wife, but she has made it clear more than once that she would welcome me with open arms if I ever wanted to. McTavish knows it, too. One of the very few wives who knows about her husband's job, and she's just as vicious as the man in front of me. Maybe even more so.

His grin disappears into a frown. "Watch your mouth, boy. Your father has given anyone permission to come in here and beat you to a pulp as long as you are still breathing at the end of it."

"Yes, but notice how, after the first three fine gentlemen that tried that had to be taken to the infirmary, no one has bothered me since. But please, be my guest. I'll gladly let you try to get a punch in."

"No, thank you." His tone drips with disgust, looking me over and clearly not seeing enough damage for his liking.

"What do you want then?" I ask dryly.

"You're being moved to a more romantic location for your date with your witch tonight." His satisfaction with the situation is palpable. Yeah, well, so is my anger. I launch to my feet from where I am sitting on the hard floor, take three wide steps toward him, and grab the bars, making him jolt backward out of reach. Coward.

"If anyone hurts her, I will kill all of you." I think on it for a moment, then I add wryly, "If she doesn't beat me to it." I have not seen Talliana in action before in person, and every time we have tried to get a video, it always vanishes or turns up ruined, but I have no doubt she is a force, given the number of bodies she always leaves behind.

She'll be okay, I reassure myself. She has to be okay.

"Yes, well, your father wanted me to lay out the rules. You play by them, and she won't be hurt. Too badly, anyway. If you don't play by them, we will put a bullet in her head without hesitation," McTavish explains.

My jaw clenches. I wouldn't put it past my father to decide to kill her anyway, or use me to get information out of her first. I don't care what happens to me, and I won't let her give up her secrets or risk her family's lives for me either.

"I've made an arrangement with her that after she answers three questions, we will let you go. So, first, you will continue the act of a clueless boyfriend. Second, we will question her, and you will be full of fear the whole time, taking hits like a champ. Third, once I am done questioning her, you will be released as promised, and we will throw her in a cell. I suspect her people will rescue her, and we won't put up much of a fight. Then, you will complete your task. We will expect a piece of useful information every two weeks after the first month. If information is not received and we find out that you have told her anything, both of you will be dead." McTavish's words are clipped and direct, almost like he is pretending to be my father by speaking just like him.

When I narrow my eyes at him without a word, he adds, "Let me repeat myself. If you do anything to mess this up, we will put a bullet in her head. Do you understand?"

Through gritted teeth, I respond, "I understand, you piece of shit."

He snaps his fingers, and four men open the door to my cell and pull me out. They shove me unnecessarily through the halls, outside, and into a black SUV waiting to take me to Talli.

My stomach knots at having to continue tricking her, knowing that this act I will have to put on will be unforgivable once I find a way to tell her the truth safely. I can't think about that now, though. I need to get through this, keep us both safe. Then together, we will figure out the rest.

CHAPTER 48

TALLIANA

CASPIAN AND I HAVE spent a lot of time in Glenna Park. It's a wonderful place for a stroll or grabbing a bite of ice cream from the small stand that sets up every Saturday. Clearly, this spot was intended to show me how closely we have been watched.

Coventina and Draven land a mile north of the park. I dismount and look at Greer. "*Wait for my signal. Don't get trigger-happy because you start to worry.*"

"*I don't like this, so please be careful. Chief Lu should be leaving now with the troops,*" Greer replies.

Entering the park, I head for the parking lot on the other side, assuming that is where they will be. Sure enough, a black SUV is waiting for me. The back door slides open as I approach, and two men come out holding a whole lot of accessories for me to wear. The man in the driver's seat lowers his window and says, "Ms. Hoffmann, we are your chauffeurs for this evening's festivities. Please get in the van so we can take you to your date."

Fucking idiots think they're funny.

"Any attempt to fight or escape will be his death sentence. Do you understand?" The man adds. His voice is calm, borderline amused as he talks to me like I couldn't kill him in one second if I wanted to.

I breathe deeply, trying to calm myself, and nod once. The man closest to my right shoves a pair of iron mittens on me, forcing my hands into fists in order for them to clamp on. I've heard about these, but I've never seen them in person before. The Brethren think they can block magic, but they are sorely mistaken. Now the man to my left puts a cloth bag over my head.

Ick. This thing smells terrible.

Rough hands pat me down for weapons, then lead me into the van and onto the hard metal floor before I feel the truck driving off. I open up my senses and latch on to each man around me, feeling a mix of smug satisfaction, fear, hate, and—*gross*—arousal.

Oh, Cas. This isn't his fight. I never wanted him involved in any of this, but now he is. He is probably confused and afraid for me, if not *of* me yet, if he believes the lies that they are undoubtedly trying to fill his head with. Except, they don't have to lie. My power, the horror these men have witnessed me inflict upon their soldiers, needn't be exaggerated. Even if they don't talk to him, he is about to see my true nature, and all my secrets about who I am will be revealed.

I'm going to lose him.

I've been wallowing in fear for the last few days about needing to break up with him before he gets hurt, but it's too late. It has probably been too late for a while. I need to find a way to keep him safe after all this, because he'll be in danger until I end this war.

And they cannot have him.

I feel like I have been in this van for at least two hours, being tossed around like a sack of potatoes for the last fifteen minutes traveling on what feels like a dirt road. We come to an abrupt halt, and I nearly topple over but manage to keep myself upright. I hear the door slide open, and someone roughly grabs my upper arms, pulling me down a gravel path. I can smell the pine trees and hear the sounds of undisturbed creatures going about their lives around me, so we must be in a forest somewhere, at one of their cabins.

We stop for a minute, and I hear a door loudly creak as it opens a few paces ahead of me from what I can guess. I'm pulled inside, almost tripping over the entrance, where there is some raised trimming at the frame, then I'm stopped again. Someone finally pulls the bag off my head, and I'm left blinded by the startling light.

I blink away the last of the spots in my vision, and I don't even have to look around before I spot him. Cas, on his knees six feet away from me. I only sense that he is sore and minorly injured, bruising and a busted lip, but nothing major or life-threatening.

He makes a muffled sound as he tries talking through the gag in his mouth, fear pouring off of him. He jerks and struggles in the grasp of two guards holding onto his shoulders to keep him still.

I breathe through the rage, keeping my control in place. Then say as calmly as possible, "Cas, it's going to be okay." I lift my chin, and with the most stuck-up tone I can muster, I ask, "Well? I'm here. What questions do you asswipes want to ask me?"

The man to the left—we'll call him Dumb—moves to elbow me in the ribs, but I throw my body backward, releasing the other man's—we'll call him Dumber—hold on my arm, and I dodge the blow. Dumb stumbles with his miss, and I sweep out my leg, catching his and causing him to fall to his face.

"Try hitting me again and it will be more than your ego that gets bruised," I snarl.

Dumb scrambles to his feet, his pale face turning a dark shade of red, murder in his eyes as he starts to charge me.

"Stop," a deep voice, the one from the phone, rumbles through the room, causing Dumb to halt. Dumber quickly gets a grip on me again and stands at attention. I track the newcomer's every step as he enters the room. His scrawny frame, awkward mop of black hair, and nose the size of a boulder make him even uglier than Dumb and Dumber. But clearly, he has some level of authority here. He slithers forward until he is standing in front of me.

"Talliana Hoffman. I'm Arnold McTavish, your captor for this evening." His head gives a slight bow, and then he levels a look at me.

"Mr. McTavish, you're even uglier than your voice led on through the phone."

A small chuckle leaves him as if I said something amusing. "Cute. Your reputation for having a smart mouth precedes you. Glad to know that I have entrapped the right witch."

"Do you plan on chitchatting all night, or are you going to get on with your questions?"

"Impatient, too. What do you see in her?" He walks toward Cas and pats him on the head, eliciting a growl. I have never seen Caspian lose a grip on his anger before, not like this.

McTavish wrinkles his nose, removes his hand, and then says, "Maybe you two are made for one another."

He turns toward me again and nods at the guards. Dumb grabs the chain between my handcuffed hands, while Dumber grabs a chair from the corner. I take this moment to get a quick look around. We are definitely in a wooden cabin. The walls are all wood planks, and from what I can tell, it's primarily just this room, which contains a small couch, a table with two chairs pushed to the side, and a little kitchen in the farthest corner from me. There seems to be one attached room that looks small and dark from here, and that's pretty much all there is to see. There's nothing on the walls, no pictures or knick-knacks; it's mostly empty.

The chair Dumber was getting is behind me now, and he pushes me down onto it. Dumb and Dumber make quick work of tying my legs and arms down to the metal chair. The rope bites into my skin, but I don't even flinch. I just hold the staring contest I find myself in with McAsswipe. He is the first one to look away, and I almost smile in victory until I see him pull out a knife, and quicker than I can react, he slices into Caspian's arm.

I'm going to kill him. I repeat this like a mantra in my head, focusing on every word and its promise. The darkness pulses, begging to expand and snuff out the last bit of my control, but I push it back into its place.

Caspian doesn't move or react past a slight tensing in his shoulders and locks his eyes on me, telling me how much he loves me in that gaze. I return it, hoping he knows I'll do anything to save him, hoping he will not forget the love he feels now once I get us both out of this.

"What do you want to know?" I ask venomously.

"Everything. I want to know everything." His grin is wild, like the scent of Caspian's blood trickling down his arm made him feral.

"You need to be more specific than that," I force out.

He leans down in front of Caspian again and wipes his blade on his shirt. A shirt I see already has blood on it and is torn at the edge.

He stands back up and walks around me and my chair. I'll let him think that he is the predator here for now, but soon...soon, he will learn otherwise.

"Let's start small." He rubs his chin like he is thinking. "Your kind has different abilities, yes? What is your skill?"

Okay, I can answer that to an extent.

"I'm a Healer. I can sense people's pain and know exactly what's wrong without them telling me," I answer flatly.

Caspian's eyes widen, but McTavish smirks. "That's...adorable." He laughs out loud, prompting Dumb and Dumber to laugh with him.

I check in on Coventina, *"How's it coming?"*

"Lu is close."

"Last I recall, though, you also have an ice ability, is that right? My General seemed to recall such a thing," McTavish prompts.

I grin at him. "How's his leg?"

He frowns. "It's fine."

"I bet it's hurting him real bad. Pass along a message for me? Next time I see him, I'll make sure my ice cuts through his throat instead. To save him the pain of having an injured leg, of course."

He grabs my jaw with a vice grip, nails digging into my skin as he pulls my face close to his. "Perhaps your people are failing because they refuse to leash their women."

"I bet you don't say that to your wife." I look down pointedly at the small gold band around his ring finger.

His fingers dig in tighter. "My wife knows her place."

"And I also bet it's not in your bed."

He lets go of my face, but his palm connects with my cheek a moment later. The sting is uncomfortable but manageable. It was a weak hit from a weak man.

"Don't you touch her!" Cas erupts.

I look past McTavish to see that he has managed to get his gag out and is now fighting and struggling with the guards who were just holding him down. He head butts someone in the knee, and I'm worried that may have damaged him more than the other guy, but before I know it, he is on his feet and racing toward me. He doesn't reach me, though. Dumb and Dumber grab him and pull him away back to his spot, where his guards get a good hold of him again.

Pride swells in me at his reckless and downright stupid actions, but that man, that fighter, is *mine*.

McTavish strolls over to him and kicks him right in the gut. Cas doubles over onto his side, the wind knocked out of him, and McTavish kicks him again in the ribs.

I feel the crack of one of his ribs as if it happened to me, and it takes every ounce of willpower to hold still.

"Next question," I force out between my teeth.

To my relief, he turns away from Cas and back to me. "Where is that rain coming from? The one that appears almost every time we make an attack on the Northeast communities. Is it an ability? Technology of some kind? What?"

My stomach drops. Time to dance around this question. "Are the big, bad men scared of a little bit of rain?" I stick out my bottom lip in a mock pout. His hand raises again, and for Cas, I lie, "We have Water Elementals that can pull water from the atmosphere and Air Elementals who can move clouds. Do the math."

He lowers his hand and nods, apparently satisfied with the answer.

"Last question, and your pet can walk free. Got it?"

"Yes."

"Good. Now, tell me the source of your magic."

My eyes widen in shock as I stare at him. Seriously? This is what they are after? I can't help myself as I burst into laughter. "I can promise you it is not some magic well that you can throw some explosives down to end our magic. It is much more complicated than that."

McTavish does not look amused as he replies, "Enlighten me then."

I lean forward like I am about to share all my secrets, and to my delight, he leans in a little too, as I respond, "Our magic is connected directly to the devil. So you'd have to kill him if you want to kill us."

McTavish smirks, backing up a couple of paces, then turns toward Cas, and I lose control as he plunges his knife right into Cas's right thigh.

CHAPTER 49

CASPIAN

HER SCREAM SEEMS TO come from everywhere.

The two small windows are blown out by a blast of water, sending glass flying through the room. The men guarding her take the brunt of the impact, and they both fall forward, splashing and grasping at the glass lodged in the back of their heads. I look back up at Talli to find her breaking free of the iron gloves that look frosted over with ice, and her eyes...They are dark around the corners, while her irises are glowing. Actually glowing, like there is a light coming from inside of her and through her eyes.

She raises her now free palms in front of her, and I watch in awe as ice shards fly from them and impale the men holding me down. The water is already reaching for my waist when McTavish drops to the floor in front of me and tries crawling around me and out the back door. I try to grab him, but remember my hands are bound and there is still a knife in my leg.

Shit, that hurts.

I watch as Talli finishes off the men at her feet next with more ice shards that appear from nowhere. The front door is forced open as five more men rush in, and she kills them all with ice in the blink of an eye. When it's clear no more men are coming in, Talli turns in my direction, but her eyes latch onto something behind me. Or rather, someone.

McTavish is lifted from the floor by the water and pushed up against the wall behind me. The raging water turns to ice, and it holds him in place up against the wall. Talli takes a step toward him when Greer comes through the door, a sword clenched in one hand and a black cloud wrapped around her other. She assesses the situation, but before she can say or do anything, Talli says in a voice I don't recognize, "Get him out of here."

Talli doesn't turn or acknowledge either of us but keeps her movements steady as she prowls toward McTavish. Once she walks past me, Greer surges forward and helps me up and out of the cabin, while I try hopping on my good leg and calling after *my heart*. I want to fight Greer, yank this knife out of my leg, and go to her, but I can't be obvious about how skilled I am at fighting through an injury. It hurts like hell, but I know I could get back to Talli on my own before I bleed out.

Greer's expression is cold and silent as she ignores my calls for Talli. Why is she leaving her in there? I mean, she clearly has the situation under control, but is she in control of herself?

Taking in my surroundings, I realize it's the middle of the night. The moon is well into the sky, but several car lights are aimed at the cabin, surrounding it and making me even more disoriented. Greer helps me to what looks like a camping chair, so I turn my gaze from the cabin door to the chair so I can sit and—

What in the actual fuck? Nope. Nope. The Loch Ness Monster is definitely *not* a couple of feet away from me.

I'm frozen in place, and Greer lets go of me since I'm hovering over the chair. Falling down hard into the seat, the knife in my leg rattles, making my head swim with the pain.

"Caspian, meet Coventina. She's Talli's bonded dragon." Greer waves with her hand toward Nessie.

Dragon? These people make friends with dragons? Wait. Not even friends, but bonded. What the hell does that even mean? I knew some of them liked their cats, but that is *not* a cat in front of me.

Oh God. Why is it looking at me like that? The dragon, with its alarmingly dark eyes, with almost impossible-to-distinguish black slits in the middle, gives me a narrowed look like it's assessing me or considering eating me. A nervous chuckle rises as I suddenly realize that Talli could feed me to her dragon once I tell her the truth about everything.

Yep. Bleeding out would definitely be for the best. If only I could reach the knife.

Greer flashes me a sympathetic look and says, "Sorry to do this to you, but it can't be helped."

A massive, dark gray dragon lands next to Nessie, looking a lot more like a dragon and a lot more terrifying. I swear the thing is smiling at me when Greer adds, "This is Draven, my bonded dragon."

Draven opens his jaws wide and blows out a puff of smoke? Shadow? Black fog? Whatever it is, he aims it at my face, causing me to flinch.

Greer clicks her tongue and smacks the beast's nose. "Bad dragon. That is not the way to treat Talli's boyfriend."

The nervous laugh returns. I gulp down my fear, which I'm sure they can smell, and ask, "So, does everyone have pet dragons in your community?"

Her eyes sharpen on me, and I realize my mistake immediately. I used the term community with ease. I try to recover by saying, "That's what it's called, right? Whatever you and Talli are a part of? That's the term they kept using in there."

She relaxes slightly and responds, "No, we are the only ones bonded with dragons. The only ones in the world."

Well, that makes me feel only slightly better. "What do you mean by bonded?" I ask, genuinely curious. How did the Brethren not know any of this?

"She'll explain everything soon," Greer answers and steps toward me, finally untying my wrists from behind my back. I clamp my hands down around the knife protruding from my leg hard enough to try to stanch the bleeding around the blade. Then I turn around, noting the few people running around doing different tasks of clean up, erasing any evidence of anything bad happening here, and trying to avoid the water pouring out of the cabin from all sides. Efficient, I'll give them that. Apparently, there is a lot I don't know about these people. How have I been with a woman for nine months without knowing she had a pet dragon?

Said dragon starts moving, and my heart nearly jumps out of my chest. It's walking toward the cabin. Talli. Is she alright? Greer sees the alarm on my face and says calmly, "She's okay."

"How do you know that?" I demand, and she gestures to the door. I turn my eyes back to the cabin, and there she is, stroking the dragon's long snout like she's a horse. She's safe. Thank God. She turns her head and locks eyes with me, the light in them slowly fading into her normal dark blue.

I don't even know how to comprehend the different version of Talli I saw today. The one I knew had to exist, but could never imagine—the deadly assassin. She is devastating like this. I should be terrified of her, but she has never looked more beautiful. If my leg wasn't injured, I would consider falling to my knees before her and worshipping the ground she walks on.

Her hair blows wildly around her as she walks toward me, like she controls the wind as well, with confidence in every step. And suddenly, I feel mournful for all the time I've spent getting to know her, but not getting to know this side as well. Her eyes, which are now completely back to normal, never leave my gaze as she approaches me. She doesn't say anything as she bends down in front of where I am seated, pulls the knife out of my leg, and presses a ball of water she holds in her hand against the wound.

It feels cold, then warm, then starts to tingle. After a minute, I have to hold my leg still as it feels like it's on fire. Then, she pulls the ball of water away, and I'm astonished to see my wound healed. Skin entirely knitted back together like nothing happened. I tentatively touch the spot like it's not real, but it's my skin.

Talli stands, and I hold my leg out, stretching it. It feels completely fine. I stand and bear weight on it, still fine. How is all this possible? How is she possible? I have already lost count of all the things she has done tonight.

She can only sense people's pain, my ass.

Talli gives a halfhearted smirk at my apparent disbelief. "I'll get the rest when we get home safely."

"Talli, are you okay? What happened in there?" She takes a step back, clearly trying to keep distance between us, making my body ache.

"Not here," she replies as she shakes her head. She goes to Greer a few feet away and has a quiet discussion with her, then another Hawk joins them. A tall man, about her age, with long hair tied into a bun. He keeps looking her over, as if concerned, and I don't like it. I don't like him and his concern for *my heart*. But the conversation ends quickly, and all three nod at each other. Talli gestures for me to come to them.

"I hate to ask you this after all you have been through, and with considering your fear of heights, but we need to go, and we have to take Covey. It's for your safety. Greer told me you already met?" Talli asks me as Greer walks away.

Covey? It takes a second for me to realize she means her dragon. I really need to stop calling her Nessie in my head, or I'm bound to say it out loud by accident.

Whoa. Wait.

"Take her? As in ride?" I ask, trying to push the fear out of my voice.

"Yes. She does have a saddle with an extra seat. There are straps that will hold you in so you can't fall."

We walk over to Coventina and go to the other side of her, where we are wedged between her and the cabin's exterior wall. Talli starts stuffing her iron gloves into the saddle bag attached to the dragon, but I recognize instantly that her breathing is heavy and inconsistent.

"Talli." I grab her hand from where she is fussing with the saddle strap. "Please look at me." I use my other hand to cup her cheek, careful not to touch the large cut there or the smaller fingernail-shaped ones, and guide her face toward mine. Then I say to her softly, "I'm not going to pretend that I understand what's going on with anything right now," not a lie, "but I can say with absolute certainty that I love you. No matter who you are. Please, don't doubt that, and don't shut me out."

Tears start to well up in her eyes, and when she blinks, two tears fall down her cheeks. I pull her to my chest and hold her for a minute before she pulls away, looking at me.

"We have to go, but I'll explain everything this time, I promise." She sniffles. Those are the exact words that I set out on this mission to hear. But instead of bringing relief, they bring dread.

She effortlessly climbs up Coventina's back and settles in the front of the saddle. I do see the second seat behind her, but I'm more than hesitant to get into it. The lights go off all around us, and I see everyone packing up quickly, getting into different vehicles, and driving off. There is a reason we are in a rush, I realize.

Oh fuck it.

I need Talli to see that I can handle this, handle all of who she is. But a dragon? A rainbow-eating unicorn would have been much more believable and easier to cope with. I take a deep breath and square my shoulders, then climb into the saddle.

Talli twists in her seat to grab the straps dangling next to me. They are made of thick leather with carabiners on the ends. She clips one on a belt loop on each side of me and screws the safety into place, then turns back to face forward, and with no warning at all, we shoot off into the sky.

CHAPTER 50

TALLIANA

I FOUND PERFECT BALANCE tonight.

When Cas got stabbed, the darkness surged to take over, but I was faster. I grabbed onto the faint light surrounding my heart and pulled with all my might. For the first time in a long time, the light inside of me grew, meeting the darkness halfway. Their edges danced together like long-lost partners reunited once again until slowly, so slowly, they mixed enough that the edges blended into a shade of gray that I have never seen before. Unlike the shadows that Greer wields, this gray seemed to glow and pulse. I was flooded with more magic than I thought possible. The feeling was...life-changing.

There was no willing water or ice to do what I wanted. It just happened. They were like an extension of me, a connection that couldn't be broken and a magic that could never be depleted. Even now, with the magic flowing within me only a small trickle compared to earlier, I feel strong. Much stronger than I have ever felt before.

Will it wear out eventually? Will the darkness and the light eventually separate themselves and slink back into their opposing sides of me? Or, once balance is achieved, is it there to stay?

"Magic is not meant to be used in its purest, balanced form forever. A human body cannot handle it. It will fade from your veins shortly," Coventina answers.

"Covey, what happened in there...I thought the light would control the darkness, but my actions were just as brutal as if the darkness had control."

She hesitates, but then she confirms what I already know. *"The light did control the darkness, but it didn't control you."*

My mind conjures the moment Greer got Cas out of the cabin.

I had an ice spear in my hand, ready to drive it through the evil man's heart, but I paused, allowing him to realize what was about to happen. He took in a few deep breaths and gained some semblance of coherency. He saw me then, death incarnate.

"This is what I do to those who touch what is *mine*." Without another thought, I threw the spear right through his heart. He died instantly.

Now thinking back, I was merciful, considering what he deserved. What they all deserved. This is the third time they tried to trap me, and it won't be the last. But this time, they went after Cas, and in doing so, they unleashed something much worse than the Order's Assassin: *the world's most powerful witch.*

Cas's arms squeeze a bit tighter around my waist, bringing me back to more pressing matters. He has been kidnapped, beaten, and starved. His world has been completely turned upside down, and now he is riding a make-believe creature. His terror is palpable, but he has on a brave face and is dealing with it. My perfect resilient fighter.

I decided on the van ride to him that I would make it all go away if he showed signs of cracking or not handling it all well. Honestly, I am still considering it anyway because how could I let him be a target like this? How could I let him fall for me? Fall for a killer?

The life I have to offer him is not a fair one. I wish more than anything that I could be an ordinary woman for him. He deserves that, an ordinary woman, and I could leave him so that he would at least have a chance at finding that. The look in his eyes right before we left, though, and what he said, it all makes me want to be selfish and keep him. But I have to give him the choice. I won't choose for him, at least not right now.

Resolution settles in my heart, and I know what to do, but fear isn't far behind it. Because what if he does choose to forget what he knows about me, or worse, chooses to forget me completely?

He is using me as an anchor right now by holding on, but I lean gently back into his chest, using him as an anchor for my heart.

Thankfully, flying via dragon turns a two-hour drive into a fifteen-minute flight. We land at Trey's tree by the lake and dismount Coventina.

"Thank you, Covey," I say out loud for Cas's sake.

She nods and walks into the water, where she submerges. I turn around to see Cas watching her with wonder and disbelief.

"Are you sure she's a dragon and not the Loch Ness monster?" he asks.

That is the last thing I expected him to say. I can't help but laugh, appreciating the way he just lightened the mood. "I'm sure. Plus, she looks nothing like Nessie."

His eyes swing to me and widen. "Have you met Nessie?"

That makes me laugh harder. "Of course not. But the pictures of Nessie look like a green dinosaur head coming out of the water. Covey has a blue head with lots of fluffy hair. Oh, and her neck is not nearly that long."

"Alright, you have me there." Cas turns and stops. I walk to his side, and I see that he is looking at Trey's gravestone. He asks quietly, "He was like you?"

"Yes," I nearly whisper back.

"Did he die because of whatever is happening in your world?" He turns to me then, searching my face.

"Yes. He died saving me from evil men like the ones that took you. A coward tried to take a shot at me—well, both of us—from far away while he was trying to carry me to safety after being hurt. Trey saw it in time to turn and take the arrow himself."

Cas tenses, going stiff as a board. "I'm so sorry," he says softly, then looks back at the gravestone. He walks to it, avoiding stepping on any red poppies, and my breath catches at the sight. He bends down and places a hand on top of it. "Thank you. Thank you so much for saving her."

My heart plummets. I don't deserve this beautiful, understanding man.

He rights himself, walks over to me, and takes my hand, and we walk to the house together. After a couple of minutes of silence, he asks, "Whatever happened to the man who killed Treyton?"

"I killed him." It happened what seems like an eternity ago. After the battle, when I regained my strength, Greer and I hunted him down, and I killed him with an arrow. Unlike him, though, I stood right before him as I took the shot. I wanted him to know who finished him, to look into the eyes of the person who took his life.

"McTavish. His men. You killed them all?" he asks, still looking ahead at our path, and I guess it's best he knows the monster he walks next to.

"Yes."

One heartbeat. Two heartbeats. Five heartbeats.

"Good," he replies, and I nearly fall over at the word. He must see my shock because he stops and turns toward me, but I back away, letting go of his hand. I don't understand why he is not running to get away from me, why he is just accepting who I am. I don't deserve his warmth and comfort, at least not until he knows everything.

"The house isn't far."

He nods, and we continue the short walk. I keep my distance and wrap my arms around myself, trying to keep the fear from swallowing me whole. The darkness is back in its cage, and the light has receded back to my heart; their job is done for the night, and the lack of power has left me feeling weak, as if a small breeze could push me over. This complete control changes so much, but does nothing for the situation with Cas.

We go through the back door, and Mom and Dad are in the kitchen. Mom runs toward me. "Talliana! Oh my God. Are you okay?" She hugs me and then looks me over. Clearly, it doesn't matter if I can heal myself instantly in the shower. She is still Mom, ready to fix any injury.

"I'm fine. I'll heal up as soon as I get upstairs," I answer, shrugging.

Mom moves away, and Dad steps in front of me. "Glad you're okay. Rest, and I'll see you tomorrow for your report and...decision." Dad looks behind me at Caspian. It's obvious he's referring to a memory wipe of everything Cas has learned over the last couple of days, if not wiping me from his mind altogether. I wish I could say for certain it won't be needed, but I'll give him the choice.

"Okay," I reply. I walk past both my parents and lead Cas up to my room. I shut the door behind him and go straight to the bathroom to start the shower.

I walk back out to see him standing in the middle of my room, unsure of what to do. He turns to me and asks, "Is Greer going to be home soon?" He knows we share a room, but seeing the two beds in the space likely made him wonder how much privacy we would have tonight.

"No, she's staying at Ash's tonight. She knows we need space to talk," I answer.

"Right. Makes sense."

"Now please get in the shower. You should get cleaned up, and I want to finish healing you."

He doesn't argue, just moves slowly while he undresses. I try to busy myself, not looking directly at him, but I keep glancing over, cataloging all the injuries and bruises. There is so much dirt and dried blood caked to his skin. The water earlier only seemed to smudge it. Anger rises in a sharp sting to my gut, but I swallow it down. Once he is bare, he walks into the bathroom, and I hear him climb into the shower. I grab his clothes and toss them into a white trash bag for washing.

A gentle knock sounds at the door. I open it and find Mom with some of Dad's clothes.

"Thank you." I take the offered bundle from her and hand her the trash bag before shutting the door again. I set the clothes on the bed and walk into the bathroom. Pulling back the shower curtain a little to peek my head in, I explain, "I need to heal you. It will take a minute to heal everything, so stand as still as possible while the water works."

"Not yet." He reaches out, opening the curtain more, and unzips my leather jacket. He pushes it down my arms and removes my bra in the next movement, then I take off my own pants and underwear. Cas grabs my hand, pulls me in, and places me under the hot, steaming water. "Please heal yourself first."

"I'll heal myself after, I promise." I step closer to him and place both hands on his chest. His arms slide around my waist, and I realize that I'm breaking my rule of no touching before the truth. I just can't help myself when I'm around him. It's so natural I don't even realize I am doing it, as if his body is an extension of mine.

I close my eyes, concentrating on the water, moving it around me and molding it over each bruise, scratch, and exterior injury on his flesh. After a minute, I open my eyes and inspect my work. Aside from old scars, his skin is without flaw.

"Alright, this will feel weird for a minute, like when I healed your stab wound earlier. Stay still." I gather a ball of water in my hand, take a deep breath, and press it into his chest. The water sinks into his skin, and I will it to heal his cracked rib. About two minutes pass, and I pull the water back out and let it fall from my hand. His breathing is ragged, and I look at his face. He looks...astonished? Afraid? Freaked out? I do one last check of him, but don't sense or see anything else wrong. I lower my head and hands. I feel defeated and tired. My energy level, along with my magic, is low, and there is still so much to do.

I feel Cas's hand on my chin, lifting my face. "Now you," he says.

Without moving my eyes from where they are locked on his, I soak in the water as it beats down on me. Everywhere it touches, it heals. Cas reaches out his hand, cupping the water, then brings it to the cut on my cheek, letting the water flow through his fingers. I can feel it heal as the water slides down my skin. He watches my flesh knit itself back together, transfixed. I don't take my eyes off of him as he reaches back up to my cheek and rubs his fingers over where the cut was.

A smile plays on his lips. "Now I know why you always know everything at school," he teases.

I release a breath. "Yeah, I'm a bit of a natural at it." I meant to say it in a light tone, but it comes out rough. I feel something crack inside of me. "Cas. I'm so, so sorry you got roped into my world. I wanted to tell you everything for so long, but I was...I didn't..." I choke on the words, and he pulls me to his chest, rubbing my back in gentle circles.

"Let's finish getting clean and head to bed. I don't know what time it is, but I suspect it's late. We can talk tomorrow."

I nod into his chest. I don't deserve this. He was kidnapped, beaten, told things he could never understand, found out magic is real, found out his girlfriend is a murderer with magical powers and a dragon, and here he is, trying to comfort me. I've been lying to him our entire relationship, for fuck's sake.

We wash up and dry off. He hesitantly takes Dad's clean clothes but only puts on the lounge shorts. We get into my bed, and I'm fully aware of how much smaller the twin is compared to Cas's queen-size bed. His body is pressed into the back of mine, and his arms keep me close against him. I had offered to take Greer's bed while he slept in mine, but his "No," came out so fast, it startled me.

I let a few minutes of silence surround us, but I can't help but ask the one thing eating me up the most. "Are you afraid of me?" It comes out in a whisper and I instantly hope he didn't hear it. His answer might break me in two, but it's the answer I would expect anyone to give in this situation.

"No, my heart. I know you better than that."

My tense body instantly relaxes, and I let myself cry in his arms until I fall asleep.

Shaking. I'm shaking. Wait. No. Cas is behind me, and he is shaking. I try to turn around, and I find that his arms are wrapped around me still, tense, muscles bulging. He's asleep, so he must be having a nightmare.

He has rarely had any nightmares since I gave him that moonstone rock. At least not that he has said anyway. I'm not going to pretend that the fact he is having one with my necklace still close by doesn't stress me out, but I shove all my fears aside, and in a practiced movement, I slowly rub his arm with my hand. Not enough to spook him out of it, but enough to comfort him so that he relaxes.

His hands shoot out and grab my wrists, pinning my arms in a crossed position over my chest. I take a deep breath and recheck him. Still asleep. His hold is bruising. I test out my ability to get out of it and away from him as quickly as possible, but as I twist my wrists a little, I hear a low guttural noise from him, almost a growl. "I won't let you take her," he slurs.

I freeze instantly. He's not afraid of me. He's afraid of something happening to me. God, I was so worried about him being scared of me, I didn't think about how having me hurt in front of him would impact him. It probably tears him apart, like it has done to me.

I always keep a cup of water on my nightstand in case of an emergency, so I position my wrists as carefully as I can, facing out. I pull the water out of the cup, and right as I let it fall on his face, I throw my body forward, and his grip releases. I hit the ground and scramble to the other side of the room, staying crouched. The water does the trick, and he is awake, gasping for air and wiping the water away from his face.

"Talli? Where are you?" he asks in a panic. He frantically looks around and finds me in a second. "What happened? What's wrong?"

I stand up and answer gently, "Nothing. You had a nightmare. I couldn't wake you up. You—" I stop. He doesn't need to know what happened. I continue, saying instead, "I'm sorry if I scared you." I try to hand him a towel for his face, but he grabs my hand and pulls my arm toward him. He sees the red around my wrist and then grabs my other hand. I feel his horror, like a wave rippling off of him.

"I'm okay," I reassure him.

"You're not okay. I hurt you...I'm no better than them," he says the last part in a whisper, like an admission.

How could he think that? He was asleep, he was afraid. He would never hurt me, not consciously.

"Cas, what was your nightmare about?"

"I uh," he sputters before finding words. "They took you. They were going to hurt you again."

"And you were trying to protect me?" I ask, already knowing.

"Well, of course. I..."

"You will never be like them. What you did was an accident. You would never lay a hand on me to harm me on purpose. Those men are evil. They only know how to hate and kill. They don't know what love and compassion are. You do. You are a good man, one I don't deserve, one I have never deserved, but one I want so badly. I have been selfish in trying to keep you and not telling you the truth. You were in danger this whole time and didn't even know it. Caspian, please walk away from this life. I can take away the last few days from you, wipe your memory, and we can have a clean break so you can move on. Or I can take away every memory of us, and then you won't even know that you lost anything. Please let me give you your life back."

"Fuck no. I would never walk away from you. I don't care about being in danger, what you have done, or what life with you involves. I'm in. I've always been in. The only thing I care about is you." His hands are gentle as one cups my cheek, and the other strokes my hair on the back of my head.

My voice shakes as I admit, "I was so afraid you would leave me and want nothing to do with me once you found out. I was so scared to tell you."

"Don't be scared anymore. Tell me. Tell me everything."

We settle into a comfortable position on the bed, facing each other, and I tell him everything. I tell him about the Order, my abilities, my destiny, Treyton, Coventina, all the men I've killed, and who I really am inside. I tell him about the darkness and my battle to gain control of it. I let him see me for the first time, and he isn't running.

CHAPTER 51

CASPIAN

TALLI TOLD ME EVERYTHING. I listened and absorbed it all, only asking a few questions here and there. When she was done, even though it was light outside and clearly morning, I pulled her into my arms and let her drift back to sleep. We only got maybe two to three hours before my nightmare woke us up anyway. We both needed more sleep, but I couldn't turn my mind off.

So here I am, just lying next to her, watching her soft, peaceful face, listening to the steady rhythm of her breathing, and smelling her shampoo. If I fall back asleep, she might be taken from me again, and I might...I might hurt her again.

I can't hurt her again.

How am I going to avoid it, though? I will hurt her when I tell her the truth. She will hate me, and I won't blame her. I wanted to tell her so many times while she was talking, but my father's threat kept ringing in my head.

Images from my nightmare flash across my mind for the hundredth time. My father has her in his grip, knife to her throat. She already looks like she has taken a beating, and I am helpless to do anything. He is threatening me, threatening her, and all I can think about is how I will kill him for it.

I need to find a way to take him down before he can really hurt Talli. How? Fuck if I know. My father is the most untouchable man of all the Brethren and getting near him is impossible. Could I kill him? If it came down to his or Talli's life, without a doubt. But if there is another way, I need to take it.

Talli stirs in my arms, then looks up at me. Instead of the sleepy smile I usually get in the morning, she has a crease between her brows.

"You're still here," she breathes, and my chest feels heavy.

"You can't scare me away."

"Even after...after everything you know now? I thought that once it all sank in, you would run."

"Never. Do you not remember our conversation last night? I will never run from you, no matter what," I reassure her.

"Cas, I am not a good person, if that hasn't been made clear enough yet. I have murdered an unimaginable amount of people, and by the time this war is over, I have no doubt that a lot more blood will have stained my soul. You don't want that. You don't want me. No one should want me."

I sit up in the tiny bed and pull her up with me. "Stop trying to tell me what I want. I grew up never knowing what I wanted until I met you." I kiss her gently and then pull her to my chest and lay us back down.

KNOCK. KNOCK.

"Talli, I need to talk to you downstairs please." Aaron's voice sounds through the door.

"I'll be right down," Talli calls out. She climbs out of bed and goes to the bathroom. She emerges a few moments later in sweatpants and a shirt. "I'll be back in a few minutes. I'll bring back some food."

As soon as she opens the door, a giant ass German shepherd races in, jumps on the bed, and sits at my feet, eyeing me with alarming intensity.

"Seth, this is Cas. Cas, this is Seth." Talli makes the quick introduction before shutting the door behind her.

I eye the dog back. "Are you a family pet or one of them?"

He huffs.

"One of them, then. If you excuse me, my future is at stake at the moment, and I would like to hear about it."

He doesn't move, but I get out of bed and go to the door. I open it up slowly and poke my head out. No one is around, but I faintly hear Talli's voice. I step carefully out of the room and go to the top of the stairs where I can hear the conversation below much better.

"You're making a mistake. You don't know him well enough!" Aaron shouts.

"I do know him! Regardless, he was just kidnapped because of me. He is involved in all of this. I told him everything last night, and he still wants to be with me. Dad, I love him more than I thought was possible after Trey," Talli argues. My chest warms at her words. Never has someone defended me before.

"How do you plan to keep him safe, Talli? Now that they know who he is and that he is your weakness," I hear Rose ask.

A moment of silence passes, and Talli announces, "Dad is going to let us move into one of the spare houses."

My mouth drops open. My father's plan to expedite my mission has worked beautifully. I will be positioned to see and hear everything that happens here, not that I have any intention of using anything I learn.

"I will not! Those houses are reserved for emergencies and new couples after they get married. Are you planning on marrying this human, then?" Aaron challenges.

I freeze, anxious to hear Talli's response.

"Not now, no. Maybe one day, when everyone is safe. But you will let us move into one of those houses, or I will find another community willing to house us instead."

Another moment passes, and Talli adds, "Dad, he is in danger because of me. It's my duty to keep him safe now."

"If he is to move into the community, then he needs to go through all the tests first," Aaron says sternly.

Tests? What tests?

"No. What he went through last night is test enough. No one will touch him. Are we clear?"

"Fine, but he is not going to just sit around doing nothing either. He will contribute to the community like everyone else."

"I understand, and I'm sure he will be happy to do whatever you ask," Talli agrees quickly.

There is a loud sigh. "Ask Ash to help you teach him everything he needs to know about living here, and find some help getting him moved out of the apartment. The Brethren are likely watching it, so be careful. I will have keys for you in a few hours."

"Thank you." Despite her words, her tone is curt. There is something going on with her and Aaron. Or has what I've seen of their relationship so far been a show?

I tiptoe back into Talli's room and close the door. I turn and find Seth still watching me, now with a judgmental look. "You should know that I love her very much, and she loves me. I won't have a problem with you if you don't have a problem with me."

Seth lies down, putting his head between his paws.

"Good boy."

His head lifts again and growls.

The door opens in the nick of time, and Talli comes into the room with a plate of food in her hand and my clean clothes over her arm.

"You two getting to know each other?" Talli asks, handing me the clothes.

"You could say that." Looking back at Seth, his tail wags at the sight of Talli.

She moves to him, scratches under his ear, then kisses his nose. "Seth has been through a lot. He just lost his bonded Hawk, and he decided to stay here. I don't know if he plans to be with me for a little while or to stay permanently by my side, but he is very important to me, so I hope you don't mind him."

"His bonded...Was he the one who just passed? The one you were so upset about before everything happened?"

"Yeah." Her face contorts with sorrow. "Mr. Simon was my trainer and like a father to me. He was the one who helped me learn control over the darkness. And just like Mr. Simon, Seth has always been right there to help me when I need it. I owe them both so much."

I move to her and grab her empty hand. "I'm so sorry, Talli. If he wants to be beside you, too, then I will move over and make space for him. I mean, what difference does a dog make when I already have to share you with a dragon?"

Talli smiles, and it lifts my heart to see it. I kiss her softly, then start getting dressed while trying to ignore all the holes and tears in my clean clothes. "Is everything okay with your dad?"

"Yeah, about that..." Talli replies slowly as she starts munching on a piece of bacon. "So, I know this has all been a lot, but the fact of the matter is, you're in danger. The Brethren know who you are, and they know they can use you to get to me. You're not safe going back to your apartment."

I sit on Talli's desk chair and ask, "But they came after me once, and it didn't work out well for them. Do you think they are stupid enough to try it again?" Yes, they are stupid enough. I know it, but I also know they won't come after me because it's not part of the agreement they bullied me into, one I have no intention of keeping.

"You don't know these people like I do. They will do anything to get to my kind, and they won't stop until we are all slaughtered. They don't learn from failure, they just throw more bodies at us hoping someone will manage the kill. Like seriously, they have tried to trap me three times now, and it has gotten them nowhere."

She's not wrong about the latter half of her statement. She's also terrified, and I don't blame her. When she sees me, she sees Treyton. Someone who will die because of her, die *for* her, and I don't want her to feel that way. "What's the plan then?"

"We keep spare empty houses in the community in case of emergencies. Dad is getting us keys to one."

I fake surprise. "Are you asking me to move in with you, Talliana Hoffman?"

Her cheeks redden. "Well, not moving in with me per se, but moving into a new place with me. To live with me so that I can keep you safe."

I laugh. "No offense whatsoever to the female population, but I never expected I would need to live with my girlfriend so that she could be my bodyguard. I've always prided myself on being able to keep other people safe if the situation arose."

"And for a human, you are an amazing fighter, I am sure. This is just a unique case."

"Everything to do with you is a unique case, isn't it?" I tease.

"Yeah, mostly," she admits.

"Alright. I will live with you and let you keep me safe on one condition." She lifts her eyebrows in question. "You stop doubting how much I love you."

Talli jumps from her spot on the bed and places the plate of food on the desk, then climbs onto my lap. Wrapping her arms around my neck, she kisses me deeply, and I pull her toward me, my body immediately responding to her.

Pulling away slightly, she says seductively, "The houses are all furnished with a king-size bed in the primary suite, a large tiled shower, and a very nice tub."

"Hmm...this arrangement might be my idea of heaven." She laughs and kisses me again.

Heaven for how long, though?

I need to find a way to get hold of a memory potion, the one the Order uses all the time on our men. I'll steal one, pay a visit to my father, slip it into his drink, make him disappear, tell Talli everything, and then I will get on my knees and beg her not to hate me. That's the best chance she has at ending this war, and the best chance I have at her forgiving me.

It's a solid plan that only has about a hundred things that could go wrong.

Chapter 54

CASPIAN

I'VE NEVER HAD AN army at my disposal to help me move before.

Greer and Ash are on Draven circling above the apartment complex to keep an eye out for danger, while Talli, five other people from the community, and I are all boxing up my apartment. Considering this is my stuff, I feel rather useless standing around and watching everyone pack up my few belongings. Talli is at least organizing everyone and labeling boxes.

Soft fingertips brush my shoulder, and Talli circles me, looking up into my eyes. "This is a lot. Are you sure you're okay?"

I allow a smile to cross my face as I pull her to me. My chin rests on her head as she buries herself into my chest. My words are honest when I answer, "This is all unexpected, and I'm still wrapping my mind around everything, but once I see our toothbrushes occupying the same holder, your sock drawer next to mine, and your pile of clothes in the corner of our bedroom, then everything will feel as it should."

She smiles up at me, but it falters after a moment. "If at any point you change your mind about my world, just say the word. I would never hate you for it."

I can see the fear in her eyes that I will do just that, but that couldn't be further from the truth. Pulling her face close to mine, I place a small kiss on her lips. "Not a chance. You're stuck with me."

She smiles again, but I can see that it is forced, so I add, "Let's finish getting moved so we can spend all night long testing out our new bath." Her smile turns into a real one, and then she nods and returns to labeling boxes.

It's been two days since Talli and I moved into the house. Everything is settled and unpacked, and now I have the privilege of allowing Ash to show me around the community. He really is the best tour guide. He knows everything about everything and answers every question I have without me even having to ask.

We start the tour by entering all my information into their system. This includes information that would be found on a job application, such as my date of birth, social security number, and photo. The information is apparently for the emergency services officers and police so that they know who I am and don't mistake me for "a Brethren trying to cause trouble," as Ash put it.

How ironic.

I do my best to retain all the information that Ash gives me, but I have no doubt there are things I will forget. I can't stop reeling about all the new information, all the things the Brethren couldn't have even imagined about their operation and safety measures. The only question that hasn't been answered is what that mysterious rain that keeps stopping the fires and attacks on the community really is, but there is no way to ask that without raising suspicion; and anyway, I have a feeling that Talli is at the root of it and that what she told McTavish was a lie. She seems to be at the root of everything.

"Ash, I do have one question." He swings his gaze to me, eager to hear it. "When the Brethren had Talli and me, they asked her where the magic comes from. Talli told me about the story of the Great Hawk, but I am still not clear on that answer."

"Oh, that's easy. Magic comes from nature. Nature created the Great Hawk and gave it the authority to bestow magic on a group of humans and provide them with the Order. Their purpose, if you will. The magic lives in their bloodlines, and through connecting with nature, they are able to use it."

I run my fingers through my hair, swiping it out of my eyes. "Well, that is a much more comforting answer than the one Talli gave during the ordeal."

"What did she say?"

"She alluded to magic being from the devil."

Ash laughs. "Of course she did. That is what many of the Brethren believe, and probably the reason they still attack. They think Hawks are evil, devil worshipers, witches, and many other things I won't say aloud."

I nod because it's all true. That is the belief that formed the Brethren, and I personally know many who still believe that. But my father? I think he uses it as an excuse, as fuel for the men, but for him, this war is all about glory—winning a centuries-long war when no one else could, nothing more. Unlike the many generals before him, he couldn't care less about religion.

Ash turns down a corner to leave the community building, and I see a stairwell going down. "Where does that lead to?" I ask innocently.

"Oh, my parents' lab and some prison cells in case we need them," he answers easily and keeps walking.

Bingo. That must be where the memory potions are. Now I just have to figure out how to get to them.

Ash leads me out of the building and crosses the street, and I follow behind. He gestures to a large white building. "This is the medical center. I assume you would like to see if they could use you here? Given your schooling?"

I look at him, confused. Schooling? Oh! Oh no. "Actually, I was considering switching majors. I have realized that I'm not actually good at any of it."

"Really? Okay then. I need a new plan for where to place you. Is there anything else you have experience with or like doing?"

"Will I be any real help around here without magic?" I counter.

"Absolutely. No one fully relies on magic for everything around here. There is always a need for manual labor." His eyes light up, and he looks me over. "Actually, I know exactly who might need your help."

Ash walks back across the street and farther into the community. I follow behind him until he stops at a dark-green house. It looks like all the other houses around here, except the garage is triple the size of everyone else's. The garage door is open, and I see two men working in there. Ash walks up the driveway, and one of the men stops working and smiles at him. His reddish-brown hair is straight and long, tied into a ponytail at the base of his neck.

"What can I do for you, Asher?" the man asks in a kind tone. He wipes sweat from his brow onto his shirt sleeve, and now that we are closer, I can see they are working with wood.

"Mr. Salo, are you in need of any help? I have a strong friend here who needs a job."

Mr. Salo's eyebrows raise, and he looks at me. He removes his gloves and offers me a hand. "Don Salo. As you can probably guess, I'm the community's woodworker."

I take his hand. "Caspian Stewart."

"Did you just move here, Caspian? What community are you from?"

I dart my gaze to Ash, unsure of how to proceed. He didn't tell me if I had a particular story I needed to follow or who I was supposed to be. To my surprise, he answers with the truth. "Caspian is a human like me." Don's eyes widen, and he looks at me again, but Ash continues, bringing his attention back to him. "He's Talliana's boyfriend. Unfortunately, the Brethren tried using him against her and...well, he's going to be staying in the community from now on. Elder Hoffman wants him to be put to use, and I thought you could use the most help in light of recent events." Ash's voice loses its strength toward the end, and I assume "recent events" means the attack that resulted in Talli's trainer's death.

There is a glimmer of sorrow in Don's eyes; it's clear he was impacted by Simon's death, too. He nods, though, and responds, "If it weren't for those residing in the Hoffman household, I would be a lot busier." He turns to me, then continues, "I'm sure busier is what most people want in the human world, but for us, being busy as a woodworker is not a good thing. I don't know if anyone has told you, but Talliana is a hero. What she did during the March on the community a few years ago saved my son's life. So if you have her love, then you will have ours too. We'd be happy to have your help."

My heart swells with pride. She tried so hard to convince me that she is a monster, something to be afraid of, but every interaction I have had with her people over the last couple of days has shown them looking at her with respect and reverence. She's a hero to them all.

Talli did tell me that she healed those who were injured during the attack that took Treyton's life, that it took an extraordinary amount of power to do it. My brain wanted to fight the information, because there is no way any of it should be possible, but it is. How she healed my leg and how these people, *her* people, look at her—it's clear that it's all true. The Brethren have no idea what they are up against.

"Thank you. I don't know much about woodworking, but I'm strong and happy to do any work you need," I reply.

He smiles at me. "Be here tomorrow at eight and wear something you're not afraid to get dirty."

"Thank you, Mr. Salo," Ash says as a goodbye.

Don waves, and Ash and I resume our walk. After a few moments of silence, Ash breaks it by saying, "It will take a while, but you'll eventually get used to it."

"What?"

"Everyone sharing how Talli has saved them or their loved ones at one time or another. How she is a blessing from the Great Hawk himself. How much they love and adore her. It will be something spoken about for centuries."

"She told me she healed a lot of people with her magic after bonding with her dragon. She even told me about the darkness she had to use to do it. But she didn't detail exactly how she did it, and the way he was talking about it...I have a feeling she was downplaying it," I admit to him.

Ash's answering smile is sad. "It's not a day she likes to think about, but it's the one day everyone insists on still thanking her for."

I stop, turning to Ash. "What did she do?"

"She made it rain."

The words bounce around my head, and realization settles in as I put the pieces together. Talli is the mysterious rain that keeps thwarting many of the Brethren's attacks. Her water ability, her healing, her dragon...

She's the answer to everything.

"Do these people know what else she does for them?"

Ash lowers his voice and answers, "Not completely, no. Only elders and a select few others know exactly what Talli and Greer do. Everyone else thinks they are memory-wiping the leaders. Which they did at first, but then they realized that even if they relocate the Brethren who get wiped, many are still coming back. Their people are bringing them back somehow. So now they've had to resort to the permanent way of dealing with their targets."

That is why Talli is a killer. I remember when the soldiers started disappearing and popping up in different locations with their memories gone. I thought that was something completely different, and I had no idea it was how they tried dealing with the Brethren before resorting to murder. The only reason my father can find all his people is because he microchips them for "insurance." That's why I have one in my arm, showing my father exactly where I am. Not many know where they get implanted to avoid them trying to take them out and run. I hadn't known I even had one, until one day, when I was fourteen, I found a scanner and scanned myself head-to-toe until I found it. It is something I will have to remove soon, right before I tell her the truth.

Ash's words are also a reminder of the biggest flaw in my plan of how to deal with my father. I have no doubt he has some kind of record of what he needs to know if his memory ever gets wiped. So, in addition to wiping his memory, I need him to disappear. I need to put him somewhere no one can find him.

"It's a shame they don't know. Maybe they would start thanking her for a lot more than just that day," I say.

I feel a breeze brush against my neck, and Talli's voice causes me to jump. "If the people saw what it really took to save them, they would no longer call me a hero. Instead, I would be branded a villain, and wouldn't that be relief?"

Talli must have come from down the other sidewalk, and neither Ash nor I saw her coming toward us. But before either of us can comment or argue with her, she walks past us and doesn't look back.

"I don't understand why that would be a relief," Ash admits.

"Because it's hard to have people love you for something that you think they should hate you for."

I've never understood Talli as well as I do in this exact moment. She believes she is a villain hiding in a hero's costume. And here I am, the actual villain in this story, doing just that, letting people label me as a good person when I am a fraud, a liar, and a murderer. I want to tell her, tell her I understand better than anyone how she feels, tell her that she isn't a villain, just a good person doing what she must to save the ones she loves, tell her that I am the real bad guy who needs to take the blame for everything she has had to do.

I should have done more. I should have fought my father harder. I should have prevented that March on the community. I should have. I should have. I should have. But I didn't. And all I can do now is try to save her so that she can save everyone else.

I can't tell her the truth.

Not until this is over. I'm more sure now than ever before. I will do everything in my power to help her save her people, then I'll rip off the hero's mask and give her someone to blame for everything she has had to do, because that is what she needs. Someone other than herself to blame.

I turn and head home, going after Talli.

Ever since they took my son away from me as a means to control me, my abilities have not been the same. Small pulls of the water have led to giant waves. Any attempt at healing has sent the injured person into shock. They are watching me day and night, so if i continue like this, they will destroy me.

I must smother the burning rage inside, dampen it with a woolen blanket so no one else can sense it. My only hope now is to find a way to control the darkness, because if i let it lash out again before I'm ready this time, my son will never be safe.

- Journal of Katarina Lehmann

CHAPTER 53

TALLIANA

June

"*IF HE KEEPS LOOKING at me like that, I am going to splash him.*"

"Cas, you're making Covey uncomfortable." I look over to where he is sitting on the bank of the lake with me. He is watching her with a wary look on his face. I add, "I promise I won't let her eat you." It's something I have said a hundred times now, but he still gets this look sometimes like he is worried that she will.

He finally looks at me and then puts his arm around me. "Sorry, to both of you. I know I've had a month to come to terms with it, but I still can't believe she is real."

"It's alright. Everything is new to you. Many people here are still nervous around her, despite having had three years. Just maybe try to be more subtle in your disbelief, or I'm afraid she will shoot water at you."

"How about you? Can I stare at you instead? Or would that make you uncomfortable as well?" He kisses my neck right on my sensitive spot.

I laugh and push him away playfully. "You could never make me feel uncomfortable. On the contrary, you make me so comfortable that fresh air feels like a rare thing since we started living together. But we really should be getting fresh air."

"Fine. Fresh air is good for the lungs, I guess." He sighs.

I hear a distinct noise, like paws digging in the dirt, and turn around to find Seth clawing at the ground. He digs and digs, then spins three times, digs a little more, then plops down into his little hole.

"Seth, if you get yourself filthy again this week, so help me, I'll ask Covey to give you a bath this time," I warn him.

"*Gladly.*"

Seth lifts his head, looks at me, then at Coventina in the lake, then plops his head back down, unfazed by my threat.

"I'm still going to have to take your word for it that Seth is a great guard dog. All he does is sleep, or make himself a comfortable place to sleep," Cas remarks.

Turning to face him, I watch a blue-colored dragonfly land on his knee. I offer it a brief smile and gently brush it away. "Don't let him fool you. He can tear through a person's limb in one bite. He is extremely vicious when he needs to be," I warn.

"Again, I'll take your word for it."

"He really likes you, though. I can tell. It's strange for a creature capable of bonding to latch onto a human, but he follows you around like he used to follow Mr. Simon. I also think you like him, too." I grin at him.

"Yeah, he's grown on me."

Before I can say something to tease Cas further, my phone beeps.

Dad: *I need you in my office now. We have an unwelcome guest.*

"What is it?" Cas asks quickly.

Coventina makes her way out of the water toward us. I show him the text. "Go to the house with Seth, please. I need to deal with whatever this is."

"You want me to hide?" Cas asks, irritated.

Coventina shifts to her lizard form and climbs up my body until she takes up a place on my shoulder.

"Not hide, just wait in a safe place until I know the threat."

Cas's face is not amused, but he dutifully walks in the direction of our house.

"Love you!" I shout to him, and without looking back, he answers, "Love you too, even though you are hiding me."

I race toward the community building and right to Dad's office. Greer is at my heels as I knock on the door and open it upon Dad's call to come in. I am not at all prepared to see what is in front of me.

Zander.

I knew. I just *knew* this man would haunt me again one day, and here he is with a big grin on his face.

"Ah, Talliana. Just the woman I wanted to see. Your father and I were discussing our marriage arrangement."

"How dare you come back to my home and ask for something I have repeatedly denied you. You are a slimy, power-hungry, sorry excuse for a Hawk. How you ever managed to weasel your way into your position as an elder is beyond me," I practically spit at him.

"As I was just telling Elder Zander here, we do not deal with blackmail regardless of what he believes he knows, and I will be personally requesting a vote for his removal from his position for it," Dad explains firmly.

"And as I told you, even if I have little proof of what your daughter is, my accusation alone will result in her being tested for multiple abilities. They will find out about the memory-seeing, and she will be contained due to her having too much unchecked power."

He's finally figured it out and decided to come forward about it, then. I'm surprised it took him this long.

"There has to be something else you want besides marrying Talli," Greer argues.

"I want powerful children. I want to be secured as Massachusetts' closest ally. I want my name to be right next to Talliana's in history. All those things require her hand in marriage."

"You fucking son of a bitch. How about I just kill you now?" I barely have a grip on the darkness, and I am on the verge of ripping open its cage. It would be a pleasure—no, my honor—to rid our people of this man.

"If you kill me, I have many close associates who will release the information about you to everyone. My death will only doom you further."

Before I can argue, Dad stands from his desk, hands braced on either side of it, and says, "We need time to consider your offer."

"We do not!" I protest.

"You have until tomorrow, Elder Aaron," Zander warns, and it takes everything in me to stop myself from strangling him on the spot.

"Let me make something clear to you. I will give you an answer tomorrow, but you are not a guest here and will not be treated as one. You came into *my* community and threatened *my* daughter. You will be under guard, and your phone will be tapped. So don't you dare step out of line." Dad walks around his desk, opens the door, and calls out for guards to escort Zander out. He promptly shuts the door and deflates against it. "I had truly hoped that he was too smart to try to pull something like this," Dad admits despairingly.

I release a loud *HA* and Greer asks, "Do you have a plan?"

Straightening, Dad answers, "No, I don't. We could use Mei-Lien to have him tell us exactly who knows so that we can wipe their memory of it, but I'm afraid we wouldn't be fast enough. Talli, if you had better control over your ability to change memories, that could be another option, but I'm afraid we would just run into the same issue."

"I wouldn't put it past him to have had his backups create backups as well, just in case of us trying something like that. That's what I would have done anyway," Greer adds.

"Then let him tell the truth about me. If they take me, we will have to tell them that I am meant to end this war. They wouldn't want to lock up their only hope," I reason.

"No. Even if we can convince them of that truth, it would still put you and the community under far too much scrutiny. Decisions regarding what you do and how you do it would suddenly be everyone's concern, and nothing would get done," Dad argues. I can't help but wonder if he means that *he* would be under far too much scrutiny.

He seems to think for a moment and then shakes his head again. "You girls go home and discuss this with Ash. He always has ideas. I'll have an emergency meeting with Orsen and Kasumi to see if they have any thoughts as well."

Greer and I nod rather soberly and leave the office.

"I have an idea. It's a little out there, though, and it comes with some risks," Ash offers.

"I'm open to any idea at this point," I reply.

Greer, Ash, Cas, and I have been sitting around the living room for two hours, stuck in a cycle of throwing out an idea and someone knocking it down. I'm feeling more hopeless by the minute, but out of all of us, Ash has contributed the least to the idea pool. So if he truly has something that he thinks might work, it is likely our best bet.

"Cas can challenge Zander to a duel."

I stand corrected. Everyone erupts at the same time.

"Excuse me, what?!" I exclaim.

"Your people still duel?" Cas asks.

Greer simply laughs.

Ash, choosing to answer Cas, says, "Technically, no, but we used to. You see, when the Order was still new and there weren't a lot of bloodlines to go around, men would often fight over a woman's hand in marriage. Eventually, an elder decided to create a rule where if two men wanted to claim one woman, they would duel until one conceded defeat, and that would be that."

"What makes you think he would agree to one?" Cas asks.

"He wouldn't have a choice. The law was never changed. People just forgot about it, if I had to guess. If you challenge him under the rule that if he loses, he can't have Talli or share her secret, he can't say no. He either has to fight you or forfeit and be trapped by the same rules anyway," Ash explains.

"That's extremely convenient," Greer comments.

Stopping this before it goes too far, I say, "Stating the obvious here, but Cas does not have abilities. Zander could send him into the sky with his air ability and let him drop to his death within the first minute."

"Actually, abilities are forbidden in duels. It is hand-to-hand combat only. Weapons aren't even allowed because the elder didn't want to have unnecessary blood spilled."

"If Zander loses, what would keep him from sharing Talli's secret anyway? We already know he doesn't care about honor," Greer asks.

"The two dragons in the room can correct me if I'm wrong, but they can bind the rules of the match so that he would not be able to speak about Talli at all afterward."

I look toward Coventina, where she is perched on the coffee table, but it is Draven who answers, *"He's right about that. Covey can't, but I can. It requires one drop of my blood for each person bound."*

That's good to know. Greer relays what Draven says to the room.

"No, no, no. This whole thing is ridiculous," I protest.

"I'll do it," Cas says definitively.

"No, you won't. I am not going to let you duel an unhinged man because of a mess I made. He could seriously hurt you out there. Can't I fight for my own hand?" I ask Ash.

"Someone tried that once and it didn't end well, so they added an amendment to the rules stating that women can't fight for their own hand or interfere if a challenge is made."

"I'll fight for her hand," Greer offers.

"Yes! How about Greer?"

"Women are not allowed in a duel, period."

"Ugh! These sexist men. Just a bunch of pigs thinking women are a commodity to be bargained for," I mutter.

"Well, consider the time period this whole thing came from. Under the circumstances, we are lucky no one has updated it to current times, or else it undoubtedly wouldn't exist anymore," Ash explains.

"Regardless, I am not letting Cas fight my battles."

"Can Talli and I have a minute?" Cas asks, his tone calm.

Ash and Greer don't hesitate to grab the dragons off the table and head into the kitchen, leaving Cas and me alone. Well, Seth is here too, but completely unwilling to move from his spot.

Cas turns to me and grabs my hands. "I am not going to let someone blackmail you. Regardless of whether or not it was a mess you made, your mess is my mess. Your battles are my battles. So you're going to let me fight for you."

"Cas, we are trained at birth to fight and defend ourselves here with or without abilities. I've never seen him fight, but I have little doubt he is more than capable," I explain, needing him to understand how dangerous this could be.

"I have been training for a long time, too. I know I can take him on and win."

His confidence is so sexy, and I want to take him upstairs and show him exactly how much I think so, but he needs to back down from this idea.

"When we trained that one day, you did seem skilled, but I could have gotten out of any of those holds way faster than what I did."

"I know it's hard to believe, but I was going easy on you that day. If I really wanted you trapped, I could have done it."

I narrow my eyes at him. "You have never really seen me fight hand-to-hand."

"I watched you train with Greer that one time."

"Training with Greer doesn't count."

"Talliana, I need you to trust me. I know I can beat him, and it seems like the only solution to make him go away and save you at the same time."

"If you lose," I make a face before finishing, "I'd have to marry him."

"I won't lose."

"Then I'll have to marry you one day."

He tucks a strand of hair behind my ear and asks, "Is that such a bad thing? The idea of having to marry me one day?" His question is teasing, but it still makes my pulse quicken. The idea of marrying this man, walking down an aisle toward him, toward a happy future, brings me a wave of joy I cannot dissect right now.

"No...it's not."

"Then it's settled." Cas kisses me and then shouts, "She agrees!"

Chapter 54

TALLIANA

"I CAN'T BELIEVE I am letting you do this," I mutter to Cas the next morning.

We are all in Dad's office, waiting for the guards to escort Zander to the room.

"It'll be okay," Cas reassures, but it doesn't help.

Dad is currently studying the book Ash brought, which explains the duel. He lifts his face and asks, "It says the duel has to happen at sundown. Tell me, Ash, where do you plan to have this take place?"

"The Range felt like the obvious choice," Ash answers. Dad nods, putting down the book. Right on cue, a knock sounds at the door, and Zander enters the room with arrogance seeping from his pores.

"Have we come to a decision?" Zander asks coolly, while looking around the room. His eyes find Cas, and they narrow. He adds, "Talliana, I see you brought a lot of witnesses today for the moment you decide to give yourself to me."

Cas snarls at him, "Over my dead body." I nearly jump at the feral noise.

"Zander, I would like you to meet Mr. Caspian Stewart, a human who has the great misfortune of truly being in love with my daughter," Dad says despairingly. Cas calms slightly, and his grip on my hand loosens somewhat.

"So you're telling me no, then? You would really risk your daughter's imprisonment?"

Cas steps forward. "I challenge you to a duel for Talliana's hand in marriage and for her secret to be kept safe."

Zander's face contorts into confusion, then outrage. "You cannot be serious. Duels don't happen anymore, and for good reason, I might add. They are archaic and outdated."

"You don't have a choice." Ash takes the offered book from Dad and hands it to Zander. "You either agree to the terms and fight, or you forfeit, and you still lose Talliana and the right to share her secret."

"You are going to sit there and allow this?" Zander asks Dad incredulously.

"You have left me no choice."

Zander looks at all of us in disbelief, and I smirk at him as I lean in more toward Cas. He wraps a protective arm around me, and I let him to piss off Zander more.

"Fine. When is this to take place?"

"At sundown. The guards will ensure you have everything you need and go over all the rules with you," Dad answers. The guards open the door and escort him out of the room.

"Caspian, you really think you can beat him? You've never seen him fight," Dad asks.

"No need. I know the type well enough. I can beat him," Cas answers without hesitation.

"Alright. Greer, make sure he is ready for tonight, teach him our ways and our tricks. Ash, find him something to fight in. Talli," Dad hesitates, looking at me. "Go home and don't leave until someone comes to get you." I open my mouth, infuriated by the order, but Dad stops me. "I cannot risk this whole thing being a waste if someone thinks you are interfering."

Cas turns me around to face him. "It'll be alright. Trust the three of us to do this for you." His lips brush mine gently, and I don't argue as I go back home to sit restlessly.

It's Mom, of all people, who comes to get me. She takes one look at me and says, "No, you are not wearing that."

I look down at my simple blue top and jeans. "What's wrong with my outfit?"

"Two young men are literally fighting for you tonight. You should give them something to fight for." She grabs my wrist and hauls me up the stairs.

"Mom, I am not a prize to be won, and I will not dress up as one either."

"What happened to you? You used to love putting on nice dresses," she asks, as she lets go of my wrist and starts looking through Cas's and my closet.

"I became an assassin, remember?" I remind her, deadpan.

"But you're still a woman, capable of looking nice for the man you love, right?" Mom throws a dress at me.

"I'm pretty sure Cas prefers me in no clothes."

To my surprise, Mom laughs. "Don't most men."

Resigned, I start changing as I say under my breath, "Today is just becoming more and more out of my control as it goes on."

"It's good for you. Consider it character building," Mom quips.

"My character doesn't need any more building."

"Everyone's character could always use more building." She stops her frantic searching for shoes for a moment and adds sincerely, "Including mine. Talli, I'm sorry. I've let your Dad wrap me up in all his games lately, and I've lost sight of what's important," she pauses, meeting my eyes, then continues, "supporting you. No matter what you choose to do or who you choose to do it with, I should have been supporting you all this time, not trying to help your Dad control you. I hope that someday you can forgive me for my part."

I grab her hand, my frustration toward her that I've held onto for too long finally fading away. "I forgive you. I'll always forgive you. Dad on the other hand..."

"I'm working on him," Mom reassures me. She turns back around and pulls out shoes to match my dress and tosses them onto the floor at my feet. Thankfully, they're flats. I slip them on and turn to the mirror.

Mom picked out a fitted emerald green dress, something I wore for Christmas one year. It has silver stitching that follows the dress down to my knees and flows down the long bell sleeves. It's a bit fancy for this ridiculous occasion, but no doubt women used to wear full gowns when duels were still the norm.

"Much better. Now let's go before we are late." She rushes down the stairs, and I race after her. We keep up a good speed as we make our way to the Range using the forest path until we reach a crowd of people making their way over there as well.

I look to Mom. "No. What is this? Why is the whole community here?"

She doesn't look surprised as she explains, "Your dad thought it was best if everyone saw Zander make a fool of himself."

"But what if he doesn't?!" I argue.

"Don't worry. He will. Your dad will make sure this goes the way we want it to. I know he hasn't been fair to you or deserving of your trust, but I can promise you that he will keep you safe from Zander." Her tone is low so that no one overhears.

It's a small comfort knowing that Dad has a backup plan, but it won't be needed. Caspian will win. I know it.

We work our way through the crowd and come to the clearing at the Range. I immediately spot Cas, his sun-kissed torso on full display, with a pair of Order-issued black leather pants hugging his body in a way that leaves nothing to the imagination. He looks like one of us, and it's surprising to see how well he fits here. It's like he was meant to be a part of this all along.

Zander is a couple of feet away, dressed in the same fashion with pale skin that would be reflective if the sun were still fully in the sky. They are both standing at attention as Ash says something to them.

Dad comes up to Mom and me, and says quietly, "A stand was erected for us to sit at and watch. Come with me."

Sure enough, on the side, in the middle of the field, is a wooden stand with five seats sitting upon it. Three seats for the elders and two for Mom and me. We will all sit up there like royalty. The idea makes my stomach churn with disgust, and all I want to do is end this entire thing. Dad must be reading me because he grabs my hand and says into my ear, "I want Zander to feel as small as possible; it will make him angry and cloud his judgment during the fight."

"It could also push him to be more violent."

"Your guy can handle it. I saw him with Greer earlier, and I think she might have finally met her match on the mat."

I look at him in surprise. Cas said he held back with me, but how does someone control that much strength and skill if he truly has it? If he is a match for Greer, that means...he's better than me. It's not jealousy that finds me at that knowledge, but concern. How did I not know how good he is at fighting? Why didn't he ever tell me? How did the Brethren get the jump on him so easily? There had to be a lot of them, I reason, but something still doesn't feel right.

Reef meets me at the bottom of the steps and holds out a hand, not giving me any other option than letting him help me climb the steps to the stand. "If I knew dueling was an option for your hand, princess, I would have been the first to sign up," he teases.

Reef really has turned into someone much more tolerable, even if he still insists on teasing me and calling me princess. Thankfully not in front of Cas, though. I find a level of comfort in his presence now instead of unease. I take his hand, faintly realizing that all eyes are on me, and reply, "Feel like blackmailing me? It seems that's the way to get a spot on the list."

Reef's silver eyes swing to me sharply, but before he can ask, I'm at my seat, and it's time for him to walk off the stage with Odel following on his heels. I guess Dad doesn't tell Reef everything like I once thought.

I take my seat slowly and watch as the elders and Mom do the same. I find Cas again, and his hazel eyes lock onto mine as he slowly drinks something out of a silver chalice. Draven is in front of them as they drink, and I know this has to be the binding with Draven's blood. Ash didn't go into detail on what it entailed, but I can't imagine what else it would be. My nose threatens to wrinkle at the idea that they could very well be drinking a drop of Draven's blood right now, but Cas has me in a trance.

I snap back to reality when his eyes leave mine. I check for Coventina, but realize she is close too. Then she is suddenly beside the stand, her head turning to me. She says in my mind, *"I'm old, but even I haven't been to one of these."*

That does cause me to chuckle a little to myself.

"Don't enjoy it too much," I respond.

"Oh, I will."

Seth walks up to her fearlessly and sits down in front of her, facing the field. She chuffs at him, but he doesn't move.

I look back at Cas and find that both he and Zander are in front of the stand now, looking directly at me.

CHAPTER 55

CASPIAN

I WAS RAISED FOR one thing: to fight the Order and be as skilled as one of their own. I was taught to be as strong, fierce, and intelligent as they are. I'm putting all that training to use today, but never would I have thought it would be in this way, under these circumstances.

I bow deeply to Talliana, who is sitting like a queen on a throne before me. She is breathtaking. Problem is, she isn't a queen, and I'm not a knight. I'm just a bad man hidden under all this armor. And she? She is a goddess amongst these lesser Hawks. One I am willing to serve with every ounce of myself.

There is little doubt in my mind that the dress was Aaron's idea. This idea of a duel might have been Ash's, but turning it into a spectacle meant to put Zander in his place was his. I have gained a lot of respect for him over this last month. He is as clever as a fox and as fierce as the cat beside him now. I noticed him slip into the gym earlier and watch as Greer and I trained. If I am not mistaken, I even saw a small glimpse of respect creep onto his face.

Beyond giving me the chance to beat Zander's ass for what he is doing to Talli, this entire scenario also gave me the exact opportunity I needed to steal a memory potion. Ash brought me to the bottom floor of the community building to get me this ridiculous pair of Order-issued black pants out of their storage, which happened to be right next to a crate full of memory potions. I snatched three while Ash's back was turned. Whoever labeled every single item in that storage unit with neat stickers should be given a raise. I had already planned to sneak in late at night to steal some this week, but I was saved the trouble. Now I just need to find a way to get Talli to let me out of her sight long enough so I can meet with my father and finish my plan. But that's a problem for tomorrow.

Moving my eyes from the ground back to my goddess, I notice her anxiously biting her lip. I place my hand over my heart and mouth the words I know she needs: *my heart*. Her eyes soften, and with regret, I turn away from her and make my way to the middle of the field. All around the field are rows of people pressed together to try to get a good view of the show. If I'm not mistaken, the whole community is here. I have come to know many of them. Word spread fast of the new human who has their hero's heart, and they didn't hesitate to make excuses to visit Mr. Salo's shop during work hours to see me.

I'm used to everyone knowing who I am because of my role as the General's son, but I'm not used to everyone showering me with the same love and kindness they show Talli. These are truly good people, and I understand why she willingly sacrifices herself for them. I am surprisingly finding myself willing to do the same.

A couple more steps to the middle of the field, and I spot a group of young girls on the other side, huddled together and giggling. I flash them a dimpled smile, and they squeal, which makes me laugh.

Finally reaching the middle, I turn again to face Zander, spread my legs to widen my stance, and force the young girls, the people, and the world around me to disappear. All there is now is me and him. My enemy. Talli's enemy.

Aaron's loud voice booms through the field. "Start!"

Zander lunges for me with murder in his eyes. I tilt my upper body back, letting his fist sail past my head, then I land a swift punch to his gut. He pivots, twisting his body to try to grab the back of my neck, but I am behind him now, using my right foot to send him straight into the ground. The crowd cheers, momentarily breaking my concentration. I allow myself a quick smile toward Talli. Then I regain my focus and quickly step back a few paces as he climbs back to his feet.

Zander's face is red as he bares his teeth at me. This man is all hot rage and a short fuse. I've fought hundreds like him. "Look, no one would blame you if you wanted to concede now and save yourself further embarrassment," I say.

"You are a worthless human, at the bottom of the food chain, who needs to be put in his place," he responds.

"Suit yourself." I shrug, then get back into my stance.

He runs and jumps this time, extending his leg out to kick me in the chest. The force knocks me over, but I grab hold of his ankle and twist. He screams and scrambles away from me. I push off the ground and get to my feet, then spin, catching his fist with my left hand and punching him in the jaw with my right. To his credit, he pulls his fist out of my grip and keeps throwing punches. Left. Right. Left. Undercut. I deflect most of them, but I take one to the shoulder.

Zander is all length and minimal bulk, so I have no doubt he is trying to wear me out with deflecting while trying to keep himself out of my grasp. I let him land a small punch to my stomach and use his proximity to grab hold of his head, and send his face straight into my knee. He bounces off it and falls backward.

He wipes the blood gushing from his nose with his arm, then asks me in a sneer as he slowly gets back up to his feet, "What do you even see in her? She is nothing but a little whore."

Red fills my vision, and I reach for him, catching him off guard, and pulling him by the neck straight into my swinging fist. He goes down again, but I don't give him a chance this time to get up. Instead, I throw my body onto his and pull his arm back until I hear it make a distinct *pop*, then I hold it there. He tries squirming out of my grasp, but I have him pinned.

"You win! You win!" Zander squeals like the swine he is. I make him suffer for a moment longer, then let go. It would serve him right to have his arm broken, but I am choosing to be honorable today with everyone watching. I step back as I hear Aaron call, "Caspian Stewart is the winner!"

Well, that was easier than I thought. I turn to Talli and find her grinning wildly. She obviously did not hear what Zander called her, and I'm glad because it couldn't be further from the truth.

I am going to rip that dress off of her the first chance I get. I make that promise evident in the smile I give her, and am rewarded with her cheeks pinkening. But then suddenly, her hand shoots out, and something flies past my face. The crowd gasps, and I spin on my heels to find Zander on the ground, crying like a baby with a spear made of ice protruding from his shoulder.

Just as fast, shadows encircle his wrists and ankles, pinning him to the ground. The ass tried using his magic on me when I wasn't looking.

I should never have turned my back on him. That was clearly a mistake. In a fight with another human, I would have felt them come up behind me and I could have stopped them, but I have no sense of when magic is coming toward me.

Talli is suddenly standing over him, with Greer at her side. She clutches another ice spear in her hand that towers far above her head, and her stance is more rigid than my own was the moment before the fight started.

"You asshole! I don't know how anyone could have less honor. I should slit your throat right now for making a move against Caspian with his back turned." Her voice is low and odd. Not her voice, I realize, but the darkness.

Aaron appears on the scene. Folding his arms over his chest, he asks the sorry excuse for a man at his feet, "Have you learned your lesson yet?"

"You will all pay for this," Zander spits through gritted teeth. A bird swoops down to land on Zander's chest, like the Pheasant can defend him on its own.

"Give it a rest already! You have lost," Greer says. She carefully places a hand on Talli's shoulder, and I notice Talli relaxing at the touch, her spear dissipating into a puddle next to her. That's my cue. I grab Talli's hand from behind, and she spins toward me. Not before I see a dark substance receding into the corners of her eyes. Placing a hand on her cheek, I ask, "Talli?"

A moment passes, and she nods, then wraps her arms around my neck. I lift her up off her feet and hold her close to me. She pulls back and kisses me deeply for all to see. Her hand runs through my hair and fists it tightly. My nerves are lit with so much energy that I have to fight the urge to put her on the ground right here and make her scream my name for all to hear. I want everyone to know she is mine, and I am hers.

Getting a grip on myself, I put her down, but don't let her go far as our lips break away. She must feel similarly because she clings to one of my arms, both of hers wrapped tightly around it. I grip her hand, and we face Aaron and Rose.

Rose nudges Aaron in the side, and he extends his hand to me. I take it, and he says, "Good work, Caspian. You saved my daughter today, and that is something I won't forget. It seems she found herself a human warrior worthy of our cause." Rose nudges him again as he takes his hand back. "When you do ask for her hand one day, you already have my blessing."

I nearly stumble back from shock. Not if, but *when*. I do want that. I would be honored to call Talliana my wife, but I have to tell her who I am first, and I doubt she will feel the same way afterward. I doubt any of them will.

I force myself to smile, though, and reply, "Thank you, sir."

"Now, if you excuse us, I want to take my warrior home and feed him some dinner," Talli says, tugging me away from her parents.

We head toward our house, the anticipation of "dinner" making me grow hard in these impossibly tight pants, when Greer and Ash catch up to us, Seth and the dragons following close behind. Talli smiles brightly at them, no trace of darkness left as we keep walking. "Thank you both for helping Cas do this. I now have no doubt he could have done this without any help, but I appreciate you both just the same. And Ash, a special thank you for finding these pants for him." Talli steps away from me to make a show of ogling me. We all laugh, and I pull her to my side again.

"Yes, thank you both for helping me," I say gratefully.

Ash gives me a pat on my shoulder, and Greer gives me a rare smile. A moment of silence passes between us all until the trail ends, and we are at the main road.

Talli claps her hands together, looking at her sister and friend, then says way too loudly, "We are so grateful, and we love you both, but please leave us alone for at least twenty-four hours. I have plans for this man that no longer require an audience."

They head in a different direction without argument, Seth pouting but following them too, and Talli pulls me into a run toward our house. Her face is aglow with happiness and a light I have never seen before. She really is breathtaking. There is nothing more beautiful that she could wear than happiness.

Yanking me into our house and slamming the door behind us, she pounces. Her fingers are in my hair again, pulling me to her lips, which are greedy and devouring. I want her to devour me, to have her way with me, to do whatever she pleases, but I know what this is, so I pull away. Panting, I ask, "Talli, are you okay?"

"I need you." She reaches for me again.

I pull back, stopping her short. "You can have me, but I want to make sure you are okay first."

"I'm fine!" she snaps. I watch her take a step back, then visibly breathe. "I'm fine," she repeats more gently. "I'm just coming down from...from the fear of you getting hurt."

"You don't have to pretend with me. I saw it in your eyes earlier."

"You saw me lose control," she admits solemnly.

I pull her back to me. "I saw you regain control. I can't imagine how hard that is. Roles reversed, I would have beaten him to a pulp and smiled about it."

The corner of her lips turn up slightly, but it fades as she explains, "I thought I figured out control, balance even. But apparently not. It feels like an addiction that I have to constantly tread lightly with. The moment I give in to the urge of feeling strong emotions, it surges faster than I can cage or try to balance."

I can see in her eyes that it takes a lot for her to admit this to me. She isn't used to being open about what's going on inside of her, and I will not take that trust for granted.

"I suspect it's like anyone who struggles with an addiction. You can't just say you'll never touch alcohol again and move on with your life. You have to work at it every day and celebrate the small wins." A tear slips down her cheek, and I wipe it away before it can reach her chin. "Tell me what you need."

Her eyes flash, causing the blue of her irises to deepen in color. She hesitates and then says, "I'm not capable of being gentle right now. My control is still wavering and—"

"Tell me what you need."

"I...I need you, and I need you to be rough."

My heart rate speeds up at the thought, and she immediately looks at my chest.

"If you don't want to, I...it's probably not safe...I should..." She turns, but I grab her arm.

"I can take it. Let go of control for me."

Her lips part, and I take the opportunity to crash my mouth against them, letting go of all the restraints I have ever felt like I needed to have in my life. I have always considered myself a generous man in bed, even prided myself on it. I always ensure the woman finds every bit of pleasure first before seeking my own. I am always gentle and considerate, and I am always aware of my strength and size. But if Talli wants rough, she is the one woman I know who can handle it. Handle me. Like I know I am the one man who can handle her and the easing darkness that is still stirring inside her. So I hold her to me like someone is trying to pry her away from me.

Someone did try to pry her away from me, but I didn't let him. I protected her, and I will always protect her—my goddess, my love, my heart.

CHAPTER 56

TALLIANA

I HAD BEEN AFRAID to ask this of him, worried he wouldn't understand. But God, isn't my worry my worst enemy? Cas has always been everything I needed and more. He has always understood me.

Without thought, I bite down on his lip, licking the blood welling there and plunging my tongue back into his mouth. This sets something off inside of him. He grasps my dress in between us, and I hear the sound of fabric ripping, followed by the feel of it, and delicate lace pooling at my feet.

I fumble with the button and zipper of his deliciously tight pants until I finally set him free. He kicks them off the rest of the way, then picks me up, grasping my ass with a bruising grip, and places my entrance right over his hard cock. A gasp escapes me as I'm pushed against the wall and he drives into me. His pace is relentless. All I can manage to do is hold on for the ride.

"I hope you don't plan on using your legs for the next week," he growls in my ear.

Cas pushes me right to the edge of an orgasm, my legs trembling around his hips, but he stops abruptly, eliciting a whimper from me in protest. He laughs, clearly amused by the torture he is subjecting me to as he pulls me from the wall and carries me away from it. He sets me down on the dining room table and captures my lips with his again while his hands start to massage my breasts.

I moan into his mouth, and with my hands braced behind me, I try to push myself into his touch even more. His kisses move around my face until he reaches my neck and that favorite spot of mine. He sucks right over my pulse, scraping his teeth over the sensitive spot, causing my body to jerk in an electrified reaction. I stretch my neck out, giving him better access, and he nips at the skin, causing me to cry out his name. He licks the spot, trying to soothe the pain, but I don't want to be soothed. I lean down, pressing my mouth to his shoulder, and bite him. Hard.

His breath hitches, and he pulls himself away from me to place a palm on my sternum and pushes until my back is flat against the table. His eyes move over me, caressing me. "A feast worthy of a god," he breathes.

"A feast worthy of you." I spread my legs out wide, letting him see just how wet I am for him. Though, the evidence of that is all over his glistening cock, still fully erect and ready for me.

There is a fire in his eyes that no amount of water could put out, so I am surprised when he replies, "I'm no god. Just a thief that doesn't know when not to take things that don't belong to me."

I furrow my brow. Does he really think that? "Cas—" I start to argue with him, tell him how wrong he is, tell him how he is my equal regardless of magic and blood, but before I can get out the words, he lowers his mouth to my center. His tongue strokes me as his hands push my legs even farther apart. He sucks on my clit hard using his firm lips, then his teeth. I squirm in his grasp, my back arching and legs clenching.

He grabs my legs and moves them over his shoulders so that they are on either side of his head. He pulls my hips toward the edge of the table, toward *him* in a swift tug, his fingers biting into my thighs as he holds me down and continues tasting me. His tongue plunges inside of me, then out, in and out, then back up to my clit. My body begins to shake, and my hands reach down to find his head. I hold onto his hair, simultaneously wanting to pull him closer to me and push him away as everything feels like too much and not enough.

"Come for me, my heart," he says with his mouth still pressed against me.

Between the moans, I manage to reply, "Always. I will always come for you." I mean it wholeheartedly in both ways. My body will always come undone for him, and I will always come for him in times when he needs me. He is mine and I will do anything, fucking *anything*, to keep it that way.

I know he must catch my meaning, because his strokes and movements with his fingers intensify until I am wound up so tight that my body is fighting to stay in control. But with one more press of his tongue in the right spot, I shatter.

"Cas! Fuck...I...oh my God...Cas..." I sputter as he uses his finger to work me through the waves of pleasure, slowing down in time to my body's needs. Once he pulls his finger out, he licks away every bit of come that pours out of me. I can hardly breathe at the sight of it. At the sight of him drinking me like I am the elixir to immortality.

He stands up and runs his fingers through his hair, shaking it as he reaches the ends. To my shock, small pieces of frost fly in every direction as he does so.

"Oh...I...Are you okay?"

I can't believe I let my magic slip like that. I could have hurt him. I could have...

"I'm fine," he reassures me with a small chuckle.

Seeing the worry edging my face, he leans back down to kiss me until I feel it melt off of me like the ice in his hair. He roughly pulls me the rest of the way off the table, and once my feet hit the floor, I shove him hard. In his surprise, he falls back into one of the chairs, and I lower myself to my knees before him, his eyes trailing me intently the entire way down.

"I don't care who or what you are. You are my light, my equal, my everything. I need you to understand that no one in this world is more worthy of my love than you," I vow, then close my mouth over his cock. His whole body shudders as I take him until he reaches the back of my throat. Sucking hard, I pull all the way to the tip, then take him again.

"So fucking competitive," he grounds out between deep, throaty breaths.

I hum in agreement, causing his cock to jerk from the sensation. I cup his balls with my free hand and do it again. My mouth and hand work in tandem as I suck him, swirling my tongue around his length as I go. His hands fist into my hair, and I feel his thighs squeezing tightly around me as I continue to take him, doing everything in my power to keep my gag reflex at bay.

He must be close, because he abruptly lifts my face away from him, has me back on my feet, and then pushes me down onto the table on my stomach. He pulls my hips back, and my sensitive nipples drag across the woodgrain, sending another surge of heat through me at the sensation. He smacks my ass, leaving behind a sharp sting, and I only have a moment before I feel his cock slam into me, pushing me into the table. I cry out as he reaches a depth I have never felt before.

"You're so perfect," he hums out as he slams into me again. "From every strand of hair on your head," slam, "to the shape of your toes," slam, "from your stubbornness," slam, "to the love you have for your family," slam, "everything," slam, "all of you," slam, "fuck, I need to keep you forever."

I scream as I orgasm again, clutching him tightly inside of me. He shouts my name and slams into me one more time, then pulses inside me, filling me completely with his come. I feel him hunch over, pressing his sweaty chest against my back. His breathing is ragged, and I am completely boneless underneath him.

After a moment, I look up and see that the table has turned into a frozen landscape before me.

"I guess I am going to need to look into this," I say dryly.

"A tomorrow problem."

He stands, and on shaky legs, I attempt to push myself up from the table. Before I can fully stretch, he picks me up and carries me to the couch. He sits down with me on his lap, then lies down, pulling me down with him so that I'm lying on his chest. I yank at the blanket on the back of the couch and cover us up. I kiss his chest, and he moans again. He grabs my sides and pulls me up so that he can lock his lips with mine. Even though we are both still out of breath, he sweeps his tongue into my mouth and I accept him, touching his face with my hands softly. He pulls away after a long moment, and we rest in a comfortable silence for a while.

Unable to stop myself, I look up at him and ask, "Do you have a foot fetish I should know about?"

"Out of all of that, that's what you focus on?" He asks incredulously, but I also detect humor behind it.

I shrug and lay my head back down onto his chest. "Can't be too careful nowadays."

He laughs, shaking my whole body in the process. "Fair enough."

Eventually, he sits up, pulling me with him. He gently touches my neck, looking me over. I know there is a mark there, a mark he left. I look at his shoulder and see the mark I left on him.

"Do you want to take a shower?" he asks.

I smile at him. "No, I want to wear it with pride for as long as I can."

A feral smile spreads across his face. "All you have to do is ask if you want another one."

"Hmm...how sacrificial of you," I purr. Reaching my arms up, I wrap them around his neck and curl up against his chest. He grabs my ass, gently this time, and stands, lifting me with him. I bury my face in his neck, peppering it with soft kisses, tasting the salt coating him.

He huffs a laugh. "Wicked thing." I don't stop as he carries me up the stairs and into bed. He unceremoniously drops me on it, and I flail in surprise. He climbs onto the bed next to me and lies on his back. Then he says, "I'm starving."

I burst into laughter, turning my head to look at him. "Come on. Let's get cleaned up, and I'll make something for you."

He smiles, reaches over to give me a quick kiss, and heads to the bathroom. I study him as he goes, feeling a mix of emotions. The thought I had earlier is circulating again, and I don't know what to do about it.

He looks like one of us.

Granted, if someone lives among a group of people long enough, they do start to blend in with those people, from adopting their mannerisms to talking like them. I believe that is a scientific fact, but a month? That's not possible. He fits in well, he fights like us, and aside from the dragons, he never seems to have trouble understanding or believing different things he learns. I promised myself that I wouldn't tune into his emotions deliberately, so I only catch the occasional feeling here and there if he is projecting. But he rarely has the outbursts that most humans do. It's almost as if...*as if he is shielding.*

I hear the shower turn on, and I come to a decision. Moving quickly to avoid losing my nerve, I climb into the shower with him. Cas's smile is nothing short of smug. "Already ready for me to mark you again?"

My cheeks flush, and I let him move me into the water. His eyes are fixed on my neck as I feel the water tingle over the mark he left and heal it as if it never happened. If only the water could heal my mind as if that terrible thought had never entered it.

He looks like one of us.

While he is distracted, I take a breath and tune into him. I immediately feel satisfaction and lust, no steady hum of static or complete void of emotions. Good, that's how it should feel. Perfectly human.

Go further.

The thought didn't come from the darkness, but from something deeper inside of me. It wants me not to just sense, but to look. All Hawks are taught to sense emotions, but only a few know how to look with our inner eye. I only know how because several years ago, when Ms. Horn taught me how to build a better shield, she also thought it wise to teach me how to do this as well. It was something I used on Trey too many times when I was concerned about him hiding things from me. Now I am about to do it to Cas, too.

I open my inner eye, and relief surges through me as I come face-to-face with nothing more than two little clouds pulsing and floating in front of me. One is colored a deep red-purple, lust. While the other is an orangey color, satisfaction. There is no wall, no haze, nothing covering these little clouds. I look around, but in the distance, I see more clouds. Their color impossible to make out. I approach them, but as I get within two feet of them, I slam right into something. Nothing? There is nothing here, but something stopped me. I put my hand up against it and feel smooth glass.

I gasp. There is no way.

There is a glass wall protecting his other emotions behind it. I take a step back. I have never seen anything like it. I didn't even know such a thing was possible.

A hand caresses my cheek, and I tune back out to find Cas studying me in front of my actual eyes.

"Are you okay?" he asks.

My head is spinning, and my heart is racing. Who is this man in front of me? He has to be a Hawk and a skilled one if that shield is any indication. But why? Why would he hide who he truly is from me? Even if he didn't know who or what I was at our first meeting, he could have told me once he learned the truth, but instead, he continued the act of being a human. For what? Nothing makes sense.

"Talli? My heart?" He's trying to catch my eyes, and I meet his with a start.

"I—I'm sorry. I got lost in a thought for a moment," I stutter.

I can't voice any of this. I need to figure out who he is first and then confront him. I can't let him know that I suspect him.

Cas pushes my wet hair back from my face and hugs me to him. "I was worried for a moment." I turn my head and come face-to-face with the mark I left earlier. I pull back, remembering myself. Without question, I will a small bead of water to his shoulder and heal the mark there.

"Hey, I planned on keeping that," he chides, trying to look at his newly healed shoulder.

I force a smile on my face. "Well, all the more reason for me to give you another one later." He laughs and captures my lips in a long kiss. We finish our shower and head into the kitchen to make dinner. I find my phone sitting on the kitchen counter where I left it before the duel. I grab it and type a message into it.

Me: *I need your help. Discreetly look for Cas in our database. He might be going under a different name. Start with Colorado.*

Asher: *What's going on?*

Me: *I'll tell you tomorrow.*

Asher: *I don't like this.*

My phone flashes with a different text.

Greer: *I don't like this either.*

Cas's arms encircle my waist, causing me to startle in surprise. "What does Greer not like?" he asks, resting his chin on my shoulder.

I quickly lock my phone and set it back down. "Dad needs Greer and me in a meeting tomorrow morning," I lie.

Cas groans. "So much for twenty-four hours of not leaving this house."

I turn in his arms. "I'll be quick, then I promise I'll climb right back into bed with you after I am done. You won't even notice that I'm gone."

"I always notice when my heart is not nearby." He kisses me before turning to the fridge to look for food.

What am I going to do?

ELDER MEYER TOLD ME MY SON PRESENTED AN ABILITY. HE IS AS KLAUS WAS, A MIMIC. I'M GRATEFUL THAT HE WILL NOT BE USED AS I HAVE BEEN, BUT I AM DISHEARTENED KNOWING HE WILL BE ANYTHING LIKE THE MAN THAT FAILED HIM AS A FATHER.

I THOUGHT MY SITUATION COULD NOT BECOME MORE DISMAL, BUT THE ELDER ALSO INFORMED ME THAT I AM TO BE MARRIED AGAIN TO SEE IF MY ABILITY WILL BE PASSED ON TO MY SECOND CHILD INSTEAD—SOMEONE THEY COULD TRY TO CONTROL FROM THE BEGINNING. BUT I REFUSE TO BE MARRIED OFF AGAIN FOR BREEDING LIKE A BROODMARE.

- JOURNAL OF KATARINA LEHMANN

Chapter 57

TALLIANA

THREE DAYS LATER, I open the back door to Greer and Ash. They come in, and I shut the door behind them. Cas is at work today helping at the woodworking shop. If he is to be believed, it's something he has really started to enjoy, working with wood. Maybe he is an Earth Elemental. It's my best guess because he doesn't seem to have an affinity for anything else.

"Please tell me you have something." We met that morning after I texted them, and they have been researching ever since, trying to find out who Cas is.

"The lack of it, actually," Ash replies.

"You didn't find anything?"

"No. If he is a Hawk, he isn't a part of any community and never has been."

"Or someone erased his file somehow," Greer remarks, and Ash looks at her, alarmed.

"Why? Why go through all this trouble?" I ask, throwing up my hands in annoyance.

"To get to you. You've turned down every Hawk that has shown up at the doorstep, so maybe he was desperate enough to find a different way for you to give him a chance," Greer reasons, using her Strategist's mind.

Rejecting that idea immediately, I say, "No. Cas is not the power-hungry type. I mean, I'll admit that the start of our relationship seemed very intentional on his side, but he explained all that, and he never tried rushing things or pushing me. The exact opposite, really."

"Talli, we can keep researching for you, but we have already searched everywhere for a trace of him. I can try to reach out to each community with his description to see if anyone knows him, but—"

Greer cuts Ash off by saying, "But. You should confront him and get this whole thing over with."

I sigh, slumping up against the wall by the back door.

"We can wait outside when you do it in case you need backup," Ash offers.

"He won't hurt her," Greer says with no doubt lacing her tone.

I look at her. "I don't think we can assume anything about him." Even as I say it, I know that's not true. Greer is right. I know he would never hurt me. Whatever his excuse is for pretending to be a human, he loves me, and I love him. I'll be angry for a while, but we'll get past this.

We have to.

Cas came home in the evening with a big smile on his face. Over dinner, he told me about the rocking chair he is learning to make and how excited he is to show it to me.

"Next, I am going to build you bookshelves for your collection of books. We can make you an entire library in one of the guest rooms if you want. I'll even figure out how to make one of those rolling ladders." My heart warmed at the idea of having a house full of furniture that he made himself. It still feels warm at the idea. We could make this house truly ours, and when I end the war, we could make a family and build a life that we love. That is something I have always wanted, even though I lost hope that I could have it a long time ago. But I have to do this first.

"Cas?" I ask quietly as we lie in bed together.

I feel him shift toward me in the dark and bury his face in my neck. He kisses my sensitive spot, then replies, "Yes, my heart?"

I hesitate, not wanting to ruin this, but I don't have any other choice if I want that future with him. "Are you hiding something from me?"

He freezes instantly. After a long moment, he pulls away and turns on the lamp on his nightstand. He sits up and looks at me. I watch as a war takes place behind his eyes and sit up myself, slightly inching away from him.

"What makes you think I am hiding something?" he asks carefully.

"You're not denying it?"

He shakes his head, and my stomach falls. Now facing the reality that I am right, my fear triples.

"Whatever it is, I'm sure I'll understand if you explain it to me." These are words I need to believe because I have come to a point where I can't live my life without him. Trey's death nearly killed me, but if something happened to Cas? There would be no return for me.

"I'm afraid you won't. Even if you let me explain, I don't know if there is any chance of coming back from this." His head drops slightly as he stares at the bed. He won't even look me in the eye. "Just please know that I truly, deeply love you more than I have ever loved anything. I have wanted to tell you. I have almost a hundred times, but I've been so fucking terrified of losing you." His glassy eyes meet mine, and all the hope that I just built my courage up on fades away. I know without a doubt that this is going to break me.

"Tell me." My voice cracks, and tears flow down my face in streams as I prepare myself. He hesitates, and I burst out, unable to bare this any longer, "Are you one of us? Did you pretend to be a human to get to me?"

His eyes widen, but I keep going, the words falling out of my mouth. "Because you blend in so well around here, and you have taken everything in stride. You even fight like us and look like us. Dad accepted you quicker than I expected. Does he know who you really are? God, did he orchestrate this as a way to control me?"

Cas touches his hand to my cheek, and I fight every urge to lean into it like I have done what feels like a thousand times before. A tear slides down his cheek as he answers, "I wish more than anything that I was one of you. I wish more than anything that I were just a simple med student who fell in love with a magical woman who exists in a world that shouldn't be possible. But I am neither of those people."

I take in his words. If he isn't a Hawk, and he isn't a clueless human...

"NO." A sob racks my chest. "No. You can't be." I pull my face away from his hand and scramble out of bed, putting my back against the wall. My control slips, and I feel the darkness reaching for my heart as it shatters and falls. It coats it completely, then claws up my throat until I can't breathe.

"You can't be!" I scream, my voice not my own.

"Let me explain. You need to know the truth. But please, you need to breathe first." His tone is desperate.

Looking down through the black haze in my eyes, I see an ice dagger clenched in my fist. Oh God. I can't let it go or make it go away. My hand is not my hand as it clenches it tighter. I look back up at Cas, panic only making the darkness worse.

"I can't," I wheeze.

Cas moves slowly toward me, like he is approaching a wild animal. Another dagger forms in my other hand, and he stops. "Talli, come back to me. Please, my heart."

"Don't call me that!"

He lunges for me, causing me to drop both daggers, and pushes me to the floor. He straddles me, pinning my hands above my head, but two more daggers reappear in my palms, and I slice his hands. He recoils, and I'm forced to climb back to my feet. The darkness strikes out at him, and he catches my wrist once more, twisting my arm to my back so I lose grip on the dagger again. He pushes me up against the wall.

"I don't want to hurt you!" he screams.

"That makes one of us!"

His grip is so loose that my body spins and shoves him to the ground, putting me on top of him instead. He holds up his hands in defeat, unwilling to really fight me. My blade presses against his throat, but as my eyes find his, the darkness stops. I stop.

Those beautiful brown and green eyes, eyes belonging to the man I love, the man I feel connected to by a thick metal chain, my light, and everything that has brought me happiness. Those eyes aren't looking at me in fear. They are looking at me in regret and love despite what I am doing right now.

I feel the darkness recede, its grip loosening on me. I make a cage around it and will the icy blade in my hand to shift into water, drenching his neck. He closes his eyes and takes a deep breath. Before he can open them again, I punch him hard, knocking him unconscious. I climb off of him as quickly as I can manage and push myself into the corner.

I hear a whine and a scratching at the door until it opens, and Seth comes in. He immediately goes to Cas and nudges his face with his nose. He whines some more and lies down, resting his head on his chest.

"He lied to us, Seth. He's one of them. He's a Brethren." I choke on the word. Seth doesn't move, though.

I focus back on what's going on inside of me, and I force myself to keep breathing until the burn of the darkness completely subsides. I reach up to my nightstand and grab my phone to text Greer.

Me: *It is so much worse than we thought.*

Greer: *Shit. OTW*

I look over at Cas again, lying helplessly on the floor, with a million things running through my head. I try to shove everything away and focus on my next steps. Starting with getting dressed.

It's not long before I hear a knock on the door, and I run downstairs to answer it. No one says anything as I lead them upstairs. Ash gasps at the sight of Cas. "What did you do to him?"

"I hit him. Hard."

"If he is still unconscious after a hit like that, you probably did some severe damage—"

"Ash! I am the Healer here and the med student. I know I did damage. I intended to do damage."

"But—" I cut Ash off, "He's a Brethren."

They both look at me with wide eyes. Greer says in disbelief, "But what I saw…No, that can't be right."

"It doesn't matter what you saw. Really, the only thing that matters right now is getting him in a cell before he wakes up."

"Are you sure? We can question him here and figure out the whole story before we drag everyone else into this, especially Dad. Maybe he has a good explanation," Greer suggests.

"No, there is no explanation good enough for what he is or what he has done to me. He deserves a cell."

Greer stops arguing, and between the three of us, we get him dressed, handcuffed in Greer's shadows, and out of the house where Draven is waiting. We throw him over the dragon's back, and we all walk in silence to the community building. Seth follows behind us, determined not to leave Cas's side. Once we reach the community building, Greer gets two of the guards on duty to help us get Cas inside and into a cell.

The guards look startled, knowing who Cas is, but don't question Greer's orders. They gently set his limp form on a cot in one of the cells, and Seth follows behind them and lies down on the floor next to Cas. Greer looks at Seth and then at me, looking for an answer to what to do. I nod, and Greer shuts the cell door, locking it in place.

I stand at the cell bars, unmoving except for the shake in my hands, and watch Cas closely. He will wake up soon. Greer hesitates next to me.

"Go, I'll be okay."

Greer nods once, knowing not to argue with me anymore tonight. Ash is the one to hesitate further, but Greer grabs his arm and pulls him along.

Once they are gone, I grab one of the water bottles on the shelf meant for prisoners, open it, and use the water to heal his head and the small cut on his neck. I tell myself it's because I want him to be in good shape to answer my questions, but I know it's something else entirely that makes me do it.

He's only unconscious a moment longer, until he groans and grabs his head. He takes in his surroundings, lifting his head, which is pointed away from me. The cot is up against the left-hand wall, so his feet are toward me. I hear him mutter, "Damn it, Talli."

"Care to say that to my face?" I'm stone cold. I will not let him get the better of me.

He whips around to see me, and his expression surprises me. He looks relieved rather than frustrated, as his tone suggested.

"I told you I would tell you the truth. I would have willingly let you put me in this cell. You didn't need to knock me out," he says as he shifts himself to a seated position.

"Clearly, you don't know me. I don't take my chances when it comes to monsters like you. Especially knowing what you're capable of. Although I think that's all I actually know about you at this moment." Bitterness drips from my every word.

His mouth opens and closes, choosing his words carefully. Cas sighs and then begins, "My name is Caspian Stuart Campbell. Stuart is my middle name, not my last name." Seeing my eyes widen, he confirms what is clearly going through my mind. "Yes, that Campbell. My father is General Campbell, the leader of the Brethren. Ask me anything, and I swear I will give you the truth."

I gasp at that knowledge alone. I see it now, the resemblance—the same sweep of the hair, same jaw line, same nose.

"So, what is this? Daddy didn't give you enough attention, so you wanted to piss him off by dating a witch?"

His jaw clenches. "No."

"Was this some mistake? We fell in love, and when you learned who I was, you didn't know how to get out of it, so you've just been trying to hide who you truly are?" It feels like a stretch, but I reach out for it just the same.

He drops his head into his hands. "No."

There is only one more possibility running through my brain, and it's the worst out of all of them. "Dating me was a ploy, a way to get to me. So that what? You could kill the famed assassin of the Order? I hate to break it to you, but you've had hundreds of opportunities and failed each time."

"My mission was to gain your trust and learn as many secrets as possible about the Order."

The blood drains from my body. Oh, how he has succeeded then. The things he knows could be the end of the Order.

"But I haven't told them anything, I swear," he says.

"Was any of this," I gesture in between us, "real for you? Or just a sick game?"

"Everything was real. From my initial interest in you to every kiss. My love for you is more real than the sun rising every morning and setting every night. That's why I haven't shared any of your secrets. I decided a long time ago that I couldn't do that to you. I chose you, Talli. Before I even said those three words, I decided that my love for you was stronger than my loyalty to the Brethren."

My stomach turns. I can't do this. I can't face this tonight. I have so many questions, but I can't do this. "I thought I could do this, but

I can't. Not tonight." Without giving him a second glance, I turn and start walking down the hall.

"I knew him. Treyton," he calls out. I stop mid-step, and the breath I was about to take halts in my throat. I'm frozen in place. I don't turn around. I don't look at him. I stand there, not sure I can believe my own senses that are telling me he is speaking the truth.

"Did he ever tell you why we went through the trouble to take him prisoner instead of just killing him?" Cas asks when I don't move.

I do move then, march right back up to his cell, and look him straight in the eye. Vibrating with uncontrolled rage, I force out between grinding teeth, "I saw his scars, you piece of shit. I asked, but circumstance prevented him from telling me."

Cas visually flinches like I cut him with a knife. He takes a deep breath. "They," he stops and starts again, "We. We needed information on how to hide our thoughts and feelings so that they could not be read. So that we could infiltrate the Order from the inside."

"Trey would never have betrayed us like that, regardless of what you did to him."

"I know. He didn't, not to save his own life. But yours. Your life was worth more to him than anything else," he pauses for a minute to stand up, scrubbing his face with his hands, then continues, "He saved your life more times than you even know. He didn't believe at first that we could really reach you, then when you broke your arm, he never doubted again."

The weird car accident that left me with a broken arm shortly after Trey left. Trey told me it was them who had done it. They did it to get to him. So many pieces fall into place. "You were in the jewelry store that day, not shopping for your girlfriend, but trying to stall me."

"Yes. I also stole your keychain from your purse. I used it as a means to convince him I could...touch you if I wanted to," Cas admits, sounding disgusted.

My head spins. Now, this is really too much.

"*You alright, sad one?*"

"*I will talk to you later.*"

I feel Coventina's presence lighten in my head, and I grab onto the bars of the front of Cas's cell, gripping them tight to try to dampen my anger.

"Did you ever lay a hand on him yourself?" I ask evenly.

Silence.

A sound escapes me, one born from the truest feelings of grief. I've fallen in love with Trey's captor, his abuser. My voice is weaker than I have heard it in a while when I ask, "Why me?"

"I didn't want it to be you. I initially picked out an easier mark, but then we figured out your identity, so my father changed the plan. I argued with him that Trey might have told you about me, tried changing his mind, but he wanted me to learn everything you knew and then kill you after. Taking out two birds with one stone." He takes in a pained breath and stops his pacing.

He was supposed to kill me. After he got everything he wanted from me. Despite his claim of changing his mind, I feel betrayed. He promised to help me heal my broken heart. And he did just that, conveniently placing himself inside it so he could manipulate me.

He is silently watching me, like I am watching him. I break eye contact first and walk away from the cell without another word. He calls out, "I could never figure out how a man could love a woman as much as Trey loved you. It was a mystery that plagued me every day, until we had that first dance at the club. Then I realized that loving you would be as easy as breathing."

I don't stop my pace this time. I keep walking, allowing tears to streak down my cheeks. I don't hide my face or try to wipe them away as I pass by all the guards. I only want to curl up in bed, but I can't go home. The image of him and his smell are all over the home we shared together. I wouldn't be able to escape him there. My feet move me in the opposite direction instead. To the lake. To Trey.

Once I arrive at our spot, Coventina is standing there, waiting for me. Her head lowers, and the last grip I have on my emotions slips. I run the rest of the distance to her and press my face against hers. My hands find the base of her jaw, where her hair starts, and I pull her to me as much as I can. A sob rolls through me, causing my body to tremble and my tears to grow into the size of heavy raindrops.

"*How do I survive this?*" I ask her. Thunder rumbles in the distance, mimicking my sobs.

"*By learning from your past mistakes,*" she answers. That makes me cry harder, because that is exactly what I want to do. Shove all my emotions deep down and muffle them until I can't hear or feel them.

A drop of water splashes onto my head, and I pull away from her to look up. The clouds break open and rain rushes out, instantly soaking me to the bone. Coventina nudges me toward the tree, and I don't argue. I move under the willow tree where Trey's gravestone is and curl up next to it, laying my head against the cold stone. Coventina lies down next to me, only her upper body under the coverage of the tree.

My body is shaky with shock, and I have no idea how to process everything I have learned. There are so many moments, lies, and emotions to sort through and try to understand through the new lens of the truth. It's all too much, so I sit there letting the tears continue rolling down my cheeks, dampening the stone, and listening to the rain splash into the lake. Then, when I feel ready, I start to talk to Trey like I used to. "Hey there, handsome. I'm sorry it's been a while. I met someone, and God, I don't know if I can honestly say that I wish I hadn't. I want to say that and have it be the truth, but Trey, I'm such a mess. I miss you so much. If you were still here, none of this would have happened."

I continue like this, telling Trey everything about Cas and what has happened. I keep reminding myself that Trey knows Cas already, but it doesn't stop me from telling him anyway. Saying it all out loud is helping me process, helping me wrap my mind around it. Because Coventina is right, if I don't get it all out somehow, I will go back to where I was before Cas came into my life. A hollow version of myself with all my emotions that my body and mind are craving to feel buried away. I have to let myself feel them to get past them. But how does a person get past this? This betrayal, this pain, this grief? He said it's always been real for him, but how can I believe it? I can't trust myself to be sure of the truth anymore.

The rain continues to follow the stream of tears that flow from my eyes, and Coventina doesn't move during any of it. She remains a comforting companion as I pour my shattered heart out.

CHAPTER 58

CASPIAN

I LISTEN AS TALLI'S footsteps take her away from me. I hear a door slam shut, and with it, my worst fear comes to life. I whirl and send my fist flying toward the concrete wall. I need something to hurt more outside than how I hurt inside. Before my knuckles can collide with the wall, an iron grip of shadow appears around my wrist, stopping the blow. I jump back, turning to see Greer coming out of the shadows against the wall outside of the cell, Draven on her shoulder.

"If you plan to break your hand in hopes Talli will come fix it, you have way too high an opinion of her," Greer says. She steps back and casually leans against the wall, not covered in shadows this time.

"Have you been here the entire time?" I ask indignantly.

"Yes, but only because I knew Talli was coming down from a darkness high, and I wanted to make sure she didn't do something she would regret."

"Ha! Well, she almost slit my throat when she found out the truth. I'm not sure what stopped her, and I'm not sure I'm glad that it did."

"Love is a powerful thing. Much more powerful than anger and hate. You'd be hard-pressed to convince her of that, though," she replies.

Running my hand through my hair in a nervous gesture, I admit, "I didn't know how to reach her. I thought she was going to kill me."

"I have no doubt you could have stopped her, even if you couldn't reach her."

"I didn't want to hurt her."

"Because you already hurt her enough for one lifetime."

My anger rises. "What do you want, Greer?"

She pushes off the wall and says, "I'm not going to ask for your story. That right belongs to Talli first and foremost, but I am going to ask you not to give up. She needs you more than I think anyone can guess right now, and you need her, too. Despite how this all started, I know how this will end. So don't you dare start sulking and throwing yourself against the walls in despair. You need to sit your ass down and figure out how to reach her."

"Despite what you think of me, I won't ever give up on her. I just don't know how to get through to her if she won't even listen to me."

"If you are clever enough to hide who you really are for this long from all of us, you are clever enough to find a way to get her back."

My mind races, and I remember something. "Give me your knife."

She looks at me incredulously. "Again, that is not the answer."

I hold up my forearm to her. "I have a chip in my arm. If I stay in one spot for too long, my father is going to think I have either been killed or thrown in a cell. I need to take it out."

She examines my arm as if she can see the chip if she looks hard enough, but she eventually sighs and hands me her small dagger.

I slice my arm open in the exact spot I memorized when I found it so many years ago. I hand her back her knife and push around on the surrounding skin, and slide the little chip out. "You cannot destroy it. If you destroy it, he will think I am running. He can't know there is something wrong, or he will bring his army here again." I place the chip in her open palm.

"I'll make sure it moves around the community and nothing happens to it. Call out to the guards if you or Seth need anything. You are a prisoner, and you will stay in there for as long as Talli says so, but we aren't monsters like the Brethren. You'll be provided food and water. Pen and paper if you want that, too." Then she turns and walks away.

Pen and paper.

"Greer!" I call out, hoping she is still within earshot.

"Consider it done," she calls back to me.

I lay myself down on the flimsy cot, my arms folded tightly in front of me, while I lie on my side and try to close my eyes. I know sleep is impossible, but I need to calm myself. I can't help but think about the man who had Talli first and the very reason why I am here now. There are so many memories with him, so many hours spent having him teach me exactly what I needed for this whole thing to be possible.

My mind lands on one. It was after I met Talli for the first time at the jewelry store. I was confused and upset afterward, because even then I had felt a connection with her. Something that pulled at me and made me not want to leave her side. I let the memory replay...

I strode into the room I had grown to hate more than anywhere else on the planet. I closed the door behind me and pressed the red folder against his chest. He took it but didn't open or move it. I circled around the seat that his legs and waist were tied to, like a shark circling its prey.

"Go on, open it," I told him.

Treyton looked at me with distrust, but he did what I told him to. I stopped in front of him and watched as he went through the contents of the folder I had so carefully put together: the picture of the wrecked car, Talliana in the back of the ambulance with Asher right next to her, and medical records from the hospital detailing her injuries.

When he was done, his jaw was tense, and he ground out, "I was told if I left willingly, you wouldn't hurt anyone in my community."

"And you believed us? I told you time and time again that if you didn't cooperate, she would get hurt. That you should have believed. Now she has gotten hurt. She will heal, but this is your only warning. Next time, we will grab her and hurt her in front of you. Do you want that?" I practically yelled at him.

I felt rage at the idea that if he had just done as we had asked, we wouldn't have had to hurt this girl. One that looked as if she couldn't hurt a fly. The word "innocent" crossed my mind, but I knew better. She wasn't innocent, none of them were. These people were evil, using their unnatural powers to hurt those who *were* truly innocent.

"You are all monsters," he seethed, throwing the folder at me.

"If she gets hurt again, it will be on your conscience. It will be your fault, not mine." His silence and hateful eyes only made me angrier. "I don't want to hurt her! It wasn't my call to hurt her in the first place."

Still, I was met with silence. So I changed tactics. "I see why you love her. There are so many reasons to. Is it the way her freckled cheeks redden at the slightest attention? Maybe it's the way she smells? Like rain-kissed leaves. How about the shiny pink gloss she wears on her lips? Her plump, perfect lips." I saw that I was getting to him, so I continued, "She was very nice, helping me pick out my fake girlfriend a present. Picked out a beautiful heart necklace after I asked her to show me what she liked. I bought it, too, since she seemed to like it so much. Maybe I'll give it to her one day."

"You're lying!" Treyton shouted.

I smiled and pulled out of my pocket something I hadn't been able to quite let go of. I threw it at him. His eyes widened as he took in the small keychain. It was a butterfly with "Best Sister" engraved on it and a colorful tassel attached. I swiped it off of Talliana's purse while she was looking at the necklaces.

"Still think I am lying?"

His voice was low as he promised, "I am going to kill you one day."

"Well, today is not that day. Nor will it be tomorrow. Do as I ask, and no more harm will come to Talliana."

"I don't even know if it will work."

"I'm not asking you to make it work. I am asking you to teach me so that I can see if it works."

"If it does work, what will you do with it?"

"That is my business, not yours." I smiled, knowing I had won. When I reached the door, I said to him, "Be ready. Lesson one in shielding begins tomorrow."

Pulling myself from the memory, I shift myself onto my back and stare at the ceiling instead.

I hated him. I hated him so much. I still would if it wasn't for the fact that he saved Talli's life, and I can't bring myself to hate anyone who saves her. God, he was so proud of his love for her, too. One day during training, he saw my jealousy and mocked me for it. "People like you don't get to know love like the rest of us," he had told me, and then laughed in my face.

At the time, I didn't think he was wrong, either. What I saw in his eyes every time I gave him a new picture of her was unlike anything I had ever seen. I thought he was a fool, but I still felt jealous nonetheless. I'd never felt even the slightest bit of warmth toward another person, let alone love. I wanted what he had, but we both thought I would never have it. I guess the joke is on both of us, seeing that I got exactly what he had, and I did get to know exactly what love feels like. I got to know what *her love* feels like.

It has been hard not to wonder these past months if what he felt was the same as what I feel now, or if it was different somehow. If the love she felt for Trey is the same love she feels for me, or if that's different, too. All I do know is that I will never feel like this toward another person in my life. If I survive this, Talli will always be exactly what I call her.

My heart.

CHAPTER 59

TALLIANA

I MUST HAVE FALLEN asleep at some point, because I wake up in the same spot with my head resting against Coventina's scales. I sit up and stretch out my neck, trying to work out the knot that has formed at the base of it, when I find a blanket draped across my lap. I look up and find Draven curled up into a ball, Greer and Ash both tucked into his side, asleep with their own blanket.

Despite the pounding in my head from crying so much, I smile at them. I may not know *how* to survive my heart shattering for the second time in my life, but I will, I have to.

Not just for myself, but for them.

Coventina lifts her head, and I turn toward her, holding her deep blue eyes for a moment before she looks past me toward Draven. "*I told him not to come. I demanded that he stay at the den with the other dragons and let me walk my path alone. But he has always been a terrible listener.*"

I look back at the sleeping dragon. He has never looked young to me, but in this moment, I can picture him as a small boy, one who is afraid of losing his sister and is determined to follow her through everything.

Coventina continues, "*I love him all the more for refusing to listen to me. Because like humans, dragons aren't meant to be alone. You need them, Talliana, as much as they need you. The moody one who cannot swim well, the smart one who talks way too much and never enough, and the one who is your light. You cannot end the war without them.*"

I abruptly stand, my sorrow starting to simmer into anger again. "*Greer and Ash will have to be enough.*"

"*If they were enough, then you would have ended the war already. They are only two pieces in a large puzzle. He is a third. And there is more to discover yet. But you will need every piece if you want to fulfill your destiny.*"

"*If you have all the answers, then tell me what all the pieces are so we can get this over with already,*" I retort.

"*That's not how it works, and you know it.*"

"*Well, it should be. Because I am tired of having a sledgehammer taken to my life in the meantime. If it is meant to be some kind of motivator, it is having the opposite effect.*"

"*All will work out as it's meant to.*" Her words are meant to bring me comfort, but I only grow more frustrated.

"*I no longer believe that.*"

"*Then your people are doomed. Now, if you'll excuse me, I need to wash this filthy dirt off my scales. I feel disgusting.*" She gracefully stands on her four thin legs and walks off with a swish of her tail toward the lake.

I catch a stir in the corner of my eye, and see that Ash is awake and trying to carefully step around Draven's tail without waking anyone. He's successful, and once he reaches me, he asks in a low tone, "What can we do?"

I allow myself to give him a sad smile. "There is nothing anyone can do. Cas lied to me throughout our entire relationship. There's no coming back from that, despite what Greer and Covey believe. I just have to decide what to do with him, then that will be that."

Ash nods solemnly. "There is no denying that he is Trey's opposite in every way possible, but one way has stood out to me as I've gotten to know him." I raise an eyebrow, uncertain of where he is going with this, and he continues, "Cas understands you in a way Trey never did. Never could. He sees you for exactly who you are and loves every part of you. I'm afraid my brother wanted to shelter you from the dark parts of yourself."

"How do you know, Ash? Clearly, he is good at pretending to be someone else. How do you know he wasn't faking that, too?"

"Because his true emotions are written all over his face, like yours are. And I don't have to be a Hawk to see exactly what he is feeling."

"Even if you're right, we can't trust him anymore."

Greer stirs, and Draven stretches like a dog after a long nap. His arms stretch out in front of him, his back arching, then rolling until his backside is straight in the air. Before Greer gets the chance to give me my third lecture of the early morning, I leave and go toward my house to take a shower. *My family's house*, I clarify in my mind.

I can't go home. Not yet.

When I leave the bathroom, Greer is waiting for me with arms crossed.

"I checked on the prisoner. He gave me something for you." She extends a white piece of paper folded in half. I open it to find the whole page scribbled with Cas's messy handwriting. I close it quickly, not wanting to read anything on it. Moving to my nightstand, I toss it into the drawer and shut it.

Greer watches me, but surprises me when she says, "Let's go train."

"I'm exhausted, and I have a kink in my neck that I can't quite manage to heal. So no." I plop down on the bed and pull the covers up to my chin.

"Fine. If you plan to lie here and wallow all day, then I am going to join you." She drops to her own bed, but instead of getting under the covers like me, she sits up against the wall and stares at me.

I shoot her a glare, then switch to my other side, giving her my back. Her eyes burn a hole into the back of my head, and no amount of covering myself with my old comforter is helping. "Greer, would you kindly fuck off, please?"

"Not a chance. Last time I gave you space. I'm not making that mistake again."

Groaning loudly, I sit up and face her again. "Why can't you just be supportive of my decision? Why does everyone have to insist that I am in the wrong for being upset about this?"

Her stern face softens. "No one thinks you are wrong for being upset. We just don't want to watch you throw away something good just *because* you are upset."

"I know you were there last night, lingering in the shadows. You heard our conversation. You know *who* he is and what his plan was. He is our enemy, Greer. How do you, of all people, not see that?"

"All I can see is the vision I had when I first met him. It is a future that I cannot let you mess up for yourself. You two—" She stops short and clamps her mouth shut like she just narrowly avoided saying something she shouldn't.

"Greer—" I warn.

"I can't. You know—" I cut her off. "Don't you spit out your change the future shit. Tell me." I feel like a small child on the verge of throwing a temper tantrum if she doesn't start talking fast. Trying to keep my anger at bay, I don't say another word, but fix her with a glare that usually gets her to do as I ask. Or demand.

She sighs audibly and spits out, "I can't tell you the specifics, but I saw both of you in the future, happy, starting a family..."

"You mean..." I gesture toward my stomach, and she nods. The world tilts for a moment, and I feel like I might have a complete breakdown from this bit of news. Greer's visions have never been wrong, and they have only been stronger since she bonded with Draven.

Fuck. I am completely and utterly fucked.

My mind starts to scramble, trying to recall my last period. Ah yes. It ended right before the duel, and I'm also on the contraceptive elixir. I breathe deep and let it out audibly.

"Whelp, the only explanation is your vision was mistaken."

"What?!" Greer exclaims.

"Clearly, I am never letting him touch me again, and I know I am not pregnant now, so it must be wrong, or maybe you saw someone who looked like him but isn't." I force myself to believe this, and even though I am still wary, I feel satisfied with my reasoning.

Greer narrows her eyes at me, a dark look that I am ninety-nine percent sure she got from Draven. She replies slowly, "Just because you don't want to believe me or Covey, doesn't mean that we are wrong."

I huff and I feel the sting of tears behind my eyes, but thankfully, none come to the surface. I suppose I cried them all out last night.

Greer strides into the bathroom and comes out a moment later dressed in her black athletic gear. She chucks my own athletic clothes at me, and I catch them in my hand before they can hit my face.

"Training. Now," her demand sounds like a snarl.

"Greer—" I warn for the second time. She is really working toward a record today.

"You're holding on tight to your anger, so I am giving you an outlet. Maybe once you're exhausted, you'll be able to think clearly again." Her hands are on her hips now, sternness in her brow.

"Throwing punches at you is not going to change my mind."

"Yeah, but it sure as hell will feel good. Or have I not pissed you off enough yet?" Her thin black eyebrow lifts, inviting me to argue. Instead, I huff and get changed.

By the time thirty minutes is up, I feel defeated. Even though I have practically killed myself trying to become a better fighter over the last three years, Greer will always best me. I have gotten her back on the mat many times, but it is always short-lived.

"Thinking clearly yet?" she asks as I pick myself up off my back for the tenth time already this morning.

"How am I supposed to think clearly when I am trying not to get my ass handed to me every five seconds?" I groan, rubbing said ass for emphasis. In reality, my mind does feel lighter even though I am pretty sure she has given me more bruises than I care to count.

Greer hands me my water bottle, and I take it, drinking it slowly so I don't make myself sick. After breathing for a minute, I say, "I love him, Greer. I didn't think I was capable of feeling that way again. We've been together for longer than I was with Trey, and even though he has deceived me, I still...I still love him." I let my head fall into my hands. I'm so exhausted. Bone-deep exhausted. "But I'm angry at him! He played me, all the talk about being in love before having sex, all

439

the times he made me practically chase him, and then when he was kidnapped...I feel like such an idiot!"

"You are allowed to be angry. You are allowed to feel like an idiot. You are allowed to feel any way that you do. But take the time to feel those things and then decide what you want. Don't rush into a decision based on how you're feeling right now. Then, regardless of the decision you make, I promise to support you," she replies.

"Even if I decide to wipe his memory and dump him on the side of the road somewhere?"

"You're my sister first and foremost. I may not agree, and I'll probably yell at you about how it's a mistake, but I'll support you, even then."

I nod, but my stomach feels like it's tied into a big knot. If Greer won't stop me from making the biggest mistake of my life, then it truly is on me to make the right decision.

CHAPTER 60

CASPIAN

"CASPIAN STUART CAMPBELL." My head shoots up, and I see Aaron Hoffman round the corner with that cat of his slinking at his side.

He stops in front of my cell, a large smile plastered on his face. "The infamous General's son is in my prison. I thought something seemed off when I read your thoughts before that first date you took Talli on, but I brushed it off, deciding you were just nervous. Clearly, that was a mistake."

Read my thoughts?

"Yes, I can read thoughts. Some mental shields can block me out, and I'll admit, yours is impressive. I've seen very few shields made of glass, and it's something even the best Hawks can't manage."

I ignore his comments and lock my shield firmly back into place. "I already told your daughter that I would tell her anything she wanted to know, but that courtesy applies to her only."

His cat eyes me like I'm a mouse it wants to play with. I try not to shudder and hold firm in my spot on the cot. I notice Seth stand and place himself slightly in front of me, at attention.

"I know. Once she has come to her senses and decides to get rid of you, I will have her ask for everything we want to know, or we will interrogate you, whichever you prefer."

"Then what will you do with me?"

"We will wipe your mind of all memories, ship you off to a sister community in a different country, and then they will drop you off at some homeless shelter or a ditch. It'll depend on your cooperation."

Seth lets out a low growl, a clear warning. "Does your daughter know your plan?" I ask, even though I know she couldn't possibly.

"She will soon enough, and she will fall in line when the time comes. I think your betrayal is exactly what I needed to get her to see things my way, so thank you."

"I doubt that," I mutter.

He frowns and looks to where Seth is with his teeth still bared in his direction. "His bonded Hawk was a close friend and the most honorable man I knew. After your people killed him, I think I lost the last remaining capacity for being..." he seems to search for the word, almost as if he is too tired to think, "...compassionate. I'm tired, Caspian, as you can tell. I'm tired of each generation having to live with a target on their back, always looking over their shoulder. I'm tired of kids losing their parents and parents losing their kids. This ends now, no matter how dirty I have to get my hands to accomplish it."

"Don't you mean no matter how dirty your daughters' hands have to get for you?"

"They can blame me when it's all over. I hope they do." The man I have known for almost a year is suddenly back. He looks like someone who has seen too much and done too much for the sake of those he loves.

Both his cat and Seth calm down.

Just when I think he is about to turn and leave, he adds, "I did like you. As much as I wanted Talli to marry a Hawk, I meant it when I said you had my blessing. You made my daughter happy and healed her broken heart. It's a shame you broke it again." Then, with that, both he and his bonded walk away.

My heart falls, and I feel like my chest is caving in where it used to be. *Talli, when are you going to come back to me?* It's been two days, and I need to talk her. I need to explain.

I want to feel confident that she would never let her father wipe my memories completely, but my memories of her? Yeah, she might let him take those. I can't lose her like that. It will be as if I never loved her at all. My body will just hold an echo of her touch, with no memory of where the echo came from.

I can't. I can't live like that. I need to reach her.

I go back to the desk and get to work on another letter.

He's hurt her. He's going to kill her. I'm not going to be fast enough.

I jolt out of the cot, flinging myself onto the concrete floor. I fall hard onto my back, and it takes me a moment to reacquaint myself with the real world again before I try to move. Closing my eyes, I try to rub the sleep from them, and when I open them, Seth is looking down at me with an expression that says, "You're an idiot." Before I met Seth, I didn't realize dogs were capable of such expressions, but he certainly is.

I sit up, cradling my head, which feels like it's been split open from the fall. "I am not going to ask the guards for a moonstone. I dealt with the nightmares before Talli gave one to me, and I can deal with them now. It didn't even completely work when I had it. It only helped." The German shepherd gives me another look, and I say through my teeth, "I'm fine, Seth."

Standing, I stretch all my aching muscles. My entire body hurts from being stuck in here for four days, sleeping on a cot, and not being able to truly get some exercise besides pacing and the occasional push-ups and sit-ups I do when I feel like I'm about to lose my mind. I look over at the desk and see last night's letter folded and ready for Greer to pick up.

Every time she visits, she gives me a small shake of her head and takes it. Either Talli is reading my letters and just being stubborn about coming to talk to me, or she isn't reading them at all. I can't blame her either way. I should have told her the moment I chose her, back in December; she'd probably hate me less if I had. She would have walked away from me then and never looked back. But now? What we have between us is so much more than the sparks of new love. We are bound to one another, whether she wants to be or not.

One of the guards, Nelson, starts unlocking my cell like clockwork to bring Seth out for a walk. "Good morning," he says gruffly.

"Morning. How's the weather today?" I ask.

"Still raining. It hasn't stopped much this week." Seth walks through the open cell door and trots alongside the tall man toward the door.

The rain started after Talli left me in this cell. It seems to start in the morning and end late into the night. There seems to be occasional breaks in the downpour, but not many. I'm not sure how, but she must be affecting the weather. It's a clue into how she's feeling at the moment, but when it stops completely, will it be a good sign, or a bad one? I have no idea. It could mean that she is ready to forgive me or that she is ready to move on without me. One thing is for sure, though. She is still deciding, and that means I still have a chance.

I move to the desk, ready to start on another letter for the day, when I hear footsteps.

That was a quick walk, Seth.

I move into the back of my cell to give Nelson room to put him back inside, but it's not Nelson and Seth.

"Stella? What are you doing here?" I ask in disbelief.

Her curly dark-brown hair is swept up into a tight bun, and she's wearing a lab coat. Her blue eyes, a mirror of Ash's, soften when they look me over, and she signs, "I wanted to come talk to you."

I sign back, "Does your husband and son know you're here?"

She shakes her head.

"Thank you for keeping my secret. Even if it meant lying to your family," I sign.

"I owed you a favor for helping me."

"You don't owe me anything for doing the right thing. I should have done more. Fought harder..." My signing trails off as I am not sure what else to say to her. I am filled with so much regret from that time.

"It is not your fault. You are a good man. I know that, and she knows that too. Give her time. Would you like me to tell her what you did that day?"

"Thank you, Stella. You give me more credit than I am due. But no, she doesn't need to know that you knew me all this time and kept my secret. She's been through enough."

Stella nods solemnly. She looks around, picks up a plate of food I didn't even notice her put down earlier, and then hurries up to the cell. She extends a plate of food to me through the opening, and I take it from her.

"I overheard what Aaron is planning. Under the bread is a vial. Take it if things go wrong," she signs.

I set the plate down so that I can sign back to her and ask her what it is, but by the time I look up again, she is gone. A moment later, Nelson and Seth are walking down the hallway. Nelson lets Seth back inside the cell and then looks at my plate of food. "Well, that saves me a trip." He locks the cell door back in place and leaves without another word.

Seth curls up onto his bed in one of the corners of the cell. The morning after being put in the cell, Greer brought him his bed, bowls for his food and water, as well as a big bag of dog food. I don't understand why he's still here with me, but he is, and I am grateful.

Grabbing my plate of food, I sit down on my cot and pull out the small elixir bottle from under the bread. It is the size of a finger with a silver liquid inside. I wish I knew what it is, but I stuff it into my pocket just in case. As I eat breakfast, I think about the kind woman I desperately tried to help, what feels like an eternity ago.

I was sixteen at the time, shadowing my father in his office when they dragged her in. She had tried helping Hawks escape by distracting the guards with shouts of alarm about a fire in the lab my father forced her to work in. The men who brought her in were asking for my father to pass judgment on her. I stood there as he did, presiding over the case as the judge and jury. All I could think during the trial was that she was a human. She wasn't a witch, and she didn't deserve to be punished like one. Stella's eyes had been so full of defiance, and her words were like sharp knives. But aside from those things, she wasn't a real threat.

She was small and delicate. Nothing like the hardened, battle-ready witches I had seen.

My father made his decision, and I watched in horror as one of his men got out a knife. I didn't think before I threw myself in front of her, begging for my father's mercy. I pointed out that the Brethen protected humans from witches, and we didn't hurt them. My biggest mistake was saying, "If we hurt her, then we are no better than them."

He got out of his seat swifter than I had ever seen before and punched me, putting me on the ground. In the next moment, I was being hauled out of his office toward a cell, and Stella's screams followed me all the way there.

I starved and rotted in that cell for a month, and was regularly beaten until I swore to my father I would never fail him again. I had meant it at the time, but I believe a part of me always knew I would.

Even though I was frequently at the prison, I didn't see Stella again until I needed to ask for her help. I remember walking into Treyton's cell to try once again to get him to talk when I found him barely breathing. I couldn't figure out what was wrong. He was my responsibility, and I needed him to stay alive. So I panicked and found Stella. I asked her to help me and she did. She figured out what was wrong with Treyton and saved him from his magic depletion. My father never found out, and even though Stella had gotten help from Killian to check on him, Killian never met me. He never saw my face. Only Stella had seen me. As a thank you, I visited her when I could and brought her things when she needed them. I learned sign language so that I could talk to her discreetly, and when it came to the night she and Killian had escaped, I held back the guards and made sure they got away. She doesn't know that last bit, but I felt like it was the least I could do for not fighting harder for her that day. That was the second time I had helped people escape that prison.

When I had to move into the community last month, I did my absolute best to avoid Ash's parents. I knew she would recognize me, and she did. Talli and I ran into her at the grocery store picking up some supplies one night. Her eyes widened, but when Talli's back was turned, I quickly signed that I would explain later. For some crazy reason, she trusted me. I saw her the next day when she showed up at the woodworking shop and explained everything to her. It felt good to get it all off my chest, and she continued to trust me enough to tell me that she would keep my secret.

With all these memories fresh in my head and my breakfast plate empty, I move back to the desk and start on the next letter.

I feel so much sorrow for Katarina. Everything has been taken away from her. Her freedom, her son, and now i've been ordered to use my ability to take away her memories. i'd argued for her to retain everything up to the point of her marriage to that wretched Klaus, and the elders agreed it was best for the sake of not having to restart her training from scratch. But i know what taking every memory away can do to our people, and it is not safe.

I despise using my ability in such a manner. Being a Memory-seer is one of the highest honors the Great Hawk can bestow, and using it against someone who was considered worthy enough to wield something even more powerful, the only one of her kind, feels like a violation of our Order. But it's my most genuine hope that Katarina is able to heal once she can no longer hear the siren's call of her memories—the good and the bad ones. Maybe then, the darkness will finally release its grip upon her.

- Journal of Irene Hoffman

CHAPTER 61

TALLIANA

"HE SAYS HE LOVES you and sends another note." Greer throws the letter at me. I grab it and put it in my nightstand next to all the other unopened letters, which makes four. Despite Greer's claim that she would support me no matter my decision, she is mad at me, and frankly, I am mad at her too.

Her tone is accusatory as she asks, "Are you ever going to read them?"

"What happened to, 'I'm your sister first and foremost' and 'I'll support you no matter what'? It's been five days, Greer, not a year. You're the one who told me to take time to feel what I needed to before deciding. But fine, you want me to decide, then go get an elixir for him."

"You're acting like a child! Do you need to be reminded that you kept your secret from him, too, and only told him once you had no choice? You both kept secrets from each other, and I'm sick of you acting like you were the perfect one in this relationship." Shadows pool at her feet and edge her face.

Infuriated, I grab the stuffed dragon on my bed and wind my arm back, ready to throw it at her face. But Greer's phone rings and I stop mid-throw as she answers it. Okay, maybe she has a point, and I am acting like a child. I huff at the thought and throw it as hard as I can to the floor instead.

"*I am considering that as a personal attack*," Coventina comments. I haven't seen her much this week, and if I am being honest, I've avoided her like I have avoided everyone else.

Before I can reply to Coventina, Greer's eyes turn lethal as she listens to the person on the other end. "Send it through now. I need to see it." She hangs up the phone and looks right at me. "Mei overheard Dad ordering an interrogation room to be set up for Cas. Then she looked over the prison security tapes." Greer's phone dings, and she holds it out so we can both watch the video she just received. It is of Dad becoming someone I don't even recognize as he threatens Cas.

The darkness breaks out of its cage, then rolls through me, stretching and expanding. *Oh no, you don't.* I grab onto the light and pull it in time to meet the darkness in the middle. They fill both halves of me, electrifying me with true power once again.

"Shit Talli! What is wrong with your eyes?" Greer exclaims.

I move to my mirror and find my eyes are darkened around the edges, but my irises are illuminated. It looks like the sun refracting in the water.

"Nothing is wrong. This is what complete control looks like." Straightening my back, I turn to face her again. "This is what magic looks like in its most powerful form." I march out of the bedroom and down the stairs.

"Where are you going?" Greer catches up behind me.

"It's time I figure out what the hell Dad is up to."

"Maybe we should think first."

"All I've done is think. Now it's time for reckless action."

Exiting through the back door, Coventina is there, ready for me. Ash comes around the corner of the house. "What's—" he starts, but stops once he sees me. He turns to Greer. "What did you do now to piss her off?"

I climb onto Coventina's back, and Draven lands in the backyard too, letting Greer on.

"No time to explain. Jump on," Greer orders.

Coventina takes off and flies me straight to the community building' roof. Greer and Ash follow me as I send ice at the lock on the roof door. I kick the knob and it comes off in a crunch. It only takes me a few seconds before I'm at Dad's office. I don't knock, but instead I push the door open and snarl at those sitting at the table.

"Talli." Dad's voice holds a warning, but I ignore it.

"I need to speak to you. Now."

Everyone leaves quickly, except for Reef. He looks between me and Dad, then opens his mouth as if whatever he is about to say could defuse the situation, but Dad cuts him off, "Reef, go." He reluctantly does as he's told, shutting the door behind him.

A long ice spear forms in my hand. I don't pull water from the air or anywhere else. It just appears, as it did when I rescued Cas from the Brethren, coming from the ice already inside of me. It should be impossible. No Elemental can make an element appear; they have to draw from something. But this must be what it's like to be in complete control. I have power. Impossible power.

Dad notices, but I don't let him speak. With my free hand, I toss Greer's phone with the video on it down on his desk. "What is this?" I ask fiercely.

"I was having a conversation with General Campbell's son," he answers through gritted teeth.

"Who are you? Because you sure as hell don't look like my dad in this video."

"Talliana. How are you still so naïve? You are so wrapped up in this boy that you can't see that he is the exact tool we need to end this."

"He's a human being."

"He's a monster! Just like his father."

"How are you any different? How are we any different? You are a monster just like they are, and I have let you turn me into one, too."

"Talli, you don't understand."

"Understand what? Uncle Cyrus told me the stories about you and Aunt Delilah messing with people when you were younger, playing with people's minds. Your *own* people. What is wrong with you?"

Dad throws up his hands in frustration, and a dagger made of ice forms in my empty hand. I grip it tightly, and he finally meets my eyes.

"You've done it then? Figured out how to control it. How?"

I'm not surprised that he knows about the darkness, even though I haven't spoken about it, and I know no one would have told him either. "The man who truly treated me like a daughter helped me figure it out, while you were too busy finding ways to use it to your advantage."

"You don't understand," he repeats.

"If I don't understand, then explain it to me!"

He drops back down into his seat. "There was an old woman who visited the Florida community when I was a kid. She had foresight that allowed her to just know things, random answers to questions no one ever asked." He looks to Greer and adds, "Greer, she was your great-grandmother," then turns back to me. "She took one look at your Aunt Delilah and said, 'It will be a Hoffman's dark blood that will end the curse and bring peace to those most troubled.'" My skin prickles. "Your Aunt thought she meant her. She started obsessing over it, trying to figure out how she was going to do it. I caught her with her shields down one day and read her thoughts. I confronted her, and she brought me in on her secret, which we agreed not to share with anyone. We researched together, tested out her powers, and came to the conclusion that her ability to manipulate memories with her compulsion had to be the answer. But she wasn't powerful enough to manipulate every Brethren into forgetting their past. So we researched again, trying to find another way until she found it."

"The darkness," I guess.

"Yes. The woman said, '*dark blood*' and Delilah realized it was the key to becoming more powerful. She let it consume her until she convinced me that we should capture a Brethren to test her abilities. I agreed to help her, and even though we caught one during the next attack, he overpowered us and killed her right in front of me. After that, I realized the prophecy could not have meant her; maybe it had to be me. I moved here in pursuit of help when I met Greer's father. He helped me with my theories, but ultimately was too preoccupied with the girl he had fallen in love with. I, too, got distracted by your mom, and then we had you. It wasn't until you were two and started showing a strange affinity for several abilities that I realized the prophecy must have been about you. No child has ever held magic that young, let alone magic that could be used in so many ways. I panicked."

"What did you do?" I ask.

"There were rumors about a Hawk with compulsion who could compel the individual to not be able to use their abilities." My ice spear and dagger morph into water and splash down on the carpet beneath my feet. I know where this story is going to go, but I have to hear him say it. He continues, "Rumors were that he was in the South African community. Angeline Waterstone had ties there and helped me find him. He compelled you not to use any of your abilities, except for healing."

"Does Mom know?"

"She did. But she was hysterical after she found out what I had planned to do. She thought I wanted to get rid of a gift given to us by the Great Hawk, but she didn't understand that it wasn't a gift. It was a death sentence for you. I had her memories taken away of you using your other abilities. After that, I did everything I could to keep you away from the fighting and the politics. I have been working tirelessly to try to end it all before you had a chance to realize your place in it. Before the darkness had a chance to find you."

"You tried to take her destiny away from her," Greer spat.

"No." The word falls out of my mouth before I can catch it. "You were trying to save me from it."

Dad nods. "You were so full of light and joy. The idea of my little girl falling prey to the darkness was not something I could allow. It was my job to protect you, so I did, the only way I knew how."

"Does Angeline still know? Did you tell anyone else about this?"

"Yes, she does. She is the only one still alive who knows."

"Alive?"

"Allow me to finish my story."

I nod, uncertain, but I need to finish learning the truth even if it hurts.

"I tried so hard to protect you, but I saw what was happening to you after Trey disappeared. It was like watching my sister all over again. At that point, I realized I couldn't save you from it, and I had to try to help you. That's why I suddenly taught you how to use a bow and let you fight and learn more. Then Trey came back, and he told me everything that happened to him, how the Brethren threatened your life, how he wanted you to go into hiding to keep you safe..."

"He knew?" My voice cracks, and the strength that I strode in here with fractures.

"Our goals were aligned, and I knew he was already willing to risk everything to save you."

"You used him!" I scream through my tears.

Dad stands up suddenly. "It was his choice! He wanted to protect you and save you from the monsters outside the gate and the monster inside of you. He was so confident." Dad scoffs. "He thought his love was enough to keep you from going dark. I knew better, but I let him try. If only to buy me more time. Then the March happened, you bonded that dragon, and when you woke up, I knew you were gone. The darkness had taken you from me, and something had unlocked your abilities again. The only choice I had left was to do everything I could to lessen the burden on your soul. I wanted you to be an unconscious weapon that could place the blame on me once it was all over."

Willing the tears off my face, I meet Dad's eyes and bring myself to say, "You should have told me."

"I know."

Anger boils up inside of me, and I let the darkness latch onto it. The balance falters, and I show Dad the monster inside as I say with barely controlled rage, "If you hadn't been so obsessed with protecting me, then I could have been more prepared. I could have been involved."

"If the Great Hawk ever blesses you with a daughter, you will understand."

I can't stand to look at him a moment longer. I turn on my heel and storm out of the room. Greer is right behind me. "Talli, we need to stop and process what we were just told."

"I need to get him out of here."

"Okay, let's all get out of here. Take him and go—"

"No. Wait out front for him with Draven. Take him to pack his stuff and get him to Uncle Cyrus. He'll keep him hidden and safe. Then come back, and we will figure out our next steps."

"We can protect him. Talli," she stops me, "you love him, and if you don't want to send him away, we can protect him."

"I can't protect him against me! Even if I have figured out control and balance, the darkness can still take over. It...I can still hurt him. Can't you see, Greer? Yes, I've spent the last few days hurt and upset by what he did, but I've also spent this time reliving the moment the darkness almost killed him. Over and over again. He's not safe around me. He needs to go, and he can't find out the real reason why. Otherwise, he'll never leave."

"You should at least read his letters before you make the biggest mistake of your life."

"Allowing myself to fall in love again was the biggest mistake of my life." We both know I don't mean it, but I don't say another word as I make my way to the prison cells.

Chapter 62

CASPIAN

I set the pen down on the desk, finally done. After four letters, this is the last one I need to explain it all. The words have not been perfect, but that was never my goal. I just wanted them to be honest.

I fold the paper and set it on the side of the small desk. Before I can stand to start my post-note pacing around the cell that I do every afternoon, I hear the door at the end of the hall open and close.

Either I've lost track of time today, or Nelson is early tonight with dinner. I stand in the middle of the room, hands clasped together behind my back as I listen to the footsteps. Those aren't Nelson's or Greer's.

Ash comes into sight. He has visited me every day after dinner since I have been put in here, and I'm always grateful to see him. But there is something wrong with his expression. It isn't the same sad resignation that he usually wears. This one looks nervous. I move closer to him. "Ash, what's wrong?"

"I don't know, but something is wrong with Talli. Greer told me to stand guard at your cell before she and Talli marched into their dad's office. I think the elders are planning something, and you're not safe here anymore." His eyebrows draw together as he thinks, then looks up at me. "I'll do what I can, but I don't know if I can protect you if Greer doesn't make it in time. The only thing I have going for me is that no one wants to face Greer's wrath if they hurt me. Other than that, I'm pretty useless."

"Ash, there is nothing useless about you. You are the smartest person I know. I actually like that you aren't lethal like the rest of us, and you have been a great friend to me. If something does happen, don't risk yourself for me. Stand aside and let them do what they have to," I tell him.

"I—" he starts, but the door at the end of the hall slams open. I take a deep breath, preparing myself for the worst. I am not going to fight. I'll let them take me, and I'll deserve whatever treatment they inflict. But to my shock, Talli is suddenly there, standing next to Ash on the other side of the cell.

"Talli! You're here! Are you—" She holds up a hand to cut me off. She looks tired. Even when we were both captured by the Brethren and tortured in that cabin, she has never looked so beaten up. Her face is red and blotchy, her eyes watery.

I did that to her.

She turns to Ash and says, "Greer's outside. Go help her."

He glances back at me one more time and leaves without a word. Talli walks to the door of my cell and opens it, letting the door swing wide.

"What's going on?" I ask, trying to reach her under her icy exterior.

She stands there by the open door, not saying anything and not looking at me. My stomach sinks. This is not right. She's not okay.

When I don't move, she says quietly, "You're free. Go to the house, pack quickly, and leave with Greer. She will take you somewhere safe. Don't ever come back. Don't..." Her voice breaks, but she regains her icy composure and finishes, "Don't ever seek me out. I don't ever want to see you again. If I do, you'll be treated like every other prisoner and have your memory wiped—all of it."

"Talli, don't do this." My throat constricts, and desperation like I've never felt before threatens to tear me apart. "Did you read my letters? Please, read them and read my last one!" I snatch the paper off the desk and try to hand it to her. She rips it from my hand and throws it on the ground.

Her tone is venomous when she replies, "No, I haven't, but they won't change anything! You need to go so I can do the one fucking thing I'm supposed to do."

"And what's that, Talli? Killing more people in the name of peace? I don't know about you, but I'm sick of murdering innocent people," I challenge. She looks away, unable to meet my eyes. "Please just read them. They will help make sense of everything. Leave me in here for another week, a month, I don't care! As long as you are willing to hear me out."

She ices over right in front of me. The Talli I know is instantly buried, so I can no longer see her. "You don't belong here! You don't belong with me! Don't you get it? We are on opposite sides of this war, and it doesn't matter if you want to be on this side or not. You aren't one of us. You will never be one of us, no matter how hard you pretend you are."

"Who cares?! What side we started on doesn't matter, having magic in our veins doesn't matter, what we should or shouldn't do doesn't matter. What we want, what we feel for each other, that's what matters," I argue.

"If you don't leave on your own, I will have you dragged out."

"Please. I love you."

Her eyes stay fixed on the floor between us as they harden so much that her soft tone shocks me when she says, "For what it's worth, despite all my efforts, I can't figure out how to stop loving you. And I'll carry that love with me all the way to the end."

I close the distance between us and grab her upper arms, letting her feel the shaking in my bones as I reply, "That is worth everything to me." She meets my eyes for a minute, and I take the opening, "You are worth everything, Talliana Hoffman."

My heart is going to beat out of my chest, but neither of us move. I know that if I do, I'll startle her. I can't tell if the look she is giving me is because she is on the verge of kissing me or killing me.

"Nelson! Gage!" she shouts down the hall, and the two men come running toward us. "Please escort Mr. Campbell to Officer Meyer outside."

On that order, the two men grab my arms, pulling me away from her.

"Talli, please listen to me! We are both just pawns in our fathers' war! They will use us until we are both just one more hollow sacrifice in the large graveyard of them. At least let me help you fight them!" The men keep pulling me down the hall, farther away from her. I could throw both of these guards off of me, but I don't want to hurt anyone.

"I'm no one's pawn. Not anymore," she whispers.

Nelson and Gage shove me up the stairs and hand me over to Greer outside, where she waits next to Draven.

"No. No. No!" I shout to the air. "Greer, you have to do something! Talk some sense into her."

Her face hardens. "We need to get you out of here. You're not safe."

There is a whimper behind me, and I'm relieved to see Seth. The large dog bumps into my leg in a gesture I have come to learn means he is here for me, and all the frustration and desperation I feel right now lessens just enough to keep me breathing evenly. Then I hear the familiar sound of my Jeep and see it coming down the empty street. It parks next to us, and Ash jumps out, throwing me the keys.

"Get in the Jeep and go back to the house with Ash. We need to get you packed." Greer climbs onto Draven in the next breath, and I decide not to argue further. For now, anyway.

Seth, Ash, and I take the Jeep the short distance to the house. My mind races as I let them help me pack my bags with the necessities. I have almost planned my escape to find Talli, when a banging comes at the front door. We all freeze and look at one another. Greer points to the bathroom and gestures for me to hide. I hesitate, but Ash pushes me in that direction, and I give in.

I listen as Greer opens the front door, and her tone is low as she answers, "He's gone. We've already gotten him out."

It's Aaron's voice that replies, "Step aside, Greer."

A warmth settles over my feet, and I look down to see shadows seeping into the room from under the door. I back up, uncertain of the shadow's intent. It follows me, growing in size until my back reaches the corner of the small half-bath.

Then it swallows me whole.

Chapter 63

TALLIANA

I HOLD MY BREATH until the guards and Cas are out of sight. The door slams closed, and I suck in air like I have been underwater for five minutes. I reach out blindly for the cell door, still open, and hold onto it to steady myself.

I had to do it. I had no choice. He isn't safe here. He isn't safe with me.

Hollow sacrifice. I always thought Cas had a unique way of painting pictures with his words. But that...that term struck me right in the chest. Both sides have made outrageous sacrifices in attempts to get even slightly ahead of the other, but we are still on equal footing. All of those lives I have personally taken, thinking they would make a difference, but they haven't. All of those sacrifices over the hundreds of years have been pointless, needless. And they will continue to be until the war is ended once and for all.

Until *I* end this war, once and for all.

Gage walks in and approaches me. He was in Treyton's school year, one of his friends. The idle thought jars me back to life right before he asks, "Are you alright, Talli?"

A strange laugh rolls past my lips. "I don't have any other choice."

He nods, then bends down to pick up Cas's letter. He looks at it thoughtfully for a moment, then hands it to me. "He spent a long time on this one. Mostly staring at it." He shrugs. "But I think it would be a shame not to read what he spent so much time trying to write."

"Thank you, Gage." I fight the urge to crumple the folded paper in my grasp while I watch him walk back to his post.

Holding onto my anger is the only way to keep Cas safe, and myself safe from more pain. I stuff the paper into my pocket and leave this space that still smells of oak and sunshine.

By the time I reach Greer's and my bedroom, I feel like the letter has burned a hole in my pocket. I yank it out and toss it onto the floor next to the stuffed dragon. The unreasonable part of me feels a little surprised to see it's not actually on fire. I eye it for a minute to make sure it won't combust as soon as I turn my back, then I drop back into my bed.

I toss and turn. I should feel at least some relief that he will be gone soon, but all I can think about is how my traitorous body wanted to lunge for him earlier, and not in anger. His words to me, his plea, his grip on my arms. Too much. It was too much, and I almost lost my hold. Turning again, I come face to face with my nightstand drawer, which is slightly ajar, paper and scribbled black words staring back at me.

Can I handle more truth tonight? More stories that will change everything? Am I an idiot for hoping for exactly that? But even if that's what they are, it won't change a thing. What I said to him was true. I still love him, and nothing can change that or the fact that he is better off without me. Or the fact that I am better off without him.

"*Do you really think that?*" Coventina chimes in with her two cents.

"*I don't have any other choice,*" I repeat the words I said to Gage a few moments before.

"*Talliana. Listen to what's inside of you. He is your strength and your reminder to live. He will keep your path lit when things go dark.*" When I don't reply, she adds, "*It's not a weakness to need someone. It's courage.*"

I feel a distinct crack inside of me, but instead of wallowing on how broken I feel, I grab his first letter.

Chapter 64

CASPIAN

EVERYTHING IS BLACK.

It feels like I have been transported to a whole other world. I can't see anything, but I can still hear. The bathroom door opens, and someone comes in, then quickly leaves. The shadows don't move, though, and I don't dare to either. So I wait and think. And wait and think. And wait, and decide.

Just when I'm on the verge of moving, if only from the fear that if I don't move soon, I'll be trapped in the shadows forever, the black starts to thin out. I look down, and it's like they are melting off of me, pooling back at my feet, then away from me toward black leather boots. Greer is standing there at the bathroom door, looking out of breath.

"I liked you a lot better when you shielded. Do you know how much shadow I had to cover you in to smother your emotions?" she pants.

I slam my shield back in place, and she straightens. "They're gone. We are safe for the night, but we need to finish packing."

I push off the wall, allowing myself my first full inhalation in what feels like an eternity. "I'm not leaving, Greer. You can't make me leave her."

"You are leaving. But not without her."

Her words shock me for a moment, and then I let immense relief flood me. "You're going to help me?" I ask.

"Yes, but let's be clear. If I ever find out that you lied to her again, I will wrap you in my shadows and never let you out. You will rot in them until you take your last breath. Do you understand?" she threatens.

"If I ever hurt her again, I want you to do much worse," I answer without hesitation.

"Noted." She turns on her heel and runs out of the bathroom.

I finish packing my bag while Greer packs Talli's. Ash is in the kitchen, packing a small bag with food and cash, which Greer stole from Aaron's safe. I also grab the money I still have from working at the club, but I know that neither will last us long.

"Alright, what's the plan?" I ask Greer the moment we all finish packing.

"You and I will go get Talli. And Ash," she looks to him, "make sure Dad doesn't come home until I text you. He should be preoccupied with the manhunt for a while, but text me if he heads toward the house."

Ash nods and runs out the front door, while Greer dashes for the back door. I reach the back door myself in time to see a big puff of smoke, and then Draven is there in all his gigantic glory. Greer climbs on his back like it's the most natural thing in the world.

When she sees I still haven't moved from the door, she yells, "We don't have all night!"

"Doesn't he have a saddle like Covey?"

"He does, but I don't carry it around everywhere I go. You'll have to go bareback." Seeing my skeptical look, she adds, "Look, it will only take a second to get to the house. I won't let you fall."

Before I can question my judgment, I run to the most terrifying creature in existence and climb on his back, taking up the seat behind Greer. I can barely debate if I should hold onto Greer when shadows gobble us up, and I fearfully grab her waist before I fall.

I'm coming, Talli, if this dragon doesn't kill me first.

CHAPTER 65

TALLIANA

My heart pounds as I read what he wrote about what really happened to his mother, that our people killed her in an attempt to kill his father. Which doesn't make sense, but I keep going. I read about his childhood and what his father put him through to learn how to be a Brethren—a witch killer. He was given his first torch and went on attacks at the age of twelve. An age way too young to be forced into murdering people.

I finish the first letter and take a deep breath, closing my eyes against the hurt I feel for him. He was just a boy, and already he was being used as a weapon meant to kill. After taking a moment to collect myself, I grab the next letter.

This one is all about Trey. How they threatened him, his conversations with Trey about me, and how Trey taught him how to shield and project the emotions he wants in a way that no one can detect. My heart leaps out of my chest when I read that he was the reason we safely escaped the night we found Trey at the prison. He had a room on that same level as Trey's cell, and he woke up when he heard a commotion. He had access to the cameras guarding Trey and watched the whole thing. He could have raised an alarm, could have stopped us, but he erased the footage instead and let us leave.

Water splashes onto the letter I'm hovering over. I didn't realize I was crying until now. I read the letter three more times, unable to comprehend why he let us go. If he hadn't, we could have all been killed. At the time, I thought how it must have been the Great Hawk watching over us, keeping us safe somehow. But no, it was Cas, and his only explanation as to why he did it was that he knew that I would die if he didn't.

I drop the letter to the floor and, through watery eyes, find the next one. I'm not prepared when I read, "*I was sent twice to kill Treyton.*" After we escaped that night, the General ordered him and another to kill Treyton after they killed me right in front of him. The first time, Cas found us at the same mall where I first met him. Trey and I were in the parking lot, walking back to the car, but before his partner could pull the trigger aimed at my head, Cas killed him and let Trey and I walk. The second time, we were at prom. He was there that night. "*I saw you, all long red curls, ruined blue dress the same shade as your eyes, and the moonlight making you glow like an angel that didn't belong in this world. You looked frantic, and I knew you were trying to find him.*" He was supposed to grab me, but he couldn't. He knew before he even embarked on the mission that he wouldn't be able to. But the General was so furious, so Cas had planned to recapture Trey and find another excuse as to why I got away. But he ultimately decided he couldn't go through with any of it and told one of the men to deliver a message to rey instead.

My body starts to shake with the realization that I would be dead so many times over if it wasn't for Cas. He saved my life time and time again, and I didn't even know he was there. He acted against orders, he lied, he killed to keep me safe, all when I was his enemy. I angrily wipe the tears away and try to unlock my clenched jaw. I should be grateful, but all I feel is anger. Because I. Just. Want. To. Be. Angry. At Cas. At myself. At Trey. At everyone.

I crumple the paper into a ball and fling it across the room. Then, before I can change my mind, I grab the fourth letter and read. This one is about our relationship. His side of every moment, every admission, every touch. He writes about the moment he realized that the Brethren were wrong, the moment he chose me over everything, the moment he decided he was going to help me end the war, and his final plan to give his father the elixir.

After reading these letters, I know now that he is someone just as broken as I am. Someone who may truly understand me better than anyone else ever could. His father made him into a monster like mine did with me. I have been spiraling, fighting myself between thinking everything was just a game and believing him when he said it wasn't. Now I know for sure that it wasn't. Not really. He was as real with me as I was with him.

I want to scream. I want to race after him and tell him thank you a million times over for how he saved me. For how he saved Trey. I want to punch him for not being the perfect normal guy I thought I had fallen in love with. I want to wrap my arms around his neck and kiss every bit of the pain he felt in his life away. I want. I want. I want.

But I still can't bring myself to do any of it. Because I still can't make the image of my hand holding a knife to his neck go away. Finally, though, I grab the last letter.

CHAPTER 66

CASPIAN

DRAVEN SWOOPS LOW, CLIMBS back up, then does a tailspin. I can hear Greer cackling in front of me. This is a fucking test. She's going to put me through hell and expect me to think straight once I get to Talli.

I am not going to fail. I am not going to puke.

Three tailspins, five sudden drops, and two loops later, we land at the house less than half a mile away. I have no doubt that we already passed the Hoffman house a few times before Draven decided to land.

Fucking dragon. Fucking Greer.

My hands are trembling, and it takes effort not to slide right off him as I attempt to climb down. I feel instantly better on my feet, and I look to Greer. "Alright, what's the plan?"

"You're going to go inside, and you're going to tell her you're sorry."

I burst into a disturbing sort of laughter. It's awkward and does not sound right to my ears. When I look at her, there isn't even a hint of humor on her face. "You're not serious. If it were that easy, I wouldn't have been in a cell for days!" Greer is supposed to be the Strategist. She is supposed to have a good plan. That's not a plan at all. That's a death sentence!

She folds her arms and stands taller. "Look, you idiot. She is in our bedroom, crying her eyes out because she just read your last letter. Her heart and intuition are at war with her stubbornness and self-preservation. You," she jabs me in the chest, "are going to go in there and tip the scales."

"How? She could kill me on sight or worse, make good on her promise to wipe my memory."

"You'll know how to reach her in the moment."

I pace for a minute, running my hand through my hair at least ten times before I square my shoulders and nod at her. She walks with me through the back door of their house, and I come face to face with Rose, looking very human with her hands covered in soapy dishwater. To my surprise, she only points to the staircase and gives me a small smile.

Greer and I reach the bedroom door, and I hear it, the sobbing. If my heart wasn't already shattered, it would break into a million pieces right now.

Before I can panic, Greer knocks on the door and instantly disappears into the shadows.

"Go away, Greer! I don't need another lecture right now!"

Gently opening the door, I take one step in, but before I can even get a look at her, a plate sails straight for my head. I instantly duck to the left, and it smashes against the door frame.

Shit, that would have hurt.

I gulp and try again. A glass this time. I decide to try once more, but I'll take whatever hit she intends for me this time. I freeze when a fork sails right past my eyes and embeds itself into the wood. I should be afraid to go farther, but I know that miss was intentional, which gives me some comfort.

Opening the door wider, I step around the fork, bracing myself, but nothing comes. I open my eyes and see her, looking as broken as the plate on the floor. She's on her bed, hugging her knees to her chest, her head resting on them, crying harder. I cross the room to her and spot a dinner knife on her nightstand. I quietly take it and toss it under her bed as I go to my knees on the floor.

I stay quiet and wait. Five minutes pass, and I finally decide to ask, "So you read my letters?"

She nods with her head still down, but makes no move aside from that.

"I think it still needs to be said again; I am so sorry." She lifts her eyes to me, and those deep blue orbs connect instantly with mine.

She speaks then, sniffling through the sentence. "I believe you, but how can I trust you going forward?"

I'm surprised by myself when I know exactly what to do. I gently grab her hands and place them on each side of my face. "Look at them—any one you want. Look at them all. Please see the truth for yourself."

"Love should be enough for me to trust you. I shouldn't have to look. What if I see something I don't like and hurt you like I did before?" She cries harder, and I realize now that I think a part of why she is so upset is because she's mad at herself. Mad at losing control and almost killing me.

"Talli, please. I want you to see all of it. I have nothing to hide from you." I keep a firm grip on her hands, keeping them on my face.

She sniffles again but nods. I let go of her hands and brace myself, unsure of what to expect.

"Close your eyes. Then take a deep breath in and out," she instructs with a slight quiver, adjusting her hands slightly so her fingers press into my temples.

I do as she says, and as soon as I exhale, I feel like she literally jumps inside my brain. It's itchy and uncomfortable, but not painful. I can see, though, every memory she pulls and watches. It's like I'm forced to relive them, being put back in my body, but having no control over myself.

I have no idea how much time passes, and I have lost count of how many memories she has gone through, but as quickly as she hops out of my mind, she hops into my arms.

Chapter 67

TALLIANA

I saw and felt so much. Every memory with his father was laced with hate, every memory with Trey laced with regret, and every memory with me laced with love.

So much love.

I tried sending him away. I tried making him leave my life. All because I am a coward. I'm still terrified of hurting him, but seeing his perspective of *us* has truly reassured me that we'll be okay. If anything is proof of that, it's the moment we shared after the duel. He handled the darkness when it wasn't caged, and I have to trust him to do it again.

As soon as I disconnect, I can't help but throw myself at him. The force pushes him off balance, and we fall together. I am undeterred as I find his lips and try to express my apology, my pleading for his forgiveness, and my love for him. He takes it all and expresses his forgiveness and love right back to me.

Tears are still streaking my face and soaking us both as I pull away, trying to catch a breath. As soon as I look at him, I realize he is crying too. I lift a hand to his face and do a horrible job trying to wipe off all the water. "I'm so sorry, Caspian," I say earnestly.

"Let's not say any more 'I'm sorries' tonight, okay?" He brushes some of my hair out of my face and says, "You are so beautiful, even if your face is all red and blotchy."

I laugh. He always knows how to make me laugh when I need it the most. He pulls himself off the floor and offers me a hand to stand as well. I take it and stand in front of him, in awe of who stands before me. My love, my partner, my everything.

"You really were going to let me walk free, even before you knew the whole truth?" he asks.

"I told you that I couldn't stop loving you. To me, that means making sure you're safe, and you're not safe here," I explain. Then suddenly I remember... "I have to go." I grab my fighting leathers from my drawer and start to change.

Cas looks at me, startled. "Where?"

I don't answer until I have my jacket zipped up. "I'm going to go kill your father," I say it as if I'm just running out to the store for milk.

"You're not serious."

I give him a sharp look that indicates I am very serious, then walk out the door. He follows me down the stairs, close on my heels. "Talli. Don't do this. You can't just run off and kill him. He has six personal guards that practically follow him into the shower, then more surrounding the house."

I ignore him. We pass by Greer in the kitchen, eating something. Mom is at the sink drying dishes. I ignore them both, too, and keep walking. My mind has been made up.

"Glad to see she didn't kill you," Greer says casually to Cas as we walk by.

"She's trying to run off to kill my father instead. Some help would be nice," Cas retorts urgently to her.

"What the hell did you say to her?"

I don't hear their argument as I continue out the door. I'm halfway to the shed to grab Coventina's saddle when a wall of shadow appears in front of me. I cut a hole right through it with the ice that appears in my hand, and then I climb through it and continue on my way.

"Talli, Cas is right. Remember last time we tried to kill the General? You got shot, and I almost drowned," Greer says to my back.

"That's why I am going alone," I throw over my shoulder.

Reaching the shed, I try opening the doors, but shadows cover the lock that's on it, and I can't get to it. I turn on my heels and bare my teeth at Greer. She doesn't back down. Doesn't she know this needs to be done? If we kill the General, then the whole operation will destabilize, and we can win this thing. I also just really want to kill him.

"Get out of my way, Greer." The darkness and the light immediately fill me up in perfect balance, and the air around us instantly drops in temperature.

"No." Her power may not be a match for mine, but her stubbornness sure is.

My rage boils over. "He is responsible for everything! He is responsible for so many deaths! He is responsible for Trey. He is responsible for hurting Cas. He is going to come after us, if he isn't already on his way. We are past the deadline he gave Cas."

Cas walks right up to me and grabs my face. "He is. He is the cause of all the suffering you have been through. I promise you that I will do everything I can to help you get him. We will get him together. We will end all of this together. Just not tonight, even if we are past the deadline."

"Oh my God. Why are your eyes glowing?!" Mei-Lien asks in alarm. The surprise of her presence turns all our tense expressions toward her.

"Mei, what are you doing here?" Greer asks.

"Talli...you have never looked more badass in your life," she breaths. Cas steps back from me, but grabs my hand, keeping me tethered to this earth, tethered to him.

"Mei!" Greer snaps.

Mei-Lien's head swings hard to Greer, and she rushes to say, "Reef."

"What about Reef?" I ask quickly.

She looks back at me. "I overheard him talking to someone on the phone. He said, 'things are worse than we thought,' and something about 'Hoffman's out of control.' Oh! And 'I need backup right away to deal with the situation.' I think he was telling someone about you, Talli. I think he's been spying on you all along."

I suddenly feel like I might throw up. There's no way. I really thought...Then I remember, Reef saw my eyes when I went to confront Dad. Cas is behind me, wrapping his arms around me, holding me steady.

"You have to leave, Talli. You and Cas need to go now. Your bags are already packed. You—" Greer starts.

"The Russians!" Ash cries out, running toward us.

"The Russians?" Cas asks.

"I saw them! They were meeting with your dad and Chief Lu!" Ash stops and catches his breath, then chokes out, "I ran down to the lab and found empty tanks. A LOT of tanks meant to hold gas."

"The gas meant to mix with the shadows?" I clarify.

Ash nods. "Yes, and there were rows of elixirs. I presume they are meant for your water, Talli."

"We have to do something," Greer says.

"I already did." Ash grows pale at the admission.

"What did you do?" she asks, going rigid.

"Something reckless..."

BOOM.

We all jump and immediately look toward the community building, then stare at Ash.

"I pulled the lab's fire alarm and made sure everyone got out before I set the fire," Ash reassures quickly.

Greer takes three long steps toward him and kisses him more passionately than I have ever seen before.

"I would say that tonight couldn't get any crazier, then I re-member, there are two dragons standing behind us right now," Cas remarks.

"You all need to leave," Mei-Lien urges. "Between the search for Caspian, what Ash just did, the Russians, and who the fuck knows will be coming for Talli, none of you are safe. You need to leave now and hide."

Greer pulls away from Ash, and we all freeze at the realization that she is right.

We need to leave our home. We need to leave the Order. We need to run and hide.

Cas moves first, pulling me toward Coventina. "Greer, Ash, go pack. Talli and I will get our bags and Seth, and meet you both back here. Mei-Lien, make sure the fire keeps everyone busy."

We all move on his command, going our separate ways. Cas and I climb onto Coventina, making the quick flight to the home that we shared for too short a time. Only a month, but the best month of my life. Cas grabs the bags, strapping them into Coventina's saddle while I eye Seth, trying to figure out how to make this work.

"How do you propose we strap his old ass onto a dragon's back?" Cas asks me frantically.

"*Yes, I would also like to know,*" Coventina says.

"Trust me. Both of you." I eye the saddle and the bit of rope I have dubiously, then it comes to me. "Help me get him onto the saddle."

Seth looks at us warily, but allows us to try to boost him onto Coventina's back.

"*Watch the claws!*" she shouts. By the low growl Seth gives in return, I can tell he must be responding back to her.

"*Covey, are you going to be able to handle this much weight?*" I ask.

"*I'll manage for a while. Draven will have to take turns with me,*" she answers, clearly annoyed at the situation but thankfully not refusing.

I climb into the saddle in front of Seth and direct Cas to climb in behind him. I feel a furry head rest on my shoulder, as I hand part of the rope back to Cas, and we work together to wrap it around ourselves, then tie each end into the saddle. Cas's hands wrap around both of us, gripping my hips in a reassuring squeeze. This will be uncomfortable, but we'll make it work because no part of our family will be left behind.

Coventina takes off and lands us back at my parents' house. Greer and Ash are just finishing getting their bags strapped to Draven, when Mom comes rushing out the door.

She has a Healer's satchel in her hand, and she reaches up to hand it to me. "Mom, I really don't think we need healing elixirs," I tell her.

"There are burner phones and more cash inside," she explains.

My eyes start to well up with emotion, and I force out, "Thank you."

She reaches for my hand and squeezes hard. "Be careful. All of you. I'll do what I can here." Then she lets go.

This is really it. We are really running. No turning back now.

"Let's go!" I shout.

Coventina and Draven take off under a cloud of shadows, carrying us...somewhere. Both the Order and the Brethren are officially after us—officially our enemies, so I'm not sure where we'll be safe or how long it'll take for us to figure out how to fix this mess. But together, all seven of us, we'll find a way.

Even if it means that we never return home.

KEEP READING FOR A BONUS CHAPTER IN GREER'S POV.

GREER

May

"THERE IS NOTHING MORE you could have done," Ash reassures for the hundredth time.

I keep my eyes fixed to the carpet, pulling out tiny pieces of lint that are as stubborn as I am feeling right now.

"You can't hold yourself responsible for every bad thing that happens around here," he tries again.

My fingernail breaks, and I swear under my breath. Bringing my finger to my mouth, I rip the tip of the nail off the rest of the way with my teeth.

"The Brethren shouldn't have been able to disable the alarms, but they did, and that's not your fault. That's not anyone's fault."

I go back to pruning the carpet and keep my gaze averted from his as I finally admit, "I was out patrolling an hour before. I should have seen them."

Ash's face softens, but his words are pointed as he replies, "It's not your job to be out flying, looking for trouble while everyone is sleeping. That is someone else's shift. You should have been home sleeping, too."

"I can't..." My voice wavers, and I hate how weak I sound. But it's the truth. I haven't slept much more than an hour at a time since the March happened almost three years ago. So, instead of sleeping, I patrol. It makes me feel more in control, like patrolling the skies with Draven will keep the Brethren from coming after us again with an army. But after what just happened, it seems I was wrong in that line of thought.

THUMP. THUMP.

A soft knock comes from the front door. Ash moves to answer it, but I beat him to it, welcoming the distraction from this conversation.

Opening the door, I find Trisha on the other side of it, dressed in black. I have never seen her wear anything other than pastels and creams, so the sight is a bit jarring. "I'm sorry. Mom's not home right now." Dad and Mom are both gone, dealing with the cleanup effort. I should be out there too, doing whatever I can to help the community, but my true duty lies in staying close to Talli. She needs me more than anyone, and I need to make sure she doesn't do anything reckless.

Her smile is sad as she replies, "I know, sweet girl. I just left her. I'm actually looking for your sister. Is she home?"

"Not at the moment, no. Is there something I can do for you?"

She reaches into her purse and pulls out a book, extending it to me. Its brown leather cover is marked up and worn to the point of tearing at the corners.

"Simon would want her to have this. Please make sure she gets it and reassure her that it does not need to be returned."

"Of course," I answer, taking the book from her.

"Thank you. Take care of yourself, Greer." She hesitates, then adds, "There are many things to fear in this world, but loving with all that you have should never be one of them."

I stare after her as she walks away, trying to wrap my mind around those words. Why did she say that to me? My shields are up and locked as they always are, but her words...they have completely disarmed me, and I hate that feeling. I shove it away instead, and try to find my neutral feelings again. Feeling a little more comfortable, I look down at the book in my hand and close the door.

"Why would Mr. Simon want Talli to have a book?" Ash asks from behind me.

"That's exactly what I am wondering."

"You need to go talk to her. *Really* talk to her. You've both been in the habit of keeping secrets from each other, and it's getting us nowhere," Ash insists.

"I hardly think today is the day, Ash." I drop the book on the small entryway table meant for keys and mail, then head toward the kitchen to get something to drink.

Caffeine. I need caffeine.

Ash follows on my heels and persists, "Today is absolutely the day, because you need each other and I need us all on the same page again."

I lift an eyebrow at him. "You're being melodramatic."

"Am I? Does she know you don't sleep, that you spend most of each night in the sky because you're terrified of another attack? Does she know that your nightmares came back? Does she know about the vision you had of her losing control and threatening to kill hundreds of men with a flick of her wrist? Does she—"

"Enough!" I explode, smacking my hand on the counter. Shadows fly across the room, plunging us into complete darkness for a brief moment, before returning to me.

He crosses his arms over his chest, giving me a knowing look. "You need to talk to her."

A single traitorous tear falls, and Ash is there in a moment, wiping it from my cheek. "Together." He places both hands on the sides of my neck, "We are all stronger together."

We make our way to the lake, hand-in-hand, where I know Talli is. I normally enjoy the walk down the path to the lake, especially when Ash is by my side, but today everything feels wrong.

"I don't feel right. Maybe we should wait," I voice out loud.

Ash squeezes my hand tighter. "We are already on our way. Everything will be okay."

I continue to walk, but the feeling won't go away. I feel like someone is watching me. Ash steps on a branch, causing a loud CRACK to echo through the trees. A black shape darts in front of our path, and I throw myself in front of Ash on instinct. The black shape turns out to be a bird—a raven. It lands in the middle of the path, blocking us from Talli. The raven gives me an intelligent look, as if trying to convey something to me, then it ruffles its inky black-blue feathers and flies off.

My heart pounds in my ears as I try to decipher what this could mean. Ash places a gentle hand on my shoulder, and I relax, just enough for Ash, but my guard is still up.

"It was just a raven," he says in an attempt to comfort me.

"That was not *just* a raven. That was a bonded creature, or one capable of bonding," I explain as I look around, trying to find it again.

He's silent for a moment, and I don't have to look at him to know he is thinking, calculating, pulling all the facts from his brain. Finally, realization finds him, and he breathes, "The Meyer family bond." This is not something I have ever talked to him about, but I know he must have read it somewhere. "It's a real thing?" he asks.

"Yes. Dad told me about it when I was little. The Meyer bloodline was known as the 'Raven Bloodline' for centuries because of it."

We start walking slowly toward Talli again, my eyes never leaving the tree line in case the raven *was* actually trying to warn me about something, as I suspect.

"And that was because ravens only bonded with Meyers and vice versa? Until you, I mean."

"There are a few reasons why we were called the Raven Bloodline. That is one of them; another is that our foresight is considered a direct message from nature itself. Ravens have always been regarded as messengers of nature, as well, much like a hawk is."

"And the other reason?"

"Meyers always have raven-black hair." I snort, always thinking that was an odd fact for Dad to have shared with me.

I finally glance at Ash, and he looks puzzled, causing my lips to pull up at the corners. I love it when he looks puzzled, because that means he is about to do his best thinking. His mind is breathtaking.

"I don't understand why you are the only Meyer in history who didn't bond a raven," he admits.

"My best guess is because my mother was a human, making me less of a Meyer." I shrug. I've never cared about the Meyer name or its bloodline. The only reason I let Dad convince me I should keep it is out of respect for my father, and the fact that I am the last living Meyer. If Ash and I have kids one day, they'll carry the blood too, but it will be even more diluted with human blood, so who knows if they'll even inherit the foresight ability.

"*There is nothing 'less' about you. You bonded a dragon. You bonded me. And I am way cooler than a stupid bird,*" Draven growls into my mind.

"You think the bond only applied to pureblooded Meyers? That's why it ended with your father," Ash guesses.

Despite Draven's protest, I nod. We are almost at the lake, almost to Talli.

"What do you think it means that you saw a bonded raven? Do you think there might be more Meyers out there?"

I stop to allow us to finish this conversation before we reach Talli. "I don't know if it means that or not. But I do believe it was warning me."

"Of?"

"Change is coming."

ACKNOWLEDGEMENTS

It has been a wild few months since I released my debut novel, Blind Thoughts. I am blown away by the love and support I have received from strangers who took a chance on me. So, first, a big thank you to all my readers for spending your precious reading time flipping through the pages of Blind Thoughts and Hollow Sacrifices. Your positive reviews, kindness, and willingness to share my work with others have touched me in ways I can't express. You all truly are the light in this community.

To my husband, Tom, I have no idea how you put up with my antics some days, but I'm so grateful that you do. Even during all my existential crises or moments where I can't make a decision to save my own life, you stand firmly as someone who I can always rely on to talk me through it. Thank you for being my soul mate.

To my daughter, Emmalyn, my little gremlin, watching you grow is the greatest joy I could ever experience. There is nothing like the glow in your eyes when you find a bit of magic in the world or accomplish something challenging. The world is big and scary, but nothing can stop you if you keep your dreams bigger and scarier.

To my best friend, Marci, thank you for all your unhinged feedback. I never thought I would find myself arguing over gray sweatpants, but that was the highlight of editing this time around. Truly, though, your honesty and tendency to say the first thing that pops in your head are things I couldn't live without.

To my book bestie, Pattie, thank you for being the best vibe reader I could ask for. You kept me in check this round by telling me when things felt off or weird. Your endless excitement and opinions when I need them the most are always such a huge help to keep me moving along.

To all my other family and friends, thank you for always being there for me. Many of you will never read this or know anything about my books (which is how I like it LOL), but you are excited about every achievement I reach anyway, and I truly couldn't ask for a better support system.

To my wonderful editor, Haleigh St. Paul at Grim Girl Edits LLC, thank you for being so amazing that I would feel lost without you. You have not only fixed my mistakes in my manuscripts, but you have also helped me to improve so much as a writer. I'm so grateful to call you not only my editor, but my friend.

To my cover designer, Moonchildreams. The magic you can create in your illustrations will always blow me away! Thank you for continuing to work with me.

ABOUT THE AUTHOR

C.L. Sharp considers herself a firm believer in happily ever after and loves writing stories with bumpy roads and banter-filled dialog.

When she isn't writing in her Virginia home, she loves spending time with her husband, daughter, and two dogs. She enjoys working with her hands for many different hobbies and is a frequent visitor to zoos, aquariums, and theme parks, where she insists on riding every roller coaster.

If you enjoyed Hollow Sacrifices, be sure to join her mailing list and follow her on social media for upcoming titles!

Website: www.clsharp.com

Instagram: @c.l.sharp_author

TikTok: @c.l.sharp_author

Facebook: Pages/C.L. Sharp

www.ingramcontent.com/pod-product-compliance
Lightning Source LLC
Chambersburg PA
CBHW020538120726
47903CB00001B/29